The Heights
of Rimring

Duff Hart-Davis

The Heights
of Rimring

JONATHAN CAPE
THIRTY BEDFORD SQUARE LONDON

First published 1980
Copyright © 1980 by Duff Hart-Davis
Jonathan Cape Ltd, 30 Bedford Square, London WC1

British Library Cataloguing in Publication Data

Hart-Davis, Duff
The heights of Rimring.
I.   Title
823'.9'1F   PR6058.A6949H/
ISBN 0 224 01837 X

Photoset in Great Britain by
Rowland Phototypesetting Ltd, Bury St Edmunds, Suffolk
and printed by St Edmundsbury Press
Bury St Edmunds, Suffolk

'Great things are done when men and mountains meet;
This is not done by jostling in the street.'

William Blake

The Heights
of Rimring

One

The night's storm had almost blown itself out, but ragged banners of black cloud were still flying on the dawn wind. Between them the sky was just beginning to lighten. As Bill Stirling opened the door of the Land Rover, a cold, damp blast surged into the warm cab.

'Come on, Spot,' he whispered. 'Out.'

The bitch leaped out into the darkness and shot away down the grassy track that led into the wood. While Stirling got ready he let her run about at will, so that she would work off steam and calm down a bit before they went into action.

For a few moments he stood still and listened. The wood was full of wind-noise; from close at hand a hissing in the conifers, and from farther down the valley a deep, surging roar among the old beeches at the back of the park. Then in a lull he caught the sound he was hoping for – a heavy, sonorous snorting-cum-grunting, as if a giant pig were rootling somewhere down to his left. Even after years of experience, he still found the call pure magic: with these primeval groans, a fallow buck was proclaiming its supremacy on the rutting stand.

Stirling reached into the Land Rover, picked up the binoculars and looped them round his neck. He took the .270 from the gun-rack behind the front seat, pulled five rounds from his ammunition belt, loaded them into the magazine, slid one round forward into the breech, closed the bolt, set the safety catch and slung the rifle on his shoulder. For none of these actions did he need to see, so often had he done them all before.

He checked his pockets for other essential equipment.

Knife – yes. Dragging-rope – yes. Dog-harness – yes. Gloves – yes. Some people thought it soft of a deer-stalker to wear gloves. But for him there was a purely practical reason. Gloves increased his chances. If his hands became frozen, he could not shoot; it was that much more efficient to keep them warm. Besides, grey-green hands were less conspicuous than pink ones: there was no point in sending semaphore warnings to the deer every time you raised your binoculars.

He took out his stick – a fine, straight hazel stem nearly six feet long with a leather thong threaded through it near the top, so that when he let go of it suddenly it would hang by the loop from his wrist. Finally he closed the Land Rover door with a careful, deliberate movement.

Spot, having indulged in some mildly illicit pursuit, returned and circled him panting.

'Sit down!' he hissed. 'You horrible brute. Behave.'

The bitch sat down with her tail thudding on the path. Though she could tell from the tone of her master's voice that he was not angry, she nevertheless judged it prudent to make slight fawning movements, lifting her nose upwards and backwards, twisting her face away from him. From above, all he could see was her eyes, her teeth and the white spot on her chest which betrayed the fact that although her mother had been a pedigree Labrador, her father had been a collie with a penchant for unofficial marriages. Happily the combination had made Spot a perfect machine for tracking deer.

He bent down, chucked her under the chin, and set off. Man and dog slipped into the dark wood like shadows. The morning was ideal for the job. The noise of the wind would cover any small sounds which the forester might make, and the overnight rain had left the ground soft and yielding: the leaves that had fallen early were too wet to crackle.

For the first half-mile there was no need to be on the alert, so Stirling walked fast to warm himself up. Spot made quick dashes to either side, following lines of scent for four or five yards and then returning to her station just behind him. Through long practice she had geared herself precisely to the needs of these early-morning forays: as the speed of their advance decreased, she progressively reduced her own manoeuvres until in the end she was creeping at Stirling's heels.

Reaching the top of the old beech wood, he paused to listen again. For a few seconds the setting moon sailed out brilliantly white between the clouds. The sky had lightened imperceptibly. Down here, in the shelter of the valley, the wind was quieter. He stood and listened. Below him in the old park were the ruins of a great house which had stood there long ago. Now nothing remained but a pattern of ivy-covered walls and the ghost of a formal garden . . .

There – the noise reached him again: a sudden outbreak of groaning, louder and clearer than before. Now he could tell exactly where the sound was coming from. The deer were farther along the hill than he had expected, drawn into the hollow, no doubt, by the sharpness of the wind.

Again he moved forward, but more slowly. He thought of the old woodland stalker's adage for advancing on deer at close quarters: one step forward for every two backward is the pace at which to proceed. On he went, testing the ground before putting each foot down lest he should crack a twig, freezing on to each tree-trunk as he reached it. Spot shadowed him soundlessly.

Outside in the park the light was already strong. Here beneath the trees the mysteries of the night lingered. Stirling's eyes swept back and forth, trying to read the secrets of the forest. That black lump above him on the left: animal or tree-stump? Almost certainly a tree-stump, but worth a check. The binoculars revealed it to be neither, but a clump of waving ferns.

The groaning ahead of him grew louder. Without being able to see the deer, he knew what they would be doing. The master ·buck would be parading his chosen territory – an area no bigger than a tennis court – and around it, in a state of high excitement, such does as he had been able to round up would be preening themselves, while the lesser bucks hovered on the perimeter, lusting but not quite daring to plunge into the fray.

It was not the master buck that Stirling planned to shoot. On the contrary, he had known this animal for the past three seasons and had watched it grow into splendid maturity. No: he was after a poorer animal – a lame buck, with only one antler – which he had glimpsed two nights before. To shoot the big buck would be all too easy, as he insisted on advertising his presence *fortissimo*, and was so well alight with the fires of procreation that his normal vigilance was much reduced. The cripple, on the other hand, would be more difficult to single out.

Stirling eased carefully forward. The light strengthened. Through the binoculars he could see his first objective – an old, mossy bank running up and down the hill, at right-angles to his line of approach. The bank should be in range of the rutting stand. If he could reach it unobserved, he would be in an ideal position from which to observe and, if the chance came, to shoot.

Down by his boots, Spot gave a sudden rumble. She had smelled something that he had not seen. Some creature had crossed the wind ahead of them. Not a rabbit or a deer, for she would not growl at either of them. A fox, perhaps . . . Stirling searched the floor of the wood with his glasses and caught a slight movement, a flash of lighter colour. He followed the animal, which was moving downhill. The stronger light in a clearing revealed it as a badger: Brock coming home from the night's excursion. It stood for a moment with its bowed front legs resting on a fallen branch and its striped face turned in his direction, before continuing on its way.

Crawling the last few yards, Stirling reached the cover of the bank. He laid the rifle on top of the smooth, mossy hump, and settled to watch and wait.

To the naked eye the wood ahead was still impenetrably dark; but through his binoculars he could make out sudden movements as black shapes flitted through the thicket. How strange it was, he reflected, that the deer returned every autumn not merely to this wood, but to this very patch of ground. Every October, as the first frosts began turning the beech leaves to gold, some immemorial instinct drew the bucks precisely to this spot, and to half a dozen others round about. What brought them to the favoured places? Was it pure memory and instinct? Or did the earth itself exhale some particular scent, in a few special places, that made the deer feel at home?

Stirling lay still, enjoying the sweet, damp smell of the moss, and the heavier, richer breath of earth and leaf-mould. Here in the wood he felt perfectly at ease, in tune with the surroundings and part of them: the hunter in the forest. As he waited for the light he amused himself by composing advertisements, such as might appear in country magazines, for luring deer on to new rutting stands: 'Excellent rutting area, situated on s. facing slope, well away from all roads. Good natural drainage. Overhead cover at preferred height. The whole amounting to forty acres (16 ha.) and guaranteed conducive to copulation . . . '

Now through the glasses he could see the master buck, churning up and down in a patch of bushes that had grown through the branches of a fallen tree. Ten yards out and ten yards back he went, grunting all the way. Occasionally he paused to beat hell out of the bushes with his antlers: one, two, three, four savage swipes, and then he was off again. His harem of does was scarcely visible: an occasional movement in the surrounding thicket gave one away, but Stirling knew there were more beasts on the stand than he could see. As usual, the buck he wanted was nowhere in evidence.

Suddenly the whole place seemed to erupt. One doe came out into the open and flaunted herself brazenly before the master. At once he tried to mount her, but she would not have it, and skittered away through the bushes with the buck in close pursuit.

In his brief absence a younger male, three or four years old, rashly sought to occupy the centre of the stage. The master buck, returning, took one look at him and charged. The clash of antlers echoed through the trees. The two animals hurtled crabwise through the undergrowth with a great crashing and snapping of branches, as though an elephant had stampeded. The fight scattered the does and the junior bucks, who rushed about in a state of frantic excitement. After a few seconds' wrestling the would-be usurper retired beaten, leaving the master buck supreme in the middle of a ring of circling acolytes.

Stirling lay still, enjoying the spectacle. As fights went, this one was short and not particularly spectacular; but the power and ferocity which the deer could let loose always impressed him. Yet the whole business seemed an amazing waste of energy. Copulation was the object of the exercise. Everybody wanted it, but hardly anyone ever got it. So much groaning and roaring and parading and fighting and chivvying and rushing about: so little actual sex. The frustration of it all seemed scarcely tolerable.

His mind wandered from cervine to human problems. Who was he to criticise the deer's love life, when his own was in such a mess? He saw a close parallel here: certainly he felt just as frustrated as the big buck roaring away out in front of him.

He tried to remember when things started to go wrong between him and Ann, but he could pin-point no particular issue or event. It was just that she had become gradually colder and harder, less sympathetic, less interested in him. Her looks had scarcely changed since the day they had been married; she was still just as slim, to the point of being skinny. Yet that was precisely what had attracted him: a tall, slender ash-blonde with a lithe figure and a face that was perhaps a touch bony and boyish, yet also attractive in a strongly feminine way.

Maybe he should have seen at the time that the face and the person might both turn very hard. That's what they had done now, anyway. Often Ann seemed to be made of wood. Ash blonde, ash wood. A hard, clean, white wood. That was her. Perhaps everything would have been different if they had had children. Surely maternity would have softened her?

But she had always refused, putting her career first. To hell with her bloody career, he had thought a thousand times. But she had always maintained that a year away from school, or even six months, would seriously damage her prospects as a teacher. He didn't know whether to believe it or not. But what he did know, deep inside him, was that their respective careers formed the heart of their problem.

He was exasperated by her refusal to start a family. She despised him for being merely a forester, and for not doing something more intellectually demanding. She had no feeling whatever for the country, the woods, or the strong, simple things that gave him satisfaction. She was just an intellectual climber, without much to justify her ambition . . .

Sue, on the other hand . . . Sue was utterly different, warmly responsive to whatever idea or task he told her he was busy with. She set him on fire physically as well. Yet there she was in her wretched little matchbox in the town, stuck with a crazily possessive husband, and two children whom she adored. There was no question of Stirling going off with her, as she could not entertain the idea of abandoning her boys. Stalemate there as well.

Abrupt movements between the trees jerked Stirling's mind back to the present. Through the glasses he glimpsed a large antler passing between two rhododendron bushes. For a moment he thought it might be his quarry – but no: a longer sight of the beast showed that it was a stranger – a mature buck, lighter in build than the master, but still too good to shoot.

Stirling relaxed again. So things at home were bad. And now something else had happened to unsettle him even more. The day before, a letter had arrived in a plain envelope with a London postmark. But though the letter had been posted in Pimlico, it had come originally from a remote village in the Himalayas, from a former college friend whom Stirling had not seen for years. 'I want you to join me at once,' Andrew de Lazlo had written. 'Something very much in your line has come up.'

The idea of a trip to the Himalayas was immediately attractive; but there was also something disturbing about the whole proposal. Stirling saw that the letter had come through the Diplomatic Bag, and certain phrases in it had made him realise that they were trying to draw him back into the old game . . .

The master buck made another unsuccessful attempt to cover a doe. A stupid rhyme jingled insistently in Stirling's head:

> Poor buck
> No luck
> Never a . . .

At his elbow Spot gave a whine. He looked sharply to his left. Eight yards away, uphill, stood the cripple he was after, so close that he could see its eyes moving. For half a second the animal glared down. Then it took off at an awkward canter, straight into the middle of the rutting stand. Its precipitate arrival broke up the party as though a bomb had burst. Leading the retreat from the front, the big buck took off first. Away went all the other deer with him. Does and lesser bucks as yet unseen poured out of the thicket. Altogether Stirling counted thirty-six animals as they charged through an open glade along the hill.

Cursing, he levered himself up off the bank and sat back on his heels. Had he not been daydreaming, he might have seen or heard the cripple coming. Even if he had lain motionless, he still might have got a chance at it, for his hat, gloves, jacket and trousers were all grey-green, and the beast might have taken him for a log.

'Sorry, Spotto,' he said to the bitch. 'Snafu.'

Spot was shivering, partly from cold but more from excitement. She wriggled closer to him. He himself was cold and stiff. As soon as the last deer was out of sight, he stood up and stamped about. Then he got down again and did twenty press-ups, with his feet on the bank, higher than his hands.

All was not lost. At any other season of the year, given a fright of that kind, the deer might have gone a mile or more. Now, however, they would settle after only four or five hundred yards. His carelessness just meant that he would have to stalk them all over again.

Presently he started forward once more. This time luck seemed to be with him, for the big buck had taken up station in a shallow bowl within range of an overlooking ridge. After a careful short stalk Stirling eased himself up on to the roots of an ancient beech tree and found he was looking down on the deer close in beneath him. Now it was just a question of waiting for the bad buck to present itself.

As he lay there, the sun rose over the woods on the horizon, and its first rays, striking horizontally into the bowl, lit up the scene with theatrical effect. The master buck was caught in a Landseerian blaze of glory. The points of its antlers, polished by repeated assaults on the undergrowth, shone cleanly white, and its coat took fire with a russet glow.

In a few minutes the one-horned buck reappeared, hustling two or three does among some privet bushes. Stirling slipped the covers off the telescopic sight and aligned the rifle on the group. One doe was standing perfectly, broadside on. He laid the thick crosshairs on the spot where her heart would be. At this range, one could hardly miss. The buck had vanished again, and he searched for it with the sight, not bothering to use the binoculars. There it came again, but hellishly restless, always moving, turning, jumping about, never standing still. At last it did stand, but back-end on to him: useless. Then it turned, broadside at last. He brought the cross on to its shoulder and held his breath.

No, he told himself at the last possible instant. There was another beast behind the buck, in line: a doe. He could see its legs. Two beasts, in fact. Lucky he hadn't fired. Then all the deer moved again, changing the pattern as if they were pieces in a kaleidoscope.

The target reappeared, higher up the bank. Its head was

hidden by a low beech-bough, but Stirling knew from the size, shape and colour that the body was the right one. Quickly he brought the rifle up, aimed and touched the trigger.

The heavy crash went down the valley like a clap of thunder. Before the echo had returned from the opposite hill, he knew that the shot was good. He saw the deer buckle as the 150-grain bullet took it in the ribs. The animal went two steps backwards, then tottered forward and disappeared behind the bushes. All the other deer took off at a gallop.

Approaching cautiously, Stirling peered round the side of the bushes. The buck lay dead, with its one antler twisted beneath its neck. He snapped his fingers to release Spot's brakes. The bitch raced forward, found the quarry instantly and began to tear round it, barking. He came up, congratulated her with a pat and a little fuss, and deftly set about removing the deer's intestines, glad to have culled such a wreck of an animal.

He finished his messy task by lifting the deer's head high off the ground so that the blood collected inside its chest ran out on to the grass. As he did so, he realised that Spot had disappeared. Odd: normally she sat rooted and slobbering, waiting to get a piece of heart or liver.

He stood up and whistled. No response. He whistled again. Still nothing. Then, far up to his left, in the conifer plantation, he heard her yapping. Blast, he thought: that could mean only one thing. He must have wounded some other animal as well as the one he had killed, and Spot had gone off on its line.

Quickly he tried to reconstruct the scene. The bullet had gone straight through the buck, certainly: he had found a sizeable exit-hole in its ribs. He went to the place on which he thought it had been standing and searched the ground behind. Yes – there were the pins, or bristles, from its coat, and some tiny chips of bone, blown out by the bullet. Now he had the line of the shot exactly, from here to the roots of the beech tree. He searched up the line and soon found another bunch of pins, and a few drops of brownish blood. Stomach blood: the second beast had been hit in the guts. He had been criminally careless in not rechecking that the background was clear.

The yapping had ceased. He gave a few prolonged whistles. Soon he heard Spot charging back through the dense plantation. Out she came, bounding and dancing and inviting him to follow her. There was blood on her muzzle: she had had hold of the wounded animal.

For a moment he thought of putting her harness on and working her on the long cord, but the young spruce in the plantation was so thick as to make the idea impossible. All he could do was keep her close in front of him and follow the line she took.

The bitch led straight up the hill. Climbing through the serried ranks of trees was hard enough, but the physical labour of the ascent was intensified for Stirling by the fact that he could not advance silently. Even though he was wearing a soft Loden jacket, he could not help scratching and swishing as he fought his way through the interlocked branches. Unless the beast was moribund, the noise would be bound to set it off again.

As he feared, he heard a sudden crash and tearing of branches twenty or thirty yards ahead. Following up, he found the place where the deer had been lying: the undergrowth was pressed down, and there in the grass was a pool of blood – but not a very big one. The beast was still strong. Hoping that Spot would bring it to bay again, he sent her off after it, but this time in desperation it kept going, over the crest of the hill and down the other side.

The further he went in pursuit, the greater became his vexation. The territory for which he was responsible ended in the next valley, and across the bottom the land was owned by an irascible farmer with whom his relations were already strained. He did not want to have to administer the *coup de grâce* on Martin Godfrey's land. Not only did Godfrey set snares for deer illegally: he shot dogs that strayed on to his ground, put down poison for them, and generally made himself an undesirable neighbour.

Yet in a minute Stirling could see that there was going to be no alternative. As he emerged hot and panting on to a clear space at the top of the hill, he heard Spot in full cry, already across the boundary. Taking a deep breath, he gave a piercing whistle that meant 'Down!' The yapping ceased: the bitch must have dropped to the ground where she was. Although he could not see her, he knew she would keep still until he called her again.

He sat down on the grass, caught his breath, and with his binoculars scanned the open forest on the far side of the valley. Presently he caught a movement. There it was – the back of the wounded beast, by then walking heavily, dragging itself along, with pauses to look back. Watching steadily, he saw it go into a hollow and lie down.

Having given it more time to weaken, he made his way slowly down. There was a chance that the beast would die. Failing that, he would try to finish it off by hand. He did not want to fire a shot out there if he could possibly help it.

A yard at a time he advanced on the little pit where he had seen the deer last. Then he moved a foot at a time, then by inches, silently over the damp grass. At last he was at the lip of the pit. With infinite caution he raised his head until he could see the doe's soft, furry ears. They were cocked. Though sick, the animal was still alert. He could easily put a bullet through the back of its neck, but the noise would bring the farmer out for sure.

A sudden burst of barking erupted from where Spot had lain down, a hundred yards away. The deer half rose, looking round anxiously. Stirling ducked and cursed beneath his breath. What the hell was the dog doing?

The wounded animal settled again. He stepped back and got out his knife, locked the blade open and advanced again. The deer's head was still up, but facing away from him.

With a sudden spring he launched himself out over the stricken animal in a flying leap. The beast saw him coming and tried to rise, but it got only half-way up before it was hammered back to the ground by the impact of his body. One horrible harsh scream escaped from its throat. With his left hand he clamped its muzzle shut and with his right he drove the knife deep into the base of its throat.

Blood spurted out over his hand. The doe heaved and roared again, but this time only deep inside its throat. He held it down, feeling the life ebb out with the blood. In a minute the struggles weakened, and in another they ceased.

He got up, shaking with reaction at the primitive murder that circumstances had forced him to commit. Yet it was not really the killing that offended him: in an emergency of this kind, Neanderthal tactics came easily to him. What upset him was the way everything had gone wrong because of his preoccupation and consequent lack of care.

He looped his rope round the beast's neck and prepared to drag it back up the hill, whistling the short *peep-peep* that would bring Spot back to him. He began to drag, taking the weight on the rope passed over his right shoulder; but after a few yards he realised that something was wrong. The bitch hadn't come. Normally it would have taken her ten seconds to catch up with him, at the most.

He stopped and whistled again. Still nothing. Leaving the deer, he moved in the direction from which he had heard the barking. Anxiety, beginning like a twinge of pain inside him, built rapidly into a surge of alarm. Instinctively he knew that something had happened to her.

He found her lying stretched on one side, obviously dead. Blood had trickled from her nose and mouth on to the grass. Her skull had been smashed in by something heavy and blunt – a hammer, or the back of an axe-head. It seemed odd that he had heard nothing except the flurry of barking – but she had been some way off, down the blustery wind.

For a moment shock halted him where he stood. Then he dashed forward and knelt over the small body, gasping for breath. Godfrey. It must have been that bastard Godfrey who'd done it. He had no proof – but it couldn't have been anyone else. Just because Stirling had come on to his land. His hands clenched desperately on the rifle as he fought down impulses of fury – to spray bullets through the windows of Godfrey's house, to set fire to his car, his combine harvester, his barns full of hay and straw.

With a great effort he controlled himself. He realised that Godfrey might easily be watching. No wonder Spot had barked. Only her incredible discipline had kept her anchored to the place when the stranger approached. What a pathetic end!

It would be the work of a few moments to go and wreak havoc in Godfrey's farm-yard, and then, when he came running, to beat hell out of him too. But if he did that, Godfrey would sue him for assault. Even so, on any other day, Stirling might have gone and taken direct revenge. Yet now a better alternative instantly presented itself. This disaster was all he needed to launch him on a new trajectory. He would get the hell out of the place altogether. Why stay? This was the final straw.

He picked up the limp, warm body and carried it in his arms over the frontier, back on to his own side. At the top of the hill, in an open space that commanded a view of the valley, he laid it on the grass and went back to the Land Rover for the spade. Beneath the turf cropped short by rabbits he buried his beloved hunting partner, and with her that phase of his life.

Two

Driving home, he found himself haunted by the one spectre from his past which he always had a struggle to keep down. Sometimes in the night it would return to plague him, and although in the day he could generally keep it buried beneath a covering of mundane chores, anything like the shock he had had this morning brought it back with the clarity of a news-reel.

Belfast was unusually hot that summer morning. By eleven o'clock a heat-haze was shimmering above the pavements, and even on the roof-top where Stirling was stationed scarcely a breath of wind moved the heavy air. Anti-sniper duty was always both nerve-racking and tedious: hours when nothing whatever happened, hours whose every second might produce an attack. He was supposed to have been training a boy who had just come out from the U.K. but the lad had gone sick that morning, and Stirling had had to man the post himself.

At 11.14 – he remembered the time exactly – he heard on the army radio set that the local E.O.D. teams – the bomb-disposal men – had been called out to a suspected car-bomb in the Falls Road area. A few seconds later the crump of a heavy explosion shook the city. It came from the direction of the Falls, and then, almost simultaneously, there was a radio report of a second bomb somewhere out on the road to Londonderry. Clearly the terrorists had set up a major sequence of attacks.

In the middle of it he had seen a young man in jeans and a black leather jacket sidle up to a supermarket on the corner below him and deposit a white carrier-bag outside the door.

Having set the bag down carefully, the youth moved off almost at a run.

Instantly Stirling radioed down to one of the foot patrols, ordering them to get the front doors of the supermarket closed and all the customers out the back. He should also call for an E.O.D. team, he knew, but because of the multiple bomb-scares he felt certain none would be available.

Even the infantry seemed to be tied up elsewhere. For a minute he got no answer to his call, and when a reply did come, it merely said that nobody was immediately available, as the nearest patrol was covering a house-search.

Up on his roof-top, he began to feel desperate. People were pouring in and out of the supermarket. If a bomb went off there, the slaughter would be appalling. He watched another sixty seconds tick by. Already it was more than three minutes since the bag had been put down. Apparently no one had noticed it. By the standards prevailing, three minutes was a relatively long delay: the bomb might go off at any second.

There was only one thing for it. From his own training he knew that with luck a rifle bullet should shatter the bomb's detonating mechanism and render the whole thing ineffective; so he took his rifle, set it for single shots, waited till no one was in the immediate vicinity, and gave the bag three quick rounds.

Women screamed and ran. Men ran too, but then stopped when they heard no more firing. Other people emerged from the supermarket, unsure of what had happened. Gradually a crowd collected, staring at the carrier-bag.

Stirling stared at it too, through binoculars. To his horror he saw some liquid seeping out of it on to the pavement.

He was down through his derelict building and out on to the street in a flash. A few seconds later he found that he had riddled – and more or less blown to bits – not a bomb, but a new-born baby.

The shock had been so traumatic that he had applied for a P.V.R. – premature voluntary retirement. His application had been granted on the grounds that his nerve was impaired. There was no exact clinical explanation for the change that had come over him; he just wasn't any longer fit for the kind of secret role in which he had been operating.

Time would heal, the psychiatrists said; and so it had. Yet Stirling spoke to no one about that episode in his life. He had never told Ann about it, never would. It was not that he felt ashamed of what he had done: having analysed the incident a thousand times, he still felt that his action had been the only logical one. Rather, he wanted to forget; and it was only when something like this morning's disaster occurred – or yesterday's letter came – that the past forced itself to the surface of his mind.

Yet now he was being drawn back into the service. The old firm was putting its hooks into him again. He felt the half-sickening, half-exhilarating excitement start to burn inside him. Of course, he could refuse: not being in the armed forces any more, he could decline the job if he wanted. But he had already accepted it. The discreet telephone call, coming within half an hour of the arrival of the letter, had caught him off balance, and he had accepted at once.

As he headed for home, his mind ranged farther back over his army career. From school he had gone straight into the Special Air Service, a regiment renowned for its toughness and for the outlandishness of the assignments which it undertook. He had joined the S.A.S. thinking that it was purely a sort of paratroop commando unit, and only later had he discovered that paramilitary intelligence tasks also came within its orbit.

He remembered the ferocious physical training, first at the depot in Hereford and then over the long, smooth ridges of the Brecon Beacons, in Wales, where one of his fellow-recruits had died of exposure and exhaustion during a thirty-six-hour trek in the depths of an iron winter. Later he had learnt to parachute – an activity he had greatly enjoyed. Then came a spell of survival training in Norway, inside the Arctic Circle, where he and his companions had been dropped in pairs, with no food and little equipment, to fend for themselves for a week.

Between the bursts of specialist instruction there had been countless exercises designed to improve ingenuity and endurance. Often the S.A.S. men had to make mock attacks on targets such as power-stations which were specially guarded to prevent them reaching their objective. Anyone captured was subjected to interrogation which was supposed to stop just short of physical torture. Stirling shuddered as he remembered standing for five hours, stark naked, on a winter afternoon outside the guard-room of a barracks near Shrewsbury while his captors waited to see if they could make him talk. They failed, but he lost eight pounds during the afternoon.

For a while he had enjoyed almost every aspect of service life, with its forthright physicality, its emphasis on all-round competence, its obsession with weapons of every kind (he had always been an exceptional shot), and its cult of violence harnessed to specific ends. Yet after a year or two he realised how few opportunities there were, or would be, for real, live action. If the Russians invaded Western Europe, there *would* be action, without a doubt, for all the S.A.S. training was designed ultimately for a particular role which the regiment would play in the event of a Communist advance. But until that came about, there was no live theatre in which to operate except Northern Ireland.

Finding himself bogged down, Stirling had conceived the idea of becoming a mercenary and going to fight for high pay in Africa, or wherever his skills might be better appreciated. After all, he could shoot straight with any kind of pistol, rifle or machine-gun, kill men silently with knife, wire or bare hands, parachute, handle explosives, operate radio sets, live off the country, and generally make himself useful in any military context. Aiming to increase his qualifications still further, he took a course of flying lessons in his spare time, and had no difficulty in obtaining a private pilot's licence. He enjoyed the flying as much as the parachuting – but again it seemed to lead nowhere. For the moment, it was just an expensive hobby. He considered applying for a transfer to the Royal Air Force and training as a fighter pilot.

Then, to his surprise and delight, he had found himself posted into an altogether murkier and more secretive world than the one he had known so far – a world in which he wore plain clothes, worked with civilian members of the Secret Service, and disappeared for weeks at a time on unmentionable missions to Turkey, Egypt, Bahrain and other exotic destinations. Though often physically uncomfortable, these trips fascinated him far more than straightforward soldiering, and it had been a disappointment, after two years, to find himself drafted back into uniform, as an instructor in Belfast . . .

He had reached home. Deepwood, a Victorian gamekeeper's cottage, sat snug and warm in the morning sun, with its old red brick glowing in harmony with the soft golds and russets of the autumn trees. He drove straight to the deer-larder, hung up the two beasts, cleaned them, weighed the carcases, sluiced down the concrete floor and went in to get breakfast.

Ann, as usual, had gone to work, leaving nothing ready for him. But with three scrambled eggs, two hunks of bread and marmalade and three-quarters of a pint of coffee inside him, he felt better, and went upstairs to shave.

Watching his face twist and elongate in the mirror, he wondered what sort of person he really was. He *looked* all right. In fact, he really didn't look too bad, considering he had reached the frightful age of thirty.

He saw a wide, open, friendly face, with freckles picking up the dark red of his hair. His hair was straight and rather fine, and getting a bit long. He would have to watch it, or Ann would start telling him he resembled an ape.

He did, he had to admit, look a bit like a monkey, but that was only because he had a wide mouth with broad, even teeth and maybe a rather deep upper lip . . . Anyway, he *liked* apes. Several times in London Zoo he had fancied Guy the gorilla. What an animal! His neck, a keeper once told Stirling, had measured thirty-six inches round. Pity he was dead. Chimpanzees, too: vicious brutes, but amusing to watch. He shot out his lips and gave a chimpanzee-type grimace, with the result that he nicked his cheek.

Perhaps if he went to the Himalayas he might track down a yeti and win scientific renown: Sir William Stirling, F.R.S., discoverer of the Abominable Snowman. What colour eyes would a yeti have? His own eyes were green and flecked with hazel. Did that make him a jealous monster? A selfish one, anyway. To go off on his own would be selfish – no argument. Or would Ann find it a relief if he disappeared?

He scrubbed his nails again, dried his face and hands, staunched the little cut and got dressed in tidy clothes. After so long in casual working gear, the smart jacket felt oddly constricting, the black leather shoes absurdly thin.

Outside, the mellow October sun gilded the leaves of the oaks and chestnuts that encircled the little house. On such a morning the place was a picture. He did not like the thought of leaving it.

At the station he stood awkwardly on the platform, feeling out of place among the few late commuters with their sleek, plump jowls and fancy suits. Finding a corner seat in the train, with no one next to him, he got out the letter from Andrew and read it again. It was headed *Ghandrung, W. Nepal,* and had been written ten days before:

My Dear Bill,

You may be surprised to hear that I've gone to ground in the Himalayas, but you'll see why when you get here. I want you to join me at once. Something very much in your line has come up – something that can't wait.

Basically, the project involves a long walk through the mountains. What you'll need is trekking kit. No rubbish – only the best. Good boots, thick socks, proper rucksack. It's boiling in the day and freezing at night (literally), so you want shorts and cotton shirt, as well as a down jacket and warm trousers (e.g. ski). Storm-proof anorak essential. Compass ditto. Snow goggles a must. Altimeter a good idea. Medical pack essential too.

All the heavy stuff – tent, sleeping bag, bed-roll etc. – will be laid on here. All you have to do is get to Katmandu as soon as possible. Report to the Annapurna Trekking Co. They'll line up your Sherpas and porters, and an air ticket to Pokhara, where you start walking. *Don't bring too much stuff*. Everything has to go into your haversack and one kit-bag (latter carried by porter).

Don't worry about money. You can pick up what you need in Katmandu. Travel as an ordinary tourist. Leave U.K. as unobtrusively as possible. An open air ticket Paris–Delhi–Katmandu is waiting for you at Orly in the name of Carson. Suggest you overland to Paris. Telex 'Carson Bingo' and your arrival time to Katmandu telex no. 2254. Happy landings.

Andrew

It was the last paragraph that had instantly given the game away. Carson was the name which Stirling had used during his earlier period of service whenever he had needed special cover. The moment he saw it again, he knew he was being recruited once more. The telephone call from Henderson, coming a few minutes later, had confirmed his intuition. What puzzled him at first – and puzzled him still – was the fact that Andrew appeared to be working for the Office as well.

Andrew de Lazlo? It seemed incredible. Stirling had known him at college and had hardly seen him since. But the de Lazlo he remembered was an intellectual, a fat, aristocratic aesthete, not a man of action at all. Claret and good cigars had been essential to his survival as a student: caviare and smoked salmon as well. Stirling supposed there could hardly be an abundance of either in Ghandrung, West Nepal. Still, as soon as he saw Henderson, all would be made clear.

In London, Stirling called first at the West London Vaccination Centre in Great Cumberland Place, where he had himself pumped full of tetanus, cholera, typhoid and sundry other germs by saucy Australian nurses. Then he caught the Central Line underground to Chancery Lane, aiming for the cluster of mountaineering shops at the lower end of Holborn. Within an hour he had spent nearly £500. To minimise the chance of being remembered, he split the purchases between the three main shops and paid for everything in cash. The money was from sales of venison during the past month, and strictly speaking it belonged to the government. But since Stirling was about to tackle a job for some department, however murky, of the same administration, he saw nothing wrong in transferring funds from one budget to another.

He bought the down jacket in Blacks of Greenock. Both it and its price seemed grossly inflated: it made him look and feel like a Michelin man. But its insulation was phenomenal. Resisting offers of down trousers as well, he settled instead for less exotic woollen ones. The last thing he needed was a rucksack. All the types on display looked hideously bright and new, but as he slid them along the rack on their hangers he noticed a much scruffier, more nondescript one lying in a corner.

'What about that one?' he asked the boy looking after him.

'That one's shop-soiled,' said the youth smugly.

'How much do you want for it?'

'It's not for sale.'

'I said, "How much do you want for it?"' His tone was icy.

The boy muttered something about asking the manager, and a minute later Stirling had bought the scuffed grey pack at less than half price. Into it he crammed all the things he had already bought, and he walked away up Holborn with it slung on his shoulders. By a strange chance, the cut-price haversack was called The Himalayan.

On his way to Pimlico he dropped into a crowded snack-bar for a sandwich and a glass of milk. The sandwich tasted more of plastic than of ham, but he hardly noticed, as his

mind was on the Office and its curious inhabitants, princi-
pally his own mentor Colonel Henderson.

The place had not changed one iota. From outside it
looked (as it was intended to) like the den of some dingy
solicitor who had strayed from the Temple or Lincoln's Inn.
An ancient brass plate beside the plain black door still bore
the name Evans & Rumbold, though nobody could now
remember who those good men had been.

As Stirling pressed the buzzer and waited, he knew he was
being scrutinised through closed-circuit television. Although
built in the eighteenth century, the building housed ultra-
modern surveillance and communications equipment, including its own computer.

A metallic girl's voice from the loudspeaker grille asked his
name, and when he gave it the door buzzed open. Inside
there was a small blind hall, with another locked door, for
which the procedure was repeated. Again, he knew, his face
was appearing on the monitor screens in the control room at
the back of the third floor. This small hall could be used as a
cage in an emergency: extra steel doors, sliding down from
the ceiling, could turn it into a secure gaol at the touch of a
button, trapping anyone undesirable until reinforcements
arrived.

The second doorway was fitted with built-in sensors which
automatically sounded an alarm if anyone entered with a
weapon concealed about his person. As he went through,
Stirling was met by an incredibly tough-looking man of
about seventeen stone who greeted him politely and relieved
him of his haversack, which he took in one hand as if it were a
purse, before leading the way to the second floor. There he
was received by Henderson's secretary (a better-looking girl
than the one he remembered), who ushered him in.

Henderson himself seemed utterly unchanged: possibly a
bit lighter in the temples, but still absolutely the pukka
colonel, beautifully preserved, with his dark-blue suit, stiff
white collar, Brigade of Guards tie, striped shirt, and his neat
pink face glowing healthily beneath the perfectly brushed

iron-grey hair. Never had Stirling seen the collar less than snowy, or one hair out of place.

As Stirling came in, Henderson stood up and greeted him warmly.

'Good of you to come,' he said in his clipped yet sympathetic voice. 'How are you keeping?'

'Fine, thank you.' Stirling sat down, already feeling scruffy. The secretary brought in two cups of china tea, not offering sugar or milk.

'You look pretty fit,' the colonel said. 'Getting plenty of exercise?'

'If I ever stop chasing deer, I cut down trees, or plant some.'

'Good, good.' Henderson smiled with an inward look on his face. Stirling feared he was about to indulge his tiresome habit of quoting some Latin proverb. In this case it was bound to be about the woodman in the autumn. But the moment passed and Henderson said, 'You're up to a bit of a walk, then?'

'Certainly.'

'Excellent. Your willingness to return is much appreciated.'

Stirling said nothing, but looked steadily into the grey-blue eyes, knowing that the man would soon get on with it.

Henderson stirred. 'You've read de Lazlo's letter thoroughly, I take it?'

'Absolutely. I've just bought the stuff I need.'

'Good. Then you're all set. When do you plan to leave?'

'The day after tomorrow. But I need a visa for Nepal, don't I?'

'Of course. Here you are.' Henderson slid an old-looking passport across the table. 'I think you'll find that in order. You may also need this.'

Stirling glanced briefly into the manilla envelope and saw it was full of used £20 notes.

'Thanks,' he said. 'I've just spent nearly £500.'

'Then you won't be out of pocket. Anything else?'

'What are my instructions?'

'At the moment, only what you've seen in the letter. You'll be fully briefed in Katmandu.'

'I see. And how long will this take?'

'It depends on you. Not less than two months, I guess.'

'Can you tell me where I'm going?'

'To Ghandrung, a village in Nepal.'

'I know. But after that.'

Henderson gave the ghost of a sphinx-like smile, and murmured, 'Into the mountains. *Non cuivis homini contingit adire Corinthum.*'

'I'm sorry?'

'"It isn't just anybody who gets the chance of going to Corinth." In other words, it's the trip of a lifetime.'

'It'd just be nice to know what this particular Corinth is.'

'In due course you'll see.'

Stirling knew it was no use to press. But he wanted to know one thing. 'May I ask one question?'

'Of course.'

'Is Andrew de Lazlo working for you too?'

Henderson smiled broadly. 'If I may say so, that isn't a very intelligent inquiry.'

'It's just that he's the last person I'd have thought of in this context. I mean, if you'd known him at college . . . '

'I didn't have the pleasure of knowing him at college. But I did meet him after he'd done some extremely useful work for us in the Sudan.'

'Was it him who suggested me?'

'Ask him.' Again, the ghost of a smile. Henderson stuck out a hand. 'Happy landings!'

Happy landings! Why did everyone keep saying that?

On the train home Stirling examined the passport. Besides the new visa for Nepal, there were several expired ones and bogus date-stamps. The photograph was out of date, but no more so than in most passports. The written details were all correct except the surname and profession. Height: six feet one inch. Distinguishing marks: none. Place of birth:

Darlington. Date of birth: 3.6.50. Residence: England. The Christian names – William George – were his. Only 'Carson' and 'Businessman' were fictitious. The money envelope was no less satisfactory, containing forty of the crumpled notes.

As soon as he got back he began to miss Spot badly. In London and on the train the strangeness of the surroundings had kept the fact of her death at a distance; but when he drove into the familiar yard among the trees, the weight of his loss settled heavily on him.

Dusk was falling. Ann had not yet returned from school – the car was still out. Normally Spot would have been at his heels for every step he took on his errands round the yard, collecting the eggs, shutting up the chickens for the night, bringing in wood for the stove. Now he ran through the routine tasks automatically, numbed by loneliness. There were seventeen eggs – good for the time of year. Dimly he wondered what would happen to the hens when he had gone. Ann would never bother to look after them and sell the eggs – it would be too much trouble.

He hid the haversack containing his purchases among the odds and ends of timber that half-filled a large space beneath the work-bench in the toolshed. Ann never looked under there. By then the fever of the injections had taken hold: his left arm ached, and he had begun to shake and feel cold. He made himself a cup of tea and went to bed, where he sweated violently under a heap of bedclothes. Half an hour later he heard Ann drive into the yard. The back door opened and shut.

'Hi!' he called. 'I'm in bed.'

She came upstairs and stood in the doorway of the room. 'Whatever's the matter with you?' she asked, in a faintly contemptuous voice which suggested either that he had no business to be ill, or that he wasn't really ill at all.

'I don't know,' he muttered through chattering teeth. 'Some bug, I suppose. Flu, probably.'

'That's what comes of hanging around in the woods all

day, getting wet through. If you did something sensible, it wouldn't happen.'

She closed the door and left him to sweat. Stupid bitch! What she failed to realise was, first, that the day had been fine, and second, that he hadn't been in the woods since early morning. To hell with her.

The claws of the fever dug into him, making the evening wretched. But then, in the early hours of the morning, he sank into a deep sleep, from which he didn't wake until nearly nine o'clock.

He sprang up feeling weak but refreshed. In the middle of the morning he drove into the town with a list of further necessities, mainly small: the medical pack, sunburn cream, insect repellent, spare boot-laces, leather oil, matches, candles, a rubber-covered torch and spare batteries, rolls of plastic tape, a ball of string, a coil of tough nylon rope, and heavy-duty polythene bags for waterproof storage of clothes. The last thing he got was a bag of balloons. He had read somewhere that balloons sent Nepalese children into ecstasies of delight, and a bagful costing fifty pence seemed a sound investment.

Back at the cottage he laid everything on his bed and sorted the clothes and equipment into two piles, one for the rucksack and one for the kit-bag.

In the afternoon a strong wind arose, almost a gale. That was handy, as the noise of the wind would swallow the sound of shots. He got out the .38 Radom Special from its hiding-place beneath the stairs and went out to an old chalk-pit deep in the woods, where he fired twenty rounds at flints set up on a fallen tree-trunk. Considering that he had had no regular practice, he was in great form, hitting four targets out of five at twenty paces. The sleek black automatic, with a ten-round magazine in the hand-grip, was a bigger and heavier gun than most of his former colleagues had favoured; but it sat in his hand to perfection, and he had never wanted to change it.

As dusk came on he stood in the yard and watched the yellow leaves spinning from the chestnuts. Everything was

33

ready, but suddenly he felt seized by homesickness. By remorse, too: should he not at least tell Ann what he was doing?

Suddenly an idea struck him. Maybe he should make a gesture and take her out that evening. Over dinner, he could give her a hint that something was in the offing. Being short of money, they didn't go out often; but now he had money burning in his pocket . . .

He awaited her return with growing agitation, like a schoolboy about to meet his first date. He was in the barn, splitting logs, in spite of his stiff arm, when he heard the car draw up.

'Hello, love,' he called.

She seemed surprised to see him up and about. 'I thought you were ill,' she said flatly.

'I felt better, so I got up. Look – are you doing anything tonight?'

'Why?' She was reaching down for some exercise books that had slid on to the floor of the car. 'Well, yes, I am. I've got this pile of stuff to correct.'

'Oh. It's just that I had this bit of luck – won some money on a horse. I thought it would be fun to celebrate.'

'On a *horse*?' She sounded both incredulous and disapproving. 'I didn't know you'd taken up betting.'

'I haven't, really. It was just that I had this red-hot tip from Ron at the garage. I won £25.'

'There must be plenty of better things than food to spend it on.' She slammed the car door and walked across to the house. Stirling turned in the opposite direction, up the grass track through the spinney. Why the hell did she always do this? No *thank you* or *sorry*. Just the frigid turn-off. He walked deeper into the forest, more determined than ever just to disappear.

Three

His alarm went off at five; but, as always when urgent business was in the offing, his internal warning system had woken him well before. For nearly an hour he had lain awake looking out at the friendly stars. He and Ann slept in separate rooms, the polite fiction being that in this way his early exits disturbed her less. Even so, he knew she would hear him getting up. Therefore – to make sure he had a few hours' clear start – he must take care that everything seemed perfectly normal.

He waited a couple of minutes, got up, went downstairs in bare feet to put the kettle on, returned to shave, clean his teeth and get dressed. He put on the clothes he had chosen for travelling – old corduroy trousers, a grey polo-neck sweater and a denim jacket – and made sure that his stalking clothes were tucked away out of sight. Then he switched out the light and felt his way downstairs towards the glow that showed under the kitchen door.

The kettle had boiled and switched itself off. He made a mug of coffee and forced himself to eat a thick slice of bread and butter coated with cherry jam.

He looked at his watch and the clock on the stove. Both said five-twenty. Time to go. He washed the coffee-mug and stood it upside-down in the draining rack. He put the loaf of bread back in the bin and wiped the crumbs from the board with a damp cloth. He checked the clock again: five-twenty-two. Come on, he told himself. You're inventing things to do. Get going.

After a last quick look round he switched out the light and slipped through the back door. The air was sharp and damp and absolutely still – too still for moving through a wood. In the toolshed he had left everything ready. Without switching on his torch he reached under the work-bench and pulled out the haversack and kit-bag. Closing the door of the shed, he silently crossed the grass to the Land Rover.

The headlights swept the cottage as he turned across the yard and into the lane. He drove slowly, letting his mind run ahead. Everything seemed clear and easy.

Eight or nine minutes brought him to the outskirts of the sleeping town. He cruised through the deserted streets, turned down to the river and swung along the bank. Not even the milkmen were on the go yet. Just as well – no one to see him.

Had he gone to his main block of woodland, he would have turned left, over the bridge. As it was, he kept straight on to the railway station and drove to the far, dark end of the car-park. By eight-thirty or so the place would be packed with commuters' cars. At this hour it was empty. He parked the Land Rover beneath the line of trees and left the key in the parcel tray, with the doors unlocked. Then he humped the haversack on to his back, took the kit-bag at the trail in his left hand, and slipped through the fence, to cross the lines and climb through the wood on the bank beyond until he came to the main road heading for London.

Little traffic was moving, but after only ten minutes he flagged down a passing truck – an immense T.I.R. lorry, driven by a merry and gigantic German. *Ja*, he was going to London. *Ja*, he had space. No problem! *Bitte, aufsteigen!*

The cab was full of music – Beethoven's Ninth Symphony blasting from the stereo tape-player, the beginning of the final movement. Stirling felt his forehead and found it was bleeding: in the wood he had walked into a sharp branch. The German soon spotted that he had cut himself. 'Ha!' he roared above the music. 'You are fighting, I think.' He let go of the wheel and launched a flurry of punches at the windscreen, while the forty-ton truck pursued its own course up

36

the motorway. Then, as the chorus followed the bass soloist into the great tune of the finale, he beat out the rhythm on the wheel itself, making the vehicle twitch from side to side like a circus elephant dancing.

Stirling glanced at his watch. It was not much after six. His luck was better than he deserved. In London he called a halt to post Ann a letter in which he merely said he would be away for a couple of weeks, and then the German took him straight on to Ramsgate, where he boarded the Hovercraft for France.

Ann, lying comfortably in bed, glanced at the alarm-clock, and saw it said seven-twenty-five. As usual, she had heard Bill go out a couple of hours before. She had seen the stretched rectangles of light flare across the ceiling as he turned out of the yard. But the light and the noise had scarcely brushed the surface of her consciousness, so much were they part of his routine at this season of the year. With the luxurious feeling of having a couple of hours in hand, she had slid easily back to sleep.

Now, in slippers and dressing-gown, she went down to make a cup of tea. The kettle was still slightly warm, as usual. But as she plugged it in, she noticed something odd: Bill's belt of rifle ammunition lay coiled up on the shelf by the door. That didn't seem to make sense. How could he have gone stalking without ammunition?

Her heart accelerated. She ran out to the toolshed and rummaged among the timber under the bench. Gone! She had come on the haversack and kit-bag quite by chance, the evening Bill had been down with the fever. Though normally she didn't enter the toolshed for months at a time, that night she had gone looking for a piece of wood to prop open the lid of the deep-freeze while she sorted through its contents. Without investigating the luggage very far, she had seen that Bill had some clandestine trip in the offing. Now he had left.

She hardly knew whether to feel relieved or angry. But as

she stood in the kitchen and wondered, relief began to predominate.

The kettle had boiled. She made tea and sat at the table drinking it, struck into a daydream by this sudden turn of events. Part of her was still fond of Bill, but part loathed him for the way he had been carrying on with that slut of a North Country girl. As if she, Ann, hadn't known about it. The whole town knew about it. Maybe he'd gone off with her now. Well, he was welcome to her.

Anyway, there was one thing she ought to do: ring the emergency number. The man from the Office had given her a number to call if ever Bill suddenly went off into the blue. She found it in her diary. The code was 01, the prefix 607. Somewhere in North London. She dialled and listened to the steady ringing. Perhaps there was nobody there so early in the morning?

Suddenly a man's voice answered.

'Yes?'

'This is Ann Stirling speaking.'

'Repeat your name please.'

She gave it again. 'You asked me to call if my husband went away.'

'Yes, yes. Of course. What has happened?'

'He's taken off.'

'To where?'

'I don't know. Well . . .'

'Yes?'

'It may sound stupid, but I have the impression he's gone to India.'

'India? Really?'

'It's only a hunch. I'm not sure. I could be wrong.'

'It is no matter. What time did he leave?'

'About two hours ago. At five-thirty.'

'So.'

There was a pause. 'Is there anything else?' Ann asked.

'Thank you, no. All is in order. Thanks for calling.'

Ann rang off. Had she made a fool of herself about India?

The pack had had *Himalayan* written on it – and the Himalayas were in India. Part of them, anyway. Or was it – the thought struck her suddenly – just a brand name? Too late. But at least she had done the right thing.

Four

As usual first thing in the morning, Room 205 of the Russian Embassy in Kensington Palace Road smelt stale and uninviting. As he came in, Sergei Antonin switched on the air-conditioning with an automatic movement, wishing wearily that the authorities would rescind the ban on opening windows – imposed for sound security reasons, no doubt, but lowering to the morale of the building's inhabitants.

Before he had even sat down at his desk, the telephone gave a buzz. It was the switchboard, telling him that Comrade Ivan Konev had already rung twice that morning and wanted to speak to him urgently.

'Call him, then, please,' he said irritably. Konev, who ran a jewellery shop in Islington, was one of his out-stations. The man had contributed little or nothing in recent months. It was time he produced something. Yet even when Antonin had heard what Konev had to say, he was not much impressed.

Stirling, alias Carson, known to the Bureau as a British agent, had gone abroad. At least, so his wife had said. She thought he had gone to India.

'What else did she say?' Antonin demanded.

'Nothing, Comrade,' Konev admitted.

'Did you check back?'

'I tried, twice. But there was no answer.'

'Did she suspect anything?'

'I think not.'

Antonin told Konev to keep phoning. Meanwhile, he sent for the stock file on Carson. The photograph was a poor one, taken with a telephoto lens when the subject was in army uniform. The cap obscured much of the face and made recognition difficult. The notes were brief, but their gist was clear. Since 1975 Carson had been retired from active service. He had been kept under observation, of course, but he had indulged in no paramilitary, political or intelligence activity. He had become a Forestry Ranger and buried himself in the country. No children. Relations with wife bad. Affair with Mrs Susan Riley of 18 Beechwood Road well recorded: he visited her regularly at 1.40 on weekday afternoons, left at 3.25 punctually. There was another photograph of him, also taken with a zoom lens, leaving the back door of the house. The affair could have been useful for blackmail purposes, Antonin reflected, but so far no advantage had been taken of it. A final note recorded that the subject had been to London two days previously.

So Carson had quit. Fed up with the wife, probably. What about the mistress, though? Had she taken off too? And why should he go to India? A long way to go to escape domestic ties. Antonin sighed and lit a cigarette. This looked to him like the straightforward break-up of a marriage. Even so, there were certain steps that he should take.

First he arranged for a man to check the passenger lists of all flights leaving London for Delhi, Bombay and Calcutta. He sent another man to Heathrow to monitor the check-ins. Then he telexed the office in Delhi, requesting a check on all flights arriving from London. Regrettably, the Bureau was not represented in Calcutta or Bombay – a deficiency which was becoming increasingly tiresome as business in India built up. He also arranged for a helpful washing-machine salesman to call on Mrs Riley that afternoon, purely to see whether or not she was still there. Finally he drafted a quick message recording Carson's movement and put it on the wire for Moscow.

All these, he told himself, were routine precautions: they would lead nowhere, but never mind. With a longer and deeper sigh he settled back to read the morning papers.

His browsing was cut short, however. To his chagrin and

amazement, Moscow came on the line almost before his own signal had landed, demanding details of Carson's movements immediately. A Red Priority order! By God, he had better get moving.

What he did not know was that in the lavatorial, off-white skyscraper which houses the Moscow headquarters of the K.G.B. an ambitious First Secretary called Nesteroff had once again exercised his prodigious facility for dredging up an individual name from the sea of reports that surged endlessly across his desk. So sharp was Nesteroff's recall, in fact, that his colleagues told him the computer which he operated was superfluous: he was himself a computer.

The moment he found Stirling's name in the message from London, his mind began to work at top speed. Stirling . . . Carson . . . Stirling. Somewhere, some time, during the past couple of weeks, he had seen that name already. The mention of India completed the circuit. India – Nepal – Katmandu. A moment later he had dug out the microfiche carrying the messages which had come from Katmandu during the past month and slipped it into the viewer. There it was: on the 3rd (according to his informant in the British Embassy) a letter addressed to Stirling had gone out to England in the Diplomatic Bag.

Now Stirling/Carson was on his way to India. To Katmandu, in all probability – the normal way to fly to the Nepalese capital was via Delhi or Calcutta. Evidently he had been summoned for some special task.

Nesteroff's mind made another quick jump – to the garbled message, also from Katmandu, about the American soldier stranded in a Tibetan monastery. The story had been far from clear. He had asked for clarification, so far without result. But now he suddenly saw what was happening: Carson had been sent to get the American out. Nesteroff would have put his month's pay on it, so certain did he feel of his hunch.

Two urgent tasks therefore presented themselves: first, to arrange for Carson to be intercepted; and second, to find out precisely where the American was, so that someone else, more suitable, could be sent in, either to eliminate him, or, if he seemed worthwhile, to organise his evacuation.

Five

'I don't want to seem rude,' said Patrick Smith, 'but the sooner we get you out of Katmandu, the better.'

'Obviously.' Stirling regarded the elegant diplomat coolly. The man was a good deal older than him – maybe forty-five – but he felt that he would like him, in spite of the perfection of his clothes. The white linen suit and red-and-white polka-dot tie made his own check shirt, jeans and training shoes look uncouth, to say the least. Yet Smith was not really as collected as he pretended to be: it was clear that he found Stirling's visit not only potentially dangerous, but also rather exciting.

Smith described himself as the Liaison Officer of the British Embassy – a title that might cover any number of underhand roles. He had sent a car to the airport, but although the driver had been unobtrusive and efficient at extracting Stirling's baggage, they had become aware of a tail within a minute of leaving the terminal. Their car – ancient, decrepit and chosen for its anonymity – lacked the power to leave the pursuer behind. Besides, as they came into the city centre the streets were so choked with pedestrians, loose animals, bullock carts and bicycles that speed was impossible. They had finally shed the tail with a ruse suggested by the driver, who took Stirling to the front of the Annapurna Hotel and told him to walk straight through to the back door, where he immediately collected him again. Thus, as far as they could tell, they had reached the British Embassy undetected.

Now Stirling sat at a white cast-iron table beneath a tree in

44

the Embassy's spacious garden. Smith had ordered gin-and-tonics, and was trying to mask his curiosity behind a front of official reticence.

'Your movements seem to have been rather well publicised,' he said suavely.

'Not by me.'

'It seems unfortunate that people were lined up on the tarmac to greet you.'

'It does. What I'd like to know is who they are.'

'I'm afraid it's our friends from the Kremlin.'

'Christ. What are they doing here?'

'They're everywhere. Or at least, their contacts are. Of course, officially we know nothing about such matters.' Smith spread his hands deprecatingly. 'But in practice we can't help hearing about such things. Especially when someone such as yourself arrives. This afternoon, for instance, a man was asking for you at the Annapurna Hotel.'

Smith paused, and when he got no reply went on: 'You're booked in there for the night. But I don't think you'd better go there – do you?'

'Certainly not. What's the alternative?'

'I've got you another room at a place called the Makalu. It's smaller and less comfortable, but O.K. for one night.'

'Thanks. That sounds fine.'

'Another thing: you know your trek starts at Pokhara?'

Stirling nodded, noticing how Smith put the accent on the first syllable: P*o*kerer, not Pokh*a*ra.

'There's only one plane a day from here. You've got a seat on the flight tomorrow afternoon. But again, I think you'd be well advised not to use it. Nor even to go near the airport, for that matter. Instead, I've arranged for a car to drive you all the way to Pokhara. It's a five-hour trip, I'm afraid, but it'll be safer. Also, it'll get you there earlier. I've fixed for you to be collected at six a.m. from the hotel. You'll be in Pokhara before midday, and well clear of the place before the scheduled flight gets in at four.'

Now that Smith was warming to his task of explanation,

his manner became more openly conspiratorial. 'How good's your local geography?' he asked.

'Hopeless, I'm afraid.'

'Well, I'll show you.' He unfolded a map. 'Paradoxically, you'll be safer as soon as you get away from civilisation and into the wilds. Here's the road from Katmandu going north-west to Pokhara. It goes a couple of miles beyond the town, and there it ends. After that, communications end, too. There's no road, no railway, no telephone, no radio, nothing. You depend on your own two feet.'

'That sounds good.'

Smith grinned at him quizzically. 'You look pretty fit,' he said. 'You like walking?'

Stirling nodded.

'Your friend's at Ghandrung, right? That's there. About a day and a half from Pokhara.'

Stirling's neck began to prickle as he saw the spot heights marked in the area for which he was heading. Every peak seemed to be over 20,000 feet, many over 25,000.

'How about my Sherpas and porters?'

'They're all laid on for you. They'll meet you in Pokhara. All you need now is your trekking permit and some money for local expenses.' He reached down into his attaché case.

'I was supposed to collect the permit from the trekking company,' said Stirling, remembering Andrew's letter.

'Again, I thought it better for you not to be seen around town.' Smith smiled broadly. 'So I had the things collected for you.'

He handed over a folded document made of coarse, thick brown paper, almost cardboard, like compressed dead leaves. In clumsy English and Gurkhali printing it announced that the bearer was entitled to trek from Pokhara to a list of places that included Ghandrung.

'And here's some pocket-money,' Smith went on, producing a thick envelope. 'Sorry it's so bulky, but most of it's in small denominations – for a good reason. It doesn't do to bring out big notes in the mountain villages – gives people ideas.'

Stirling took the money and thanked him. 'You seem to have thought of everything,' he said. 'All I need now is to know what I'm supposed to be doing.'

'Well – I can enlighten you a bit. Let's go in, though. It's getting chilly.'

After the stifling heat of Delhi, the mountain air felt sharp as the sun went down. Stirling followed his host indoors to a functional, white-walled office.

'Mission Yak,' Smith began. 'That's the codename we've been using. Do you know *him*?' He dropped on to the desk-top a photograph of a strong-looking, ruggedly handsome man in his fifties, with close-cropped dark hair. Stirling shook his head.

'General Dan Sulzberger, U.S. Army. Expert on nuclear weapons, tactical as well as intercontinental. You won't remember the incident, because it was hushed up at the time, but two years back he upped and defected during a goodwill tour of China. The incident caused a panic in the Pentagon because everyone assumed the general was going to hand priceless defence secrets to the Chinese. Later, a rumour came out that he was working for the Chinese – advising them on defence.

'That was the last anyone heard of him – until a few weeks ago, when a letter reached your friend de Lazlo. It had come from a monastery called Rimring, in Southern Tibet.'

'I'm sorry, but who wrote the letter?'

'Sulzberger himself. He said he'd defected again, back to the States – or at least that he wanted to. But while he was trying to escape from Tibet he'd broken his back, and was stuck in this monastery.'

Stirling's pulse accelerated. 'So my job is to go into Tibet and get him out.'

'Not exactly. While he was in China, and later in Tibet, he compiled a dossier of all the information he'd got hold of. That's what you've got to fetch – the dossier. He calls it his

47

Bible. There's no document in the world that the Western Governments would better like to get their hands on than the Rimring Bible. It gives details of the entire Chinese defence set-up – and not only that: it covers the border with Russia as well.'

'And where is this place – Rimring?'

Smith spread his hands again. 'Sorry – I can't help you. It's not marked on our maps. But it can't be all that far inside the Tibetan border. This is where de Lazlo comes in. He's in touch with the Tibetans. He'll lay on guides to take you through the frontier. But even in Nepal you're going to have to go carefully.'

'Why's that?'

'The whole of this area here, to the north, is closed to foreigners at the moment. The government's trying to round up the remnants of a tribe called the Khampas, and they're not letting any trekkers through. The trails are closed.'

'What by?'

'Police checks. Army patrols. You'll have to work your way round them somehow.'

'What about a helicopter?'

'A helicopter?' Smith sounded slightly pained.

'Couldn't I be lifted up to some starting-point near the border? It would save a lot of time.'

'My dear fellow, I don't think you realise what Nepal's like. It's a very primitive place. Helicopters scarcely exist there. The King has one for his private use. The army have a few. But there are no commercial ones. It isn't like Europe. And anyway, flying helicopters in the Himalayas is a dicey business. You get terrific winds, sudden storms. There are no facilities for refuelling or repairs, except in Katmandu. Most of the villages are so steep – on such steep ground, I mean – that a chopper wouldn't be able to land near them anyway. Wait till you get into the hills, and you'll see what I mean.'

Stirling grunted and looked at the map. Smith cleared his throat and said, 'It's awkward. I wish we could give you more help. But the whole situation's very delicate. If the

Nepalese Government knew we were involved in this operation at all, it would be, well, difficult, to put it mildly.'

'They don't know anything about it?'

'Not yet.'

There was a pause. Then Stirling asked, 'Why don't the Americans handle this? After all, it's their affair. I'd have thought this was exactly the sort of thing the C.I.A. would be on to like a shot.'

'The C.I.A.', said Smith drily, 'are not very popular in this part of the world at the moment – especially since that farce on Nanda Devi.'

'Nanda Devi? What was that?'

'The C.I.A. tried to build a nuclear-powered tracking station so that they could monitor Chinese rocket-launches. They wanted to put it right on top of Nanda Devi – 26,000 feet or so. But the climbers failed to reach the summit, and they had to store the device in a crevasse for the winter. When they came back next spring, they couldn't find it. The whole thing had disappeared beneath the snow, including the fuel rod of Plutonium 238.

'When the Indian Government heard about it, they went off the deep end, because it's the snows of Nanda Devi that feed the head waters of the Ganges. They thought the whole river might turn radioactive for the next few hundred years.'

'What happened in the end?'

'There *is* no end. They never found the thing. They don't know what happened to it. So far there's been no radioactive leak, but the Indians are afraid that one might start any spring. You can see why the Americans aren't everybody's favourite uncles around these parts.'

'Even so,' Stirling persisted, 'I'd have thought the C.I.A. would just send some damn great long-range helicopter in and hoick the general out, regardless of what the Nepalese said or did.'

'They might – *if* they knew where to send it. But that's the point. Nobody except a few Tibetans knows where Rim-ring is.'

Smith drummed on the table top with his propelling-pencil. 'In a way, your mission's a kind of successor to the Nanda Devi fiasco. If you get the Bible out, it'll tell the Pentagon more about Chinese rocketry than any number of monitoring stations.'

The Makalu Hotel turned out to be a graceless modern building wedged into a gap between older houses. But it made up for what it lacked in style by functioning with reasonable efficiency. The reception clerk handled Stirling's registration promptly, and a boy quickly carried his luggage up to the double room, tawdry yet serviceable, on the second floor. After a shower and a change of clothes Stirling went down to the restaurant, where he was pleasantly surprised to find the curries excellent. The beer, though prodigiously expensive, was drinkable.

As he ate he studied the map which Smith had given him, starting to memorise its salient features. But although his eyes were on the names of mountains, rivers and villages, his mind dwelt on the disconcerting fact that 'friends from the Kremlin', as Smith had called them, were already in such close attendance. There had been a bad leak somewhere.

Full marks to Smith for laying on the early-morning departure to Pokhara, anyway. He liked the idea of K.G.B. agents pinned down in a futile wait at both the Annapurna Hotel and the airport.

After supper he settled his account – for the meal as well as for the room – and wrestled briefly with an urge to explore the narrow, bazaar-like streets through which he had approached the hotel. Each was flanked by dozens of tiny, wooden-fronted shops like rabbit-hutches, in which the proprietors crouched hopefully, half buried beneath their merchandise. He would have liked to join the tide of humans and animals that flowed endlessly through the pungent darkness, to feel and hear the heart-beat of the city.

But he knew that to go out would be to court unnecessary

risks. It would be crazy to end up on his first evening in Nepal with a knife between his ribs.

Reluctantly he returned to the second floor. The landing was in darkness. He tried the switch, but the bulb seemed to have gone. No matter: he felt his way along the passage to room 202 easily enough.

During his years of service he had perfected a patent method of entering strange hotel rooms, and now he adopted it again as though he had never ceased to use it.

Approaching silently, he inserted the key in the lock, turned it and the handle simultaneously, and flung the door sharply back on its hinges. There was a thump, a sudden commotion. He felt, rather than saw, the man coming at him. He just managed to crouch and make a half-turn towards the noise. There was a pop and a hissing sound right above his head. A snatch of some viciously strong smell seared his nostrils. Instinctively he blew out. An instant later his shoulder caught the man in the chest.

He carried through the short, sprung charge, forward and up. The attacker was lifted clear of the floor and flung backwards against the wall. The impact of his head on the concrete rang out like that of a cricket ball well struck. His body slumped to the floor.

Stirling's nose was on fire. Blindly he rushed into the bathroom, turned on the taps of the basin and sloshed water up his nostrils and into his mouth, trying not to breathe. As he fought the fire, his training flooded back to him. He raced back into the bedroom, groped up his torch from the bedside table, dived at the inert figure on the floor and ripped out the pockets of the trousers. Though he could hardly see, he found what he was looking for – a small aluminium container with a screw top, containing a single white tablet. He swallowed it at once, threw open the windows and dived back into the bathroom.

He was shuddering with reaction. Prussic acid! It must have been that. The K.G.B. bastards used it often. He held his face downwards in the basin of cold water, blinking his eyelids frantically. At least he had eaten the antidote. What about the sod next door? He might come round. Stirling's gun was still there. Better get hold of it.

He lifted his face out of the water. His eyes and nose still stung furiously, but his vision was improving. He could see enough. Holding his nose, he went quickly in and extracted the .38 from his haversack. The man on the floor showed no sign of recovering. Stirling closed the outer door of the room and locked it. Then he put his head out of the open window and began to take deep breaths.

In spite of the fresh air, something was wrong. His lungs wouldn't work properly. He couldn't get enough oxygen. When he tried to draw air in, his muscles seemed to have jammed. Palpitations seized him – a ghastly fluttering all through his chest. Panic welled up. He was going to suffocate. Or else it was a heart attack. He clutched desperately at the window sill, pouring with sweat.

Now his legs were shaking as well. He couldn't seem to keep upright. Paralysis: he slid down on to the floor, still grasping the window sill fiercely. His vision had gone again. The street lights were only a bright blur. He felt as if a gigantic weight was crushing him.

How long he lay there by the window, he could not tell. He came round slowly. First he realised that he could see again. He was on his back, and a pattern of light was flickering on the ceiling. His breathing seemed to be normal. He tested his limbs and found them in order.

He had got away with it, but only just. Because he had ducked instinctively as he became aware of danger, the gun had gone off above his head instead of in his face: he had caught only the edge of the gas blast, instead of its full force. Also, he had held his breath. A full breath of that stuff at point-blank range – two feet or less – caused instantaneous collapse – and afterwards left no sign. A verdict of death by natural causes would have been recorded.

He picked himself up gingerly and searched the room. First he found the light bulbs, which had been taken out. Replacing them, he saw the weapon on the floor – an aluminium tube about eight inches long with a pistol grip at one end. He remembered seeing something similar during training: a squeeze of the trigger fired a percussion cap, which in turn crushed a phial of prussic acid, releasing the gas. The assailant was always given an antidote to take immediately he fired.

Stirling fetched a towel and dropped it over the gun, wrapped it up and put it out of the way in the bathroom. Next he rearranged the beds so that it was physically impossible for the door to open. Then he turned his attention to the man on the floor. He was a young, thin Nepalese with a ratty face, shabbily dressed in Western-style clothes – yellow nylon shirt and grey cotton trousers. A local recruit, obviously, and now in a bad way, still unconscious, breathing fast and shallow. Taking no chances, Stirling trussed him thoroughly with nylon cord, forced a gag made from a ripped-up pillow-case into his mouth, and dumped him in the bathroom.

His natural inclination was to get the hell out of the hotel as fast as he could. Yet he knew he would be safer staying where he was. He strongly suspected that the man in his bathroom had not come alone: sooner or later a colleague would arrive out there on the dark landing. He might be less lucky a second time. It was better to remain *in situ*, trapped though he was, until early morning. Then, if he had to, he could shoot his way out and make a quick getaway in Smith's car. But to shoot his way out now would probably land him in gaol.

He checked the windows. Their metal frames pivoted on a vertical axis. He leant out, looking up and down. The flat roof was only about four feet above, but it had a wide overhang, which would make it impossible for anyone to climb down without a rope. A rope. The thought gave him a new idea: yes, his climbing rope would easily reach to street level. That was the way to leave, when the time came. Meanwhile, provided the door could not be opened even a crack, he was safe enough where he was.

He closed one window completely and set the other with a glass balanced precariously on the sill, so that if anyone tried to open it further the glass would crash to the floor. He made sure the beds were wedged tightly, took off his shoes, stretched out under one thin blanket, checked the .38 yet again and switched out the light.

Deep down, he was exhausted by the strain of the past few days, by the long flight and the jet-lag. But also he was simmering with tension. Although he could breathe more easily, his chest still felt tight. He concentrated on relaxing, letting each arm, elbow, wrist, finger, finger-nail even, lie heavily on the hard mattress.

His mind ranged back to Deepwood Cottage. What time would it be there? Six hours behind Katmandu? Five o'clock, then. Ann. Coming home from work. Had she fed the chickens? The boiler would be out, the kitchen cold. Sadness settled on him at the thought of his home left with no one to love it. He thought of Spot's grave in the wood. Maybe the deer were passing it as they came out to graze in the evening.

His mind turned to the mountains: high, clean sheets of snow. No people. Away from crowded cities crawling with potential killers. Mission Yak. Not a bad name. He liked the idea of a yak: a faintly ridiculous creature, somehow, but a nice one. The monastery of Rimring. Would there be priests in scarlet robes?

Suddenly he was wide awake. He glanced at the luminous hands of his watch. Twenty-five past seven. No – twenty-five to five. A noise had awoken him. There it was again: someone trying the door. He had left his key in the lock, half-turned. Another key clinked as it met his head-on.

He got the gun in his hand and lay still. Which was best – to shout out or to feign sleep? The scraping, clicking noise continued. Very slowly and carefully, so that the springs would not creak, he eased himself off the bed and stood with his back to the passage wall, listening. Now, even if somebody fired through the door, he could not be hit. What if he himself fired out through the door? By Christ, that would shift the bastard. But it would also attract precisely the kind of attention that he didn't want.

He waited, holding his breath. The prowler was obviously not going to shoot through the door: his aim was to get into the room. Another prussic acid specialist, for sure. Now he was trying to unscrew the whole lock, rather than pick it.

Stirling's inclination was to let him carry on: even if he got the lock right off, the door still would not give. He checked his watch again: not much more than an hour till he'd be leaving anyway. Maybe he could keep the man in play until it was time to go, and then do a Nepalese rope-trick on him, leaving him busily at work.

He sat on the bed and rolled over heavily, making the springs creak. Then he gave a couple of histrionic yawns. The scratching ceased abruptly. He switched on the lamp and stumbled across to the bathroom, where he went to the lavatory and flushed it. His prisoner was still alive, but not by much. Having had a look at him, he returned to bed and switched the light off again.

The manoeuvre proved successful. The attempt on the lock did not start again for nearly half an hour. When it did begin, Stirling let it continue for a few minutes, and then made another precipitate visit to the bathroom, during which he extracted the climbing rope and packed up the rest of his kit. Again, the locksmith was forced to desist.

Thus, by fits and starts, the game continued until 5.45 a.m. It was still perfectly dark. All Stirling had to do was to pull on his shoes. Everything else was ready. By then, he hoped, the man in the corridor must be convinced that his bowels were in a state of dissolution.

Covered by the noise of the cistern filling yet again, he passed one end of the rope under the thick water-pipe that ran along the skirting-board beneath the window, and tied both haversack and kit-bag to it. Having made sure there was no one in the street below, he lowered the bags carefully to the pavement, together with the other end of the rope, which thus hung double all the way down the wall. Then, holding both strands tight in his right hand, he eased himself backwards through the window and walked quickly down the wall, hand over hand on the rope. The moment he touched down, he let go the loose end and began pulling down on the other. The rope snaking over the window sill and round the pipe would make a noise, he knew. It was inevitable. But even if the man heard it, he would not know what it was.

The air in the street was surprisingly cold. Stirling gasped, partly from the effort of lowering himself, but mainly from the sudden chill. The end of the rope slapped down on the pavement and he quickly stowed it away.

Then he shouldered the haversack and took the kit-bag in his left hand, leaving his right free for the .38. But he did not need it. Round the corner, outside the hotel's front entrance, stood a car with its lights on. He walked up to it and recognised Patrick Smith's driver from the night before. Without a word he threw his luggage into the back seat, closed the door softly, climbed into the front, and indicated that they should go.

Six

Deep pastoral calm enveloped Pokhara airfield. A bullock cart with squealing wooden wheels crunched slowly along the cinder landing-strip, and grey-black water buffaloes wandered untended. One tumbledown shack did duty for an airport building. The sky was overcast, the air hot and close. The broad, green valley, flanked by scrub-covered hills, felt as if it was filled with invisible steam.

As Stirling's car drew up a man detached himself from the group at one edge of the field and came across – a slim, wiry youth of hardly more than twenty, with shiny, straight black hair and a friendly brown face split by a dazzling band of teeth.

'Sherpa Mingmar,' he announced with a shy smile. 'Welcome to Pokhara. Welcome to Himalaya.'

'Thanks.' Stirling smiled and shook hands. 'We're a bit early.'

'O.K., sair. Porters soon ready.' He indicated the group of men and seized Stirling's two heavy pieces of baggage, one in either hand. They went over to the main body of the little private army: four small, muscular men, barefoot, in ragged shirts and shorts, with a mass of stores and equipment spread out round them on the grass, arguing furiously.

The Sherpa explained in jerky monosyllables that the porters were packing their loads. Anything the sahib might want during the march should travel in his haversack; the kit-bag, containing the rest of his things, would be carried by one of the porters, and he might not see it for hours at a stretch. In the evenings, the porters probably would not reach camp for an hour or more after he had.

Stirling made a few new dispositions, transferring the .38, among other things, so that it would travel on his own back. Then he handed the kit-bag over. He was ashamed to see that it made up only part of one porter's load. The man stowed it inside a huge, funnel-shaped wicker basket along with blanket-rolls and cooking equipment, before lashing the whole bundle together with rope.

Stirling itched to be off – he was starting to get a persecution complex, and kept looking round the field for intruders. But he could see no future in trying to accelerate the careful process of packing. He looked himself over with distaste. He was a head taller than any of the Nepalese, and therefore immediately conspicuous. Beside the smooth brown limbs of his men, his own looked pale and hairy. He was sweating already. The sun, though intermittent, burned powerfully when it did come out. According to his altimeter, they were only 3,000 feet up – 2,000 feet lower than in Katmandu.

Still there were no big mountains to be seen. The post-monsoon clouds, which had rather spoilt their drive, lowered everywhere.

'Where *are* the Himalayas?' he asked Mingmar in a voice which suggested he did not believe in the existence of such mountains. The Sherpa laughed and said, 'Here, sair, all around you.' He waved all round the northern horizon. 'Here – ' he pointed almost straight up into the air – 'here Macchapuchare. Fish-tail mountain.'

'Why fish-tail?'

'Two peak, sair. Like fish-tail. Nobody climb her.'

'Why not?'

'No permit giving.' Once, he explained, an English expedition had climbed to within fifty feet of one of the twin summits before abandoning their attempt. Since then the Nepalese Government had declared the mountain a sanctuary. So Macchapuchare had remained inviolate.

As Mingmar darted from one man to the next, he rattled out commands in what sounded like volleys of curried Italian. Every short, sharp sentence had a hot ending: *ho*! or *no*! or *na-yoh!* The words flew out like machine-gun bullets. Gradually the various heaps were sorted and stowed.

As the process neared its end there was a sudden flurry. Everyone stopped work as the noise of an engine grew steadily louder. Stirling had a panic that the daily flight from Katmandu was coming in, hours ahead of schedule. But the aircraft that appeared was obviously a private one – a small, angular, blue-and-white plane which came in to land so abruptly that the water buffaloes fled bellowing from the runway. One moment the plane was high in the air; the next it had dived steeply, straightened out, touched down and come to a halt after a ridiculously short run.

From it there emerged an amazing crew – a Sherpa dressed like an astronaut, white all over except for silver trimmings down the side of his shorts and round his cap; a tall, willowy European pilot with dark glasses and bell-bottomed lilac trousers; and a stunning blonde girl with legs about five feet long, a lively behind barely contained by a pair of sky-blue shorts, and a buoyant torso that had a flame-red shirt in similar trouble.

Stirling got up off the grass, needled by a twinge of alarm. The party was heading straight for him. It was as if they had come to find him.

'My word!' cried the girl in a cracking Antipodean accent. 'How d'you be, cobber?'

Stirling grinned defensively and took the outstretched hand, catching a blast of expensive scent. She announced her name, which he took to be Kerry. He recoiled instinctively from the brashness of her approach. With her first words she had struck a false note, a jangle of excessive heartiness. He wanted nothing to do with her. But she was all over him.

'Bill, did you say?'

'That's it. Bill.'

'This your first trek in the Himalayas, Bill?'

He nodded.

'Bloody marvellous mountains! Fantastic scenery. But

jeeze, is it hot! Couldn't I just do with a nice wet in the boozer! Which way are you heading? West?'

He nodded again.

'Travelling alone?' She looked round brightly for fellow trekkers.

'That's right. You too?'

'One's company!' She fluttered her eyelashes. 'Actually, I'm on my way to meet a friend at the Annapurna base-camp.'

'A climber?'

'That's right. He's on an expedition. Not Annapurna it-self. Something smaller. Wait a minute, though. We must be going the same road. Dhampus, Ghandrung? Right?'

'I'm meeting a friend, too,' he said stonily. But the cold response didn't stop her.

'Mind if I tag along, Bill? I'd really like some company.'

Looking at her dispassionately, he could see the attraction of having those legs precede him along the mountain trails. Yet in his present state there was nothing he wanted less. For one thing he was still trying to come to terms with the emotional turmoil of the past few days. For another, he had to concentrate on the journey ahead, to learn about his new environment. To have the blonde chattering at him would be the worst possible distraction. Besides, he felt suspicious about her motives. But he had no monopoly of the tracks.

'Well,' he said grudgingly. 'Whatever you like. You have your own porters, I suppose?'

'Over there. Nima's lining them up now.' She nodded to where the astronaut-Sherpa and the pilot were sorting out a second private army, considerably larger than his own. The girl was certainly travelling in style: maybe she had a port-able bath and bidet, perhaps also a fridge and a sauna.

The pilot came towards them, his fair hair flopping on his shoulders. 'Hi!' he called. 'Haller.'

Stirling shook hands and said, 'Bill Carson.' Then he added, 'Nice plane you've got.'

'A good one for this country. Very quick up and down – no

bother.' Though Haller's English was fluent, his accent was markedly German. 'You have seen one before?'

'No – what is it?'

'Cessna STOL. You know STOL? Short take-off and landing. Come – I show you.'

Stirling glanced round again. Mingmar was still not ready. Might as well look at the aircraft.

They walked over to it. The plane was a curious combination of ancient and modern: a square, box-like fuselage, but a long, slim nose. Square-ended wings, square-tipped tail, non-retractable wheels on tubular aluminium struts – the whole thing highly functional, but no beauty. The interior was the same: eight seats done up in shiny brown-and-white plastic, with bare aluminium legs, and no decoration inside the fuselage.

'Performance is *fentestic*,' Haller was saying. 'You must know – take-off run, one hundred metres. Landing run, eighty metres. You can land – how you say? – on a sixpenny.'

'Expensive to hire, I bet.'

'Oh no – not at all. Two hundred dollars per hour. It is nothing.'

'Nothing to some people.' Stirling gave a wry glance in the direction of the blonde.

'So, I give you my card. One day, maybe, I am at your service.' He handed over a card made of the same brown paper as the trekking permit and bearing the legend 'KLAUS HALLER, Licensed Air Taxi. Special Mountain Flights. See Everest in Luxury.' At the bottom was an address and telephone number in Katmandu.

Stirling thanked him and slipped the card into the pocket of his shorts. In truth he was fascinated by the plane, and would have enjoyed a good look round it. But he wasn't going to tell Haller that, or even let on that he too could fly. All he wanted was to be on the move as soon as possible.

Now Mingmar had everything to his satisfaction. At the last moment he had been joined by his second-in-command – a sinewy, older, taller man with high cheekbones, a broken nose and a distinctly Mongol cast of feature, whose name was Pasang. With him had appeared a slip of a youth called Likpa.

'Cook-boy,' Mingmar announced. The lad had a small, pointed face and watchful, slanting eyes which kept a sharp lookout from under the peak of a large green baseball-type cap. He looked about thirteen. Like the porters he was barefoot, but he wore at least two pairs of trousers: beneath the tattered hem of his outer pair of jeans the bottom of another layer was visible.

He startled Stirling by heaving one of the heaped wicker baskets on to his puny back and settling the load so that most of the weight was taken by a broad strap which passed over his forehead on top of the cap. The porters made identical humping and settling movements, and a moment later they all set out, walking hunched slightly forward against their head-bands.

It was a big moment. Mission Yak was rolling. The girl, thank God, was still not organised. Stirling gave her a wave and called 'See you later,' hoping he never would.

Soon the basic pattern of the advance became clear. Mingmar led, and Stirling kept with him. The porters and cook-boy followed in single file. At the back came Pasang, driving off the children who swarmed about the party screeching for baksheesh.

They went up through the town along a street of uneven cobbles, between tumbledown, windowless houses. Everything looked tawdry and decrepit. Mongrels scavenged among the rubbish, competing for scraps of food with pigs and scrawny chickens. A sickly smell of decay lay heavy in the air.

Presently they drew clear of the houses and started up a drab grey valley. For the first hour Stirling felt depressed, for the surroundings were so ordinary. The valley was a mess, strewn with banks of loose stones which the river had dumped during the monsoon spate. The heat was intense and steamy. The straps of his haversack bit into his shoulders. His socks were too thick for temperatures of this order. His left boot was done up too tight, causing the laces to chew at his instep. Sweat stung his eyes and poured down his chest. It would have poured down his back, too, had not the weight of his pack clamped his shirt against him in a soggy mess. His lungs hurt unnaturally – no doubt the legacy of the gas.

But as the valley closed in, things became more interesting. They began passing beneath huge fig trees with branches hanging to the ground which he recognised as banyans. The few small houses were primitive but much neater than those in the town. The walls were mud, the floors bare earth, the windows mere openings. Chickens wandered in and out. Stirling had never been close to such poverty before, yet somehow it did not oppress him. The people who watched him go by looked adequately fed and not at all miserable. The children were extraordinarily handsome: they did not beg, but smiled at the travellers with shy dark eyes.

Presently they came to one immense banyan tree whose trunk was surrounded by a square platform of earth banked up inside a retaining wall of stone. Mingmar unshouldered his pack and sat down on the wall. 'Here rest,' he announced.

An hour earlier Stirling would have asked him not to stop, to keep going. But now he thought he had never heard a more welcome pronouncement. He too swung his pack off, and felt buoyant at the release. The air under the tree was cool. Merely to sit on the stone wall and take the weight off his feet was delicious – a simple physical pleasure in no way spoiled by the fact that curious villagers came and stood staring at him from a distance of about three feet. Some placed their hands together in front of their chins and murmured 'Namaste!', the universal greeting. The others just came and stared.

Soon the column went on and crossed the river on a primitive suspension bridge. The stream, or khola (with a hot h, as Stirling had heard the Sherpas pronounce it) was a torrent of molten, cloudy turquoise hurtling between banks of rounded ash-grey stones. The bridge was in the final stages of decay, its planks rotted and broken so that travellers could see straight down past their feet into the raging water twenty feet below. As each man crossed, singly, the structure swayed hideously from side to side.

At the point where the broad valley ended, they began to climb. This was the moment to which Stirling had been looking forward, the first real challenge. They went up gently at first, but then ever more steeply as they scaled the backbone of the ridge. The dusty track gave way to a stone staircase rising at a prodigious angle as it twisted and turned between tiny, terraced fields of stubble. Up and up and up it went, sometimes with the vertical height of each step greater than its width.

Never in his life had Stirling been so hot. Sweat cascaded off him. His thigh muscles ached piercingly. He took back every previous thought he had entertained about their progress being too slow. The map, sketchy as it was, gave no inkling of the ups and downs taken by the path. The spur they were climbing scarcely rated in the general sum of things: it was a pimple, a molehill, too small for the cartographer's attention.

The one consolation was that, as he struggled upwards, the air grew cooler. Again they rested on a stone-girt platform, and this time his altimeter gave the height as 4,500 feet. Up here the coolness of the breeze was pure delight.

Once more they climbed, but gradually the slope became less precipitous, and they went on more easily through small meadows and patches of wood in which the trees were pleasantly familiar and yet slightly strange: the horse-chestnuts falling ripe to the ground were jet-black rather than brown, and the leaves of the oaks had frilly serrations round the edges.

At four-thirty Mingmar stopped suddenly and announced that they would camp where they were. The site was a good one – small, grassy terraces commanding a steep drop, with plenty of firewood at hand and a clear stream a few yards away. Stirling's first inclination was to push on and put another hour between themselves and the airfield. But then he reflected that he should be safe enough already, where he was. The fact that he had not shown up for the Pokhara flight would certainly have thrown the hounds off his scent. In any case, he felt too exhausted to argue.

He was glad to sit and do nothing as the team went into action and built the camp. Mingmar decreed where the tents were to be pitched – Stirling's a little apart from the others – and started to build a fire. The porters dumped their loads, unrolled the bedding bundles and began to fit tent-frames together.

Taking a towel and a bar of soap, Stirling went to wash in the stream. The place where the track crossed it looked un-propitious, so he scrambled a few yards further uphill and was rewarded by the discovery of a magnificent natural shower-bath, where the water shot out over a small cliff and fell ten feet into a basin of rock. He had planned only a limited wash, but the sight of the flashing cascade was too much for him, and he stripped off every sweat-soaked garment he wore and stood letting the water hammer its great gouts and splashes into his face and shoulders. He soaped himself from head to foot, sluiced himself down again, and came out fizzing all over.

Back in the camp he found himself the owner of a complete little homestead: a tent neatly pitched, a mattress of foam rubber, a sleeping bag, a wicker stool and a plywood box for a table. On the box stood a white enamel mug of steaming clear tea, alongside it a bowl of coarse grey sugar and a saucer containing slices of fresh lemon.

He sat on the stool, topped up the mug with lemon and sugar, and drank it feeling extraordinarily content, stretched by the exercise and tingling from the shower. His lungs seemed normal again, and for that alone he felt enor-mously relieved. The first sharp taste of trekking had shown him what a violently physical task he had undertaken:

everything would depend on his body functioning well.

Wood-smoke from the Sherpas' fire drifted along the hill, bringing scents of resin. Apart from the occasional bleat of a sheep, the air was absolutely quiet. Overhead, a rift in the clouds was lit up theatrically by the setting sun. Life seemed about as good as it could be. Best of all, there was no sign of the chattering female: no chance, now, of her party overtaking them that evening. From somewhere close at hand a cicada began to whirr.

He finished the tea and started rummaging in his tent, organising his things for the night and the next morning. He was absorbed in his rearrangements when he heard a soft voice call from outside. He looked out and saw Pasang, the broken-nosed second-in-command.

'Sair,' he said pointing upwards. 'The mountain.'

Stirling emerged and followed the raised hand. He started to say something but found he could not speak, for there, riding in a cloud-gap at an inconceivable height – far higher than he had dreamed of looking during all his searches in the afternoon – was a blazing triangle of fire and ice, the summit of Macchapuchare.

The dying sun flashed from it. Blue sky framed it. Eddying whirls of mist swept round it. A giant of the earth, it was still more a giant of the sky, serene yet overpowering, fantastic in its beauty, immeasurably remote yet close enough to chill the heart.

Stirling was physically shaken by the magnificence of the sight. The mountain dwarfed him like the first rampart of a world he had never known, a new world in which his life would start again.

Seven

Although dog-tired, he slept lightly, aware of the ground jabbing at hips and elbows through the thin mattress. Also he found it hard to achieve a satisfactory temperature. With his head at the back of the tent, away from the opening, he was too hot, so after a while he turned round, with his head to the open air. Soon he was too cold, so he unrolled the tent-flaps and let them hang down, with only a small gap left open.

During these exploratory manoeuvrings he heard the Sherpas chatting quietly as they sat round the fire. Then, at about midnight, the murmur of their voices ceased and he fell asleep.

The next thing he knew, he was suddenly wide awake, aware of danger. The night was very dark. He lay still and listened. Far off in the mountains a jackal yelped. But that was not what had woken him. Silence. Then a faint movement outside the tent-flap.

He breathed deeply, feigning sleep. The tent-flap moved as a hand began to lift the canvas cautiously. The starlit sky showed through the widening gap. The .38 was in his rucksack, down by his feet, out of immediate reach. In the tent-opening a blade gleamed dully in the starlight.

Already he was rehearsing the old close-combat drill. Always pull the man towards you. He expects to be repulsed, so surprise him with a pull.

He kept up the deep breathing. Now the man was clearly outlined against the background of sky. He was trying to make out the position in which his victim was lying.

Now! Stirling struck hard and fast, seizing the man's right wrist with his left hand and twisting it up towards his body.

At the same instant he gripped the man's hair with his right hand and jerked him forwards and downwards. The attacker gave a high yelp as his knife bit into his own stomach. Stirling also shouted, partly to frighten the man but more to call assistance. Yet the intruder didn't seem to need much frightening: he lay crumpled on the ground in an inert heap.

Stirling held him down while he felt along the edge of the tent for his torch. The beam showed a dark pool of blood welling out across the grass at the tent entrance. He scrambled up and threw the man bodily away: he landed on his side and stayed there, with the knife handle protruding from his stomach.

'Mingmar!' roared Stirling. 'Hey! Come here!'

The camp sprang to life. The Sherpas blew up the fire and lit flaming brands which they held over the prostrate figure. Stirling was shaking with reaction and anger, for he thought one of his own team had turned traitor.

'Who is it?' he shouted at Mingmar. 'What the hell's he doing?'

The Sherpa held his brand low over the intruder's face. 'No seeing him before, sair,' he said.

'Not one of our men?'

'No, sair.'

A quick count bore Mingmar out. The whole party had assembled – the four porters, skinny and shivering in scraps of underclothes, the boy Likpa in striped pyjamas, and the two Sherpas, in shirts, shorts and jerseys. Their eyes gleamed in the dancing torchlight. The man on the ground gave a groan.

'He tried to kill me,' Stirling snapped. 'Ask him who sent him. But be quick, because he's going to die.'

Mingmar bent over the stricken figure and addressed it at machine-gun speed in Gurkhali. When the man did not answer, the Sherpa slapped his face and shouted louder, from a few inches' range. At last the man began to speak, forming words with difficulty.

'What does he say?'

'Sahib sending him.'

'A sahib? What sort? English?'

'He don't know.' Another volley of questions.

'One hundred rupee pay,' Mingmar announced.

'Where was the sahib?'

'In Pokhara, sair.'

The man trembled all over. His eyelids flickered open and shut. The life was ebbing out of him. A moment later he gave another shudder and lay still.

'He dead,' said Mingmar. The Sherpas searched the pockets of the man's trousers, but found nothing. Then they dragged the body to the edge of the terrace and rolled it over so that it was temporarily out of the way.

Stirling's mind ran rapidly over various possibilities. It could hardly have been the German pilot who'd sent him: he'd seemed harmless enough. Yet he was the only white man they'd seen in Pokhara . . . Unless of course someone had come up from Katmandu on the afternoon plane. That seemed more likely. Whoever he was, thank God he'd only been able to find an amateur footpad armed with a knife.

The one certain fact was that Stirling no longer felt comfortable. The makeshift torches had burnt out. Everyone withdrew to the fire for warmth and light – everyone, that is, except Pasang, whose natural bent as a watch-dog set him apart on the hillside above them, beyond the circle of light, keeping a lookout of his own accord.

'Deep sorry, sair,' Mingmar kept repeating. He obviously felt that the attack was somehow his fault, that the reputation of the whole country had been undermined by the incident. 'He very bad man,' the Sherpa repeated. He had been on twenty, thirty treks, he explained, and never had there been the slightest trouble. The Himalayas were normally a very safe place, he insisted. He could not understand how this had happened.

Stirling felt sorry for him. He didn't doubt that what he said was true. Yet he could hardly explain that this was not a normal trek. Later, he might have to, but not yet. 'Don't worry,' he told Mingmar. 'It's not your fault. I don't blame you at all. But the question is: what do we do now? Maybe another . . . another bad man will come . .'. Tonight.' He made a squelching noise and drew the edge of his hand across his throat. 'Best to go on to Ghandrung.'

'Now, sair?' Mingmar looked startled.

'Yes, now.'

'No possible,' said the Sherpa firmly. 'Too much dark. Porters falling down, breaking leg. Dhampus pass very steep. Too much dangerous, sair.'

Stirling had to respect the young man's opinion. His own experience of the Himalayas was so brief that he could not argue. Had there been a moon, it might have been different; but without one, the night was impenetrably dark. He thought of the steep and awkward stone staircase they had climbed in the afternoon. Something like that would be a killer at night, particularly going down. With only his one torch in the whole party, progress would be snail-like. They would have to stay where they were.

For a while they clung round the fire, with Pasang lurking somewhere out in the dark. Then Stirling felt sleep closing in on him again. He tried to negotiate with the Sherpas so that they would wake him after an hour and let him do a stint of guard duty, but they refused absolutely, and Pasang came to station himself right outside his tent in a way that reminded him painfully of Spot. Thus protected, he drifted off to sleep.

He was woken by the cracked, half-broken voice of Likpa outside his tent as the boy called, 'Wassing wattair, sair.' He looked out and saw an aluminium bowl of hot water steaming on the box-cum-table. The wisps of steam vanished upwards in the crisp morning air. The scent of woodsmoke still hung over the encampment.

Stirling stumbled into the open, propped his pocket mirror against the edge of the bowl and proceeded to shave. There was no real need to shave, he knew. It was just that he felt better if he did. But today, as he scraped away, he had the unexpected bonus of a vision as glorious as that of the evening before.

Huge wreaths of mist were drifting past, both in the valley below and on levels higher than the camp. As he looked up, the clouds parted briefly and Macchapuchare rode out in dazzling splendour against the blue. The shifting of the fog gave the impression that the mountain itself was moving – that the glittering peak was sailing the sky-sea above. A moment later the summit was swallowed again by the circling clouds; but then, to one side and lower, a whole new range of icy shoulders and ridges shone briefly, white and silver, through the mist. Up there, far above, was another world, of which Stirling had so far caught only the most evanescent glimpses: a world luminous with ice and eternal snow.

The sight woke him up with a jolt. He realised that Pasang was standing behind him, by the tent, waiting for him to finish packing. Hastily he stuffed everything into rucksack or kit-bag. Hardly had he emerged from the tent before it was felled behind him. Pasang and one of the porters dropped it to the ground, rolled it, stowed it and bundled up the bedding, all in a few seconds.

A cup of scalding lemon tea had appeared on his box, together with a few biscuits. He ate one of them and was sipping the tea when he noticed one of the porters hovering. 'What d'you want?' he asked. 'A biscuit?' He held a couple out, but the man smiled shyly and indicated that he was after the stool and makeshift table. Stirling surrendered them. A few moments later they had been lashed into position on top of one of the loads. The message was clear: the time had come to start.

Mingmar came up, looking lively and cheerful.

'Everything O.K., sair?' he asked breezily.

'What about our friend?' Stirling pointed to where they had rolled the body over the ledge.

'Him buried, sair.' The Sherpa showed him the place where they had found a deep cleft between slabs of rock.

They had dropped the body down and dumped stones and earth on top of it.

The porters hoisted their loads and moved off first, leaving Likpa to pack the remains of the kitchen things. At the last moment the Sherpas prowled the site like predatory animals, picking up a couple of minute pieces of paper. As a final gesture Pasang kicked out the ashes of the fire and scattered them about, so that no one else could have divined that a party of eight people had spent the night there.

They hit the trail at five to seven, and for Stirling the next three hours were pure delight. The cool, moist air was alive with the scents of the night, and it kept them fresh as they went up through woods to the Dhampus Pass at 5,500 feet. Monkeys chattered overhead in the branches of the tropical forest, and as the party rounded a corner they came on a pair of handsome, silver-grey langurs which sat on a stone wall with their long, curled tails hanging almost to the ground. Seeing the men, the monkeys scuttled along the wall on all fours and took to the trees with enviable grace and speed.

By the time the morning grew hot they were descending, so that progress was easy and pleasant. To Stirling, it seemed that he had entered some forgotten Arcadia, still basking in a golden age.

In the hamlets the houses were sturdy and solid-looking, with maize-cobs stacked high under the eaves like logs round houses in the Alps, and on the roofs pumpkins were set out to dry in rows. Out in the open family parties were grinding maize or millet in primitive mortars. At one bend of the track the travellers surprised three girls, naked to the waist, washing their hair in a stream against a background hot with bougainvillaea.

The birds delighted Stirling particularly: the parrots flashing through the tree-tops like flights of green arrows; a hoopoe alive with brilliant colours on a rock above the stream; a lammergeyer wheeling on huge, blunt wings, half vulture and half eagle, against the fiery blue sky.

Yet among all the novelty he saw many things that reminded him piercingly of home. The rhododendrons (a few still in flower) were exactly the same. So were the wild strawberry plants, the silver birches and the bracken. When a hen pheasant burst clattering out of the undergrowth, the sight and sound took him straight back to the oak copse behind Deepwood Cottage.

As he walked, he was weighing up the tactical and physical limitations imposed by such stupendous terrain. There were no roads of any kind. Many stretches of the track were impassable to horses or even to donkeys. Therefore no one could move from one village to the next faster than a man on his own feet. Nor could a message travel any more quickly, for there was no telephone or radio.

Thus it would take more than a day for news of his arrival at Ghandrung to percolate back to Pokhara. The sahib who had sent out the midnight assailant would not hear for several days whether or not his object had been achieved. By the time he did hear, Stirling would have disappeared into the high valleys to the north and west. In this country, a man depended entirely on his own strength and initiative: with mechanical and electronic gadgets denied him, he was thrown back on fieldcraft and physical stamina.

Stirling's reverie was interrupted by Mingmar calling a halt. 'Breakfast and lunch,' he announced. 'Brunch.' Since they had already been walking for three hours, with only a couple of brief halts, the idea seemed excellent, particularly as Mingmar had chosen a lovely place. A small stream ran through a pool in the middle of an open meadow, and the slope of the field faced out over miles of blue-green valleys and ridges.

With extraordinary speed and efficiency the Sherpas built a fire and began to cook. Stirling found it hard to keep still for the smell of frying. To distract himself, he took off his boots and sat with his feet in the stream. As usual, his shirt was soaked with sweat, so he took that off as well and draped it over tufts of grass to dry, enjoying the hot sun on his back.

Soon he saw Likpa heading his way with a tray. 'Rumble-tumble!' the boy announced proudly, setting the food down on a rock. He went off with a sly glance behind him to see what the sahib would do.

Stirling didn't hesitate. The rumble-tumble was a mighty omelette with strips of onion in it, accompanied by fried potatoes. There was also a heap of freshly cooked pancakes, thick and heavy. To go on them was raspberry jam, butter, and – an incredible reversion to childhood, this – *peanut* butter. Peanut butter! It must be twenty years since he had tasted the stuff. He spread a layer an inch thick across one of the flapjacks and topped it with as much jam as the structure would support. After two such depth-charges and three mugs of lemon tea, he felt fit for any number of further hours on the trail.

It irked him that the Sherpas expected him to eat in state, on his own. He would rather have joined them round the kitchen fire. He decided that for the moment he had better fall in with accepted etiquette, but when he had finished eating he got out his little Gurkhali phrase book to start learning a few words.

When Likpa came back to fetch his tray he said carefully, '*Sahrai ramro.*' The boy looked astonished. Then he beamed and said, 'Vairy good! *Ramro sahrai.*' Stirling repeated the phrase the right way round. The boy was delighted. A bridge had been built.

As Stirling began to replace his stockings and boots, he found two creatures like fat black worms anchored to his bare calf. Leeches. He suppressed a shudder and controlled the urge to tear them off. If one did that, he knew, their jaws remained embedded in one's flesh, and the wounds were liable to fester.

Instead he walked over to the fire and enlisted the help of Pasang, who drew a stick out of the embers and deftly gave each leech a touch with the red-hot end. Instantly they let go their holds and fell to the ground, where, to show what they had been doing, the Sherpa squashed one on a flat stone.

Bright red blood spurted across the grey surface – not the leech's, but Stirling's.

Ghandrung was still three hours ahead. As they went on Stirling began to think pleasurably of seeing Andrew de Lazlo again. Arrogant, physically idle, greedy and sybaritic, Andrew was many things that Stirling didn't like; he came from a higher social stratum, and knew it. But the unattractive qualities, it seemed to Stirling, had always been tempered and overcome by a naive enthusiasm which made Andrew amusing company. The two men had always got on well, their relationship being based on the exchange of bantering insults and mutual abuse. Yet Stirling still could not imagine what had brought Andrew to live in such a remote and backward area.

Early in the afternoon they reached Landrung, a village strung out along the side of a steep hill, partner for their objective; and soon Ghandrung itself came in sight, on about the same level, but on another mountain, across a great chasm of a valley. According to Mingmar, it was still an hour away.

Down they went, steeply, almost perpendicularly down, into the valley of the Modi Khola, a fast river which flowed straight from the glaciers and snowfields of Annapurna. With every step the heat increased, and once again Stirling sweated prodigiously. By the time he reached the bottom he felt he was going to dissolve.

Yet when he reached the river itself he felt instantly revived, for the sheer, sensuous beauty of the khola was something beyond his imagining. The stream was a plunging, rolling torrent of molten turquoise. The banks were huge slabs of smooth grey rock, sculpted by centuries of erosion into long sweeps and scallops. There was something primeval about the simplicity of each element: the blueness of the water, the smoothness of the rock, the rage of the current. Seeing it, he felt irresistibly drawn to the river.

He looked back. The porters were still high up the hill behind him, picking their way down. He would have to wait for them anyway. He looked at the stream again. The main body of the stream was travelling dangerously fast, but in front of him was a small bay in which the water eddied slowly backwards: an ideal spot.

Stripping to his underpants, he waded in, watched by the Sherpas with incredulous hilarity. The water was shatteringly cold. Never had he given his metabolism such a shock. He felt as if he were wading into liquid ice. A moment later, as the water reached his midriff, he realised that he was doing precisely that. The river, straight from high glaciers, was barely melted ice and snow. He immersed himself once and came up gasping. A second ducking almost made him faint – a sensation both stunning and delicious. A third plunge produced shooting pains in his legs, so he turned and splashed quickly back to shore. The Sherpas did not disguise the fact they thought him crazy, but the bathe had been something to remember.

Galvanised by it, he easily climbed the steep ascent into Ghandrung, which proved more prosperous-looking than its neighbour Landrung. The houses were bigger, and many had slate roofs rather than thatch. The steeply rising street was paved with cobbles – another sign of affluence.

As they went up it they collected a steadily increasing swarm of children, who danced round their heels like terriers. But then, as they rounded a bend in the street, a man with red tags on the shoulders of his khaki shirt stepped out of one of the houses and challenged them.

'Police check,' Mingmar explained. 'Your trekking permit, please.'

Stirling unshouldered his rucksack and dug out the pass. The policeman took it and scrutinised it for some time, both from close range and at arm's length, in a way that would have seemed more professional if he had held the document the right way up. Then, no doubt to save face, he withdrew into the house, indicating that the others should wait outside.

Stirling sat on a low wall. The crowd of children had become enormous – easily a record to date. He considered making a trial issue of balloons, but rejected the idea on the grounds that he might be able to move off at any minute.

Time passed. The porters came plodding up with their loads, peering upwards from the forward-tilted attitude that their head-bands forced them to adopt. One by one they backed up to the wall and lowered their bundles on to it. Stirling was amazed by their strength and stamina: they were all short, lean and wiry, yet they carried eighty-pound loads for hours on end. He, though much larger, found a thirty-pound pack enough of a burden. He had good boots, too. Three of the four porters were still barefoot, and the fourth wore only an ancient pair of plimsolls eroded into enormous holes.

The policeman reappeared and let fly a stream of instructions. When it ran dry, Mingmar began to interpret. Because of the Khampas – very bad mens – the trekking routes to the north were closed. It was not possible to go up the Kali Gandaki, or even up the Modi to the Annapurna basecamp. The government had forbidden it . . .

Stirling interrupted. He had heard all this before. 'Tell them we don't want to go north,' he said. 'Tell them I've come to make a trek with Sahib de Lazlo.'

'Sahib Lazair!' The name produced a flurry of discussion.

'What's the problem?' Stirling asked.

'Sahib Lazair not here. He going away.'

'Where to?'

'Don't know, sair.'

Stirling felt a stab of anxiety. Surely Andrew wouldn't have taken off without leaving him a message?

'Ask him where we *are* allowed to go.' He unfolded his map and began firing off names interrogatively. 'Deorali. O.K.?'

'*Ho!*' Yes.

'Ghorapani?'

'*Ho!*'

'Chitre?'

'*Ho!*'

'Tatopani?'

'*Hoiná!*' No.
'Dana?'
'*Hoiná!*'
'Chingkhola?'
'*Ho!*'

The picture was clear. Everything to the north was out of bounds, but the villages to the west were clear. It was as Patrick Smith had warned him.

'O.K. We'll go west. But first we must find Sahib de Lazlo's house.'

As if to make up for the earlier delay, the policeman now insisted on accompanying them to their next objective. The sight of the large, pink-faced stranger escorted by the constabulary roused the children to a frenzy of enthusiasm, and Stirling felt like the Pied Piper as he towed a cavalcade of urchins cavorting up the hill.

From the outside, Andrew's house looked little different from any of the others, although its environs were neater and its shutters in better repair than any of the neighbours'. Yet the door was locked, and knocking brought no response.

By then word of Stirling's presence had evidently gone round, for as he stood irresolutely in the road a man hurried up and introduced himself as the local schoolmaster. Sahib Lazair, he said, had left a *chitthi* for his friend, a letter; it was in the post office, and a man was bringing it immediately. They should all go to the school, where they could wait in comfort until the letter arrived.

The school was a modest little place, but it occupied a wonderful position, sitting on a spur that jutted out over the valley. Primitive classrooms surrounded a small yard. As if in response to the party's arrival, the afternoon clouds began shifting and parting to reveal glimpses of Annapurna. Immense walls of ice loomed high above the town, dazzlingly close; the school seemed to be facing the mountain at point-blank range.

The Sherpas and porters filed into the yard, but the schoolmaster used his authority to ban the children. Another wait began, punctuated by the teacher's excruciating conversational sallies, which were designed to practise his English. Then Stirling said, 'Do you know Sahib de Lazlo?'

'Certainly, sair. Everyone in Ghandrung know Sahib Lazair.'

'What does he look like? Big?' He held out his hands, some distance from his stomach. 'Fat? Red face? Long hair, like this?' He indicated hair down to shoulder level.

'No, sair.' For once the schoolmaster looked nonplussed. 'Mr Lazair very thin man, like so.' He held his hands about six inches apart. 'White hair. Very short, like lama. Mr Lazair is guru, sair. He holy man.'

Andrew de Lazlo a guru! Only by a great effort did Stirling stop himself laughing. The idea was preposterous. He began to wonder if they were talking about the same person. What had happened to the corpulent and florid friend he remembered?

Speculation was cut short by the arrival of the letter. It was from his Andrew all right:

Dear Bill,
    Sorry to miss you, but I have had to push on to
Khibang. Keep going and catch me up there as soon as
possible. Hope you've had a good trip so far.
    See you soon.

    Andrew

P.S. Our contacts have got a bit ahead of schedule, so step
    on it.

Stirling felt suddenly deflated. He had been looking forward to the reunion, and to company. Now he was faced with another long march on his own. He felt tired and depressed. The bloody schoolmaster was still chattering, too.

Khibang, the Sherpas said, was four or five days to the west. But as soon as the name was picked up by the porters, one of them began haranguing Mingmar in a sullen voice.

'This mans no wanting go Khibang,' the Sherpa reported.

'Why not?'

'Too much western way. He liking go Kali Gandaki.'

'Well, tell him we can't go that way because the police won't let us.'

'I telling him, sair.'

'What does he say?'

'Not going Khibang.'

Stirling started to feel angry but realised he had better be careful. If he made too much of a scene, he might be left without transport altogether. Better to have one man on strike than four. Even in this minor crisis he couldn't help feeling amused by the idea of a man walking out on him. It wouldn't be like in England, where a striker had only to stroll to his car in the park and drive home. Here the man would have to walk out literally, thirty or forty miles at least.

Further argument was saved by one of the other porters volunteering the services of his sister, who lived right where they were, in Ghandrung. The man went off to fetch her.

Hardly had he left when a fresh commotion broke out among the children outside. The gate opened. To Stirling's chagrin, in strode the absurd astronaut-Sherpa, followed by the blonde in blue shorts. The sun had touched up the tan on her legs to a devastating apricot brown – even he had to admit that. But again the sight of her made him uneasy. He had the sensation of being followed.

Compared with the first time he had seen her, she seemed rather subdued, and when he asked how she was getting on, she answered angrily, 'All dead buggers!'

'Sorry?'

'Bloody police. Refused to let me go on up the Modi. They say all the tracks to the north are closed. I can't even get to Annapurna. What's the *matter* with them?'

'They're rounding up bandits or something.' He was deliberately vague.

'Have they screwed up your plans too?'

'Not at all. I'm going west in any case.'

'Boy, you sure can rattle your dags, anyway.'

'What's that?'

'You get a move on. My word!' She paused, and he knew what was coming. 'I wonder, Bill . . . would it be too much of a drag if I came along?'

Yes, it would be a monumental drag. Yet he could hardly tell her to push off unless he gave some good reason – and he couldn't give her the one very good reason that existed.

'It might not work out,' he said evenly. 'From your point of view, I mean. The thing is, I'm in a hurry. We're going to have to travel pretty fast. Also, I'm not sure where we're going to finish up. You might find yourself miles away and running out of time. How long have you got?'

'I – well – I've not got any deadline, really.' She pushed the dark glasses right up on top of her head and looked at him appealingly. 'Maybe I could come for a few days anyway. If I can't keep up, I'll have to quit – that's all.'

Now that he saw her whole face for the first time, he was surprised to find how attractive it was. She had big grey eyes and a fine, intelligent forehead that belied the brashness of her manner.

'Up to you,' he said. 'But don't blame me if you take on more than you can handle.'

'Don't worry. I'll look after myself.' She gestured towards her Sherpa and porters. 'After all, we're a self-contained unit, Nima and me. We could come back on our own.'

Stirling cursed himself silently for not being tougher.

'Is it all right then? Can I come?'

'I suppose so.' To cover his irritation he began burrowing in his rucksack. 'We'd better get going. We've still got to find somewhere to camp for the night.'

The chill of evening had already settled on Ghandrung, at 6,500 feet, and every step they took that evening would raise them higher still. Stirling felt uneasy and annoyed. He should have sent the girl packing. Maybe he would have, if he had not been distracted by the business of the porter defecting.

It was too late to worry. The man's replacement had arrived – a strapping, square woman with one gold ear-ring, wearing a coarse linen skirt and shirt, but no shoes. Out of deference to her sex a few items were removed from the load which her predecessor had carried, and were redistributed among the three men; but the bundle which she hoisted on to her back was still enormous.

'Is she all right carrying that amount?' Stirling asked Mingmar. The Sherpa gave a shrug which indicated that to him the porters were beasts of burden, and it made no difference whether they were male or female. Far from appearing solicitous, he let forth a tremendous burst of *ho*-ing and *yaso*-ing, and drove the column back into action with blasts of abuse.

Stirling presented the schoolmaster with a battered paperback thriller. Outside the gates he distributed a dozen balloons among the pack of children, from whom there arose piercing screams of pleasure as they discovered the delights of blowing balloons up and then releasing them, so that they spiralled wildly in their brief, spluttering flights.

He wished he felt more secure. The delay had been a long one. By evening the whole of the village would know that a sahib with red hair had passed through, and that a blonde sahiba had gone with him, on their way to Khibang. If anybody was following up his track – as the attacker of the night before must have followed up – he would soon discover their route. For this reason he decided they must not camp on or beside the track, but must move some distance off it before settling for the night.

It was difficult, without revealing the cause of his anxiety, to explain the necessity to Mingmar.

'Very good camping place near track,' the Sherpa protested. 'Away from track, no finding water.'

'I'm afraid a bad man may come in the night again.'

'Bad man dead, sair.'

'I know. But another one.'

'Here no bad mens, sair. Here very good people.'

'Yes, but you never know.'

They trudged on, climbing through a forest of feathery pines. The vast white ramparts of Annapurna South and its outlier Hiunchuli towered beyond the screen of branches. The apparent proximity was an illusion, Stirling knew, for the map showed that the summits were ten miles off to the north; yet the air was so clear that the eye could hardly accept the fact. The snowfields, rock-faces, crevasses and sheets of ice all seemed within touching distance, so sharply was every detail defined.

Stirling's party led in its usual order. Then came the girl and her little army. She herself did not deign to carry a pack: that was left to one of her minions. But at least she kept going and did not call for extra halts.

At last Mingmar began casting about for a camping place. They came to one spot that would have been ideal, had it not been right beside the track. A stream of clear water crossed the path, and on either bank of it there were small level areas that would have done well for the tents. When Stirling rejected the site, Mingmar was naturally annoyed: he stared hard with a calculating look in his eyes which suggested that the sahib was getting neurotic.

'We've just got to find somewhere less obvious,' said Stirling firmly. 'Come on. We'll look up here. Tell the porters to wait till we come back.'

Mingmar gave the porters a couple of bursts – of what, Stirling could not tell – and followed him sulkily up the hill. Fortunately for everyone's sense of honour there was no need to go far. After only a couple of hundred yards they came on another site very like the one below – a line of terraces on either side of the same stream. Yet although it was not far above the path, the shape of the hill put it out of sight of anyone using the track.

Mingmar accepted the place with good humour. As usual, the camp went up like magic. In only a few minutes the Sherpas had fires blazing, and Stirling's tent had been pitched so as to give him a matchless view of the sun setting on the peak of Annapurna South. He sat on his wicker stool and eased the laces of his boots. The sun had already left the camp, yet the big peaks were still catching it, and the snows glowed softly pink against the fading sky. No wonder the Nepalese believed that the summits were inhabited by gods.

His reverie was interrupted by a frightful scream from the cockerel destined for supper. Pasang held the bird out in both hands at arm's length, and Mingmar, standing to one side, cut off its head with a single downward sweep of a kukri. The Sherpas laughed uproariously as the body twitched and blood spurted from the severed neck. There was something barbaric about the offhand way in which the murder had been committed, and the hilarity which accompanied it. And yet, Stirling wondered, would it have been any better if they had killed the bird surreptitiously, out of his sight and hearing?

The girl and her entourage had settled on ledges across the stream, a hundred yards or more away. He could see their separate fires. He supposed that he ought to ask her to have supper with him, but he was damned if he would.

He pulled on a jersey against the increasing cold and sat watching the sunset, physically content yet slightly on edge. Then he saw one of the girl's porters coming towards his camp. The man began talking to Mingmar, he looked round at Stirling. The visitor pointed back to his own camp.

Mingmar came across to him.

'What's the matter?'

'Sair, this porter man, my cousin, he say, lady she having radio.'

'Great. She can listen to the radio if she wants.'

'No, sair. No listen. She making message.'

The Sherpa seemed jealous of the rival expedition's facilities.

'I'll go and have a look.'

He retied his boots loosely, crossed the stream and walked along the line of terraces. The girl's tent was easily distinguished from the rest, being orange, like his own. It was pitched at the far end of the line, to give her privacy. He was amused to see that she also had a small blue lavatory tent standing on its own at a salubrious distance.

He approached stealthily and crept up to the tent from behind. The light was going, but he could make out a line of some sort running from the apex of the tent at the front away to the rock-face opposite. Washing-line? No: aerial.

The girl was sitting in the tent-opening. He could see her feet sticking out, and hear faint sounds. By stepping carefully over the guy-ropes he came right up beside her, outside the canvas, without her being aware of him. When he peeped round the corner he found her sitting almost underneath him, concentrating intently on the key of a small Morse-code transmitter.

Eight

He stood in the lee of the tent and held his breath. In a few moments he realised he could make out the individual letters she was sending. The evening was so still that each click from the transmitter cut a notch in the silence, and it was easy to pick up the pattern of dots and dashes, shorts and longs. He got an A, an L and an I. Then a pause. Then she started again: D E O R A L I. Another pause. Then the same again: D E O R A L I. The name of the village just ahead. She was sending someone her location, telling someone where she was – telling someone where *he* was! Christ almighty! He had let the enemy right into the camp.

With a quick movement he stepped over the guy-rope and confronted her. She gave a cry of alarm and scrambled to her feet, making a futile attempt to cover the transmitter with a jersey.

'Tuning in to your boy-friend, I see.'

The girl did not answer. She stood backed up against the front of her tent, with one arm braced on each leading edge.

'I'm sure he'll be glad to know you're in Deorali.'

No answer.

'Who is he, so precious he has to be kept in touch with all the time?'

At last she cleared her throat and said, 'Why shouldn't I tell him where I am?'

'No reason at all – provided it's him you're talking to.'

'What d'you mean by that?'

'I thought you said he was on Annapurna.'

'He is.'

'Well – Annapurna's there.' He pointed. 'Your aerial's aligned in the wrong direction.'

She flushed even deeper and said unsteadily, 'I expect he can pick it up.'

Stirling felt sure she was lying. He stepped forward and took her roughly by the shoulders. 'Come on,' he said sharply. 'Tell me what the hell you're playing at.'

'Let go of me!' she shouted. 'Take your bloody hands off!'

She tried to wriggle free, but he held her tight and shook her harder. 'Stop lying!' he yelled back. 'Or else I *will* hurt you.'

'Bastard!' she shouted. With a violent twist she got her arms free and gave him a back-hander on the side of the head. Stung into action, he seized her by the hair on the nape of her neck and lifted her onto the tips of her toes. She screamed with pain and lashed out wildly.

'Let *go!*'

He ignored the shout and hoisted her still higher. With his left hand he grabbed hers and twisted it round in a half-nelson, forcing it up her back.

'Calm down!' he hissed. 'They're all watching us.'

He let the pressure off her scalp. She looked round and saw the row of astonished brown faces. He released her altogether. Suddenly her resistance collapsed. Turning, she clutched at him, shaken by sobs. Suspecting a deliberate ploy, he kept her at arm's length. In a minute, however, he saw that she really was distressed. Tears poured down her cheeks, and she kept gasping, 'I'm sorry! I'm sorry!'

'Relax,' he said more gently. 'Sit down.'

He pushed her back on to her box and crouched down in front of her. She found a handkerchief, blew her nose and gradually got herself under control.

'I knew I couldn't do it,' she blurted out.

'What?'

'He paid me to spy on you.'

'Who did?'

'The Swiss.'

'What Swiss?'

'The pilot. Haller. The one you saw at Pokhara.'

'I thought the bastard was German.'

'No. He's Swiss.'

'What does he want, anyway?'

'I don't know . . . '

'You mean he didn't tell you? Is he a friend of yours?'

'No. I only just met him.'

'You only just met him, and he paid you to spy on me. Tell me another.'

'It sounds mad, I know. But I met him at a party in Katmandu and he asked me if I wanted to earn a thousand dollars. Happened I did want to, so I asked how. He told me all I had to do was attach myself to you and radio out the location of your camp every evening.'

Stirling said nothing. The story sounded a mile high. The girl blew her nose again. She seemed to be stuck in her narrative, so he prompted, 'And did he pay you?'

'Half – and half when I get back. Here.' She pulled up a purse that had been hanging on a cord under her shirt and took out a wad of notes. 'Here.' She held the money out.

'What's that?'

'Five hundred dollars. The first instalment.'

'But it's yours.'

'I don't want it. I haven't earned it.' She started to cry again. 'You have it.' Her hand was shaking. He took the money, but kept it between them.

'It's not mine either.'

'Burn it, then.'

'God, no – that would be a hell of a waste.'

A glimmer of a smile broke through her tears. 'Keep it, then.'

'I'll put it in safe custody. You might want it back.'

'Thanks.'

Until then he had felt sure she was bluffing. But the business of the money unsettled him. There was no need for her to have let on that she had the cash at all. She had parted with it so spontaneously.

88

'It was awful,' she went on. 'As soon as I saw you I knew I couldn't spy on you. But in the town it sounded so easy.'

'Tell me more.'

'Haller gave me the set and told me how to run out the aerial.' She pointed at the neat blue box and the wire.

'Do you know Morse?'

'I didn't, but he gave me this card of the letters and symbols. All I had to do was get on the air every evening from seven to seven-fifteen and keep transmitting the name of the place we'd got to.'

'Deorali, Deorali.'

'Exactly.'

He looked at the transmitter: Japanese, transistorised, a neat enough job, but heavy. He was surprised that it had the range to be any use in the mountains.

'Where were you transmitting to?'

'Pokhara. He told me to align the aerial in that direction.'

'How d'you know where Pokhara is?'

'I don't exactly. But from the map you can see it's just south of east.'

'He must have someone there listening out. Or is he in Pokhara himself?'

'No – he went straight back to Katmandu. I saw him take off.'

A discreet cough from the shadows made them look round. Nima had come to announce that the sahiba's supper was ready.

'Don't you think we'd better eat together?' Stirling asked. 'There's a bit of explaining to be done.'

She nodded, and he told the Sherpa to arrange for her table – another box – to be moved up to his own fire.

'I'll see you in a minute, then,' he said. 'I think Mingmar's even got some rum. I'll see if I can squeeze a tot out of him.'

Night had fallen swiftly and a nipping chill had set in. Beside his own fire, his box was neatly laid with knife, fork and spoon. He called Mingmar, explained that the girl was coming to supper, and asked if they had any rum.

'Yessair. We having rum. Rakshi also.'

'Rakshi?'

'Nepalese drink. Very good. Like whisky.'

'O.K. Let's have rakshi, then. Keep the rum for later.'

He hunted in his tent for soap and a towel. Taking his torch, and stepping high to evade the leeches, he went to wash in the stream. Whose side was the girl on? Maybe her confession was part of some deeper scheme of deception. And yet, that business of the five hundred dollars . . .

Back in his tent he pulled on a pair of long trousers and a second sweater. The firelight flickering on the canvas gave the place a feeling of great cosiness. Looking at his rumpled belongings, he felt a boyish sense of delight at the sheer compactness of this way of life. Almost everything he possessed was assembled in this snug retreat. Outside was the great Himalayan night; inside, his own patch. The sight of a leech advancing end-over-end up the floor hardly enhanced the tent's attractions, but he evicted the intruder and closed the flaps against further invasions.

The second box had been brought up and laid. A few moments later the blonde appeared, but looking utterly different. The obvious change was that she had put on a light-grey sweater and dark ski-pants. Yet her face was the real surprise. Maybe it was the firelight, or Stirling's imagination, but she looked far softer and more attractive. The brashness and vacuity seemed to have given way to a warm intelligence. She had washed her face and done her hair up in a handkerchief or scarf – but the change was greater than could be accounted for for by any such physical rearrangement.

'Well done,' he said. 'Have a seat.'

She sat down and stretched her hands to the fire.

'It's ridiculous,' he went on, 'but I'm not even sure of your name. Kerry, is it?'

'Kiri. It's a Maori name. Kiri Nelson.'

'Oh – you're from New Zealand. I thought you were Australian.'

'Easy mistake. A Strine éccent's not much different.' She smiled as she exaggerated the edgy vowels.

'What are you doing in Nepal?'

'You really want to hear?'

'Of course.'

'Well . . . ' She picked up a smouldering branch and dropped it into the centre of the fire. 'I suppose I'm on the run.'

'What from?'

'Busted romance. What else?'

Stirling almost said, 'That makes two of us,' but in the event he had no need to answer, for a rush of ragged waiters loomed up out of the darkness bringing their food. Nima set down a tin tray for Kiri without ceremony, but little Likpa presented Stirling's with a flourish.

'Cheecken!' he announced proudly.

'*Kukuru*,' Stirling countered.

'Bintz!'

'What?'

'Bintz!'

'What's that?'

Steam rising out of the battered aluminium saucepans made identification of their contents difficult. Stirling shone his torch straight down into the one the boy was indicating. 'Oh – beans!'

Likpa beamed with pride.

'What is it in Nepali?'

'*Simi*.'

'*Simi*. O.K., I'll remember.'

The boy withdrew, to be replaced by Mingmar bearing two tin mugs and a bottle that had seen better days. 'Rakshi,' he announced. 'Very special.' He set the mugs down and poured a generous dose of cloudy, colourless liquid into each. He waited eagerly for them to try it.

'Happy days!' Stirling raised his mug to the night and took a sip. The stuff was like rhubarb wine tinctured with diesel oil. He gulped some down.

'Same whisky?' asked Mingmar hopefully.

91

'Almost,' Stirling gasped. 'Very similar. Very good.'

The Sherpa retired satisfied and they fell on the food. The cuisine of the Pasang–Likpa kitchen was markedly superior to that of the rival establishment. Whereas Kiri had only tinned meat fritters, fried potatoes and tinned peas, Stirling feasted on roast chicken, mashed potatoes and fresh green beans. For a chef wrestling in the dark with a wood fire, the chicken was a masterpiece. Not only was it amazingly tender: Pasang had coated each piece in lightly curried batter.

'What's that like?' Stirling asked between mouthfuls.

'All right. When you're as hungry as I am, it doesn't matter much.'

'Try some of this. It's really quite something.' He speared a piece and put it on her plate. She ate it and exclaimed, 'Some chookey!'

'Chookey?'

'Chicken.'

He gave her another piece, and also some beans, which were equally delicious. By then he had drunk most of his rakshi, finding it slightly less repellent when it accompanied food. At least it had a bit of an alcoholic kick.

'Tell me about your broken romance.'

She shrugged. 'Not much to tell. He was a doctor too. Maybe that was the trouble. Too much in common. Birds of a feather flocked together, but in this case it didn't work.'

'Were you married?'

'No – just living together.'

'And you're a doctor?'

'That's right.'

'You don't *look* like a doctor.'

'What's a doctor supposed to look like?' She had a nice teasing manner. 'Sorry to disappoint you.'

'Who said I was disappointed? Go on.'

'That was all, really. We had a bust-up. I wanted to get the hell out, so I came to Katmandu with a friend. We went on a trek in the Everest area. Fantastic. Tremendous. Although I

92

don't suppose it's any less tremendous here, round Anna-purna, once you get higher.'

She took a pull from her mug, grimaced and swallowed. 'So we had ourselves a trek, and then Jane had to go home. I was back in Katmandu and met Haller at a party. I said I'd been trekking. We talked about Everest – you know, the usual chat. Next morning he rang up my hotel and asked if I wanted to see Annapurna as well . . . '

'How did he . . . what did he say about me?'

'Nothing, really. Just that he wanted to keep tabs on you. Whenever I asked anything, the answer was that I was being paid enough to get on and do the job without too many questions.'

'What about the Sherpa and porters?'

'All laid on by him. He paid for everything.'

'And what about your boy-friend on Annapurna?'

'He was a blind, Bill. He didn't exist.'

Stirling got up and pushed the fire together, adding some bits of wood from the pile left ready.

'Is that why you dressed in those skin-tight shorts – to decoy me?'

She smiled awkwardly. 'I felt terrible. Especially in front of all those porters. Did I look awful?'

'Well – kind of *striking.*'

'Too right. Bill – tell me who you are.'

The invitation was sweet. He longed to open his heart and let go all the emotions pent up over the past few days. Not since he and Sue had last made love had he been able to have a real conversation. It would be marvellous, now, to talk out his problems at home, his journey and his mission. To share it all would halve the weight he was carrying.

Yet instinctive caution silenced him. All he knew about this girl was what she had told him herself. Maybe she'd been Haller's girl-friend for years. Maybe Haller was a front for someone else. Or maybe she had been innocently caught up in someone else's plans.

In the end he just gave her the briefest possible outline:

that he lived in England, that he too had wanted a break, and had come out to meet a friend.

'But you're not just a tourist, are you?'

'Is that a question or a statement?'

'Well – both.' She smiled. 'I mean, if you're just on a trek, why's Haller spending all this money trying to keep tabs on you?'

'Ask me another. I'd really like to know. All I do know is that I got a letter from a friend inviting me to come out and trek. So I'm on my way to meet him – and that's about it.'

The Sherpas returned to clear away their plates.

'You didn't finish your meat,' said Stirling reproachfully. 'The cooks will be offended. Pity we haven't got a dog we could slip it to. Pity we haven't got Sp——'

'What was that?'

'Nothing. I said the cooks would take offence.'

'Balls to them. They can eat it themselves.'

The sudden robustness jolted Stirling out of his incipient melancholy. Hell, he thought as he sipped his tea. I *like* this girl.

'Look at the mountain,' she said.

The sky was clear, and far above them the ridges of Annapurna glowed frostily in the starlight; at night the mountain looked ghostly and ethereal, still more remote than in the day. They watched it in silence except for the murmuring of the fire. Then she said, 'There was one other thing about Haller. He seemed convinced you'd be heading north. He thought you'd go up the Kali Gandaki to Jomsom.'

'He must have known about the tracks being closed.'

'He did. But still he thought you'd go that way. He expected you to by-pass the police checks. What's more, he thought you were going to fetch something.'

'Did he! What sort of thing?'

'I don't know. But it seemed to be something pretty big. He said if you brought anything to Jomsom I was to transmit the word CARGO, and he'd come right up with the plane.'

94

'Your friend Haller knows more than I do about what I'm doing.'

'Not my friend.'

'Sorry – but he's not bloody well mine either.' He thought for a moment and asked, 'Changing the subject – what does "rattle your dags" mean?'

She gave him a mischievous glance. 'You know how sheep droppings get stuck on the sheep's backside, in bobbles? The bobbles are the dags. So when he rattles 'em, the old sheep's really going. I was brought up on a sheep station. Not a very refined atmosphere.'

Stirling laughed. 'And what's "all dead buggers"?'

'Opposite of "box of birds". If we're feeling great we say, "Oh – box of birds!" You know – all singing and lively. But if we're down, we say, "All dead buggers." You've never been Down Under?'

He shook his head and stared into the fire. He liked the way she could coarsen her accent at will. Presently he said, 'The thing is, what are we going to do now?'

'Can I stick with you for a bit, seeing I've got this far?'

'O.K.,' he said carefully. 'But I don't know what'll happen when we get to Khibang. My friend may want to take off somewhere else. He may not like having girls around. I don't know. But try it, anyway.'

'What about the radio?'

'Oh, keep broadcasting. If Haller thinks I'm going north to Jomsom, he's going to have a puzzle to sort out when he hears I'm heading west all the time.'

'Great.' She smiled. 'Thanks, Bill.'

'Forget it. But I do have one confession to make. I seem to be attracting unwelcome attention – not just from Haller, but from someone else as well. Last night someone tried to get into my tent and knife me.'

'And do *what*?'

'Knife me. That's why we climbed up here tonight – to get away from the path.'

'What happened to the man who tried to kill you?'

'I killed him.'

She looked thunderstruck, but said nothing.

'Things being how they are,' he went on, 'I think it would be safer if you moved your tent up here, next to me.'

'Am I being propositioned?' Her voice was mock-indignant.

'Not yet. But since we both have orange tents, somebody might attack you by mistake. What I'll do is run a trip-wire round both tents, so that if anyone does come, I'll get warning.'

Stirling called for the Sherpas to move Kiri's tent up, and they repitched it alongside his own. Once she had settled inside it he ran a single line of black button thread across both fronts and rigged it to a tin can full of pebbles, so that if anyone touched the thread or broke it the can would rattle by his ear. Then, having laid the .38 within easy reach, he wriggled into his sleeping bag.

The thought of her in the other tent stirred him pleasantly. Not yet, though: better wait. Or had he? What the hell! He'd watched her closely while she was talking. He could be wrong, but he trusted her. Whoever else might be working for the K.G.B., she was not. Of that he felt certain. Besides, he could get into her sleeping bag without spilling any official secrets.

'Kiri,' he called softly.

'Hello.'

'Mind if I come across?'

'Jeeze!'

'What's the matter?'

'At last!'

He leapt naked through the frosty darkness and dived through the flaps of her tent. Inside it was black as soot. He felt, but could not see, that she was stretched out deliciously warm and naked inside a capacious sleeping bag. He nestled alongside and began to feel her. He wanted a torch so that he could see her too.

'What about . . . I didn't come prepared for this sort of thing,' he whispered.

'I did.'

He began to say something else but her lips closed sweetly on his and shut him up. Her tongue speared deep into his mouth, in and out, in and out. Her hands were as busy as his own, all over the place. Her mouth came free for a second and he gasped, 'Kiri, I think you've done this before!'

'I don't think *you* have,' she muttered in his ear, biting the lobe.

The taunt drove him to kiss her more fiercely, drive into her more deeply, and scrumple her body more tightly in his arms. 'The trouble is, I'm not used to such flat ground,' he grunted between bursts of kissing. 'I normally do it on slopes of one in *one*, not one in three.'

Already they were half out of the tent and progressing further downhill with every movement. The tin can gave a frantic rattle. But it was too late to go back. Feeling grass beneath his bare elbows, he looked up and saw the spectral profile of Annapurna outlined against the stars. At the sight a surge of pagan joy went through his body like an electric charge and sent him shooting over his own precipice. Kiri was a few seconds behind him, but the force of the avalanche swept her away with him, to leave them both trembling like stranded fish on the hillside.

Stirling picked himself up, then Kiri. He lifted her gently back into the tent and zipped them both into her sleeping bag. They whispered languorously for a while, and then he muttered, 'Goodnight, honey. When I get back, I shall write a treatise on the art of making love at high altitude. For best results, I shall say, you only need four things: the most beautiful girl in New Zealand, a site 7,000 feet above sea-level, a slope of one in three, and an uninterrupted view of Annapurna.'

He leant across and made certain the .38 was where he could lay his hand on it fast.

'What are you doing?' she muttered.

'Just tucking you in,' he said.

97

Nine

Boris Ortsov shifted uncomfortably in the hot, cramped confines of the teleprinter booth. Nepalese had been smoking in here. He did not care for such close contact with coloured people.

What a dump Katmandu was! No telephone connection with Moscow. No radio link of any use. It seemed incredible that the Bureau had no communications facility of its own in a capital city. You'd have thought they'd have set up some means of keeping in touch with home. Normally, messages went out by post to Delhi. By post! They'd be better off using carrier pigeons.

Now, in the Soaltee Hotel – supposedly the most modern in the city – he had to wait for a teleprinter circuit to become available, like any other member of the public. That annoyed him. To be thrown in with the common herd was bad for his self-esteem and even worse for security.

Naturally the public teleprinter had Roman letters only – no Cyrillic. To send his message in transliterated Russian would attract unwelcome attention, especially as his call had been booked to Aden and he was ostensibly making contact with a businessman there. Therefore he must transmit in cryptic English.

He felt a little nervous, he had to admit. The message from Nesteroff had been couched in unusually aggressive terms. To issue such threatening orders at long· range was not cultured. But at least the teleprinter was more impersonal than the telephone: less chance of getting flustered. He checked the list of points that would have to be covered.

Carson's whereabouts, route to the monastery, position of same, cover story – his documents were not yet to hand.

Of course (he thought as he waited) Carson should have been eliminated before he had even left Katmandu. He would have been, too, if Ortsov had arrived in time. As it was, their native agent had had to make use of amateurs, and they had botched the job.

Ortsov also had to admit that he himself had been careless. If he had taken the trouble to find out about trekking permits, he might have caught up with Carson. As it was, he had been stopped by the police on Pokhara airfield, and again had been obliged to pay a Nepalese to do what should have been a straightforward job. At this distance, however, the chance of Moscow detecting such negligence was infinitesimal.

The machine gave a tinkle. The Nepalese clerk through the glass partition made a sign to show that the circuit was open.

'HELLO ALEX,' Ortsov typed laboriously, his stubby fingers stretching to find the right keys. 'JIMMY HERE.'

He imagined the impulses he had set in motion winging their way through the central clearing station in Aden and on over the 5,000 miles to Moscow.

The machine jumped and rattled. Letters poured out on to the strip of paper, which popped up a notch at the end of each line.

'ALEX HERE REPORT DEVELOPMENTS.'

'CONFIRM OPPOSITION ELIMINATED.'

'STATE PROOF.'

'NO PROOF BUT GOOD LOCAL REPORT.'

'UNSATIS   ESSENTIAL YOU MAKE CERTAIN PERSONALLY RETURN NORTHWARDS SOONEST.'

Ortsov swore. He had already spent one night in Pokhara, and that was enough.

'REGRET HOSPITALISED DISSINTERY,' he typed. 'NOW RECOVERING   WILL PROCEED NORTHWARDS SOONEST.'

It was true that he had had a stomach upset. It might even

have been a touch of dysentery. How could Moscow possibly tell?

There was a pause of several seconds. Then the machine began to chatter again: 'HAST LOCATED SICK COLLEAGUE?'

'RESEARTSCH UNDERWAY BUT NOTHING DEFFINITE.'

'URGENT STEP UP INQUIRIES ORGANISE TRAVEL PARTY.'

'AGREED   ARRANGEMENTS IN HAND.'

Another pause. Then: 'RECOMMEND HIRE HELICOPTER NORTHERN RECONNAISSANCE.'

'REGRET ZERO HELIKOPTER AVAILABILITY.'

'CHECK FURTHER.'

'ALL PASSIBLE CHECKS MADE. CONFIRM ZERO.'

Another pause, longer. He imagined Nesteroff saying to his colleague, 'How in hell can we shift the bastard?' Nesteroff thought him idle, he knew. Always had. It was time he asked a question. He typed again:

'WHAT PROGRESS PROFESSIONAL PAPERS QUERRY.'

'PAPERS UNDERWAY SHOULD LAND TUESDAY.'

'THANKS   INTEND LEAVING SOON AS PAPERS ARRIVE.'

There was another pause. Thank God he had taken the initiative. The professional papers were the evidence for his cover story, showing that he was about to make a geological survey. Until they reached him, he obviously could not strike out into the wilds of Mustang. But the bastards in Moscow were full of sauce. 'CONSIDERING REINFORCEMENT,' they chattered. 'REPORT PROGRESS SAME TIME TOMORROW.'

Ortsov sat back and wiped the sweat from his forehead. He had kept them off his back for the moment. Yet that 'considering reinforcement' was sinister. They were trying to pressure him by threatening to send out someone else to tread on his toes.

He signalled to the clerk that he was through, and went round to pay in cash. Then he strolled along to the hotel's main bar and ordered himself a beer.

In fact he very much hoped that Carson was not eliminated, for after his first futile rush to Pokhara he had conceived a new idea, of stunning simplicity. Seeing the

Himalayas, and the scale on which the whole operation would have to be mounted, he suddenly realised how much effort it would save him if he allowed Carson to do three-quarters of the job on his behalf. Let *him* go into Tibet and bring out the American. Then, when the Englishman was on his way back, it would be relatively easy to ambush him. The map showed very few routes through the Tibetan border: all Ortsov had to do was discover the position of the monastery and work back from there.

Thus he would spare himself a very long walk. It was not that he was lazy – God forbid. He had put on a little weight lately, it was true. He looked down critically at his belly pressing out against his shirt. But that was nothing. When it came to hiking, he could go as fast and as far as anyone. It was just that he disapproved in principle of unnecessary effort and risk. There was no point in two expeditions battling their way up on to the Tibetan plateau if one could achieve the same result.

Moscow would never know that he hadn't been into Tibet himself. So long as he came back with the American's report, and Carson never reappeared, everyone would be happy. Besides, he had thought of an excellent way of keeping Moscow at bay. As soon as his papers came, he would send a valedictory cable and go off the air. Moscow would assume he had taken to the mountains. In fact he would have a few pleasant days loafing in Katmandu before he made his way to Jomsom, in the north. He saw from the map that the place had an airstrip: that would be his base of operations, and the place from which to fly out the American's dossier.

Of course, this all depended on Carson still being alive. But Ortsov – in spite of what he had told Moscow – felt fairly sure that he was. The man he had sent from Pokhara had never returned; and surely he would have come back to claim his hundred rupees if his mission had been successful?

Ten

'Wassing Wattair,' came Likpa's husky call. Stirling rolled over in his sleeping bag and peered out. Steam rose from the bowl into another clear, still morning. Luxuriating in his and Kiri's private warmth, he lay for a minute or two gazing up into the bright sky and reviewing the events of the past three days.

They had made excellent progress, with no sign of any pursuit. The nights had been undisturbed, except by love-making. His instincts about Kiri had proved well-founded: as he had thought, her involvement with him was purely accidental. But instead of a menace she had turned out a godsend, for her skill as a doctor had greatly strengthened the mission's resources.

At every major halt she had treated patients with the most revolting sores, abscesses and deformities. Her fame seemed to go before her, and the queues of sick people grew ever greater. Her patience was extraordinary, and so was her courage, for many of the people brought to her were beyond any help she could give them, yet she did something for each one of them with amazing cheerfulness.

But nothing impressed Stirling so much as the way she dealt with an accident to one of their own party. One morning, as they were clearing up the debris of brunch, Nima, the astronaut-Sherpa, began fooling around with a water buffalo which had wandered into camp. Wielding a table-cloth in pseudo-Spanish style, he had played the animal into a state of some excitement. Then he had slipped and fallen over, and in a flash the buffalo had trampled on him and broken his leg below the knee.

102

Stirling could never have set the leg and splinted it as Kiri did: he lacked not only the skill, but also the nerve. The sound of the bone-ends scrunching across each other had been enough to make him throw up. She, on the other hand, had remained absolutely calm and authoritative, and it was she who had got the injured man loaded into a cut-down carrying basket, so that he could be transported on porters' backs to Kusma, the nearest airstrip, some four days to the south. The loss of the man did not hold them back, for they still had Mingmar and Pasang; but Stirling shuddered whenever he thought of the way the leg had looked.

He got out of his sleeping bag and pulled on some clothes, manoeuvring awkwardly to avoid Kiri in the confines of the tent. As usual, he dressed inside to avoid the stares of the audience which assembled, as if by magic, at every camp site. No matter where the party had settled, no matter how deserted the spot might seem, spectators would rise up out of the stones or materialise from the trees.

Today's house was small but keen. As Stirling emerged he found three children and an ancient man standing almost in his bowl of water.

'*Namaste!*' he muttered. The old man gave a faint answering grunt. As he sat on the stool and lathered his face, four pairs of eyes followed every movement as though there was a rigid connection between them and his right hand. The old man's face, he calculated, was four feet from his own, that of the nearest child two. To a Nepalese, two feet seemed by no means an impolite distance from which to observe a stranger – especially if the man had reddish hair and fair skin, and indulged in this amazing ritual of scraping his face every morning.

The Sherpas seemed neither to shave nor to grow any beard. Their faces were extraordinarily smooth. So were their arms and legs. Like Chinese, they had hardly any body hair. Beside them, Stirling looked as hairy as an ape. Perhaps that was what the watching children supposed him to be – a yeti. Abruptly he gave them his best gorilla-type grimace and hoot at point-blank range. The biggest child let fly a piercing scream and hid itself in the folds of the old man's coat. In an attempt to soften the blow Stirling turned his pocket-mirror round and held it towards the other two. Seeing themselves – probably for the first time in their lives – they too howled and took refuge.

'What's the matter?' called Kiri in a sleep-muffled torpor from the tent.

'It's my fans – they're rioting again. Up! Up! All good K.G.B. agents should be out and about by now.'

'That lets *me* out, then. What time is it?'

'At the third stroke, it will be six thirty-nayne precaysely.'

'Are you all right?' She stuck a tousled head out.

'Box of birds. Why?'

'What are you talking about?'

'In London, if you phone the speaking clock, that's what you get – a lovely lady with a hayghly refayned accent telling you the tayme.'

He saw her humping and bumping about as she got dressed and gave her backside a good pinch through the canvas. He cleaned his teeth – to the further stupefaction of the onlookers, whose nerve had been restored – and set about packing his things. Likpa brought tea and biscuits, and Stirling sipped and munched his as he walked about, enjoying the by-now-familiar spectacle of the camp being struck. So professional was the whole routine, so quick and apparently effortless, that he felt he had known it for years. As usual, the Blue Loo (Kiri's name for it) was the last tent to fall, and the party was on its way within a few minutes.

For more than an hour they toiled up a steep, blind climb in the full glare of the sun. To keep them going, Mingmar told them that the view from the ridge was 'vairy special'. He repeated the promise so many times that Stirling began to discount it. The result was that, when he did drag himself sweating to the top, he was overwhelmed by the grandeur of what he could see.

Now for the first time they had not one or two snow peaks

in sight, but a whole horizon full of gleaming white giants. Like a conjuror bringing rabbits out of a hat, Mingmar flung out his right arm, with the palm of his hand held upwards, as he named each one. 'Gurja Himal!' he cried with a flick of the wrist. 'Dhaulagiri Five! Dhaulagiri One! Tukche Peak! Nilgiri! Annapurna One! Annapurna Fang! Hiunchuli!'

Stirling felt his knees melting as he looked at the Dhaulagiris and Tukche, which lay straight to the north. It was through that mighty white barrier that he would be heading. 'Here is Himalaya,' said the Sherpa more calmly. 'Abode of snow. Dhaulagiri is White Mountain. Annapurna is Giver of Life.'

Stirling did not answer. He gazed in silence with his heart pounding.

They came down to Khibang in the early afternoon. The village was large and prosperous-looking, with the houses widely spaced over a fertile shoulder. Inquiries soon established that there was a sahib in the village. The party was directed to a solitary house which stood out on a ridge of its own. While Mingmar went in to make contact, the others slipped off their loads and settled in the shade of a peepul tree.

A man emerged from the house and stood looking round – a white man, rather old, with grey hair cropped close to his skull. Stirling felt a prick of anxiety: surely after all this they hadn't tracked down the wrong man, some stranger?

The man came towards them, limping heavily, and suddenly Stirling realised that it *was* Andrew – but another one, the remains of the man he had known. He got off the wall and advanced to meet him. 'Andrew! At last.' He raised his right hand, preparing for a Western-style handshake, but the gaunt stranger merely placed both palms together before his face and muttered '*Namaste!*'

'*Namaste!*' he answered awkwardly, repeating the gesture. 'Great to see you.' He hoped he did not reveal what a shock it was to find his fat friend so old, so emaciated, so grey.

'Welcome,' said Andrew curtly. His eyes had taken in Kiri and the rest of the party, but he ignored them and told Stirling to come inside.

They went into the house – a single room with a floor of beaten earth, a bed of bare boards like an open box, and two wooden shelves on the wall. In the centre of the floor a small fire was burning: pieces of split wood, radiating like the spokes of a wheel, came together beneath a simple iron ring, on which a Nepalese woman was roasting fresh maize grains in a pan. Since there was no chimney, the smoke gathered under the low ceiling and rolled out through the open windows. At the far side of the room Mingmar was talking to two other Sherpas. Motioning Stirling to wait, Andrew went across to the three men and began speaking rapidly to them in some native dialect.

There was nothing to sit on. Stirling squatted on his heels and smiled at the woman cooking. She offered him some maize and poured a handful out of the pan. The blown-up grains were hot and tasted like pop-corn. Munching them slowly, he gazed round the bare room and wondered what chain of events had brought the corpulent hedonist of college days to live in a place like this. The only ornaments were the gold ear-rings worn by the woman: plain gold hoops carried rough nuggets the size of marbles, heavy enough to drag the ear-lobes out of shape. Everything else in the house was purely functional.

Presently Andrew left the Sherpas and took Stirling out-doors, round the far side of the house to where an open terrace commanded tremendous views of the Dhaulagiri massif. Without preliminary courtesies he launched straight in: 'What the hell are you doing, bringing that girl with you? Who authorised her, for Christ's sake?'

Stirling was startled by the suddenness of the attack. 'Nobody authorised her,' he said, his anger rising. 'She just turned up.'

'I'd have thought you'd have known better than to lumber yourself with that kind of handicap.'

'I did *not* lumber myself with her. She was dumped on me by some bloody pilot from Katmandu.'

'Not Haller?' Andrew looked at him sharply. 'Not Klaus Haller?'

'Yes. Klaus bloody Haller. You know him?'

'Know him! He's the biggest menace in the Himalayas. He's a government spy – never stops snooping around. Oh Christ! Haller! How did you get involved with him?'

'Look. How about making an effort to be civil for a moment? I haven't come all this bloody way to be abused. I came out exactly as instructed. Everything went fine until I got to Pokhara. Just as I'm leaving the airfield, Haller swoops down in his plane and tips out the girl with a Sherpa got up to look like a spaceman. She says she's going my way, to join her boy-friend on Annapurna. Then I discover she's got a Morse transmitter and that Haller's planted her on me to keep a check on where I am.'

He paused. Andrew looked as though he might blow up at any moment.

'Think for about five seconds,' Stirling went on, 'and you'll see whose fault it is that we're tangled with Haller. If you weren't in on this, and if you hadn't written asking me to come out, I'd never have set eyes on Haller. I never knew the bugger existed until he dropped out of the sky on me. You needn't blame *me* for getting him involved.'

The logic took effect. Andrew made an effort to calm down and screwed up a fleeting grin. 'Sorry. I'm a bit wound up. I ought to have thanked you for coming. You made it, anyway.'

'Just about. But I'm afraid we've got problems, Haller apart.' He told Andrew about the episodes in the Hotel Makalu and the tent on his first night out. 'There must have been a bad leak somewhere,' he concluded. 'It's bloody odd, but I did nothing whatever to show that I was coming out here. I don't know how they got on to it.'

'Oh well.' Andrew looked less harassed. 'At least you seem to have lost them for the moment. Let's have some tea.'

He clapped his hands and shot a burst of machine-gun Gurkhali at the woman who came out of the house.

'I'm sorry I couldn't explain things in my letter. But maybe it was just as well I didn't. Anyway, the point is this: I've lived in the Himalayas for four years now, and in that time I've become more and more closely associated with Tibetans.'

'Here in Nepal, you mean?'

'Everywhere. In Nepal, India, and in Tibet itself. There's more contact with Tibet thàn a lot of people imagine. There are always caravans of traders coming down with salt and going back with grain and stuff.

'Anyway – since the Chinese invasion of Tibet, Nepal's been full of refugees. For the past couple of years I've been trying to give them a hand. I suppose I've become a sort of unofficial liaison officer, pleading the refugees' cause to the Nepalese Government. In particular, I've become – *de facto* – the personal representative of the Dalai Lama.'

'The Dalai Lama! I thought he was in India.'

'He is. He lives at Dharamsala, near Darjeeling. He settled there with his entourage.'

'Have you met him?'

'A couple of times. An impressive man. Through me he keeps in touch not only with the exiles here, but also with contacts still inside Tibet. Messages are passing all the time.'

The tea arrived, thick with buffalo milk, in chipped glasses.

'That's the general background,' Andrew continued. 'Now for the particular. There are two separate circumstances that brought you here. They told you about the American – General Sulzberger?'

'The outline, yes. He's stuck in a monastery in Tibet.'

'That's right. That's one factor. The other's the Khampas. You know about them?'

'The people the purge is going on against.'

'Exactly. They're a Tibetan tribe who settled in Nepal

after the Chinese invasion. They went to ground in Mustang – a province right up on the Tibetan border. Hell of a wild place. They lived in caves and tents and made occasional guerrilla raids on the Chinese border troops in Tibet. Several outside parties encouraged them, not least the C.I.A. They flew a few of them to the States for commando training. But nothing came of it.

'In any case, the Khampas have always been regarded as a nuisance by the Nepalese Government. Five years ago Katmandu announced that the last of them had been resettled – another word for captured – and that the problem had ceased to exist. Whether Katmandu believed that, or just said it for propaganda purposes, it's impossible to tell. In any case, the Khampas hadn't had it, by any means. There's still one strong group of them up in Mustang, where they've been for the last twenty-five years.

'Now. What Katmandu certainly doesn't know is that ever since the exodus from Tibet they've been harbouring one of the most priceless treasures from the Dalai Lama's former household.'

'What – here, in the Himalayas?'

'In Mustang.'

'What is it?'

'It's called the Emerald Goddess of Chamdo.'

The name seemed to resound in the far recesses of Stirling's mind. 'Chamdo,' he repeated, voicing one of the echoes. 'Where's that?'

'In Eastern Tibet, where the Khampas originally came from.'

'And what is it? You haven't seen it?'

'Of course not. I doubt if any Westerner has seen it. But I've heard descriptions of it. It's a life-sized effigy, supposed to be made of solid gold and encrusted with emeralds. I don't suppose the gold is solid – if it was, they'd never be able to move the thing. Almost certainly it's only a skin. But I'm sure the emeralds are real.

'The thing's worth millions, obviously. But to the Tibetans

that's beside the point. What matters to them is the fact that the Goddess represents freedom. If the Chinese had captured her, it would have been the symbolic end of Tibetan freedom. The symbolic value's far greater than the physical.'

'How did they get hold if it? The Khampas, I mean.'

'At the time of the Chinese invasion, the Goddess was in Lhasa, where she'd been for generations. This particular faction of the Khampas used to furnish the Dalai Lama's bodyguard. When the Chinese came, it was a case of *sauve qui peut*. Somehow during the escape the Khampas got cut off from the main body of the household, and they've been in Mustang ever since.'

'But nobody else knows about her – it?'

'Nobody *did* know.' He gave another strained smile. 'Now at last I'm coming to the point. Everything was O.K. until earlier this year. Then one of the young Khampas defected: got fed up with living in the wilderness and walked down to Pokhara, where he started to talk. Luckily he himself had never seen the Goddess and didn't even know where she was hidden. Even so, he said enough to spark off another purge – the one that's on now.

'Then the Khampas themselves got the wind up. They took divinations, and the answer was that they must move the Goddess out of the country, to the safety of India. Through me, they consulted the Dalai Lama in Dharamsala. He agreed. So that's what they're in the process of attempting: *they're bringing the Emerald Goddess out.*'

'Christ! That must be quite an undertaking.'

'It is. That's precisely the problem. They can get her so far, but if they come down to any of the towns with her, the army or police will pick her up in a moment. Therefore they must lift her out from one of the mountain airstrips. To do that, they need help.

'The position is this: I've done a deal. Verbal only, but binding all the same. We need help – or rather you need help – to get through the Tibetan border and find the monastery of Rimring. They need help to arrange an air-lift. So I've said that if some of them act as guides for you, we'll set up an aircraft to come and collect the Goddess from Dhorpatan.'

'Where's that?'

'It's a village – town, really – four days west of here. There's a cinder airstrip. Also, there's a big camp of Tibetan refugees there already. So Tibetan activity in the area is quite normal.' He paused and then added quietly, 'I must admit that the involvement with the Khampas is something I've brought on us myself. No one else knows about it – neither the Office nor Katmandu. But it was the only way I could see of getting you to Rimring. Have you got a map?'

'In my pack. I'll get it.' Stirling got up with his mind spinning: not one hair-raising project, but two. He found Kiri hemmed in as usual by invalids.

'Sorry, love. This is going to take some time.'

'It's all right. I'm busy. Are we going to spend the night here?'

'I don't know – we might.' It was already half-past three. 'I'll let you know as soon as I can.' He went back with the map.

'Here we are,' said Andrew, 'in Khibang. There's Dhorpatan – due west. There's Mustang – way to the north-east. And there's the border of Tibet. Normally, you could have gone straight up the Kali Gandaki to Jomson – there – and then forked right to this place Muktinath, where the Khampas are going to meet you. But because of the purge they've got police or army checks on all the main tracks, so you'll have to take a roundabout route . . . '

'Just a minute,' Stirling interrupted. 'You're talking a lot about *me*. Why don't *you* do the job, or at least come along? You know so much more about it.'

'Two reasons.' Andrew smiled ruefully. 'One, I'm too well known. I'm watched all the time. The place is alive with spies. If I went missing, it would be like turning on a red light in the Ministry of the Interior in Katmandu. They'd know at once that something was happening. But the second reason is the real killer – this.' He stuck out his right leg and patted his knee. 'I can't walk any distance now. I have to be carried, like a millionaire.'

'What happened?'

'Very undramatic. I just fell down some rocks one day and smashed my knee. It might have been all right if I could have got some treatment. But there was no doctor within a hundred miles, so nothing got done about it until too late.'

'I'm sorry. I noticed you were limping.'

'Don't worry. I'm used to it. But you see what I mean. Where were we? Yes – your route. Your first problem is to get past Annapurna and Dhaulagiri. People in the West think that each is just one mountain. They've no idea. Look at this.'

With a pencil he superimposed some lines on the map to show the extent of each massif. 'Dhaulagiri's got six main peaks, Annapurna five. But there are literally dozens of others. Dhaulagiri goes from here to here – what's that? Forty miles? At least. Annapurna's the same. Another bloody great lump of mountain forty miles across, with scarcely any way through. There's the Kali Gandaki, in its gorge between them. With that closed, you've got problems.

'But there are various factors in your favour. One is that the authorities aren't expecting the Khampas to come this far south. All the government's trying to do is to keep tourists out of the Khampa area, so that they don't see anything embarrassing, like prisoners being marched off in chains. Therefore, if you go north through one of the high passes, off the main tracks, you should be all right.'

He drank the remains of his tea and added, 'I'm sure you realise that in these mountains communications scarcely exist.'

'That's an advantage in our kind of operation, I should think.'

'Exactly. There's a primitive police radio network, but it's only got a few stations, and there's no way of contacting the villages in between. Ninety-nine per cent of the villages are out of touch altogether. The army's hardly got any helicopters either. Most of the ones they have got are out of action – can't get spares. In other words, once you take to the mountains, you should be relatively safe.'

'I'd be happier if I knew what our friends from the Kremlin are up to.'

'Well – you seem to have given them the slip so far. There's one or two things we can do to increase their confusion, too. Tomorrow, for instance, you ought to leave here in the dark and disappear north. I'll go on towards Dhorpatan in the middle of the morning. Sooner or later someone's going to turn up here in Khibang asking where you went, and with any luck he'll be told that you went west as well.'

'What about Haller? What's he doing?'

'Yes – Haller. He's not as bad as I made out. I over-reacted a bit there, I'm afraid. Sorry. He's just a sort of amateur spy: nothing to do with the K.G.B. He farts about trying to sell the government information. The air taxi gives him an ideal excuse for hopping around the mountain air-strips and picking up rumours.'

'Yes – but why's he so interested in me?'

'Probably he got wind of the fact that you were someone special. Special mission, etcetera. He may even have heard something about the Emerald Goddess. Maybe he thinks he can collar her and sell the jewels, or ransom the Tibetans or something.'

'That makes sense. He gave Kiri – the girl – the impression that he expected me to be fetching something heavy.' Stirling paused. Then he said, 'You might as well take the transmitter too.'

'What's that?'

'The radio that Haller gave the girl. If you take it, and broadcast the name of the place you're at each night, he'll think I'm there too.'

'I doubt if anyone will pick up the signals at this range. We can try it, though.'

'Do you have a route for me?'

'Not really. But it's simple enough. All you do is go straight up the river from here, due north. The Myangdi Khola. There it is. The track goes through a very high pass – 17,200 feet – there it is. How are you at that sort of height?'

'Never tried it. I'll just have to hope for the best.'

'You should be all right. You'll have to get used to it, anyway. Once you get on the Tibetan plateau you'll be at 13,000 or 14,000 feet for days on end.

'Either on your way to this first pass, or just beyond it, you'll be met by two of the Khampas, who've come down to act as guides. They'll take you up to the main body, which is still somewhere in Mustang. They'll detach a raiding party to go with you into Tibet. Then, on your way back, you'll rejoin the others and come down to Dhorpatan together.'

'With bands playing and flags flying,' said Stirling with mild sarcasm. 'You make it sound like a Sunday-school outing.'

Andrew ignored the remark. 'I'll make sure I'm there when you get back,' he went on. 'I spend a lot of time in the refugee settlement anyway. People are used to me being there. I've already got an aircraft lined up to come in and lift the Goddess out to Bhairawa – that's a town down on the Terai, the plain. All you need to do is send a messenger on a couple of days ahead of you when you're coming within reach of Dhorpatan.'

'How long will the trip take?'

'A month at best. Six weeks maybe.'

'If anything goes wrong, will I be able to contact you?'

'No.'

Stirling got off the stone wall and walked up and down.

'What are you thinking about?' Andrew asked. 'Money?'

'No. I've got plenty of money. Weapons, for one thing. I've got an automatic, but we need more than that.'

'I've got some rifles and grenades.'

'Ah. What sort?'

'I haven't looked at them yet. But they must be British – they came from a Gurkha depot. A friendly quartermaster wrote them off.'

'How about a decent map? This one's practically useless –
and anyway it doesn't cover Tibet.'

'There is no decent map of the area you're heading for.
You'll have to rely on the Khampas.'

'What about an interpreter? My Tibetan's non-existent.'

'You needn't worry. Dawa Wangdi, the Khampa leader,
was one of the people the C.I.A. took to the States, so he
speaks English quite well.'

'How many men shall I take?'

'I'm hoping you'll make do with the Sherpas you've
brought with you. Porters I can let you have.'

'One of my Sherpas will come, anyway.' Stirling's instinctive reaction was that he would rather take Pasang than
Mingmar. The older man had a core of resilience and loyalty
that Mingmar lacked. 'The boy's useful, too,' he went on.
'He'll come. No – I don't need any more Sherpas. Porters,
though – yes.'

'I expected that. So I've got you six, all good men. One big
advantage is that they've all done a bit of military training, so
they'll be able to handle rifles. What about the girl? You'll
send her with me, I suppose?'

Stirling was ready for that one. 'No,' he said coolly. 'She'll
come with me.'

Andrew stared at him with a pitying look. 'Come on, old
man. Do you realise what sort of a journey you're in for?
Everything you've done so far has been a doddle in compari-
son – a honeymoon. From now on the going will be tough.
You'll be very high – in the snow a lot of the time. There
won't be much to eat. If anyone gets hurt, you'll be many
days from the nearest doctor.'

'That's just the point,' Stirling cut in with satisfaction.
'The girl *is* a doctor. That's why she's coming. Whether or
not any of us get injured, it's certain that the American will
need treatment. If he broke his back weeks ago, and nothing's been done about it, he must be in a bad way. Do you
have any medical supplies?'

'Yes, I have.' Andrew sounded reluctant to admit it, as

though the medical pack's mere existence acknowledged that Stirling's decision was right. 'Anyway, we'd better stop talking and start doing something, otherwise we'll be benighted.'

At the front of the house, Stirling found Kiri disposing of her last patients.

'Done any good?'

'Not much. I lanced one septic finger, and one boil. Apart from those I was pretty helpless. It's all things like T.B. and thyroid deficiency. Pathetic, really.'

'Come over here a minute. I've a confession to make.' He led her off a few yards, away from the other people. 'I've got to head north,' he said quietly. 'A long journey, and a dangerous one. From now on it won't be a jaunt any more. I'd like you to come, but only if you want to. Don't come for my sake. The alternative is to go to Dhorpatan with Andrew and fly out to Katmandu from there.'

'You really want me?' She looked at him steadily.

'You'd be worth your weight in gold.'

'I'll come, then.'

He said nothing, but pressed down hard on her hand against a warm bank of earth.

'When do we start?'

'Before dawn tomorrow.'

'Is it Tibet?'

He nodded. 'How did you know?'

'It's been in your eyes for days.'

'How could it be in my eyes, crazy?'

'It was.'

He tackled the Sherpas next. As he expected and hoped, Mingmar opted out, making specious excuses. But Pasang had no hesitation in signing on. Nor did the boy Likpa.

Andrew addressed the porters in fluent Gurkhali. The journey to the north was expected to last at least thirty days, he told them. Their daily rate of pay would be half as much again as normal. For extra days, over thirty, that the trip might take, they would get double. If anyone wanted to leave

116

now, he or she would be paid up to date, and for the days needed to get back to Pokhara.

The proposals set off a buzz of discussion. Only four men elected to go back. The rest, including the husky woman from Ghandrung, voted to carry on.

'How much did you tell them about what we're doing?' Stirling asked.

'Nothing. As far as they're concerned, a journey's a journey.'

'What about their clothes – for cold weather, I mean?'

'I told them they'll be in the snow. They're used to that anyway.'

The last hour of daylight vanished in a fever of packing. The porters' old loads were laid out in a yard behind one of the houses, and new loads assembled. Sacks of maize and rice were parcelled out into individual bags, so that each man carried his own rations. The rifles – old British army .303s – were distributed among potential users, but packed inside loads, so that they should not attract attention prematurely. The ammunition posed a problem because of its weight: this too was divided up to spread the load. The box of twelve grenades was yet another heavy burden, but essential. So too was the medical pack – a useful and comprehensive selection of drugs, including morphia.

Everything they did not positively need, they jettisoned, the Blue Loo first. Though of no great weight, it took up valuable space. 'I never asked for the damn thing anyway,' said Kiri. 'Throw it out. I'm just as happy going behind a rock.' Stirling had refined his own equipment so carefully that there was hardly anything he was willing to abandon; but he rearranged things so that he carried more weight in his own pack and left less for one of the porters.

The sun was setting by the time the last of the loads had been assembled. The members of the party had found accommodation in one house or another, so there was no need to build a camp. All the same, out of sheer habit Pasang lit a fire in the courtyard where they had done the packing, and they sat round it after supper.

'One thing I would like to know', said Stirling, 'is why they chose me. Am I right in thinking you suggested me?'

Andrew looked at him with an air of amusement. 'You are. I knew you walk like hell. I thought you'd enjoy it. Particularly as I gathered things weren't too good at home.'

'How did you gather that?'

'The Office.'

'The Office!' Stirling felt a surge of irritation at the ubiquity of the Office, and the never-ceasing intrigues of the bland, smooth, impossibly efficient Henderson. So they had been keeping an eye on him all the time, even though he was no longer on the strength. They must know about Sue. Snooping bastards. He poked the fire savagely.

'How did they get their hooks into you?' he asked.

'In the Sudan, first. I was teaching there, when a man from the Embassy appeared and asked if I could do one or two things for them. Then I came out here, on a trek to begin with, and when I decided to stay, the same thing happened again.'

'But how did you get involved with the Tibetans?'

The question let loose a flood of political invective about the iniquities of the Chinese invasion of Tibet: how, in the name of freedom, an age-old civilisation had been all but eradicated, how countless people had been murdered and unspeakable barbarities committed, and how the frontiers of Communism had thereby been pushed closer to the great soft sponge of India.

'Doesn't this sort of thing worry you?' Andrew asked almost savagely. 'Don't you care when you see freedom being ground under?'

'Of course I care. It's just that I haven't ever been involved with Tibetans before.'

'Well – bloody well *get* involved. You're about to be involved, anyway. People in the West don't realise what freedom means. They've got it. They take it for granted. But if it was taken away from them, by God they'd scream.'

Andrew's eyes glittered. 'As soon as you meet the Khampas, you'll see what I mean. They're *marvellous* people. Incredible courage. Tough as hell, but laughing with it. They're full of jokes. You'd expect them to be miserable and embittered – not at all. You can't help liking them. Unless you're a Chinese Communist or a Nepalese bureaucrat, of course.'

'What about Tibet itself? I thought it was opening up again.'

'Not really. They let in one or two carefully chosen people and show them a few carefully chosen things, like in Russia. But in fact Tibet under the Chinese is far more a forbidden country than ever it was under the Dalai Lama. No strangers are allowed in without special permission.'

'What do *we* do, then?'

'You find a way round the border posts. Between them, rather. The frontier's not continuously manned, thank God. Everything's on too big a scale. It'll be a question of finding a pass that's not occupied. The Khampas are pretty good at that.'

'They'd better be. And we'd better get some sleep.'

To Stirling's surprise, Andrew suddenly, awkwardly stuck out his hand. 'Thanks for coming,' he said abruptly. 'I hope you don't think me too odd – going native and everything. I must have changed a lot since you last saw me.'

'You have,' Stirling told him. 'But so have I.'

Eleven

Like its owner, Klaus Haller's office in Katmandu exuded ambivalent sexuality. The walls were flame red, the carpet lemon, the furniture (imported at vast expense) made mainly of chrome and glass. A calendar featuring naked boys graced one wall, a series of lesbian posters another. A one-way mirror ensured that the person sitting at the desk could observe people entering the secretary's cubby-hole next door without himself being seen. Winter and summer an exotic, musky scent hung in the air, though whether it emanated from joss-sticks or from Haller's exceedingly attractive secretary, visitors found it impossible to decide.

'Maus,' he said, running his fingers over the taut little globes of her behind, which a semi-transparent blue sari did nothing to protect. 'How can I possibly see this man? I have to leave now for Lukla.'

'He says it is important,' said Kailasha pertly. 'He is very upset.'

'So will my clients be if I am late.' He looked at his watch. 'So. O.K. I give him five minutes. After five minutes, interrupt, please.'

The girl switched her long black hair over one shoulder and glided out, her sari rustling and the fine glass bracelets tinkling on her dark wrist. Over the primitive intercom she called down two floors to the waiting room and asked the client to come up.

His steps clonked on the wooden stairs – a stocky, powerfully built man with a sallow complexion and brown, badly cut hair. The sight of Kailasha stopped him in his tracks, but he recovered quickly and handed her a card. 'James Adair Junior,' he announced. 'Call me Jim.'

'Thank you, Mr Adair.' Her manner was smooth as honey. 'I'm afraid Mr Haller is in a great hurry, but he will see you for a moment.'

She took the visitor through, and after a brief exchange of formalities Haller said briskly, 'Tell me your business, please. I have to fly important Japanese clients to Everest region, and I must leave – how you say? – pronto.'

Adair began to explain. He was a geologist from Princeton, studying the composition of glacier moraines. He had come to Nepal to further his researches. He slid over the glass-topped desk two off-prints of learned articles under his own name, reproduced from scientific journals. Haller, screened by his dark glasses, looked at them briefly, glanced covertly at his watch, and peeped through the one-way mirror at Kailasha, who was filing her nails.

'The thing is,' Adair was saying, 'there's only one place in the whole goddam world where the rocks I want to study *exist*. That's in Mustang, up in the north. I come all this way, and now they tell me nobody's allowed up there, for Christ's sake.'

'That's right. For foreigners, entry into Mustang is forbidden just now.'

'Why's that?'

Haller shrugged and drummed on the desk-top with his long, elegant fingers. 'Politics, I suppose. They don't normally give reasons for these things.'

'What I was wondering,' Adair became ingratiating, 'was whether you could fly me up to that place on the river. What's it called – Jomsom? Yeah, Jomsom. Then I'd be ... '

'Please!' Haller interrupted, spreading his hands. 'How can I fly you there, Mr Adair? You have no permit, no? You need a permit to go to Jomsom. And anyway, what would you do when you got there? Unless you have authority to make exploration there, you will be arrested and sent back. So – it would be useless.'

'In that case' – the man's voice became positively conspiratorial – 'could you – er – help me get the necessary permission? I heard you could sometimes make arrangements . . . I could make it worth your while . . . '

'Perhaps, next week, something is possible. But now I have no time, you understand. Already I am late for my journey to Lukla.' He looked at his watch, openly this time, and shifted in his seat. But Adair was not easily deterred.

'I really have very little time, too,' he said anxiously. 'Couldn't you use you influence to get things going on my behalf? Just make a couple of phone calls, say?'

'Unfortunately, these things are not so simple. To make an arrangement might be possible, but it would be a question of personal visits to the correct government office. Please: I do my best to help you. But you must wait until I am back – yes? Two days, only.'

'Sure, sure. O.K.' Adair nodded resignedly. Then he added in a casual voice, 'Say, Mr Haller. D'you happen to know an Englishman named Carson?'

'Carson?' Haller did not move, but behind the dark glasses his eyes came round sharply. His fingers stopped drumming the desk.

'Yeah. Bill Carson. Funny thing – I met him once on a seminar in London. I haven't seen him in years, but yesterday I heard someone say he passed through Katmandu recently. Is that right, I wonder?'

'Carson,' said Haller, pretending to search his memory for the right person. 'Yes. I think you are right. In fact, I am quite sure of it. I saw him at Pokhara. He was just leaving for a trek. You are missing him, I think.'

'Pardon?'

'You miss him. He is gone eight, nine days now.'

'Which way did he go, d'you know?'

'Oh . . . ' Haller was vague. 'Where to? How can one say? On such treks, people go where they will. It is impossible to tell, exactly. But, you must know, he cannot go in northerly direction. As you say, that is forbidden. He can only go to the west.'

There was a pause. Kailasha rustled silkily into the room

and reminded Haller that he should go, but his frantic haste seemed suddenly to have evaporated. He waved to the girl, to show that he was coming, and said, 'So you know Carson! A strange coincidence – yes? Tell me – where have you been meeting him?'

'Gee, that's a tough one. It was at some seminar. In London, I guess. I was over there a couple of years back. Something to do with trees and fossils. He's a forester, I think.'

'Excuse me?'

'A forester – you know, *Forstmeister*.' He pronounced the German word with a murderous American accent, and laughed louder than was necessary. But at least he seemed to sense that he had outstayed his welcome. He got up to go, promising to call again on the following Monday, when Haller would be back.

The Swiss ushered him to the door. 'Where are you staying?' he asked. 'The Soaltee? That's fine. If there's anything we can do to help, only call Kailasha here. She will be delighted. For example, if you want to see Katmandu's night spots . . . she knows them all. You will find her a pleasant companion, I think.'

His tone was nakedly suggestive, and so were the movements with which the girl preceded the visitor through the door and took him downstairs. As soon as they were out of sight, Haller hopped about the room searching for the papers he needed and whipping them into his black kid briefcase.

'Mäuschen,' he said as Kailasha reappeared. 'A job for you. That man stinks – his story, I mean. I do not know what he does, but it is something, how you say? Fishy? Find out. O.K.? First he say he wants to go to Jomsom. Then he wants to find Carson. It is too much coincidence. Find out who he is and what he wants. Use your charms on him – but not too many of them, *hein*?'

He drew her long, supple body to him and kissed her hard on the lips. She nestled against him for a moment and ran her hand down his chest. 'O.K., Klaus,' she murmured. 'Klaus's Maus will manage.'

'His story stinks,' she added, drawing away, 'and he stinks, too. He smells like a Russian. Cheap scent and bad cigarettes.' She sighed. 'One day, Herr Haller, you will trip over your own whatnot.'

'Excuse me?' In the abstraction of collecting papers, he had only half heard what she said.

'So many irons in the fire. It's all getting too complicated.'

'No, no. Not at all. It is quite simple. The girl is with Carson. The radio tells us where he is – on his way to Dhorpatan. So, the Goddess is coming there also. We have our man on the airfield. He tells us when the Khampas arrive. Then – *klatsch*! I fly in and pick it up.'

'What if a message comes while you're at Lukla?'

'No, no. Not yet. The Khampas cannot reach Dhorpatan yet. Another week, at least. Concentrate on that man, Maus, and when I come back, tell me who he is.'

Twelve

Mission Yak approached the bridge five minutes ahead of schedule. Overhead, the stars hung bright in a clear black sky, and at ground level darkness still cloaked the terraces so thickly that the path was hardly visible. But the noise of the water grew steadily louder, and by the time they came down to the river bank the roar of the stream was such that no one could possibly have heard them pass. As Stirling crossed the bridge he reflected that the people living on the bank must be almost totally deaf. How else would they endure being battered continuously by such a volume of sound?

Looking down at the white water beneath, he felt exhilarated by the violence of its movement. Like the stream, he was free and on the move, with his private army pared down to a manageable unit and himself firmly in command. With Mingmar present there had been a certain ambiguity about the command structure, but now there was no doubt about the relative positions. Stirling was the platoon commander, Pasang his sergeant, the porters the rank and file. Kiri and Likpa fell outside the normal structure, it was true, but neither looked likely to lead a revolt.

Stirling had been pleased by the way Pasang got the party on the move that morning. Without Mingmar's flamboyance, without agitated *ho*-ing and *yaso*-ing, he had lined everyone up in just as short a time. Now they turned upstream well before light began to show. When dawn did start to break, it came as a luminous glow behind the mountains to their right, for they were heading due north into the heart of the Dhaulagiri massif.

As soon as the light was strong, Stirling halted the column

and, through Pasang, ran over the drill for action if an aircraft should appear. If anyone heard an engine while the party was in the woods, the men were to freeze on to trees until the aircraft had gone. If they were caught in open country, but on broken ground, they were to freeze on to rocks or in holes. But if they were in a place that offered no cover at all, Stirling and Kiri would freeze while the rest went on: shorn of its European contingent, the column should pass as an ordinary party of Nepalese on its way home for the winter.

As Pasang spelled out the instructions in words of one syllable, grins spread over some of the porters' faces. 'Tell them it's not funny,' he ordered sharply. 'Not a game. Tell them there are bad men in the machine-bird who'll shoot them if they don't do what you say.' This news produced a gratifying increase in concentration, and some of the men began casting furtive glances at the sky.

As a further precaution Stirling sent one lightly loaded man on ahead, giving him a quarter of an hour's start. If he met anyone coming, or saw anything untoward, he was to return and give the main body warning. Otherwise he was to come back at sundown.

The party advanced steadily up the western bank of the Myangdi Khola. Although Stirling was anxious to cover as much ground as possible, he did not want to stretch the porters unduly at such an early stage of the journey, so he tried to set a medium pace that would suit everybody. At first he found the column stringing out in a long line behind him; but later, as the ascent steepened, and the sun rose higher, the men seemed to close up automatically. His own heavier load, he realised, was slowing him down.

In his pack, besides some of the rifle ammunition, he now carried a missive from the Dalai Lama to Dawa Wangdi, the Khampas' leader, given him by Andrew. Not until he had watched Andrew writing a letter for General Sulzberger the evening before had he realised that, according to the Nepalese calendar, the year was 2039. It seemed strange that by arriving in the country he had both landed in a place sustained by medieval methods of agriculture, and at the same time jumped fifty-odd years into the future. Yet even 2039 seemed a relatively civilised date compared with the Tibetan name for the same period: the Year of the Iron Monkey.

All day they toiled on up the river. The higher they climbed, the more barren the tiny fields became. At the spot which Pasang picked for the mid-morning break a few terraces had been scratched out of the stony hill, and maize had been harvested on them; but between these pock-marks of cultivation the ground was almost pure rock, supporting nothing except a few spiky plants whose leaves were sharply serrated.

'Look,' said Kiri at one halt. 'Hashish.'

'Are you sure?'

'Absolutely. We found some on our other trek. Smell it – you'll see.' She broke off a leaf and crushed it in her fingers, to hold it under Stirling's nose. The harsh, sweet smell brought back vividly the one occasion on which he'd smoked a joint at home, only to be violently sick.

'Why doesn't anyone harvest it?' he asked Pasang.

'Too much here, all around.' The Sherpa indicated that the stuff grew everywhere. But he said the local people made money by selling what they could collect to smugglers, who took it down to India.

'Police no catch them?' asked Stirling, lapsing easily into pidgin-English.

Pasang smiled. 'No, sair. They going night time. Police sleeping too much.'

With his broad grin and his Chinese-style blue cap pushed back on his head, Pasang looked younger than Stirling had at first thought. During a wait he asked how old he was, and the answer was twenty-nine.

'Are you married?'

'Yessair.' The Sherpa became rather coy. 'Two wife.'

'Two! How many children?'

127

'Three, sair.'

'And Likpa – is he a relation?'

'Yessair – son of sister.'

The last place they went through before the pass was a god-forsaken village – a cluster of smoke-blackened hovels bunched so tightly together that the roofs all seemed to be joined in one. The houses crouched low in the middle of a dun, drab sweep of upland from which all life seemed to have been drained. Even under the brilliant noonday sun the place had an air of desolation.

'By God,' Stirling said. 'I bet even old Andrew wouldn't fancy living here. What a dump!'

As they drew nearer they saw that the house walls were made of split-bamboo matting tied to a rough framework of timber. The roofs were nothing more than a loose thatch of reeds. Everything – walls, roofs, people – was coated with soot. A smell of smouldering wood or dung suffused the air.

The path twisted between the hovels, sometimes no more than a couple of feet wide, giving the sensation that every crevice in the walls harboured dark eyes. Then it debouched on to a small open yard where three ancient men, plainly under the influence of drugs or alcohol or both, sat on the flagstones with glasses of cloudy rakshi beside them. As Stirling went by, they shouted fuddled invitations to join the party, but the scene was so depressing that he carried straight on, past the decrepit revellers and the blackened women, who wore heavy gold bangles in their noses as well as in their ears. The children – no less filthy – were clad in smocks of coarse, felt-like material, with strips cut from hessian sacks wound round and round their legs like puttees, all black as night.

'These mens no good for porter,' said Pasang contemptuously as they drew away from that sooty and desolate place. 'Too much money from hashish. No wanting work.'

Stirling felt oppressed and somehow frightened by the squalor of the village. It was as if they were leaving civilisation behind. Ahead, a series of grey rock-ridges rose layer upon layer towards the beginning of the snow. Still they followed the bank of the river, but now its course was much steeper – a series of cascades and rapids rather than a smoothly flowing stream. The going became progressively rougher, as much scrambling as walking.

Already it was the longest day's march that Stirling had done. He started to feel the strain in knees and thighs. Part of the reason was the sheer distance they had come; part was the weight of his pack, and part was the height they had climbed. Starting from 5,000 feet, they had already ascended to more than 11,000.

'How're you feeling?' he asked Kiri when they halted.

'O.K.,' she replied, but carefully. 'A bit tired.'

'Same here. But no ill effects from the altitude yet.'

'You shouldn't feel anything yet – not till 13,000 or 14,000 feet. How much farther tonight?'

'Another hour, maybe. There's no question of making the pass today. Pasang says there are some yak pastures up ahead of us. He's making for them.'

Soon they went through a few moribund trees, and Pasang gave orders that everyone should collect firewood, since there would be no more above them. Stirling and Kiri took off their packs and joined the hunt. Up here the Nepalese were less scrupulous about obeying the universal law of the land that no living tree must be cut for burning: since there was not much wood on the ground, they got out their kukris and hacked down branches from the stunted pines. In a few minutes everyone had an unwieldly bundle of sticks lashed on top of his load.

Stirling found the final hour tough going. His legs only just held out, and as he approached 13,000 feet a needling ache bored through the back of his head. Breathing became a labour. He looked back at Kiri: she seemed to be going easily. Although he had said nothing to her, he was secretly scared that he might become ill at extreme heights. He wasn't sure how his body would react. At least he had the comfort of knowing that if he did fall sick, she would know what to do.

At last they came over a backbone of rock to find themselves on the foot of the promised yak pastures. Smooth grass slopes swept up to a background of vertical rock cliffs, and the cliffs in turn were backed by distant ramparts of ice and snow. Close in under the rock-faces stood a row of four low buildings, hunched into the hill. Here, said Pasang, people lived in summer, grazing their yaks and sheep, but now they had all gone down for the winter.

As the party climbed towards the huts an eagle came sailing off the cliff above, uttering explosively piercing whistles. One of the porters let fly a no-less-explosive imitation. The eagle answered. The porter replied. The bird screamed again, and for a few minutes the pastures rang with fierce, long-drawn-out cries rebounding from the rocks.

They came to the old buildings, roofless and tumbledown: but since the ground inside was covered with animal droppings, and the low stone walls offered little protection from the elements, everyone chose to camp in the open, as usual. It would have been better, from the point of view of security, to have tucked everybody indoors, but Stirling reckoned the chances of an aircraft coming over at that time of day were so small as to be not worth considering. Besides, the forward scout returned as instructed just before sunset reporting that the track ahead was clear. For the moment, it seemed, undesirable aliens had been given the slip.

The camp was pitched in the eye of the setting sun, but the moment the sun disappeared beneath the horizon, cold came biting in. When Stirling went to wash in the river, he found ice forming across the surface of a pool and he quickly abandoned his idea of having a full-scale bath. Even though he had stopped exerting himself, his headache persisted, and he found that the small physical effort of moving around the camp left him breathless.

As the light faded, huge stripes of cloud flared up orange and pink all across the sky in band upon band of brilliant colour. The effect was theatrical in its splendour, but when Stirling remarked on its beauty to Pasang, the Sherpa shook his head and said, 'No good – snow coming.'

Certainly it felt cold enough for snow, although the evening seemed deceptively still and fine. While the Sherpas got supper going, Kiri tried to build a fire out of the sticks that she had carried up, carefully breaking the dead pieces into short lengths and constructing a tiny, compact wigwam, then piling larger pieces all round it. In spite of her attention to detail, the fire stubbornly refused to do more than smoulder. She blew on it till she felt dizzy, and still it would not burn. Then she noticed the female porter from Ghandrung standing behind her with a look of faintly contemptuous amusement on her face.

'Go on, then,' said Kiri. '*You* get it going.'

The woman – who was still bare-footed – stepped forward and lifted most of the heap of sticks into the air with one snatch of her brawny hands. The carefully built wigwam was instantly flattened, the embers almost extinguished. Smiling broadly, the woman clapped down a heavy mass of wood on top of the wretched pile and roughly jabbed at it with her toes. To Kiri, the chances of it lighting seemed negligible. But the woman knelt down, took an immense breath, and by holding her lips pursed into a small round hole blasted a hissing jet of air into the base of the fire from a distance of at least two feet.

In a few seconds a small flame was spluttering, and soon long tongues were licking high up through the pile. The woman drew back and gave the heap a couple of kicks that would have extinguished any normal bonfire. Then she bent and with a final blast fanned the whole pile into a crackling blaze – whereupon she withdrew, bashfully acknowledging the applause.

'Amazing!' said Stirling. 'She must have incredible lungs.'

'Like bellows,' said Kiri. 'In fact, that's what she is – a human bellows. Let's call her that – the Human Bellows.'

'Bill,' said Kiri softly. 'Are you asleep?'

'No. I think I was for a bit, but it's difficult to breathe.'

'I know. As if there's a weight on your chest. Bill?'

'What?'

'The wind's getting up.'

'I know. Pasang said it would snow. Those stripy clouds. Are you warm enough?'

'Fine.'

He reached across and laid the back of his hand on her cheek. She had the sleeping bag tucked up tight round her neck, and turned her head slightly to kiss the back of his hand. 'If it does snow, it'll be a change from all that heat, anyway,' he said.

They lay quiet, listening to surges of wind in the guy-ropes. Then she said:

'Bill – why are you doing this?'

'Why? I don't know really. I suppose I'm a bit like you. Things weren't too good at home. I was fed up – I decided to get the hell out.'

'Are you married?'

'I was. At least, I am. But I'm not planning to go back.'

'Was it that bad?'

'Oh, Kiri.' He turned on his back, staring up into the pitch blackness of the tent.

'Sorry. You don't want to talk about it.'

'It's not that. But it sounds so banal. We just seemed to have got to a dead end – nowhere to go. She despised me because I wasn't ambitious. Does that worry you – no ambition?'

'I hate ambitious people.'

'Good. But you're a bit ambitious yourself. You went through all the slog of becoming a doctor.'

'That wasn't ambition. I felt I had to do *something*. It's all a matter of degree. What are you going to do when this is over?'

'I don't know. But love, it isn't over yet.'

'I know. Bill – are you afraid?'

'What of?'

'These mountains – they're so big, I mean. We could get lost, or snowed up or something.'

'Of course I'm afraid.'

'You don't show it.'

'Nor do you. There's no point in showing it. But only a moron wouldn't be a bit scared. As you say, we could easily get lost. We probably will. We may run out of food. We'll get bloody cold, for sure. I hope to hell we don't get ill.

'The worst thing would be to get captured by the Chinese. Think of that: God knows where we'd finish up. The next worst thing would be to break a leg and have to be carried out. Almost anything but that. It would be a drag to be arrested by the Nepalese, as well. Any of these things is on the cards. They run through my mind like a silent film while we're walking, round and round. That's life, though: it's no good letting worries get the better of you.'

'I know. Only worries come most at night.'

'Push them down. Go to sleep.' He ran his forefinger up over the bridge of her nose and along one eyebrow, gently resting it on her eyelid. 'It'll be an early start again.' Presently he heard her breathing grow deeper and more regular: but he himself lay for a long time listening to the wind and fighting the weight that seemed to compress his lungs. He must have slept intermittently, for he saw from the luminous dial of his watch that time occasionally took a jump forward; but it was a relief when the sky at last began to lighten, and he heard the Sherpas start to clatter round the kitchen fire.

'Sorry, sair.' Likpa looked crestfallen. 'No wattair. All icing.' The river had frozen a complete crust during the night. By smashing off icicles, the Sherpas melted enough water for tea, but there was no question of shaving or washing much. As dawn broke, the sky had a sinister hazy look, which Pasang again said was a sign of snow coming.

The forward scout was sent off ahead while camp was being struck, and the main party followed him twenty minutes later. Soon after six they were on their way.

As soon as they moved out of the shelter of the cliffs, an icy wind hit them, blasting down the slope into their faces. For the first time Stirling and Kiri had walked in long trousers. Even so, it was a shock to feel the cold and smell the snow coming. Overhead, the haze in the sky gradually thickened into dirty cloud, which began to obscure the highest ridges.

They had been going for nearly an hour when the storm hit them. One moment the air was clear, though the clouds were more menacing than ever; a second later they were enveloped in a hurtling rush of snowflakes, driven by a wind of redoubled force. Turning round, Stirling was startled to find nobody in sight. Pasang should have been right there, behind him. He stopped, and a moment later the Sherpa loomed up out of the blizzard, already plastered with snow. Stirling realised that he could not see more than a yard or two.

'Too much dangerous, walking!' shouted Pasang above the roar of the wind. 'Wait is better.'

'O.K.,' Stirling yelled back. 'Let's find some shelter.'

They waited where they were for a few minutes, until all the porters had bunched tight together. Then they went slowly on again until they found themselves in the lee of some high rocks which were breaking the force of the wind. As they crouched beneath the overhang, snowflakes fizzed and hissed over their heads, and some eddied back to land on their feet.

Stirling sat on his heels, leaning back against the rock with his eyes shut in an attempt to soothe his headache, which had come on again as soon as he had started walking. It seemed incredible that only the day before they had been sunbathing. Those leisurely, sun-soaked brunches seemed part of another world. Had he really swum in the Modi Khola?

He opened his eyes and looked round the beleaguered army. Kiri was dozing with the blue hood of her anorak pulled in tight round her face. She looked pale. He suspected that she felt worse than she was admitting. The faces of the porters were resigned rather than apprehensive. One or two men had pulled on pairs of battered plimsolls, but the Human Bellows still had bare feet. Didn't she feel the cold at all?

Or didn't she own a pair of shoes? The man Stirling felt most worried about was the forward scout. Would he have the sense to stop and wait, as they had, or would he feel bound to keep going, and so risk falling into a crevasse?

The storm cleared as abruptly as it had come on. The wind fell, the snow eased off, and the clouds gave way to hot sunshine. They emerged from shelter to find themselves in a world of dazzling whiteness.

For the first time they needed their snow-goggles to cut down the glare. Everything in sight was brilliantly, blindingly white, not least the great summits that speared up into the sky on three sides of them. On their right, slightly behind them, stood Jirbang, with the main peak of Dhaulagiri hidden beyond it. On their left front were the summits of Dhaulagiri Two and Three, ranged with the peaks of the Mukut Himal along the horizon. Immediately ahead a high, ragged wall dipped to a shallow V, pointing their way to the north.

Beautiful as it looked, this new white world was far more dangerous than the old one, for by cloaking the mountains in snow the storm had obscured all the fine details of the terrain. No longer was it possible to tell whether a smooth slope was earth, rock or a sheet of ice; no longer could one be sure that an innocent-looking hollow did not conceal a hole several feet deep. All trace of the path had been eliminated, and there was no sign of the man who had gone ahead.

The route was by no means obvious, for although they could see the V in the horizon, the ground they were in was exceedingly rough and broken. Even Stirling, with no experience of it, could tell that they were on the moraine of a glacier among large rocks and debris left by the melting ice. Although his instinct was to press on – as always – he saw the sense of Pasang's suggestion that they should remain where they were until the snow had started to melt. Then, the Sherpa said, they would be able to see the path again.

An ominous silence followed the storm. The wind died away, and for a while everything stood frozen and still, with the fresh snow flashing back points of sunlight. Then, as the increasing heat began to melt the snow and ice, the glacier gradually came alive again. Snapping, booming noises began to sound in its depths, and presently water started to trickle. Sheets and lumps of snow began to slide, leaving bare rock steaming in the sun: the noise of water moving constantly increased, until the Myangdi was once more a river.

In due course a fantastic world stood revealed. Translucent domes of ice, shot through with rainbow colours, arched above jumbled rocks and channels of water. Huge stalactites hung glassily from the roofs of crystal caverns. Every few minutes, with a primeval subterranean groan, the glacier would shift imperceptibly forward, shattering a whole dream palace and sending the fallen pillars to feed the embryo stream.

While they waited, Pasang stamped down a small area of snow and built a fire with wood saved from the previous night. On it he and Likpa cooked a modest brunch – maize porridge, tea, biscuits and jam. As he explained, it was not what he would have liked to serve, but it was the best he could do in the circumstances.

Stirling was just finishing his tea when he saw Kiri stiffen and turn her head. 'What's the matter?'

'I can hear something. It's either a bee close to me or an engine far away.'

'There can't be any bees up here.'

They listened, turning this way and that. The glacier gave a particularly loud and resonant boom. Then Stirling also heard the sound – a distant buzz.

'Aircraft!' he announced sharply. 'Kick the fire out, Pasang. Tell everyone to keep still.'

Pasang shouted a quick volley of orders. Stirling looked round. Ten minutes ago, they would have been in trouble, caught on a white backcloth. But the sun had melted the snow so fast that now they were in a mottled, well-broken background, with plenty of big rocks to disguise the human shapes among them.

He dug in his rucksack and got out his binoculars. The engine noise was louder now, and definitely below them, in the direction from which they had come. He looked round again. Everyone was well down, but a thin column of smoke hung in the still air.

He scanned the great void below them. 'There it is!' he exclaimed. 'Coming this way.'

'Who?' asked Kiri. 'Haller?'

'Can't tell yet. But I don't think so. No – it's a dark aircraft – a helicopter. Heading straight for us. No it isn't – it's going to pass to our left.' He too got down in a hollow and crouched motionless as the machine, painted a dull, drab grey, came clattering up the ridge. The pilot was clearly following the Myangdi, like the people on the ground, but luckily he was keeping to one side of the river. In a few seconds the helicopter went safely past, still climbing, and disappeared towards the pass ahead.

Stirling did not like it. The pilot had not seen them, he felt sure, but the aircraft had not looked as though it was on a search mission. Its appearance, rather, was that of a ferry, aiming straight for a fixed point. Stirling felt uncomfortably certain that it had been taking supplies up to some unit stationed in the pass ahead.

For the moment he said nothing about such a possibility to Pasang, but merely asked how long it would take them to reach the pass; and on being told two hours, suggested they should start right away. This they did, but they had not been on the move for many minutes when they heard the aircraft coming back. This time it appeared suddenly, shooting into sight over a ridge above them, on a line almost directly overhead, and leaving them no time to find suitable holes for concealment. All they could do was to freeze where they stood, and Stirling was pleased to see that the porters had taken their instructions seriously.

Again the helicopter went straight over, leaving them apparently undetected; but its prompt reappearance, and its return on the same course, made Stirling still more certain that the pass was occupied. He was not surprised when, half an hour later, the forward scout came padding back to meet them with the news that he had found Nepalese soldiers on the skyline.

How many? Stirling asked, through Pasang. Six or eight, the man said. He could not be sure, as he had had to watch from a distance, and the soldiers had been moving about. Had the aircraft brought them supplies? Yes – it had hovered, like a hawk, and loads had fallen out of it. Had anyone seen him? Any of the soldiers, or the pilot? No.

'Bad news,' said Stirling, returning to where Kiri sat waiting on a rock. 'It sounds like an army patrol. According to Pasang, there's no other way through. One or two people might make it, over that shoulder, lightly loaded, but not the porters with their bundles.'

'What can we do, then?'

'There are two possibilities. One is to shoot our way through, and the other is to wait. Shooting would be quick. Quite easy, too, but not a good idea. Apart from the fact that we don't want to start killing people unless we have to, it would draw all hell down on the area. At the moment the Nepalese may not know that the Khampas are here. They may only be guessing. But if we knocked out a patrol, they wouldn't be left in any doubt. Therefore, it's better to wait. The patrol will probably push off in a day or so.'

'What if they don't?'

'Then we will have to force them.' He bent down, picked up two smooth, round pebbles, lobbed one in the air, and threw the second at it as it fell, missing narrowly. 'What a start! Grounded before we've even cleared the first obstacle!'

'Where do you think our Khampas have got to?'

'They must be somewhere on the other side. If they haven't been caught, that is. Maybe that's what brought the patrol into the area: sighting Khampas on the move. But with any luck they'll have spotted the patrol, like our man did.'

Stirling's altimeter was reading 16,000 feet: too high for a comfortable bivouac. Apart from the cold, there was no fuel, and as soon as the sun went, there would be no water. Depressing as it seemed, the only sensible course was to retrace their steps and return to the yak pastures of the night before. This they proceeded to do, and the only positive compensation Stirling could find was that his tolerance of high altitude had improved. The night before, he had been exceedingly uncomfortable at 14,000 feet, but tonight, though he was still short of breath, his headache had gone.

Thirteen

'Still there.' Stirling eased himself down out of the vantage-point and slipped the binoculars back inside his anorak. 'Six men, as far as I can see.'

Pasang nodded. His lean face glistened with sweat – the legacy of their hard climb – but it was also lit up by boyish excitement. Far from resenting the extra difficulties and exertion that this game of hide-and-seek was causing, he seemed positively to enjoy the challenge. The loyalty which he had shown from the start of the trek had suddenly blossomed into a powerful additional weapon which greatly strengthened Mission Yak's resources.

Besides, he had proved a deadly shot with a rifle. Round the corner from the yak pastures, in a sheltered ravine from which the sound would not carry far, Stirling had put Pasang and five of the porters through a practice shoot with the .303s. At two hundred yards Pasang had put four shots out of five into an eight-inch bull painted on a vertical face of rock.

Now he and Stirling had climbed to a point from which they could see down into the pass. Where the path came over, a rough wall and shelter had been built of dry stones to give travellers some protection from the wind, and a bunch of tattered prayer-flags, red and white, fluttered from the tops of long poles fixed upright against the wall. The patrol had pitched one large tent inside the shelter. The smoke of a fire drifted away to the north. Clearly the men were expecting to be there for some time.

Four was the most Stirling had seen at a time, but he guessed the patrol was six strong. The soldiers wore dark-green woollen hats, jackets and khaki trousers. They were obviously not expecting any kind of attack, for they did not carry their weapons about with them or maintain a continuous alert. Their function seemed purely that of a road-block.

As such they were all too effective. Mission Yak had been at a standstill for forty-eight hours. The delay worried Stirling for several reasons. For one, the party's food supply was by no means unlimited; for another, he was afraid that the Khampas – presumably stuck on the far side of the pass – would give up waiting and move off somewhere else.

To go back to Khibang and round through some other pass was out of the question. The only alternative seemed to be to shoot their way through the pass they had reached; yet to annihilate the Nepalese patrol would give the authorities first-hand information as to their whereabouts.

The longer he lay and waited, the more Stirling came to think that the only thing to do was to take the risk and open the pass with a shoot-out. He did not want to kill soldiers if he could help it, but there might be no alternative.

One thing about which he had no qualms was Pasang's support. At first he had been worried that the Sherpa might not be prepared to open up on fellow-countrymen; but so deep had Pasang's attachment to him become that it was a case of Mission Yak versus the rest. He was happy to shoot anything or anyone who stood in the way of success.

Again Stirling searched with binoculars for a radio aerial. That would make a great difference – to know whether or not the patrol was in touch with the outside world. He guessed they were not – the distance from any base seemed too great. If he was right, the party's chances of slipping through to the north would be that much better. If he waited until the afternoon helicopter had gone and then shot his way through, *and* there was no radio, the attack would not be discovered until the aircraft returned the next afternoon – by which time they would have disappeared far into the maze of high valleys which he could already see stretching away beyond the pass.

A sea of mountains filled the northern horizon. It chilled

him to find that Pasang could name hardly any of them: already they were on the edge of the territory that the Sherpa knew. Nor was the map much help, for on their line of advance, towards the north-east, the names gradually died out. Those that did appear were printed in blue ink, and this, according to the legend, meant that their location was 'not precisely established'. Further still, beyond the curve of the Tibetan frontier, the map was entirely blank. Looking at that empty space, and trying to correlate it with the serried white ramparts in the far distance, Stirling felt he was shaping to walk off the edge of the world.

The long afternoon wound down. Ice melted slowly in the sun. Water trickled in the gullies. Between the outcrops of rock coarse brown grass sprouted in tufts, warm to the hand. In weather like this, and in the middle of the day, even a 17,000-foot pass was a pleasant enough place; but Stirling had already seen and felt enough to imagine what it would be like when the temperature plunged below zero and the wind screamed on a stormy night.

A decision was needed. 'Pasang,' he said. 'We're going to have to shoot. We'll wait till the helicopter's been. Then we'll shoot the men so that our own party can get through. Otherwise we might wait for weeks.'

Pasang nodded and ran his fingers up and down the barrel of his rifle, as though it were the neck of a horse which might perform better with a little soothing encouragement.

'Come on,' said Stirling. 'Let's get nearer.'

There was still a quarter of an hour before the helicopter was due. They moved down their private ravine and round a small hillock. The ground was so broken that they had plenty of cover, and only in the final stages of the approach did they have to crawl. They shed their packs in a hollow and wormed forward to the crest of a mound scattered with large loose stones. Here they were less than two hundred yards from their objective, and the human targets looked comfortingly large: the pillar of the rifle's iron foresight covered only half a man, instead of his entire body.

Stirling found the wait painfully exciting. He felt his pulse rate increase, and breathed deeper to slow it down. To be a hunter was his natural bent, but to be hunted as well was doubly stimulating.

One soldier emerged from the tent and stood looking towards the south, evidently on the look-out for the helicopter. Stirling laid the tip of his foresight on the man's chest and squeezed his forefinger tight on to the front of the trigger guard. So firm was his position that the rifle never wavered.

'No missing,' muttered Pasang with grim relish.

'It should be all right. When I give the word, we shoot as many as we can. They won't know where we are. No seeing us. Maybe we kill three or four. But if the last two hide in the shelter, you cover me from here while I go in with a grenade.'

The minutes crept past. Looking down at his boots, Stirling saw that the stitching had begun to fray round the toe. This, the older of his two pairs, was wearing out faster than he had expected: a good job he'd brought the new pair as well.

He looked down into the pass again. The same man climbed on to an outlying rock and began to urinate over the drop. Once more Stirling aligned his rifle and held his breath for an imaginary shot.

Suddenly, to his amazement, the man crumpled and fell backwards, clutching at his chest. Fractionally later the crack of a rifle split the silence.

'What the hell?' He looked round sharply. 'Where did that come from, Pasang?'

'The other side.' The Sherpa pointed to their right, to the north side of the pass. Another shot cracked out and a second man toppled from the enclosure wall.

'Shoot, sair, shoot?' cried Pasang hoarsely, levelling his rifle and snapping off the safety catch.

'No, no!' Stirling knocked the weapon up, out of line. 'Wait.'

The remaining soldiers pulled themselves together, got

down behind the parapet and opened fire. Bullets whistled overhead, hit rocks, ricocheted whining into the sky. But the shots were not aimed: unable to pin-point their attackers, the Nepalese were spraying the mountain indiscriminately. Echoes rolled and thundered among the ice-cliffs beyond the pass.

Through the din Stirling became aware of a different sound: the helicopter. The soldiers heard it too and began to shout. The engine-roar swelled rapidly and the aircraft popped suddenly up over the final ridge. After one short sweep the pilot came quickly in to hover low over the little encampment. The prayer-flags thrashed furiously in the downdraught from the rotor. Seen from close range, the machine looked much larger – big enough to carry twenty men, at least.

Now, thought Stirling: will the invisible marksmen take on this huge new target? If they do, they can hardly miss it . . .

But no: through the scream of the engine he could hear that the firing had stopped. The soldiers rushed about making frantic signals at the air crew. The message was plain: they did not want supplies – they wanted out.

A door in the fuselage slid open and a climbing-net dropped down. Three men grabbed their kit and went up it, one by one. A fourth man stayed on the ground, still gesticulating. A steel cable unrolled swiftly from the cabin with a canvas belt on the end. The man took it and knelt down, working hard. Then he raised his hand, and the first body was winched aboard. The rescuer repeated the process for the second corpse and scrambled up the net to the safety of the machine's belly.

The helicopter lifted away and gained height. But then, instead of turning for home, it began a wide, circling sweep of the area. Providentially, to Pasang's right a jutting rock overhung a recess. Stirling shoved the Sherpa into it and bundled in against him with his back to the opening. Too late he remembered their haversacks standing out in the open. His own was rock-grey, Pasang's a dirty crimson.

The engine faded and swelled, receded and advanced. Then it held steady.

'Hovering,' said Stirling. 'They've seen something.' He eased himself out cautiously and peered over the rock. The aircraft was stationary, but at a considerable height. As he watched it went forward again, at last heading for the south. 'It's O.K.,' he said. 'They're going home.'

Silence flowed back into the pass. Smoke still streamed from the fire, and the prayer-flags had resumed their peaceful flutter. The canvas of the abandoned tent flapped gently.

'Is Khampas,' said Pasang.

'Where?'

'They shooting.'

'The people who came to meet us?'

'Yessair.'

'Where are they, then?'

'They coming, sair.'

They stood waiting, hidden in their hollow. The air was sharper now, the declining sun cooler. Suddenly a new sound broke the silence: laughter – a chuckle. Two shaggy figures appeared in the pass. Pasang stood higher on a rock and gave a penetrating whistle, like his eagle call, but double. The strangers raised hands in greeting.

Stirling felt a huge surge of relief and hurried forward. The newcomers were small, stocky men with flat, wide faces battered by the elements into the colour and texture of old leather – dark brown and shiny. Deep wrinkles radiated from their eyes and mouths, and when they laughed or smiled their entire faces bunched into masses of good-humoured corrugations.

They were dressed in voluminous coats of sheepskin, belted at the waist, with the fleece on the inside. Their square, furry hats and clumsy soft-leather boots gave them a quaint, home-made look. They also had a powerful home-made smell, so pungent as to be almost more animal than human. Stirling fought back a smile as he remembered a remark made by the fastidious Mingmar down in the valley, after they had seen a couple of Tibetan traders: 'Teebettans too much dirty people – no wassing.' The two Khampas certainly gave the impression that they had never washed in their lives.

They talked rapidly, making bold gestures. Pasang evidently understood their dialect without difficulty and translated for Stirling in staccato bursts.

The Khampas had come to the pass that morning, he said. They had lain up all day waiting for the soldiers to move off. When they realised the men were planning to stay the night, they opened up on them, their hope being that the rest would run away. They had not known about the daily helicopter flight. They had been astonished and afraid when the machine appeared.

Why had they not shot at the aircraft too? Because they thought their bullets would have no effect on such a giant bird made of metal.

Had the pilot spotted them? No, because they had hidden under a rock.

And where had they come from that day? From a safe place in the mountains, where there were big caves – big enough for all the Khampa people to live in.'

'*All* the Khampa people? Did they say *all* the Khampas?'

Pasang repeated the question and translated again. 'Yessair – all come.'

'How many?'

'Forty, fifty. Womens also.'

Something was wrong. According to Andrew, he was supposed to have met the main Khampa body near Muktinath, a week's journey to the north-east. For some reason the tribe had moved south prematurely. He was afraid it might make them less keen to keep their half of the bargain by leading him into Tibet. If they were already well on their way to Dhorpatan and freedom, would they want to back-track so far into hostile territory?

But this was no place to argue. The urgent task was to get Mission Yak through the pass and as far as possible beyond it before daybreak.

'How far are the caves from here?' he asked.

'Three hour, four hour.'

'We must get everyone there tonight.'

'Yessair.'

'I'll go down and get the others. You stay here with our friends. If anyone else comes up, drop down to warn me.'

The sun was low over the ridges of Dhaulagiri as Stirling set out, and by going down himself he seemed to accelerate its fall. After a few minutes he was down in the vast, icy shadow cast by the mountain. Overhead, the sky again went into a menacing array of pink and bronze bars, and he needed no one to tell him that more snow was on the way. His breath shot jets of smoke into the frosty air. For extra speed he had left his haversack with Pasang, and his only burden was the rifle on its sling. For the first time at this altitude he felt really good – legs fit and going well, lungs able to cope with the thin air.

In only half an hour he was back in the frozen valley where the rest of the party was waiting. He found them lurking disconsolately among the rocks.

'Come on!' he called as he approached. '*Aunu!* Let's go.'

As if by magic Likpa handed him a mug of hot, sweet tea. Kiri got up from beside the fire and held something out to him. 'Here – Likpa and I have been giving each other cooking lessons.' She handed him a lump of doughy-looking cake.

'Spunch kek,' said Likpa proudly.

'Smashing. Who made it?'

'We both did – a combined effort. We baked it in a biscuit tin.'

Stirling ate the lump hungrily. 'Let's get going. Give me your pack. It's quite a climb.'

After a short argument he got it off her, and they set out with him in the lead, and the senior porter appointed to act as shepherd at the back of the column.

'Tell me what happened,' said Kiri.

'Keep going, and I will. Did you see the chopper?'

'Yes – up and back.'

'Hear any shots?'

'No – were there some?'

'A few.' He gave her an outline of the action. 'So, as it turned out, the Khampas did the shooting for us.'

'But you'd have fired if they hadn't.'

'We'd have had to. Otherwise we'd have been stuck in-definitely.'

She was silent for a few minutes before asking, 'How does it leave us?'

'Not good, but not too bad either. The worst thing is that the Nepalese now know there's some illegal activity going on in the area. The best thing is, they don't know it's us causing it. In fact, with any luck, they'll read the situation back-to-front. The soldiers knew that the shots came from the north side of the pass. Therefore, they must deduce that the at-tackers – whoever they were – were trying to come through from north to south. Probably they'll assume they've come through in the night, and they'll set up a terrific hunt for them tomorrow somewhere down behind where we are now.'

The dusk was thickening fast. Between the slabs of ice and gullies full of snow, solid rocks and empty holes became dangerously alike. The need for extra care made progress even slower. On the steepest part of the ascent – almost a cliff-face, up which the track zigzagged on a narrow ledge – Stirling had to wait for twenty minutes before he heard the porters wheezing and grunting and hooting their little owl-calls as they wound up the path below him. Frost bit keenly at his hands and face. His gloves were buried in his haver-sack, with Pasang, so he pushed each hand up the opposite sleeve of his anorak to conserve warmth.

By the time they regained the pass it was fully dark, but as they were reorganising themselves for the next stage the new moon rose and shone bleakly through a thin curtain of cloud, giving a dim but useful light. Pasang had not wasted a minute. He had dismantled the big tent, cut the canvas into two pieces, to spread the load, and rolled each half into a neat bundle. Inside the tent he had found one sack of maize and

148

another of rice, besides packets of tea and sugar. All this extra food he had divided up into small lots for distribution among the porters. He had also kept the fire going, and in a big billycan which the soldiers had left behind he had tea boiling. Not until Stirling tasted it did he realise that it was laced with rancid butter. He nearly choked on the greasiness of the first mouthful, but forced himself to swallow it, reflecting that the fat would provide much-needed fuel for the march ahead.

Icy stillness gripped the mountains as they prepared to set off again. To the north the limitless sea of peaks and ridges glowed faintly white beneath the opalescent moon. As they stood poised to plunge into that freezing ocean Stirling shuddered with apprehension, so vast and inhospitable was the landscape ahead, so great the possibility of getting lost, injured or killed.

He shook himself. Better keep imagination on a tight rein. 'O.K.?' he asked Kiri. She nodded, looking like an inflated pixie in her down jacket with the hood turned up.

They set out. The Khampas led, with Stirling and Kiri behind them, then the string of porters, and Pasang bringing up the rear. The track – narrow and stony and dropping steeply – demanded careful footwork, especially on stretches where snow had melted during the day and frozen again into knobbly runs of ice. Twice Stirling slipped and half fell, jarring his knee and his arm. Yet in spite of the difficulties he found himself enjoying the stealthy advance through the night.

The mountains were eerily beautiful, and he had the agreeable sensation of making good progress while the enemy's attention was diverted. Another advantage was that they scarcely had to climb: almost all the way the track ran level or downwards, and as they lost height, dropping to 16,000 and then 15,000 feet, they could feel the air growing warmer. As the night wore on the clouds gradually thickened until the moon itself became invisible and only a luminous glow remained. Later still a bitter breeze stirred in their faces, bringing a sure hint of snow.

A newcomer would have had no chance of finding his way through that maze of ridges and valleys in the dark, but the Khampas never hesitated about choosing which direction to take. Once, when the track divided, one of them pointed to the right and said '*Tukche*'. Stirling remembered that was the name of the pass that led down to the Kali Gandaki, and he guessed that the Khampas must have come through it on their way in from the north-east. Now, taking the other fork, the guides continued almost due north along the flank of a steep valley.

'I wonder where Andrew's got to,' said Stirling, thinking aloud. 'It's three days since we left him. He ought to be at Dhorpatan by now.' When Kiri did not answer, he turned to look at her and got the impression, from the way she held her face down, that she was crying.

'Are you all right?'

She nodded.

'Shall I take your pack?'

She shook her head.

'I could give it to one of the porters to carry.'

She shook her head again, and he turned forward once more, disturbed by her sadness. There was nothing he could do except leave her alone with whatever private grief it was that had welled up out of her past. Thinking of it made Stirling himself feel maudlin. For a few minutes he was back with poor Sue in her little matchbox house, hopelessly chewing over the future.

On and on the column went, with occasional short halts, and when at about midnight the snow began to fall, Pasang came bustling up the line to ask the Khampas how much farther they had to go. The answer was only a very short way – not more than half an hour. Stirling laid himself a private bet that they would have at least a whole hour more, and in the event even that estimate proved optimistic.

Towards the end the snow came on thicker – fine, small flakes driven fast by the wind so that they flew into the marchers' faces like needles. Dragging one foot past the other, Stirling hoped Pasang had given the porters an adequate explanation of the need to move at night. He hoped they were not blaming him for their discomfort (the Human Bellows had at last put on a pair of shoes, but they were thin, pointed, black-leather city shoes, utterly unsuitable for the mountains). Above all, he hoped they would realise that the snow, though unpleasant, might have been sent by some benevolent deity in answer to a prayer, for in their wake it was laying a smooth, safe blanket over the path, blotting out every sign that people had passed that way. He imagined how it must be drifting inside the walls of the enclosure up on the pass behind them. By morning, no trace would remain of what had happened during the night and the previous day.

Perhaps, thought Stirling, the power of the Emerald Goddess was protecting them. Through his daze of exhaustion, he tried to imagine what the image would be like. He saw a serene, Buddha-like figure, smiling. But where were the emeralds? In the eyes? 'With gazing fed, And fancy dies . . .' His mind was starting to skid around, like his feet. Snow gritted into his eyes and stung his cheeks. Melted snow was coming through the toes of his boots.

Suddenly he fetched up with a bump against the back of the man ahead of him. The Khampa had stopped. Through the driving flakes Stirling saw a light – a cheery, reddish light: the glow of a fire. A few seconds later he was half-led, half-dragged into the delicious warmth of a smoke-filled cave.

Fourteen

Stirling was kneeling in front of his tent, with his possessions spread out on a ground-sheet to dry in the hot sun, when he heard the rollicking, staccato belly-laugh. He jumped up in time to see an immensely broad and solid man come round the corner of the rock. Though no taller than the guides of the night before, Dawa Wangdi looked twice as wide – a rolling, sawn-off bear of a man enveloped in a huge brown fur coat, with tufts of the same fur rising from the corners of his flat hat just where a bear's ears would be.

'Well come, friend,' he cried in greeting. The English words were spoken in an American accent, but with a curious intonation, equal stress on each syllable.

Stirling had been preparing a respectful '*Namaste!*', but at the sight of the Khampa leader's boisterous, Western-style advance and outstretched arm he abandoned the idea and shook hands.

'Well come!' Wangdi gripped Stirling's hand with one great rough paw and clapped him on the shoulder with the other. 'You travelled good?'

'Pretty good, thanks.' Instantly Stirling sensed the attraction of this powerful, burly creature. The only thing not bear-like about him was his eyes: far from being mean and yellow, they were dark brown and shiny as horse-chestnuts, and they flashed with goodwill in the leather football of a face. His whole demeanour seemed to radiate amusement at the jokes life played on him.

'My friend!' He fired off his matchless belly-laugh again. 'I happy man.'

Suddenly he looked over Stirling's shoulder and made an exclamation. Kiri stood there, and Stirling introduced her as Doctor Nelson.

With a flourish Wangdi swept off his furry hat, revealing long black hair streaked with grey and swept back into a pigtail. 'Doctor. Well come too!'

Kiri thanked him prettily and complimented him on the site of the camp.

'Excuse me?'

'This place. It's very nice.'

He beamed. 'We didn't make it! The gods, I think.' He laughed yet again and raised an arm to the natural amphitheatre of mountains that enfolded the snug valley, with its clear stream trickling and its tufty grass re-emerging from the overnight snow as the sun went to work. 'Come,' he said. 'We drink tea.'

He led them to a small, separate valley – a private re-entrant between walls of naked rock – in which his own tent was pitched. Compared with those of his followers, it was a palatial home. The roof and walls were made of a thick, grey-brown fabric like felt, blackened by smoke on the inside, and the whole structure was supported by ancient, polished bamboo poles.

The visitors were invited to sit on a rug which was old but fine, with a pattern of red and blue. Wangdi sat on another, raised on a dais, giving him extra height. He pushed back the bearskin coat from his shoulders and revealed a necklace of small bones threaded on a black cord. In the centre of the tent a fire of yak dung smouldered, giving off such pungent fumes that Stirling found breathing difficult.

Wangdi clapped his hands and called for tea, which was soon brought by a tiny woman so wizened that it was impossible to judge her age: she could have been the Khampa's servant or wife or mother. From a wooden tray she set down brass bowls of steaming black tea in which lumps of butter were melting among crusty islands of grey, sawdust-like powder.

'Tibetan tea!' Wangdi pointed jovially at the bowls. 'You like the butter and *tsampa*, the barley meal?'

'Fine.' Stirling's enthusiasm was not entirely feigned: he had already developed a liking for the initially rebarbative brew. The great thing about it was that it did everything necessary: warmed you, quenched your thirst, stimulated you and fed you, all in one. Lack of variety was all that could be held against it.

A stilted exchange of compliments began. Although Wangdi spoke English freely, he understood little of what Stirling said, no doubt through lack of practice. After a while, however, he began to tune in to the strange language again, and presently Stirling brought out the big white envelope from Dharamsala, crumpled now and bashed in at the corners, but with the flame-red seals of the Dalai Lama's household still intact.

Wangdi received it with a glowing smile. He fingered the bones in his necklace rapidly as he muttered a prayer. Then he turned the envelope round and round, like a child unable to decide which way to open a present. At last he slit the envelope with his finger-nail and brought the letter out.

He read it slowly, tracing each word with his stubby index finger. Pleasure, surprise and satisfaction chased across his features. When he reached the end of the single sheet he gave a grunt and bowed his head low, pressing the paper to his forehead.

'His Holiness say, he glad we bring the Emerald Goddess to freedom. He bless our journey. He meet us in Indialand.'

'Good.' Stirling made more polite exchanges, and then steered the talk to himself.

'It was bad that the men in the pass were killed,' he began.

'Was necessary,' said Wangdi, implicitly defending his men's action.

'Yes, it was necessary. Otherwise we couldn't have come through. But now the Nepalese know that there's somebody in the area. The soldiers will be out searching.'

'Here no.' The Khampa was emphatic. 'Search Kali

Gandaki area, yes. Search south of high pass, yes. But here – here O.K.' He laughed, and as he remembered the American phrase added, 'No problem.'

'Andrew de Lazlo said you would wait for us in Mustang. Why did you come on so soon?'

'In Mustang, many soldiers – here, here.' He pointed with quick, darting gestures into every corner of the tent to demonstrate the ubiquity of the Nepalese forces.

'Did they see you?'

'No, no. No problem! Khampas travelling night-time. Very secret. *Top* secret – ha ha!'

Stirling couldn't help laughing at such robust and simple enthusiasm. He braced himself to ask the difficult question: 'It's still possible for you to take me to the monastery of Rimring?'

There was a pause, which grew uncomfortably long.

'My friend,' Wangdi began, in a voice that suddenly seemed less ebullient, 'you understand. Myself, I cannot come. Myself – I must stay with my people.'

For a few seconds Stirling had the sick feeling that he was about to be betrayed, that the whole plan was about to collapse. But then the Khampa leader continued: 'My best man take you to Rimring. Tashi, he called. He know the path.'

Stirling swallowed with relief. Wangdi had taken the question more personally than he had intended. He had never expected that the leader himself would come. 'Thank you,' he said. 'How long will it take?'

'From here you go with porters to Kali Gandaki. Three days. Beyond the river, guides come with horses. Then you go faster.' He made merry galloping motions with arms and shoulders. 'Two days to Tibet frontier. Then three, four days Rimring *Gompa*.'

'Coming back, we'll have to carry the American.'

'Excuse me?'

'The American soldier. He will have to be carried.'

'He ride horse, too.'

Suddenly Kiri, who had sat still and quiet, spoke up. 'If he's broken his back, he won't be able to ride. He won't be able to travel in a basket, even. He'll have to be carried flat – horizontal.'

Either Wangdi did not understand, or else he did not care about the finer points of the rescue operation. In any case, he brushed the detail aside as something they could sort out later.

'Where *is* Rimring?' Stirling asked, to smooth over the awkwardness. He got out his map, such as it was, and looked at the names to the north-east. 'Do we go by Thorong La?'

Wangdi waved away the suggestion and the map simultaneously. 'No good,' he said contemptuously. 'Your way is by Yak Khola, Yulokang, Peri Himal. No problem.'

Stirling shifted on the rug. The heights on the way looked formidable, the open spaces immense. When the map gave out, they would be entirely in the hands of the guides.

'What will you do?' he asked. 'Our trip will take twenty days at least. Is it safe for you to stay here that long?'

'Safe – enough.' Wangdi turned his hand back and forth in front of him, as though he was hefting something to judge its weight. 'That's why we come here. Nobody going this way in the fall. You have a saying: off the beating track.'

'Beat*en* track.' Stirling smiled. 'What about helicopters?'

'Nepalese army has very few.' Again he swivelled his hand. 'Is possible. But Himalaya very big place!' He roared with laughter and called for more tea. When the woman had filled their bowls again Stirling asked about Wangdi's trip to America.

It had taken place eight years ago, the Khampa told him. Together with three subordinates he had walked down to Pokhara, where the C.I.A. had collected them in a special aircraft and flown them via Calcutta, to Camp Hale, in Colorado. There, for three months, they had been put through commando training designed to encourage them to make raids on the Chinese frontier-posts along the Tibetan border. They had also learnt to parachute, the idea being

156

that they would drop inside Tibet and harass the defenders from the rear.

In the event the return trip had proved a fiasco. The pilot of the aircraft lost his bearings and dropped them on the wrong side of the border, back into Nepal. One man was killed when his parachute-cords became entangled, and the canisters containing arms and ammunition had drifted away with the wind, to land unseen in some high ravine, whence they had never been recovered. The highly trained Khampas were thus left with only an Armalite rifle apiece and a few rounds of ammunition. For years now, Wangdi said, the weapons had been useless, as they had nothing to fire through them. They had to rely on their own ancient rifles, bound together with leather and wire.

'How did you like America?'

'Wonderful! Americans very good people.'

'But didn't you miss all the things you'd seen there – afterwards, I mean? Cars, television, food?'

Wangdi smiled and spread his arms. 'Tibet is our home. Tibet best.' The sparkle left his eyes. 'But now, Khampa people all old people. We are too many years in these mountains. It is twenty years since we leave home. Khampa people are tired.' He paused, with his eyes far away.

'For many winters we are saying, "In the spring, we go home. English, American, Russian people – somebody makes our country free again. Then we go home." But in the spring the Chinese are still there. My friend – Tibet is prison now. It is never free. Khampa people never go home. That is why we go to his Holiness in Indialand.'

Stirling was moved, not so much by Wangdi's sadness as by the way he normally kept it down. How could anyone remain so cheerful in such circumstances? He hardly knew what to say.

'You go tonight?' Wangdi half-asked, half-stated.

'Tonight?'

'To Rimring. Yes. Soon is better. Tashi expects you. Come – I take you to him.'

They walked outside, blinking in the hot, bright sun. As Wangdi had said, the place was as safe as any upland valley could be, for the area of the camp was divided up into five or six miniature ravines, each separated from the next by outcrops of rock, and the whole settlement seemed to disappear into the caves and gullies round the valley sides. It was true that the Khampas' herd of yaks might be spotted from the air, but the animals on their own would not excite suspicion, for there were plenty of other herds in the mountains.

Everywhere in the camp men and women were at work, cooking, grinding barley into tsampa, cutting up hides, spinning yak hair, patching clothes. Every garment was homemade, from skins or rough-woven material. Both men and women had their faces smeared with red ochre, which Wangdi said was a protection against cold and insect bites. The people stared at them uninhibitedly.

'It's partly that I'm so tall,' said Stirling. He wished he could shrink a bit, for he felt like Gulliver among those Lilliputian nomads. Wangdi, he reckoned, might be five foot six, but most of the men were hardly over five foot, and the women were correspondingly smaller. Even Kiri looked like a slender giant among them. It was not quite true that all the Khampas were old, as Wangdi had said. Children of various ages were frolicking about.

In one small meadow they came upon a group of women sitting opposite each other in two short lines, rolling skin bags full of liquid back and forth between them. At first Stirling thought they were playing some game, and was about to make a facetious remark, when Wangdi said, 'Butter.'

Butter! Of course. The skins were full of yak milk. There had not been time to wonder where the ubiquitous butter came from. Obviously the Khampas made it themselves.

They went on and found Tashi – a slight young man with a huge shock of spiky black hair and steeply slanted eyes. Though he spoke no English, he had a lively appearance, and Stirling liked him at once.

It was agreed that the party would consist of Stirling's own team, reinforced only by Tashi and a second guide, Chimba. Some of Stirling's porters would carry their loads as far as the Kali Gandaki, but across the river the party would be met by other Khampas with horses: the loads would be transferred to the ponies for extra speed, and the porters would continue unloaded, so that they would be free to carry the American general out.

The porters already had rifles. Stirling gave one to each of the guides and another to Pasang, keeping one for himself. He gave the .38 temporarily to Kiri. Thus everyone in the party was armed except Likpa, who was too small to wield a rifle anyway. The distribution left four rifles over, and these Stirling handed to Wangdi, together with some surplus ammunition. The Khampa's delight was unbounded. 'Now we shooting Chinese!' he roared, as though Chinese were partridges. 'Bang bang!'

At five o'clock Stirling held a conference. The aim was to make sure that everyone agreed on the plan of campaign. The first objective was the bridge over the Kali Gandaki at Tsele, three nights' march to the north-east. They expected the bridge to be guarded, so when they reached it they were to decoy the guards away by lighting a fire some distance up the western bank of the river. The fire would also act as a signal to their contacts on the far bank.

Making oblique approaches, Stirling questioned Tashi via Pasang, on his knowledge of Rimring. The Tibetan said the monastery stood on top of high cliffs, and that it could not be seen from the track below. There was no way up to it except in some sort of basket which the lamas lowered from above. It certainly sounded as though the Khampa had been there before.

'I thought the Chinese had closed all the monasteries,' said Stirling.

'They destroy many, yes,' Wangdi agreed. 'But some are so small and so far distant that they are leaving them. Now they are making propaganda. Chinese people very tolerant, they say. Leaving lamas in monastery. No problem. Tscho!' He spat contemptuously. 'Many hundred lamas killed or in gaol, many monastery burning down. Chinese people tolerant – tscho!'

'Supposing we get the American,' Stirling went on. 'We come back to the same bridge, I take it?'

'Same bridge.'

'So if nothing goes wrong, we should be back at the river in twelve or fourteen days.'

'Khampas meeting you,' said Wangdi comfortably.

'What if we get held up?'

'They waiting.'

'What about you – the rest of you? Suppose the Nepalese find you here?'

'We shooting them!' He gave a bellow of laughter and made motions of rifle-aiming and trigger-pulling. 'No. Is possible we have to move northwards. But then guides know the new place.'

The arrangement seemed alarmingly loose. But with no communications of any sort, no one could make it any tighter.

'What time do we leave?'

'The moon, she rise nine o'clock. Go then. But first we have special Khampa ceremony. The Goddess is casting out evil spirits from your journey. One hour now. I call you.'

Back in his private enclave Stirling found that Likpa and Kiri had already dismantled the tents and packed them. They also had supper bubbling on the fire – Tibetan meat balls, Likpa's speciality. The sun had gone off the valley, and the cold came clawing at hands and faces as they sat eating round the fire.

'There's a ceremony,' said Stirling between mouthfuls. 'In front of the Emerald Goddess.'

'Jeeze! What for?'

'Making our journey safe.'

'When?'

'Any minute.'

'Christ!' She pushed futilely at her hair. 'I'd better get tidied up.'

'Don't be ridiculous. The Goddess isn't going to see you.'

'How do *you* know? I look a wreck anyway.'

'Not to me.'

'Thanks, cobber.'

She smiled at him with a wry, self-deprecating twist of the mouth that he found intensely appealing.

'Well,' he said as he finished his food, 'that was delicious. It's dried yak from now on, I should think.'

'It's yak everything,' said Kiri saucily. 'Yak meat, yak milk, yak butter, yat dung, yak clothes, yak tents. Mission Yak's going up the Yak Khola. Yakkety yak!'

'You sound as though you don't *like* yaks,' said Stirling reproachfully, knowing full well that she had spent half the afternoon fancying them.

'Oh no, I love them. There's a baby – a calf. It's so furry it can hardly see out.'

'So would you be if you had to live in this climate.'

She stuck out her tongue and punched him gently on the arm.

The cave was so dark and thick with smoke that for the first few moments they could see nothing but the fire burning in the middle and the twin batteries of butter lamps, rising in tiered rows, which flickered at the far end. The cavern was alive with a low, droning buzz as the assembled Khampas intoned their prayers. A ceaseless murmur of *Om mani padme hum* rose from all round, ascended to the ceiling, and came fluttering back down the rock walls, doubling and tripling the intensity of the original sound until the lamps themselves appeared to judder from the impact of the noise. Some incense even more pungent than the reek of burning dung smoked from among the lamps and still further thickened the air.

As Stirling's eyes adjusted, he saw that between the banks

of lamps a single figure was sitting cross-legged on a pile of skins – a lama with shaven head and yellow robe. In front of him towered a smooth, dark wall which at first glance looked like wet rock but later revealed itself as a monumental wooden box, black and shiny with age.

Round the edges of the cave loomed the faces of men and women, sitting rapt in concentration. Wangdi occupied a rug of his own behind the lama's left shoulder. Stirling and Kiri sat on another rug behind him, but Wangdi motioned Stirling abruptly to move up and sit beside him, which he did.

The suspense grew ever more taut, until the air was vibrant with expectation.

Suddenly the long, thin call of a trumpet cut through the drone. The prayers died instantly. No one in sight had blown that unearthly note. The lama in the centre raised his head, rocked backwards and forwards, and began to beat out an erratic rhythm on a small skin drum. From the shadows to the right a bell clanged once. Then a second trumpet-call sliced through the electric silence. The drum began again, with a more insistent beat. The bell clanged twice. The trumpet brayed, the drum sounded, the bell pealed; trumpet, drum, bell; trumpet, drum, bell, faster and faster until an overpowering cacophony rebounded from the rock walls of the chamber.

The lama rose to his feet and faced the shiny black wall of wood. Through the din of the instruments he began to chant in a harsh voice, all the time wielding his drum. He leant shakily to right and left and struck fiercely angled postures between the two groups of lights, drumming frenziedly into the corners of the cave.

In Stirling's ear Wangdi shouted, 'The Goddess comes!' The music rose to a crescendo. At its height the lama flung himself full-length forwards to the ground. Above him a grotesque face blazed abruptly out of the darkness, hurling back the flames of the butter lamps in a thousand green flashes.

A halo of orange hair outlined the apparition, the spiky

locks standing straight up like tongues of flame. The eyebrows also were the colour of fire. The blood-red tongue that hung out of the mouth like a dog's was flanked by vicious canine teeth. Yet it was the eyes that held Stirling transfixed – the three eyes. Two were normally placed, the third in the middle of the forehead. All three gleamed and flared green with some ancient message of hate.

A gasp rushed round the cave as the Goddess stood revealed. Stirling was aware of people prostrating themselves, but he himself remained upright, transfixed by the fury of rage that came driving at him through the smoke.

The lama sprang to his feet, drumming again. But now he turned on the cave and the people, and began to roar out words in bursts of two or three. His voice was a hoarse scream, scarcely human. Stirling could tell that the words were curses, designed to put devils to flight.

Foam flew from the priest's mouth. His eyes rolled. His body shook with ghastly palpitations. He began to make fierce, erratic rushes at the edges of the cave, wielding his drum like a madman and screaming imprecations as he came. At every charge the Khampas nearest to him rolled and grovelled in an attempt to escape his frenzy, forcing themselves flat to the floor or into the crannies of the walls. Stamping his feet, flailing his arms, he ploughed through or over the prostrate bodies.

Stirling felt Kiri's fingers clenched on his shoulder like steel clamps. His own hands were locked on to his knees. Then suddenly the lama was coming for him, straight through one edge of the fire. He too cowered to the floor to escape the whirling drum. Once, twice it whistled over his head and the raving medium staggered on.

What happened next, Stirling could never be sure. One moment he was prostrate on the rug, avoiding the infuriated priest. The next he felt a great blast of wind surge up the cave from behind him. The fire flared. The butter lamps were blown out. A boom like thunder reverberated through the cave.

163

Terror seized him. First he thought there had been an earthquake, and the roof of the cave was going to fall; then, as he looked up again, *the face of the goddess changed*. Only the uncertain firelight now glittered off the emeralds. But surely the whole face had been transformed? No longer did the features seem contorted by rage. Instead, the eyes and eyebrows and mouth seemed to have relaxed into a faint, infinitely calm smile. The expression was one of benign content.

Stirling saw it only for a second. Then the lama-medium gave three shrill, vulpine yelps and collapsed inert on the heap of skins. When Stirling looked up again, the face had gone, covered once more by the black wall of wood.

The music had ceased. The lama lay moaning. All round the cave a rustle spread as people picked themselves up and began to mutter in quick, quiet voices. Presently the lama rose and made shakily for the cave opening.

The Khampas waited as Wangdi got up and ushered his visitors out. Stirling was shaking as he hit the cold, clean air of the night, unnerved by the ferocity of the forces he had seen let loose. He heard Wangdi speaking as if from a great distance.

'So, my friend,' the deep voice was saying. 'Bad spirits are defeated. You having good journey now.'

The two men shook hands awkwardly in the bright starlight. Stirling could not speak. He turned away and got Mission Yak moving into the white wilderness to the north.

Fifteen

'Any news of Carson?' asked Haller as he swept into the office.

'Nothing.' Kailasha cocked one hip so that her crimson silk trouser-suit was nicely stretched over knee, thigh and backside. 'You're late,' she added reproachfully.

'Mäuschen – don't.' He threw his briefcase on to a chair.

'What's the matter?' She came gliding after him with an armful of mail.

'Everything. The weather at Lukla is *scheisterlich*. Half the time we cannot fly. The Japanese do not want to pay. And now, the machine is *kaput*.'

'Where?'

'Here in Katmandu, of course. I just make it back. The same thing again. Fuel starvation.'

'I'm sorry.' She straightened the things on his desk. He sat down with a groan, took off his dark glasses and rubbed his eyes. 'Any calls?'

'Many. I made a list. But most of them are from the American. He's called twice this morning already.'

'What American?'

'Adair. The one who wants to look for fossils in Mustang. The geologist.'

'Oh – him. The one who said he knew Carson.'

'You told me to seduce him, remember?'

'Did I? Did you?'

'Only a little.' She smirked and flicked an invisible speck of dust off her tunic, hoping to provoke further inquiries. But Haller did not rise to the lure, and she went on, 'If he is an American, he's a pretty odd one.'

'How?'

'His attaché case is full of papers written in Russian. I smelled he was a Russian, too. I told you.'

'You can't read Russian, can you?'

'No, but I know the script. And anyway, I took a couple of sheets and copied them.' She laid them in front of him with a little flourish. 'There.'

Haller sat up. His exhaustion lifted. 'Make some coffee, Maus,' he asked, and then added, 'Sweet, please.'

Outside on a spirit lamp Kailasha brewed strong Turkish coffee in small, narrow-waisted brass pots, expertly bringing each to the boil several times before whisking it from the heat. As she poured out the foaming black liquid she heard Haller whistle. When she took the coffee in she found him studying the photostats intently. His Russian, though sketchy, was good enough to give him the gist of what the documents said.

'Maus – this is something. The man is a Russian, quite sure. I think we have a K.G.B. agent in town.'

'K.G.B.? What for?'

'From this, I cannot tell. The paper is general instructions for foreign travel. But look at the head of each sheet. Here: this word means 'Confidential' in Russian. He drank his coffee quickly and held out the cup for a refill.

'So – what do we have? The geology *Spiel* is a front – only for show, yes? This man pretends to know Carson. That means he wants to find Carson. Also he wants to go to Mustang. Therefore he thinks Carson is in Mustang. Therefore he knows about the Khampas coming out. Therefore he seeks the Emerald Goddess also.'

The telephone rang.

'That's him for sure,' said the girl.

'Tell him to come . . . ' Haller glanced at his watch. 'I need half an hour. Tell him to come at twelve.'

While the girl dealt with the call outside, he stared at the documents again. But in a way their content hardly mattered. What did matter was that he had suddenly seen a way of earning a considerable amount of money.

'He'll be here at noon,' said Kailasha, returning.

'Good. Now, we have to think quickly. First, what reports do we have from Dhorpatan?'

'De Lazlo is there, in the refugee settlement. He's been there for a week. Kessang's last report came in yesterday.'

Haller nodded. 'And Carson? Is he with him?'

'The girl's last radio message to Pokhara was on Wednesday. Since then, she's been off the air.'

'But it came from Dhorpatan?'

'Oh yes.'

'Then Carson is there. He probably keeps her so busy in his sleeping bag, she has no time to transmit.' He gave a lecherous chuckle, and spun his swivel-mounted, black-leather chair to face the map that covered most of one wall.

'So: this confirms my theory. Now the Khampas are here in the neighbourhood of Gompa.' He pointed with a ruler at a village on the junction of three main tracks, to the north-west of the Dhaulagiri massif. 'They come by this way. Quite sure.' With the ruler he traced the path leading south to Dhorpatan. 'Carson waits to help when they come near the airstrip. It is clear.'

'One thing,' said the girl diffidently. 'After you'd gone last week there was an incident in the Myangdi Pass. Somebody tried to come through from the north. Two people were shot – two soldiers. The army made a big search, but they didn't find anything.'

Haller stared at the map. 'How did you hear about it?'

'Brigadier Bahadur phoned. He wanted to speak to you.'

'Excellent. Now I speak with him. But that incident was nothing, I guess: some Naxalites with a grievance against the army. That's all. And what about the north? What happens in Jomsom?'

'Nothing. No movement at all. Norbu reported on Saturday.'

'Exactly. The Khampas are gone from Mustang already. Therefore if our Russian friend wants to look for Khampas in Mustang, he is welcome. He can look for rocks, too. But – '

he clapped his hands – 'the permit will cost him a lot of money. *'Viel, viel Geld!'*

'D'you think he has that much money?'

'Naturally, if he is what we think, he is loaded. Cash, too, I think. Specially printed in Moscow. All we need is to get him the permit to make geology exploration in Mustang, and then we charge him a fortune.'

'But they won't give permits for Mustang at the moment . . .'

'This is where our friend the brigadier comes in. Get him on the phone, please.'

Combining as he did the offices of Minister of Defence and Minister of the Interior, Brigadier Bahadur controlled the issue of permits for trekking and all other forms of exploration. All applications from foreigners to enter Nepal passed across his desk – and indeed it was he who had tipped off Haller about Stirling's arrival.

To say that the two men worked closely together would have been a charitable understatement. In fact they were on the lookout constantly for ways of supplementing their legitimate incomes. The projected seizure of the Emerald Goddess was merely the latest – though potentially the most lucrative – of their various conspiracies. Haller, having prepared the plan, was in charge, but the brigadier was to receive a substantial cut from the proceeds in return for granting certain military facilities which would help gain possession of the image when it reached one of the airstrips.

Now, Haller felt certain, the prospect of another thousand dollars or so all round would quickly produce the necessary permit.

Kailasha pressed the buzzer. The brigadier was on the line. 'Good morning, Mr Haller,' said the high, clipped voice. 'Have you any news of our friends?'

'No, Brigadier. But everything is going well; I think.'

'We had an incident at the Myangdi Pass last week.'

'So I hear. What happened?'

'At first I was thinking it was something to do with our

project. But now I think not. Some people tried to come through the pass from the north. A patrol was guarding it, you know? Two soldiers were shot dead.'

'I am sorry.'

'Yes, it was a bad business. But I am glad to tell you that the patrol gave a plucky account of itself. The survivors deployed, as taught, and guarded the pass till a helicopter brought reinforcements.'

'So no one came through?'

'No one.'

'Good. I congratulate you.'

'It is nothing. Now – what can I do for you?'

'A small matter, Brigadier, but an urgent one. I have a foreign client, a geologist, anxious to make research in the glaciers of Mustang.'

'Mustang is very difficult now. You must know that.'

'I do. But this is a special case, of possible benefit to the State.' (This was a stock phrase used to show that there might be money in a deal.)

'I see,' said the brigadier cautiously. 'And who is the client?'

'An American professor. Adair, his name is. He is well qualified, I assure you. Excuse me?'

'His politics. He is not active politically?'

'No, no. He has no interest except rocks.'

'And what is the extent of his interest?'

'Five hundred at least. Perhaps twice that.'

'I see. When does he want to leave?'

'So soon as possible. If he gets his permit, I fly him to Jomsom, and he can start from there.'

There was a pause. Then the brigadier said, 'I think it will be in order. Do you have the man's details?'

'Naturally. My secretary gives them in a minute. What time can we collect the document?'

'Five o'clock this evening. Will that do?'

'Beautiful.'

'We shall need two passport photographs, as usual.'

169

'Of course. Thank you, Brigadier. I give you to Kailasha now – one moment.'

He switched the call through. Incredible how easily these things sometimes went. On the second line he telephoned the airfield to see how the Cessna's repairs were progressing. The news there was less good. New filters would have to be flown up from Delhi. Haller cursed briefly. But he knew the engineer was a good one, and would do his best. There was no point in shouting at him.

'As soon as you can, then, Sita,' he said. 'Tomorrow?'

'Not possible, sir. Wednesday.'

'Wednesday, then.'

He put the receiver down. Through the one-way mirror he saw that Adair had arrived already and was gripping Kailasha with a longer-than-necessary handshake. To break it up he gave the intercom button an unnecessarily long, loud buzz. He was gratified to see the man jump.

In the past few days Adair had caught the sun severely. His nose and forehead were scarlet and peeling, and his hairy arms were bright pink to the elbow.

'Getting a tan, I see,' said Haller with a smile as he offered him the chair opposite the desk.

'Stupid,' said the visitor, feeling his nose. 'I don't usually burn. I guess I overdid it. The sun sure is hot up here.'

Haller nodded. 'I'm sorry to have kept you waiting so many days. But now I have good news for you. The Ministry of the Interior is prepared to issue you with a permit for geological explorations in Mustang.'

'Oh boy!' Adair's scorched face lit up. 'That's great. Fantastic. I can't thank you enough.'

Haller held up his hands deprecatingly. 'Please. It is nothing. But you must know, it took – how you say? – a bit of doing. That part of the country is closed to tourists since many weeks. Normally, the Ministry does not issue permits for Mustang. We had to make special application. Also – you understand – we have had to make some . . . payments. Otherwise the facility is not forthcoming.' The long, elegant fingers of his right hand made slight movements as of shelling peas, and the mauve shirt-cuff rustled on the glass top of the desk.

'Sure, sure,' said Adair easily. 'I'll pay – no bother. How much is it?'

Again Haller held up a hand. 'The whole project, I am afraid, will be *very* expensive. You want me to fly you to Jomsom, I expect?'

'You bet. Is that possible?'

'Of course. But in this country, you appreciate, it is not so simple to arrange an expedition in some remote part like Mustang. You see, we have nearly no communications. I cannot telephone Jomsom from here. Nobody can. This tour of yours – how many days?'

'Fifteen, twenty perhaps.'

'So – you need Sherpas and porters for twenty days. Have you made Himalayan trek before?'

Adair shook his head.

'You realise there are no hotels – nowhere to stay? Therefore you must be always camping. You need porters to carry the tents and equipment. Sherpas to direct them. There are no porters in Jomsom now. So, we have to hire porters in Pokhara. Then the porters have to come to Jomsom. You have hurry, no?'

'Right. I do.'

'You know how long it takes a porter to go from Pokhara to Jomsom? Six days, minimum. You don't want to wait so long. So, I have to fly the men up from Pokhara. They shit the aircraft up terrible.'

'Why's that?'

'Scared. They never fly before. Think they're going to be killed. It doesn't matter. How many porters? Three? Four?'

'More. I have some quite heavy equipment, and I want to collect specimens, too. That'll make a lot of weight. Let's say six or eight.'

'O.K. Eight porters, two Sherpas. That means I have to make two trips – Pokhara to Jomsom and back, Pokhara to

Jomsom and back – before I return to Katmandu and collect you. That is three trips to Jomsom. Finally, I collect you when you are finished. So, I fly to Jomsom four times.'

'How do I get hold of you when I'm through?'

'It is easy. The control tower at Jomsom will send a radio message to the tower here in Katmandu. They pass it on to me. My God – ' he pointed at Adair's sunburn – 'you must be careful with the sun.'

'Yeah, yeah. I'll wear a hat when I get in the mountains. The thing is, when can we start?'

'Your permit is ready today. Five o'clock. But the aircraft is unfortunately not serviceable.'

'Oh Jesus! How long for?'

'Maybe tomorrow. Probably Wednesday. We have to bring spare parts from Delhi. But anyway, I send a message to Pokhara and start making the arrangements.'

'I don't want to seem ungrateful,' began Adair uncomfortably, 'but is there no other aircraft? I mean, I don't have too much time. I have to be back in New York by the middle of December.'

'Mr Adair,' said Haller soothingly, but with a hint of menace. 'Now I have started all this arrangement, it is better you stay with me. Yes? Number one, I happen to know, there is no other aircraft at all. Number two, I do not think you get your permit with any other operator.'

He waited till that had taken effect, then added, 'One thing we have not discussed – the fee. I am afraid it will be considerable.' He brought a pocket calculator out of a drawer and punched some figures into it, pretending to do his sums. But in fact he had done the sum already, and, since the exercise had consisted merely in thinking of a suitable figure, it had not been difficult.

'O.K.,' said Adair. 'How much?'

'I cannot do it for less than ten thousand U.S. dollars, or five thousand sterling.'

'Does that include the porters and everything?'

'Of course.'

With no further word Adair reached into his attaché case and brought out a wad of 100-dollar bills. Peeling a few off it, he gave the rest to Haller.

'Thank you,' said the Swiss with a smile. 'Payment is not always so prompt. I do everything I can to speed the trip up. You are still at the Soaltee? Good. As soon as everything is fixed, I call you. But first, come back at six this evening to collect the permit. Perhaps we can have a drink?'

'Fine. I'd like that.' Adair made as if to go, then said, 'By the way, you didn't hear any more about my friend Carson?'

'Nothing. But then I would not expect to. Once a trekker is gone into the hills, he is gone. We hear nothing till he returns.'

Adair bowed himself out. Haller gave Kailasha a kiss on the mouth and slid a 100-dollar bill down the front of her suit-top, between her breasts, telling her to go out and buy something special. The rest of the money he took straight round to his bank, where the Indian manager never asked questions.

Altogether Haller felt pleased with the morning's developments. The highest fee he would normally have charged for the flights to Jomsom and for setting up the trek would have been 4,000 dollars. Of that, half would cover the porters and the food. A thousand would cover the flights. Another thousand to the brigadier – and still he was left with six thousand in hand.

The best thing was the way the American/Russian had played into his hands tactically as well as financially. By demanding to go to Jomsom, he was putting himself out of range of any action that might take place. By then Haller had no doubt that Adair also had got wind of the fact that the Emerald Goddess was on the move: his talk of Carson could mean nothing else.

Maybe the K.G.B. are short of funds, thought Haller. Evidently they fancy the emeralds too. Well – as long as Adair kept looking for them in Mustang, he would do nobody else any harm.

Sixteen

'Christ, it's cold!' said Kiri. 'I don't know whether to flap my arms or keep still.' She stopped flapping and hunched back into her down jacket, pulling the fur-lined hood in around her face. Stirling too was wearing all the clothes he had been able to force on together. A bitter east wind was scouring down the valley into their faces, and although they huddled in the shelter of some rocks, it found them out.

They had reached Rimring – or so Tashi told them. There was no sign of any building in that stony upland wilderness, but the Khampa insisted that the monastery stood on top of the cliffs which flanked the north edge of the valley, to their left. Since the path ran close under the cliff-face, it was impossible to see to the top of the cliffs, let alone anything that stood back from the edge of the drop.

According to Tashi, access to the monastery could be gained only by means of a contraption which the *rinpoches*, the lamas, let down on a rope – some sort of basket. The first problem was to attract the lamas' attention, and the Khampa had walked way out across the broad floor of the valley to flash messages up at the people above by angling a plate of polished aluminium into the evening sun.

So far he did not seem to have had any luck. They could see his tiny figure moving among the big boulders. Every few minutes he would climb a new rock, hoping for a better vantage-point, and every now and then a stray signal from the primitive heliograph would flash past the party at the cliff-foot.

Stirling knew he should have gone out into the valley too, but he had felt so exhausted when they had arrived that he had idly sunk down on the track, believing that the sending of a message would be a formality, the task of five or ten minutes at the most.

Now the time for signalling would soon be done, for the sun was already low, and in half an hour it would drop behind the ridges that closed the western end of the valley. Besides, big clouds kept blanking it out, further curtailing the available transmission time.

Stirling had serious doubts about whether they had come to the right place. Even if they had, it seemed certain they would have to spend another night in the open. Pasang, coming to the same conclusion, had gone ahead along the path in search of water.

'I suppose we were due for a setback,' said Stirling. 'Everything's gone a bit too well so far.'

'Don't say anything like that. You might provoke a disaster.'

'I might. But at least I've managed not to provoke one till now.'

As he said, the road to Rimring had proved straightforward, though tough. Favoured by the full moon and clear skies, they had moved mainly by night, lying up by day and becoming almost entirely nocturnal in their habits. One evening, as the camp was coming alive in the dusk, an immense owl, with wings fully five feet across, had sped silently over their hollow to alight on a crag above them. Through his binoculars Stirling had watched it sitting there, blinking its fierce yellow eyes and twitching its tufted ears. Every now and then the great bird would turn its head suddenly through 180 degrees and look straight backwards. That, he had felt, was just what Mission Yak must be: strong, confident, silent, bold – and with eyes in the back of its head.

Two long night marches had brought them without incident to the west bank of the Kali Gandaki. The bridge was guarded by a pair of soldiers, who remained obstinately rooted to their post after the signal fire had been lit. Rather than attract attention by shooting at them, he had sent Pasang forward with money to buy an unopposed and unrecorded crossing. From a good position in the rocks not fifty yards above the end of the bridge, he had watched Pasang go down in the bright moonlight, prepared to shoot at the first sign of trouble. But the soldiers made none: 200 rupees per man persuaded them to take a stroll and investigate the fire along the bank. In their brief absence Mission Yak slipped quietly across, to find their Tibetan scouts waiting with eight small, sturdy ponies.

At Stirling's insistence they had gone on for half an hour beyond the river before stopping to reorganise the loads, just in case the bridge party had second thoughts. Then, in an empty valley, overseen only by the glistening snow-peaks, they had transferred most of their burdens to the horses, lashing them to the clumsy wooden saddles with leather thongs. The Tibetans offered Kiri a ride, which she tried for a while, but the discomfort of the hard saddle and the pony's uncertain gait over the stony path soon put her back on her own feet. The great asset of the horses was that they took the weight off the human backs, and so enabled the whole party to move faster. The professional porters responded strongly, skipping along like goats.

At first Stirling had been amused by the Tibetan who perpetually followed the horses, pouncing eagerly on every new heap of droppings the second they were produced: scarcely had a fresh consignment hit the ground before he had scooped it up with his bare hands and stowed it in one or other of the hide bags which he carried for the purpose. At Kiri's suggestion they christened the man Horseshit Harry; but though to start with they laughed at his zeal and shrank from the miasma which inevitably accompanied him, their derision soon gave way to gratitude, for in the desolate wastes which they were entering there was scarcely a tree or stick of wood to be found, and only the dung, laboriously transported, gave them fires for warmth and cooking.

So, for three further nights, Mission Yak moved steadily eastwards through the ghostly, moonlit mountains. The worst enemy was the cold. Ice froze in the nostrils, and toes and fingers easily turned numb. So long as he was on the march, Stirling found, his blood kept moving all right; but when they stopped in the freezing darkness he and Kiri had to pile on all possible clothes to conserve their body heat.

The Nepalese did the same, though with far less good materials. Likpa habitually wore at least three pairs of trousers on top of each other, sometimes four. Most of them were ancient blue jeans, as were the trousers favoured by Pasang, although he also possessed an old yet somehow fashionable pair of grey flannels, which he generally wore outermost. Stirling was glad that the Human Bellows had stayed behind with the main body of Khampas. She would have blown up the dung fires to furious blazes, no doubt; but she would have suffered direly with her bare legs and feet. The other porters improvised as best they could, mainly with strips of hessian sacking. The Tibetans were easily the best equipped for this high and inhospitable country, being swaddled in so many layers of yak and sheepskin that it was impossible to tell what shapes of men marched beneath the mounds of fur.

Wassing wattair had become a distant memory. No longer did Stirling and Kiri make jokes about Teebettans being too much dirty people. They themselves were in no state to criticise. Stirling had long ceased to shave, and his sprouting, gingery whiskers gave great merriment to Likpa. One morning, as they were eating breakfast/supper before going to sleep for the day, Stirling saw the boy laughing at him – not sneakily, but with open amusement. Pasang, questioned as to what the joke was, sheepishly confided that Likpa thought Stirling resembled a yeti.

'How do you know?' Stirling pretended to be annoyed. 'Have you ever seen one? Has *he* ever seen one?'

'No, sair.'

'Nor have I. But I'll show you what a yeti looks like.' He put down his mug, gave a couple of hoots and a grimace, and set off across the grass in a shambling run, on the tips of his toes and the backs of his fingers. The display proved a terrific hit. Likpa shouted hoarsely with laughter and rolled on his back in such a paroxysm that he singed his hair in the fire. Thereafter he addressed Stirling, respectfully enough, as 'Sair Yeti'.

In the early marches after leaving the Kali Gandaki they passed through one or two villages every night. Whenever the wind was in their faces the smell of wood or dung smoke, drifting warmly on the night air, would warn them when they were approaching some habitation. No matter how quietly they moved along the dusty tracks between the dark, sleeping lumps of houses, their passage would set the dogs barking, and long after they had drawn clear of each place strangulated yelps would continue to punctuate the frosty darkness. After once being attacked by a great brute of a mastiff Stirling armed himself with a stout, knobbly stick which he cut from a stunted oak tree struggling on the bank of a stream. Gradually the villages became scarcer, and after they had crossed the Tibetan frontier, they had seen no houses at all.

Paradoxically, Stirling had found the frontier a disappointment. Although he had not exactly wanted to meet resistance there, he had secretly hoped at least to see a Chinese patrol, and perhaps to have the pleasure of out-manoeuvring it. In the event, they had found nothing at all to distinguish the pass that took them across the border from any other. As Wangdi had promised, it was a rarely used and scarcely visible track which cut through a narrow ravine in the border ridge at nearly 17,000 feet, so that people travelling that way entered Tibet almost through a tunnel.

'Bhot,' Pasang announced – Tibet's proper name – and suddenly they entered a different world. At night its precise texture was not visible, but even in the moonlight they could see wide, barren valleys dotted with stones, and the ridges of bare rock riding high on either hand. When day broke, they saw the full desolation of the upland wilderness. The horizons were still bounded by snow peaks, but in general the country flattened out. The going was easier, the slopes less precipitous. Stirling's map had long since ceased to be of any use, but the altimeter and compass showed that they were travelling mainly north-eastwards at an average height of 13,000 feet. Without a guide they would have been in severe difficulty, for the wide, dry valleys – all very similar – lay haphazardly at all angles to each other in an endless maze, the result of some ancient geological upheaval, rather than of erosion by water, so that they were not arranged in any logical pattern.

Once they were clear of the border area, they reverted to daytime movement, for there was no one to see them pass. There was still, theoretically, a danger that a patrolling aircraft might come over, and Stirling had Pasang rehearse the new men thoroughly in anti-aircraft drill; but so vast and empty was the land through which they were advancing that the chances of their being spotted seemed infinitesimal. And so it proved: they had reached Rimring without setting eyes on any other human beings.

'Think of living here,' said Kiri grimly. 'What on earth do you do for food?'

'I'm not convinced there is anyone living here,' Stirling answered. 'What the hell's Tashi doing?'

'Still flashing,' said Kiri, who had the binoculars.

'Come on,' said Stirling. 'We can't sit here till it gets dark. Let's go down and have a look.'

They got up, cold and stiff, and set out across the gentle bowl of the valley floor. But they had not gone far before they saw Tashi hurrying back towards them.

'He must have seen someone,' Kiri said. Stirling turned and scanned the cliff-top with the glasses.

'By God! There *are* people up there. And they have got some sort of pulley – a bucket on a rope. And a gantry. They're putting it out now. Let's get back.'

'It's like the Meteora,' said Kiri as they stumbled back across the tussocky grass and boulders.

'What's that?'

'A group of monasteries in northern Greece, built on fantastic pillars of rock, half way to the sky. I think that's what "Meteora" means – "In mid air". There's practically no way up except by being hoisted in baskets.'

'You've been there?'

'Only once.'

'And you went aloft?'

'To a couple of them, yes.'

'Brave of you.'

'Oh no – we were quite safe. The monks are queer as coots.'

Stirling laughed. 'I didn't mean that. The rope. It might break.'

'There is that. The same applies here, of course.'

'Specially if the bastards cut the cable above you.'

They arrived back under the cliff, panting. Pasang had appeared in the distance, returning from his reconnaissance. They gestured upwards to show that at last they had got some action, and he broke into a trot.

They waited in a fever of impatience. Presently a few chips of rock came pattering down on to the path. Then they heard a bump above them, and, peering out from under the shelter of the overhang, they saw the bottom of a square, gondola-like leather bucket slowly descending.

Down it came, with a faint creaking of leather. Occasionally it stopped like an ill-functioning lift. Soon they could see it contained a man (though there was room for two) – an old lama, bald and bare-headed, wearing loose robes of rough brown cloth.

'*Deus ex machina,*' said Stirling quietly. 'Or his near representative.'

As the bucket touched down the reception party moved forward to meet it. The lama let go of the hide ropes on which he had been steadying himself, and stepped out. But at the sight of Stirling and Kiri his face seemed to freeze into a mask of hatred or revulsion.

'*Namaste!*' said Stirling gently, placing his palms together before his face. The lama gave no sign of a greeting. His manner was implacably hostile, his eyes hard and narrow, his face shut.

Pasang began a well-rehearsed speech of greeting: they brought messages of goodwill from His Holiness the Dalai Lama; they had come to take away the sick white man; they were grateful to the lamas for looking after him so long . . .

The Sherpa faltered and stopped. The lama remained stony and silent. Stirling wondered if he was deaf, if he had grasped what Pasang had said.

'Tell him the same thing again, but slower.' he ordered. 'Make sure he understands.' Again Pasang tried. Still the lama watched them coldly, his arms folded. At last he spoke in a weak, high voice and in an accent – or at least an intonation – quite different from that of the Khampas. The reply was very short.

'He say, no white man here,' Pasang translated. 'He never see other white mens.'

Stirling was convinced there must be some misunderstanding. 'Tell him it's the American man we've come for. The American soldier. The one who hurt his back. Say it all again.'

No response.

'Maybe he thinks we're Chinese or something,' muttered Kiri under her breath. 'Tell him we're English people, Pasang. Friends of Tibetans.'

No reply.

'Tell him I have a letter for the American,' said Stirling, producing the envelope that Andrew had given him. He held it out so that the lama could read the name on it, if he wanted to. But evidently he did not want to, for he did not even glance at it. Nor did Pasang's further explanation have any effect.

Stirling began to feel angry as well as desperate. The man's hostility was unreasonable. What harm had they done him? Why could he not at least be civil? But he kept his temper in check and said to Pasang, 'Ask him if this is the monastery of Rimring.'

Pasang put the question, and at last got an affirmative answer. 'Yessair,' he confirmed. 'This Rimring Gompa.'

'Then ask if the lamas can put me and Doctor Nelson up for the night. One night.'

Without explanation or apology the lama lifted his head in refusal and stepped back into the leather bucket, giving a tug on the rope as he did so. The interview was over.

'What the devil's the matter with him?' Stirling exclaimed as the basket went swaying up the cliff. 'Surly bastard!'

'Didn't you think he was lying?' asked Kiri.

'I'm sure he was. At least, I *hope* he was. You thought so too?'

'Absolutely. His manner was so rigid. The moment he saw us, he made up his mind to say nothing. Otherwise at least he'd have asked us where we came from. Surely someone in a place like this would be curious when visitors arrive? We must be like beings from outer space as far as the monks are concerned. When did they last see anyone new?'

'When the general arrived, I bet.' Stirling thought for a moment. 'You must be right,' he said. 'The man's behaviour wasn't natural. The American couldn't have invented the story about the monastery. He *must* be up there.'

'Unless they've killed him.'

'Why should they kill him?'

'Maybe they got fed up with looking after him. Or maybe he just died, and they're scared of us finding out. They probably think we'll blame them.'

'That's more likely. But if that lying bugger thinks we're just going to turn round and go home, he's got a surprise coming. Even if the general's dead, I'll go through every inch of the place to find his Bible.'

At that moment a single long trumpet-blast sounded from the heights above. Looking round, they saw the sunlight fading from the great white fang of a peak that dominated the eastern end of the valley – a giant without a name. Clearly the call was a salute to the death of another day.

'Now they're playing the Last Post, the bastards,' said

Stirling jovially. Suddenly, in spite of the difficulties (or perhaps because of them) he felt in top form. It was as if he had been set some ghastly initiative test, like having to move a platoon of men across a river with nothing but a bean-pole and a length of button-thread to help. The utter impossibility of the task made him inclined to laugh rather than to cry.

'Come on, Pasang,' he announced. 'We'll duff up these fucking lamas yet.'

'Yessair,' said the Sherpa staunchly, grasping the spirit if not the finer points of the exhortation.

Whatever they managed to achieve, they were going to be stuck in the open for the night. Pasang had found water about twenty minutes ahead, so they went on in the dusk. As he walked, Stirling searched for some idea that would lure down a more tractable representative of the monastery – the abbot, perhaps. Maybe they could have a serious discussion with him. Yet it was Pasang who produced the idea for a breakthrough.

'Sair.' He came up to Stirling from behind. 'I think there is other way to monastery. Many lamas living there. Food no coming up all in basket.'

'Some easier way in – yes. That makes sense. A flatter approach from the back. If that's the case, it's just a matter of getting round behind: but these damn cliffs go on for a long way.'

'Here, sair. I show you.' On his reconnaissance Pasang had found a narrow fissure in the cliff-face, a natural crack only two or three feet wide, almost vertical at the bottom but slanting over towards the top. Soon they came to it again. The split looked dark and ominous in the twilight. 'Do you think you could climb that?' Stirling asked.

Pasang hoisted himself into the bottom of the crack and reached up, feeling the walls, calculating the width and the angles. 'I think so,' he said.

'Tomorrow, perhaps,' Stirling suggested.

'That can't be their front door,' said Kiri. 'They'd never get supplies up there.'

'No – but if it got us up at all, it would do. Then we could sort the lamas out and start using the hoist properly. Or maybe we could go out the back way, wherever that leads to.'

They went on and made camp in the place Pasang had found – a dip below the path where a trickle of clear water emerged from an underground spring. Ice was forming over the channel, but they broke it away and kept the water running long enough to collect what they needed for themselves and the animals. The Khampas unloaded the horses, tied on their leather hobbles, and set them free to graze, but the ponies hardly needed any artificial restraint, so firmly were they rooted to the patches of fresh green grass that grew beside the stream.

For the humans, the site was less attractive. Each tent-base had to be cleared of stones and levelled with ice-axes, and in most places the rock was too near the surface for the aluminium pegs to be driven in. Most of the guy-ropes had to be anchored with large, heavy stones.

While Stirling struggled with the tents, Pasang and Likpa cooked supper. As Kiri had predicted, they had eaten yak, yak and yak again. Tonight they had it once more – dried meat hacked into small pieces and reconstituted with boiling water into a sort of curry, with rice and a tin of beans. As they ate, Stirling vowed that tomorrow he would shoot one of the handsome wild horned sheep which they had seen from time to time along the trail. Although the animals made off at the sight of humans, he felt sure they could be stalked. Only the feeling that he must reach Rimring as soon as possible, without wasting time, had prevented him from going after them already. Tomorrow, he thought, tomorrow he would climb into the monastery, shoot sheep, do this and that . . .

But then, after a mug of steaming tea, thickened by one of their last tins of condensed milk, he suddenly thought: why not tonight? Why not storm the monastery tonight? The sky was clear. The moon would be bright. If he appeared on the plateau and tried to enter the monastery by day, the lamas would probably repel him; but if he went up in the dark, the odds were that they would be asleep, and that he could gain access to the place unseen.

He told Kiri what he was thinking.

'Don't, she said tensely. 'You'll fall off the cliff and kill yourself.'

'I won't try to climb the cliff. We'll go up that fissure.'

'We?'

'Me and Pasang. He's a proper mountaineer, after all. If I'm right, that crack gets narrower all the time as it runs back into the mountain. So it'll be like climbing a chimney – we'll be able to wedge ourselves between the two sides. I don't think it'll be hard at all.'

'Suppose you get up. How will you know where the general is?'

'I don't know yet. Have to play it by feel. But I've got an idea. I'll sacrifice one of our grenades. Not to kill anyone, just to wake them up. If we get in there and let off a grenade – say in a courtyard or somewhere – the general's bound to hear it, if he's there. He'll realise what it is, and then he'll yell out. That should take me to him.'

'What if you do find him? You'll never get him down the fissure.'

'No. We'll have to wait till morning. Or till we get some sense out of the lamas. I'm assuming the general can speak Tibetan. He had fluent Chinese, anyway; and now, after all this time here, he must be able to talk to the lamas pretty well.'

He thought for a minute, then went on, 'Let's say that you and the rest of the party will get back to the place where the bucket comes down soon after first light. If we're not ready to come down, I'll throw a message over to you.'

'What if you don't come down at all?'

He looked at her sharply, but the fur edging of her hood hid her expression. 'Go home without me,' he said. But then he added shortly, 'I'll come down.' She stared silently into the fire.

He told Pasang what he intended. As always, the Sherpa

responded readily. 'When we go?' he asked.

'As soon as the moon rises.' Stirling extracted the 100-foot coil of climbing rope – unused so far – and got his automatic back from Kiri, since it would be impossible to take a rifle up the fissure. Then he took two grenades out of their case, and, having made sure the pins were safely taped into position, slipped them into the chest pocket of his anorak.

They sat round the fire, not talking much, waiting for the moon. Kiri was tired and low, worn down by the cold and the strain of continuous travel. Stirling felt it, but had nothing to comfort her with. The frost bit sharply, but at least the wind had died away to nothing.

At last an opalescent glow began to expand into the sky beyond the eastern horizon. 'Right,' said Stirling. 'Here we go. Sleep well, honey. Keep warm.' She gave a quick nod. He could tell that she was close to tears. He said nothing else, but put a hand on top of her hood and pressed down firmly.

In the faint moonlight the fissure looked inky black; but Stirling had loaded the last new batteries into his torch, and the beam picked up the ledges and cracks clearly enough. With no fuss or delay Pasang hitched one end of the rope round his waist and led off up the torch-beam, wedged like a spider, arms and legs splayed into either side of the fault. After twenty feet he stopped in a secure position and waited for Stirling to come up with him.

Stirling, less practised, had some difficulty. He found the effort of bracing himself continuously such a strain that his legs began to shake. Although he was very fit from walking, he didn't seem to be using his walking muscles. Another problem was that he heated up like a furnace inside his many layers of clothes, and in the confines of the fissure it was impossible to take any of them off.

At the end of the third pitch he had a brief panic that he would not have the strength to reach the top or to get down again. But Pasang seemed undaunted, and after a rest they went on. Towards the top the ascent became easier, for the fissure slanted more and more to one side, away from the vertical, so that they could wriggle upwards, rather than climb, lying on their sides. The cleft of the moonlit sky above them gradually grew brighter, and for the last few minutes there was no need to use the torch.

At the last moment Stirling had another fright. The exit from the chimney was extremely narrow, and although Pasang squirmed up through it without much trouble, Stirling could not force his body through the opening. For a few seconds he fought the rock in a panic, half-crushing his chest, bruising his knees and elbows. Then he subsided back down the neck of the chimney, carefully turning his head sideways to withdraw it through the slot.

The first expedient was to get rid of all the things which were making him even bulkier than usual – the binoculars slung round his neck and the grenades in the breast-pocket.

'Pasang,' he called softly. 'Take these. I'm stuck.'

The Sherpa's head appeared in the gap. Stirling handed up the glasses first, then the grenades, one at a time. 'Careful with these,' he whispered.

Freed from the encumbrances, he moved backwards across the chimney towards the open side, in the cliff-face, until his behind was almost projecting into space. Then once more he tried to lever himself vertically up. In this new place he did slightly better, but again jammed on his breast bone.

'Here, sair,' whispered Pasang urgently, seeing how close he was to the outer edge. He handed down one end of the rope.

'It's all right. I can't fall because I'm wedged. Give my arms a pull.' He raised his arms above his head. Pasang set his feet carefully in safe positions and heaved him upwards. His chest, elongated by the pressure, at last scraped through. Gasping, he crawled inwards, away from the lip.

After the blackness of the fissure, the moonlight seemed bright as day. The landscape up there looked much the same as below – gently undulating ground, dotted with huge stones. Stirling posted the grenades back into his pocket and slung the binoculars round his neck again, keeping them outside his anorak. Then they set off, warily but fast, towards the west.

On that icy plateau, absolute silence reigned. Every time one of them scuffed a boot against a rock, the noise sounded desperately loud; even the lightest footfall scrunched harshly on the frozen grass.

They walked fast for ten minutes, then slowed to a more cautious pace. Even so, they came on the monastery abruptly: as they advanced on to a low crest, they suddenly found a colony of flat roofs glowing dimly in the moonlight close below them.

They sat down in the shadow of a big rock to study their objective. The place was smaller than Stirling had expected – not more than ten buildings all told, grouped irregularly round a rectangular central courtyard. To enter the monastery would be no problem, for it lay defenceless, without exterior walls, as open as any village: one could just walk in.

The moonlight cut sharp, black shadows around the stumpy buildings. Through the binoculars Stirling could see the prayer-flags hanging motionless from the tops of two poles. Out on the cliff edge, some fifty yards further, he could make out the cantilever beam of the hoist. The biggest of the buildings occupied one entire side of the courtyard, and in front of it stood three small, pointed *chorten*, or shrines, with peaked, pagoda-type roofs.

Stirling began to whisper something, but at the same instant Pasang also started to speak. They both stopped, both started again simultaneously, trying to say the same thing: that the big building was obviously the *gompa*, or temple, and that the houses at the back must be the living quarters. As if to confirm their intuition, a drum began to thud from the large building, accompanied by a drone of prayer. A gleam of light showed fleetingly through a chink in one of the shutters. This would be the time to get the general out, thought Stirling – while the lamas were at their devotions. But even if they found the American, they would still have to lower him down the cliff.

Secure in the shadow of the rock, they sat and waited. An icy breath of wind suddenly brushed over them: the prayer-flags fluttered briefly, and from down in front of the temple a wind-bell sounded a sad, lonely chime. Pasang nudged him silently and pointed out over the flat ground behind the buildings. '*Jangu!*' he whispered.

'What's that?'

'Wolf.'

Stirling's heart jumped as he saw the two ghostly shapes slinking noiselessly through the rocks. The glasses brought them into sharp focus: silvery, dangerous, efficient, the predators stopped once to investigate some scent and then disappeared into a gulley. Soon afterwards an animal gave a few short, grunting bellows, obviously disturbed by the prowlers.

'*Dzo*,' muttered Pasang. 'Half yak, half cow.'

The disturbance died away. Scanning with the glasses, Stirling saw that, as they had suspected, the monastery was not cut off from behind at all. The ground rose gently towards the distant skyline.

A shaft of yellow light, feeble but warm, fell across the courtyard as the door of the gompa opened. A man came out and walked diagonally across the yard to the far corner, carrying a small, open butter-lamp whose flickering flame cast fitful illumination on his face. The scrunch of his soft slippers on the gravel carried clearly to the hidden watchers.

One by one six more monks left the temple and went their several ways across the yard. Still a light showed through the open door. Then Stirling noticed something odd: a thin column of smoke was rising from a chimney at the back of one of the buildings. A chimney! As far as he knew, chimneys did not exist in Tibet: as in Nepal, people just lit fires in the middle of the room and let the smoke find its own way out through the roof, doors and windows.

He put the binoculars on the house's flat roof: yes – a square, clumsy-looking chimney rose a few feet above it. In a

189

flash he realised that only a Westerner could have built that chimney – or caused it to be built – and that therefore the American must be in that end house. The chimney had done his detective work for him: no need to let off a grenade now.

For the first time Stirling began to question his own determination to rescue the general as well as his Bible. If he slipped in, got the book and slipped out again, no one would ever know how great or small an effort he had made to extract the human being as well. At least, no one but he himself. That was the whole trouble: he did not like the idea of living with the memory of a sick man callously abandoned.

Two more lamas appeared, and the second closed the door behind him. No more light showed from the temple building. The drum had ceased.

It was too cold to keep still any longer. Stirling stood up and rubbed himself furiously. 'Come on,' he whispered. 'Let's go.'

They worked their way round from rock to rock until they were only twenty yards or so behind the hut with the chimney. The column of smoke rising straight into the sky was the only thing that moved in the silent, frost-bound night. The rest of Rimring lay cold and dead beneath the moon.

'Lamas sleeping,' whispered Pasang with satisfaction.

Stirling nodded. His only immediate worry was that one of the lamas might already be in the end hut, sharing it with the American. It was a risk he would have to take.

'Now,' he hissed. 'Quickly.'

He and Pasang were at the front of the hut in a couple of seconds. There was a primitive wooden latch, which jammed at Stirling's first shove, but gave at his second attempt. The door opened with a loud creak. The two men slipped into the foetid warmth of the hut. Somebody moved in the darkness, and a strong voice snapped out something in Tibetan.

Stirling stood still. Then he said firmly, 'General Sulzberger?'

'Jesus Christ Almighty! Who are you?'

'A friend. Is there anyone else in here?'

'Nobody.'

'O.K., then. We can all relax.'

Seventeen

'Holy smoke!' The American voice was thick with sudden emotion. 'God almighty! Who are you?'

'My name's Bill Carson. I've come to get you out.'

'Jesus Christ! I can't believe it.'

'I'm real. Is it safe to shine a torch?'

'Sure is. Shine away.'

'What if the lamas see the light?'

'They won't worry.'

Stirling switched the torch on. The beam picked out a primitive bed of rough timber, inclined so that the head was higher than the foot. On it, flat on his back beneath a pile of furry rugs, lay a fine-looking, middle-aged man with iron-grey hair cut short in a uniform scrub. As Stirling came across he raised his right arm and the two men shook hands, like explorers meeting in the jungle.

'Who's that?' asked the general sharply as Pasang moved in the background.

'Sherpa Pasang. He came with me. You have a lamp?'

'Sure – over on that shelf. And have the Sherpa blow up the fire.'

Pasang blew the smouldering dung into a flicker of flame bright enough to give faint illumination. Then he lit the butter lamp as well.

'Bill, is it?' the general asked.

'That's right. Bill Carson.'

'But you're only a kid!'

'Some kid! I'm thirty. But I feel a hundred and thirty, I can tell you. We've come a long way.'

'How in hell did you get here?'

'I walked up out of Nepal. We started from Pokhara.'

'Pokhara? Jesus! How far's that?'

'I don't know in miles. But it's only taken us four days from the Nepalese border.'

'And you got through O.K.?'

'No bother.'

'Fantastic. Here – sit down. There's a stool somewhere.'

Stirling sat down beside the bed. Pasang squatted by the fire, adding small pieces of fuel methodically.

'General, what do we do if someone comes in? What are your relations with the lamas?'

'Easy. They won't care.'

'You're sure? We had a hell of a reception when we got to the bottom of the cliff. The fellow who came down didn't want to know us.'

'You came up in that goddam basket?'

'No – that was just it. They wouldn't have us. We had to climb up another way.' Stirling described the lama who had met them, and his surly behaviour.

'That was that bastard Lobsang. He's always like that. He thinks I'm a Russian spy, or something crazy. Also he hates me for causing so much trouble.'

'Is he in charge, then?'

'No, the abbot is the boss. He's O.K. You just picked a bad day. They have a kinda roster. I guess Lobsang was on duty when you came.'

'He told us you weren't here. Never seen a white man, he said.'

'Did he, the two-timing bastard? I'll give him hell in the morning.'

Stirling smiled at the patient's vigour. 'General,' he said, 'how's your health? Are you fit to travel?'

'Gotta be. Can't say I'm in great shape. But I'll make it if you have the guys to carry me.'

'We've got plenty of manpower. Also a doctor.'

'A doctor! Incredible! Where is he?'

'She, it is. She's down below. You won't be sorry when you see her, either.'

'God almighty! How come she's here?'

'I'll tell you some time. The thing is – how badly are you hurt?'

'Pretty bad, I guess. Smashed my back when the chopper came down. Lost the use of my legs – for the time being, anyway.'

'Are you in pain?'

'Not a thing. Can't feel a thing from the waist down. I don't know whether that's good or bad.'

'Kiri'll tell you. The doctor, that is. You said you crashed a helicopter? I imagined you just fell down the rocks or something.'

'No, sir. I could never have walked out from where I was when I quit. The chopper was the only chance. We'd been flying reconnaissance missions all day. The pilot and I had just gotten out. The old whirlybird was still hot to trot, so I jumped back on board and took off again. I knew I had just about zero fuel, but it was then or never, and I took the chance. All I could do was head south as fast as the chopper would go and hope I'd make the border.

'Boy! I flew for ten minutes with the gauges flat on zero. Ten minutes! It seemed like ten hours. Then – blip. Goddamned engine cut, and there I was – nothing but ridges and valleys in sight, still inside Tibet. At the last moment there was a kind of miracle. I saw the roofs of this place and headed straight for it.'

'But you had no fuel?'

'Nope. I was gliding on the rotor. Luckily I had quite a bit of height. But there's a limit to how far you can get. Like I said, I saw these roofs and dove straight in.'

'Where did you land?'

'In back there. In a ravine. Not the best place to touch down. I guess – the lamas had a hell of a time getting me out. But one good thing was that the wreckage was deep down out of sight.'

194

'Did the Chinese chase you?'

'Must have done. But we never saw them. They must have assumed I'd been killed and gave up looking. Say, Bill, what date is it?'

'I make it December 8th.'

'December 8? Jesus! Then I've been here two months.' He fell silent. When he spoke again, his voice was guarded. 'Just a formality, Bill, but can you identify yourself any more?'

'Who I am? I told you. British . . . '

'Military?'

'No.'

'M.I.6, then?'

'To do with them.'

'You have a passport?'

'Of course.'

'Will you show it me, please?'

'I'm sorry, I left it in camp, down below. You can see it in the morning. I have a letter for you, too.'

'O.K.' Again he paused, looking sideways at Stirling. 'How did you get the message that I was here?'

'It came down through a friend of mine in Ghandrung, Andrew de Lazlo. The letter's from him.'

'You pass.' The general smiled at him. 'I just wanted to make sure who you were. You got here just about in time.'

'Time for what?'

'You don't know? Hell, no: of course you don't. I thought about it so much myself, I kinda assume everyone knows. You heard about my Bible?'

'Of course. You've still got it?'

'Sure thing. Under the bed. That book – I can say it myself – contains more information about Chinese defence than the United States has collected in thirty years since the Communists took over. But there's one fact in it that won't wait. On January 18 next the Chinese are going in across the Soviet border: they're gonna attack the Soviet Union.'

Stirling whistled softly.

'Yes, sir. You can whistle. There's gonna be the biggest

goddam eruption since Krakatoa.'

'What's the point, though? Surely they won't get far?'

'I wouldn't be too sure. The Chinese army's far bigger than anyone in the West knows. Better trained, too. Plenty of tactical nuclear missiles. Ballistic weapons as well. They're hoping to beat shit out of the Soviets with one great big pre-emptive strike. Then they'll follow through with a few million men.'

'Why in the middle of winter, though?'

'Ground's frozen then. Rivers too. The armour can move freely. The natural barriers aren't so strong as in summer. For years the Chinese have been saying that war between them and the Soviets is inevitable. Now they ain't gonna wait no longer.'

'What can anyone *do* about it?'

'The Pentagon better do something, pretty damn quick. Either they gotta leak information to the Soviets, or they gotta persuade the Chinese that the Soviets are tipped off and ready for them. Or both. Anything to make the Chinese see sense.'

'It sounds bloody dangerous either way.'

'It is. We're on the brink, Bill: right on the brink. Boy, am I dry. Can your man make tea?'

'Of course. Is the stuff there?'

'Up there. The shelf on the wall.'

Pasang made tea Western-fashion or Tibetan-fashion, according to the circumstances. Tonight the equipment was Tibetan, so he broke a large handful of dry, black tea off the end of the brick and crumbled it into boiling water. After letting it stew a minute, he put in some pinches of salt, strained the brew through a hair sieve, added some lumps of bright orange butter and poured the greasy mixture into bowls.

'Did you get that chimney built?' Stirling asked.

'Sure did. The lamas couldn't make out what in hell I wanted it for. But without it I'd have been smoked like an old piece of bacon.'

The walls of the room were bare, rough plaster. The ceiling

consisted of clumsy wooden beams with rushes or grass laid over them.

'Where did the wood come from?' Stirling asked.

'God knows. The stuff's like gold-dust here. Originally it must have been brought up from somewhere way down in one of the valleys. But lately what they've done is cannibalise one building into another. The place used to be much bigger, with a hundred monks. Now there's only a dozen left, and they took down some of the buildings to patch up the rest.'

'Two months in a place like this! What have you done all the time, General?'

'I wrote up my Bible, number one. It was already a big book when I sent out the S.O.S. But now it's a heck of a lot bigger. I wrote something new in it every day. I figured it was better to have everything on paper, in case anything happened to me. That was number one. Number two, I read Shakespeare.'

'*Shakespeare?*'

'Yes, sir. Your bard is surely the greatest. The things he says. The way he says them. That guy's given me hope. He's given me *life*.'

'But you had a copy with you?'

'Right there.' He motioned to the table beside his bed. Stirling picked up the slim volume, pocket-book size, bound in battered, dark-red, limp leather: a complete Shakespeare, beautifully printed on India paper. 'I had it with me when I first went to China,' the general went on. 'I had it all the time. You know what? There's several of the plays I can recite straight through. Recite, mind you. No peeking! You wanna hear Macbeth? I'll give it to you, first line to last. I did it yesterday.'

'Well – some time. "When shall we three meet again?" All that. I don't know what the end is, though.'

' "To see him crowned at Scone," ' said the American instantly. 'Malcolm, that is. "Tomorrow and tomorrow and tomorrow . . . " You can guess how often I've told myself that bit.'

197

'I bet.'

'I truly think, without Shakespeare I'd have gone crazy.'

'Do the lamas talk to you?'

'Some do, some don't. My Tibetan's not that great, anyway. Conversation's pretty limited.'

'I was surprised the monastery still existed. I thought the Chinese had closed them all.'

'They did, most of them. All the guys here have stories of brothers or uncles being ripped out of monasteries and put to slave labour. Just a few places got away with it, and this was one of them. But boy, do they hate the Chinese!'

Pasang brought over the tea. At Sulzberger's behest Stirling gripped his hands, pulled his trunk upright, and wedged a sloping board behind him against the wall, so that he was propped up nearly vertical. The movement released from the bed such a dense miasma of dark human smells that Stirling caught his breath. Seeing him blench, the general apologised for the inevitable consequences of his own immobility and lack of proper nursing.

'Don't worry,' Stirling told him. 'It's fantastic that you've survived at all. You've kept shaving, too, I see.'

'Yes, sir. Had to keep up morale somehow. Couldn't let *all* the standards slip.'

'More than I have.' Stirling fingered his week-old beard. 'The trouble is, it's cold moving at night, which is what we've been doing.'

For a while they drank tea and chatted. In the firelight the general's face looked gaunt but ruggedly handsome. His dark eyes burned strongly from deep in their sockets. The longer Stirling looked at him, the more clearly he saw how impossible it would be to leave such a man behind.

Though eager to look at the Bible, he soon felt himself sinking beneath a great weight of drowsiness – brought on by the warmth in the hut and his own exertions. He began to yawn uncontrollably.

'You better get your head down,' the general said. 'Will you make out on the floor? And the Sherpa?'

'We'll be fine. As long as you don't mind having us.'

'My pleasure! What d'you figure on doing in the morning?'

'The sooner we hit the trail, the better. Don't you think?'

'I sure do.'

'First, though, we'll get Kiri, the doctor, up here to have a look at you. As soon as she's done what she can, we'll lower you over the cliff and away.'

'Sounds great,' said the general. 'Next stop Washington D.C.'

Morning revealed that the monastery buildings were all painted with red ochre, and that the gompa-entrance was surmounted by a row of horned skulls – from wild sheep, Stirling guessed. The day was brilliantly fine, the air so clear that the snow peaks on the horizon seemed scarcely an hour's march away. As Stirling stood by the gantry at the top of the hoist, his breath smoked in the frost sunshine.

He had slept fitfully on the earth floor of the hut and now felt grittily on edge. In spite of Sulzberger's faith in the good nature of the lamas, he himself sensed nothing but barely veiled hostility. The general attitude seemed to match that of the man who had come down the cliff the evening before.

As soon as the strangers had been discovered in the American's quarters, a small, curious crowd had gathered in the courtyard, and the lamas had stood there watching sullenly, fingering their chains of bone beads and occasionally muttering to each other. Even the abbot, though less churlish, had not shown the slightest warmth or interest when it was explained to him that the Englishman had come to take the general away. A dowdy and unimpressive figure in spite of his saffron robes and winged hat of felt, he had listened impassively and merely wished them a safe journey in the curtest of farewell speeches.

Stirling did not trust these men. Their isolation was so complete, their grasp of outside events so tenuous, that they might easily take him for an enemy. He kept telling himself that since they had looked after the general for two months, they could not be hostile to Westerners in principle; but what if they somehow got it into their heads that he was trying to kidnap the American? All he wanted was to get clear of the place as soon as possible.

The hoist was extremely primitive, like a medieval crane. The gantry arm, made of two rough wooden beams, projected out at an angle over the edge of the cliff. Its inner, lower end was rooted in a fault of rock that acted as a secure natural socket and also maintained the arm's angle. A rope of plaited leather strips passed from the rim of the lift-bucket up over a wooden pulley at the top end of the arm and down to a wooden drum, which was turned by hand-cranks to wind the rope in, and could be braked for descents by a simple lever. The wood, though old and whitened by exposure, seemed hard and sound enough, and the joints all looked well fitted, with the wooden pegs tight in their sockets.

As he began to direct the operation, Stirling clearly foresaw the greatest potential danger. He himself would remain on top, in physical control, until the last moment; but there would come a time when he, too, would have to descend and entrust his life to the lamas. The only alternative, to go back to the rock-fault chimney and climb down it, would take several hours and be almost equally dangerous.

First he sent the bucket down with Pasang on board, primed to return with Kiri and the medical kit. The Sherpa showed no emotion as he stepped from the solid edge of the cliff into the slender, swinging contraption of wood and leather, but Stirling guessed that he must be terrified. The two lamas on the winding drum controlled the descent carefully, one keeping the brake-lever continuously applied, and the other holding one of the crank-arms as a fail-safe. When smoke began to rise from the friction on the drum's wooden rim, they poured water on it to reduce the heat.

By counting the revolutions that the drum made, Stirling roughly calculated the length of line that had gone out. Just as he reached two hundred feet, the creaking and whining ceased and the line went slack. A couple of minutes later came the signal jerk, and the lamas began to wind in.

With the weight of two people on it, the leather rope gave alarming twitches and snaps as the thongs were pulled tighter together. By signs Stirling indicated to one of the toiling lamas that he would take a turn on one of the cranks, but the man ignored his offer. Condemned to wait in anxious idleness, Stirling kept glancing wistfully at the relatively level hinterland behind the monastery. The monks had fields of barley there, the general had told him. They even grew potatoes. A spring which emerged from the plateau ran sweetly even in the frosts of winter. It would have been infinitely easier to leave the place by the back route – had it not been for the fact that the track ran northwards only, with no connection to the south and west.

At last the top of the bucket frame reappeared, and Stirling's heart lifted as he saw Kiri's golden head come into view. She was looking good, too: much better than the night before.

'Hello, doctor,' he said brightly. 'How are you this lovely morning?'

'Flourishing, thanks.' She smiled. 'How's the patient, though? That's more important.'

'He's in great spirits, all right. Physically, I don't know. You'd better look. Take it easy now.'

Holding one of the ropes, and extending her other hand to him, she hopped nimbly ashore. The bucket swung away into space and bumped back again. Pasang handed out the medical pack, and then Stirling's haversack, which he had added to the load of his own accord. Finally he himself jumped out.

'What a ride!' said Kiri. 'And what a view!' For a moment she stood gazing round, taking in the ruddy buildings, the crane, and above all the monks, who glowered back at her – almost certainly the first white woman they had ever seen.

'Come on,' said Stirling. 'We mustn't hang about.'

He took her across the compound. As he had hoped, the

general was overjoyed by her appearance, calling her 'Miss', 'Ma'am' and 'Doctor' before settling on her Christian name, and exclaiming in amazement that so beautiful a physician should exist anywhere, let alone on the Tibetan plateau.

Stirling left them to it. The next task was the construction of a stretcher. He had considered the idea of cutting off the top of the patient's bed and using that, but the wood was too cumbersome and heavy. Instead, he had sent out a demand for lighter spars of timber, and in due course a lama had grudgingly produced the ideal answer – two ancient bamboo canes about two inches in diameter and ten feet long, both light and strong.

First Stirling spread out a large, rough felt blanket on the ground. Then he laid the poles along it, about three feet apart, and brought the ends into the middle, where he sewed them together, using the spike on his knife to pierce holes, and threading nylon cord through them. Pasang, who helped him, was neat and quick with his hands, and they soon had a serviceable stretcher.

Next they turned their attention to the business of securing it to the hoist-rope. The bucket would have to come off for the moment, and to go in its place they rigged a cat's-cradle of ropes – four equal lengths radiating from a central knot to each corner of the stretcher. As they were tightening the knots Kiri emerged from her consultation. Her face was less sunny than before.

'What's the verdict?'

'Not great. The bottom four vertebrae are smashed – more or less fused together. It looks as though the spinal cord must be crushed. That's why he can't move his legs, or feel them. But it's not that that's worrying me, really. What I don't like is that he's very run down – low pulse rate, low blood-pressure. He's lost a lot of weight. If he spends all day out in the cold air, I'm afraid he'll get pneumonia. The chances of that must be pretty high.'

'It's a risk we'll have to take. Can you give him anything to pep him up?'

'Not really. What he needs is proper nursing and some decent food. And warmth.'

'None of which he's going to get.'

'Exactly.'

'How had he better travel? Upright or lying down?'

'Lying down, definitely. Anything else would finish off the small chance he's got of being able to walk again.'

'I thought so. We made him this stretcher.'

'That'll do fine. Have you got any clothes you can spare – a sweater and a pair of trousers, maybe? The warmer we can keep him, the better.'

Stirling dug in his pack and produced a lightweight V-necked jersey and a pair of pyjama trousers which he no longer bothered with at night, preferring to sleep in his clothes. 'That'll help make room for the Bible, anyway,' he said.

The general's record was a considerable document, consisting of two substantial school exercise-books with thick cardboard covers. At first Stirling had been dismayed to find he could scarcely understand a word of what the books contained. The tight, scrawly writing was one reason, but another was the fact that the general had used a kind of home-made shorthand, reducing names to initials and words to only one letter. Some were obvious – v for very, t for the, tt for that, and so on; but without intensive coaching (which they had already started) Stirling would never have known that K.L. stood for Kai Lang, Chief of Staff of the People's Liberation Army, or that H.G. was the Hailer Gap, in western Mongolia, through which the Russians had long been expected to launch an attack. His first few minutes' study of the text had left him fascinated and excited, for he saw that the document was a gold-mine of top-secret information. Now he had wrapped it carefully in polythene bags and packed it into his haversack – the most secure place he could think of.

By the time the general had been dressed in his travelling kit, he was in sparkling form. 'All aboard for Katmandu!' he cried as they carried him out.

'Don't get too excited, General,' Stirling warned him. 'We've got to get you down the damn cliff first.'

For extra safety – should any of the lowering ropes slip – they lashed him firmly into the stretcher, with cords going right round it. As Kiri said, he looked like a sausage-roll, the man being the sausage and the enveloping circle of yak-hide rugs the pastry.

'Is there anything we can give the lamas as a thankyou present?' Stirling asked. 'We've got plenty of money, but I don't suppose that's much use to them.'

'No, sir. They can't spend it. Maybe if you had an old book or something. Even if they couldn't read it, they'd still treasure it as an oddity.'

'Don't give them your Shakespeare, anyway.'

'Jesus no! That's coming right with me.'

'Wait a minute – I know.' Somewhere at the bottom of his pack Stirling had a battered paperback copy of Evelyn Waugh's *Scoop*. He dug it out and gave it to Sulzberger, who in turn presented it to the abbot in a brief farewell ceremony. At last a faint smile illuminated the austere face, and suddenly Stirling felt that his descent of the cliff-face might be safe enough after all. Perhaps, all the time, the lamas had been more frightened than hostile. He too smiled, though more from the idea of the monks poring over the antics of William Boot in Azania than from any feeling of warmth.

The farewells were over. As they carried the general to the cliff-top, the prayer-barrels were turning busily: perhaps someone had given them a spin to speed their journey. They lashed the leather rope to the apex of the cat's-cradle, took up the weight by cranking-in half a turn, and gently pushed the stretcher out into space. The patient was a little down by the feet, but that was a good thing, and as he disappeared from sight he saluted the lamas in a way that Stirling found oddly moving.

The rope creaked and stuttered in its normal fashion, until at last the tension went out of it. Soon it twitched from the signal jerk, and the monks wound it in rapidly, free of any weight. When the end came up, Stirling retied the bucket and sent Pasang and Kiri down together. At least he could be sure that no one would interfere with their descent.

Tension mounted inside him as he waited for his own. The abbot and two acolytes stood there, politely attending until the last of the visitors had gone. The two powerhouse lamas worked the crank and brake. They all looked resigned, if not enthusiastic. Perhaps it was ridiculous to feel so scared: and yet . . .

The bucket came back. His turn had come. He bowed again to the abbot, smiled broadly, and stepped aboard. Even without the possibility of sabotage, the contraption was alarming enough. The judder in the rope which he had observed from above was immensely magnified in its effect on the passenger. The creaking and snapping sounded infinitely more sinister. The bucket turned back and forth as it went jerkily down, like the gondola of a balloon caught in a high wind.

Looking down, Stirling saw upturned faces still far below. Because of the overhang, the smooth rock of the cliff-face was ten or fifteen feet from him.

Suddenly an even bigger jerk than usual came down the rope. The bucket continued to turn back and forth, but its downward motion ceased. He was hanging in mid air. Intense fear seized him. Maybe the monks intended to leave him there. Or maybe they were preparing to cut the line. There was nothing he could do but stand and clutch the side-ropes.

At last there was another jerk and the rope began moving again. He whistled with relief, and as he finally approached the ground he felt a surge of high good humour flood through him. Now! They had reached their goal. They had found their objective. They were on their way home.

Eighteen

The first day of the return journey was idyllic. The sun shone steadily. The air was warmer than usual. There was no wind. The going was mainly level, and the party made excellent progress. The horses, enlivened by their night of good feeding, were brisker than usual, and the porters had the stimulus of facing towards home.

At first Stirling had experimented with a two-man team for carrying their patient, one porter at the front and one behind, each with a stretcher-pole on either shoulder. The advantage of this system was its compactness and manoeuvrability: the team could easily negotiate even a narrow track. The disadvantage was that the load was too heavy for two men. The general said that before his accident he had weighed 180 lb. Even now, Stirling thought, he must be nearly 150. The stretcher, rugs and clothes put the total burden back to easily 180, so that each porter was carrying 90 lb or more on two hard poles which cut into his shoulders.

Not only was the weight too great: it also fell on the men in the wrong place. Accustomed as they were to taking the principal strain of a load on their head-bands, they found it awkward to move with the weight on their shoulders. Seeing this, Stirling tried slinging the stretcher on ropes, so that the burden could be transmitted through to the headbands. With a makeshift harness the idea worked well enough for the man in front, but for the man behind it was useless. The weight, transmitted through the ropes to a back-harness and thence to his forehead, kept pulling him forward, so that he could not lean into it, as he was used to doing. Besides, the slackness of the ropes made the stretcher swing and bump intolerably.

Eventually Stirling settled for a conventional four man team, two at the front and two at the back, which worked well enough except in places where the track became too narrow for two men to walk abreast. Then, until they came to a wider stretch, two men had to carry the general anyway.

The various trials and re-riggings cost the party at least an hour, but Stirling did not regret the time devoted to research. At least he now knew what was feasible and what was not. He himself had taken a turn on one of the poles, but the experiment had not been a success, for he was so much taller than any of the porters that the stretcher became hopelessly lopsided. He regretted this on two counts – first, because he wanted to do his share of the carrying, and second because to be one of the bearers put him in an ideal position for conversing with the general: as he walked, his head was on the same level and a couple of feet in front of the patient's. When he found that his height disqualified him from carrying duty, he walked behind the bearer-party, so that he and the American were facing each other, though ten feet apart, and could still talk without much difficulty.

'I knew you'd come,' said Sulzberger at one stage. 'Not *you*, I don't mean. But someone. You British always get through.'

'Not always. Sometimes. But how did you get your letter out, anyway?'

'It was like a miracle. About my third day in the monastery these two men appeared. Tibetans. They were carrying salt, I think, on their way down to Mustang. I tried to persuade them and a couple of the lamas to take me, but no dice. Then one said he knew of an English sahib in a place called Ghandrung who was a good friend of the Tibetans. I figured that if he was in touch with Tibetans, there was a chance he'd help.'

Stirling explained how he himself had known Andrew at

207

college, and so had been drawn into the rescue.

'Why didn't the C.I.A. do something?' the general asked.

'Good question. They don't seem too popular in this part of the world. Too many cock-ups. So the Powers-that-Be decided it would be better if the British handled it. The trouble is, it's going to be harder getting out than it was getting in. We have this deal with the Khampas. They needed help, and so did we.'

He outlined the saga of the Emerald Goddess and the Khampas' reason for wanting to take the image out to India. He explained that the main party was waiting for them across the Kali Gandaki, and that the aim was to reach Dhorpatan, where Andrew would lay on an aircraft to fly them out.

The general appreciated the hazards of the situation in a flash. 'The Nepalese know the Khampas are on the move?' he asked.

'Too right they do.'

'Then they'll have closed the trails in the areas they think the Khampas are likely to be.'

'Exactly. They have. Coming out, we only moved at night.'

'Did anyone pick you up?'

'Not that I know of. But it isn't just the Nepalese authorities we're up against. We have other opposition as well.'

He told the general how Haller had planted Kiri on him, and how the would-be assassin had come after him on the first day of the trek. 'One thing I'm sure of,' he concluded. 'Tibet's a damn sight safer for us than Nepal at the moment.'

'You know what?' The general sounded matter-of-fact. 'What this party's got to do is split. Soon as we get back through the frontier, you leave me. Take off with your Sherpa and go like smoke with the Bible to meet the Khampas and get the hell out. Leave me your beautiful doctor, and we'll make out somehow. That way, at least the book of words will get where it needs to be as fast as possible.'

Stirling marched in silence. Then he said. 'It's not on,

General. I thought about this on the way out. Your book's full of information, sure enough. But your head's even fuller. We've got to get you home as well.'

'O.K. So what happens if you *do* leave me? Maybe we hit a Nepalese army patrol. I get taken into custody. O.K. They take me to Katmandu and I claim diplomatic immunity. If I give you my I.D. disc, they won't even know who I am. I'll tell them I fell off a mountain or something. How about that?'

'Let's see how we go,' Stirling stalled. Again he walked in silence for a while. Then he said: 'One thing I'd like to ask, General. When you first went into China, had you got all this planned – the double defection, I mean?'

'Of course. Why else would I go to that goddam place?'

'It was a big risk.'

'Jesus, Bill. You gotta take risks sometimes. What about yourself, come to that? You're taking crazy risks, coming after me. You could have stayed at home by the fire.'

'Not really. The fire had gone out, more or less.'

'That's too bad. But it was the same with me, I guess. Wife died of cancer. Boys off on their own. Might as well do something, I reckoned. Better than sitting on my ass in the Pentagon, anyway.'

'How did you make the Chinese accept you?'

'They needed my nuclear know-how . . . '

The conversation was suddenly interrupted by Pasang, who came loping back along the column and called excitedly, 'Sair, *na, na!*' He was pointing up into the rocks, and for an uncomfortable moment Stirling thought he had seen people. Then Sulzberger said, '*Na* is the bharal – blue sheep. They're all over the place.' A moment later Stirling spotted the row of heads with striped faces and handsomely curved horns peering down at them from a shelf above.

He had already discussed with Pasang the ethics of shooting for the pot. Tibetans regarded wild creatures as sacred, and, being devout Buddhists, would not kill them. But the Sherpas, though also Buddhists, ate meat if they could get hold of it, and so did the Khampas: their religious beliefs had been tempered by the harsh realities of their life in exile.

Fresh meat, thought Stirling, would do everyone good, particularly the patient. He looked at his watch: eleven o'clock. Nearly time for the midday break anyway. He told Pasang to go on till he found a suitable spot for a halt, and to await him there. Then he unslung his pack and lashed it on to the pony with the lightest load. He checked his pockets for knife and rope, and sent the column ahead.

Accoutred only with rifle and binoculars, he went up the hillside like a sheep himself. So long had he carried the heavy pack that its sudden removal gave him wings. He climbed effortlessly, turning back now and then to watch his little army worming on along the valley floor. Then he went cautiously out on to an eminence and looked upwards, to see the row of inquisitive heads still motionless and staring at the humans below.

As he went into the stalk, memories flooded in on him – of green-scented dawns in the forest at home, of the bucks roaring, of good shots, bad shots, mistakes, Spot. Yet mingled with the homesickness came a feeling of exhilaration at once again being the hunter. In a wider sense he was still the hunted, but for a few minutes the cares of Mission Yak fell away from him as he became absorbed in his favourite pursuit.

Moving stealthily, a foot at a time, he picked his way through the jumble of loose stones that separated the outcrops of living rock. After every few steps he unbent from his crouch and cautiously raised his head. Again and again he saw nothing but the sharp serrations of more rock ledges above him. Wondering if he had aimed for the wrong spot, he let his concentration wander and trod on a loose stone. A small, sharp clonk rang out in the silent air.

A movement caught his eye. There on the skyline twenty yards above was a pair of ribbed and curving black horns. They snapped to right and left. The owner was alert and listening intently. Again the head turned back and forth. Then it vanished. There was a scrabbling, scraping sound as the sheep made off. Then came a strange chirring alarm call, almost like that of a squirrel.

He unshouldered the rifle and scrambled up to the ledge where the animals had been. As he came up to it he smelt their rank stink. There they were: five broad, slate-blue backs moving up through the screes at a trot, white rumps bobbing.

There was no time to scan through the glasses. He dropped beside a rock in a kneeling crouch, settled the rifle and gave a whistle. The sheep stopped and turned sideways, looking back, exposing the fine dark stripes along their flanks. With his naked eye he could see that the leader was the largest – an old stager, probably tough as leather. The second was a younger-looking ram. Its body was covered by the next sheep in the line, but its head and neck were clear. Lining the foresight on the base of the neck, he held his breath and squeezed the trigger.

The crash of the shot rang tremendously among the rocky gorges. The bullet hammered the sheep flat to the ground. A split-second later splinters burst from a rock beyond, and still the solid projectile continued, whining away into the sky. The surviving sheep departed at a gallop, giving no second chance.

Stirling went forward with a glow of satisfaction. Some people would say he had gratified his blood-lust. Yet in his own eyes he had merely done a useful job efficiently. He had caused no suffering, and had supplied the expedition with meat.

The bold amber eye of the ram was still bright, and blood was oozing out of the long, blue-grey hair on its neck. Stirling plunged his knife into the base of the chest to increase the flow, pulling the carcase round so that he head was lowest. Considering the barrenness of the habitat, the animal was amazingly sleek and fat. As he waited a few moments for it to bleed, he became aware of a familiar sound: ravens gurking gently overhead. He looked up and saw two, already circling, apparently summoned by the shot. Above them, far bigger birds swung in a wider orbit: vultures.

He slit open the animal's belly, left the entrails on a flat stone for the scavengers, and set off downhill with the sheep flopping behind him on the end of a rope. When he reached the track again he tied front and back feet together so that he could sling the carcase over one shoulder. He hurried on along the path, trying to estimate the dead weight that flopped against him. Fifty or sixty pounds, he thought: meat for everyone for a couple of days, at least.

He found the party comfortably installed in a sunny, sheltered hollow whose amenities included not only a clear and musical stream but also liberal quantities of small, brittle, scrubby plant which Pasang called *burtse*. Fuelled by its dry and crackly twigs, three separate fires were blazing briskly in merry contrast to the normal slow putter of pony-dung. In a flash Pasang had the sheep's liver cut into strips and frying in a pan.

The smell was such as to make waiting a torment and conversation impossible. 'My God!' groaned the general. 'You ever smell anything better than that?' No one answered. 'My God!' he repeated. 'If you'd lived on potatoes and goddam maize for nine weeks, you'd know how I feel.'

They fell on the smoking liver and ate it ravenously, as if none of them had seen food for a month. But the liver was only the hors d'oeuvre. After it, in the pan Pasang sizzled up steaks cut from one of the sheep's haunches. The Khampas, not bothering with a pan, had cut their meat into chunks and skewered them on pieces of wire, to roast them in the flames. Prodigiously delicious smells wafted up from every side, so strong that Stirling imagined the vultures would be gathering above the feast at any moment.

'Even better than a two-tooth ewe, I do declare,' said Kiri between mouthfuls.

'What the hell's a two-tooth ewe?'

'A hoggett – a second-year ewe. The best mutton there is. But it was never as good as this.'

'You probably weren't as hungry.'

The general ate as strongly as anyone, propped up with his

trunk vertical. Before the meal Kiri had made him do violent arm exercises to help expand his lungs, and after it he leant back pleasantly comatose.

'Don't doze off, General,' said Stirling with mock severity. 'We've got to do some work.' Having wiped the grease off his hands, he unwrapped the Bible and opened the first volume at the page where he had left a marker. 'We're still on the Old Testament,' he said. 'We'll have to get a move on. What's U.L.P.?'

'Underground launch platform.' The general came sharply awake. 'Can also be in the sides of cliffs. Plenty of them are. The Chinese have built a whole lot of dummy missile sites out in the open, for other people to see. Those are the ones the satellites pick up – and the ones the Soviets will hit in their counter-strike. So when you see *D*. U.L.P., you know it's a decoy. O.K.?'

'Fine. What about A.T.M.?'

'Anti-tank mines.'

'And *N*. A.T.M.?'

'Nuclear anti-tank mines. You talking about the Amur River complex?'

'That's right.'

'O.K. There the Chinese have a fantastic set-up – belts of nuclear mines ten miles wide, staggered one behind the other. Boy, will they blow shit out of the T72s!'

'What are they?'

'T72s? Russian battle tanks. You look on a bit, you'll find a detailed drawing and description. I saw one in Harbin earlier this year.'

'How did it get there?'

'Captured. The Soviets were monkeying about near a town called Fuyuan. This tank came across the frontier and didn't get back. There's plans of the mine-belts in the book, too.'

Every time Stirling turned a leaf he set the general off on some new avenue of disclosure. The store of knowledge inside that grizzled head was immense. But again and again he returned to the certainty of war, the imminent Chinese attack.

'It's just the latest move in what you British used to call the Great Game,' he said. 'You know that?'

'I've never been quite sure what the Great Game was,' Stirling confessed.

'Well – I guess it's the struggle for power in Central Asia. A hundred years back the main players were yourselves and the Russians. Now they're the Russians and the Chinese. Even without an actual war, both sides have been manoeuvring like crazy. For example, two years back the Chinese opened a new highway from Yarkand right through to Rawalpindi in Pakistan. A fantastic engineering achievement: the eighth wonder of the world, they call it – the Highway of Friendship. Horseshit!

'There's no goddam friendship between Pakistan and China. But each needs the other. Most Pakistan weaponry comes from China. If the Pakis got into another war with India, they could be resupplied down this new road. Equally, the Chinese need to keep a grip on Pakistan, just to stop the Soviets getting in there first. Ever since the days of the Tsars the Russians have wanted a warm-water port. Karachi's the one they've got their eye on. That's why the Soviets moved into Afghanistan and put 60,000 troops there. They wanted a forward base in the area. Next stop the North-West Frontier and Pakistan . . .'

After half an hour, Stirling closed the Bible reluctantly. He found himself absorbed by the mesh of international intrigue into which he had stumbled. But it was time to push on. He roused Kiri, who had gone to sleep in the sun with her fair hair tousled all over her face. She came to suddenly with a cry of 'Jeeze! Where am I?', and Stirling had to bring her back to reality.

Pasang and Likpa were still squatting by the fire, drinking tea. The Khampas had peeled off their *shubas* as far as the waist and were evicting lice from the fleecy linings with absorbed determination. The ponies were grazing on the rushy grass by the stream. Gradually everybody pulled together and re-sorted their loads for another stage.

The afternoon passed without incident – and with many quotations from *King Lear*, which the general at that moment was trying to recite entire. By chance, or perhaps by gentle cheating, he reached a perfectly apt passage just as they were ascending a ledge that climbed diagonally across the face of a precipice, and recited:

How fearful
And dizzy 'tis to cast one's eyes so low!
The crows and choughs that wing the midway air
Show scarce so great as beetles . . .

His high spirits persisted through the golden afternoon, and only when the cold struck at sundown did he go quiet. At Kiri's insistence they camped at the first good place they found, even though it was not yet dark. She wanted the patient under canvas before the full bite of the night cold came on, and fussed about him in a way he greatly enjoyed. For supper they had the remains of the sheep spiked with curry sauce, and as Stirling fell asleep he looked back on the day's progress with satisfaction. They had not gone as far as he had hoped, but all the same they had done well. Looking back later, he realised that the day of *King Lear* was the last really good day that Mission Yak enjoyed.

In the morning they woke to find the weather entirely changed. The brilliant, frosty sunshine had given way to icy mist which eddied and swung with disconcerting changes of direction. All day it cloaked the high valleys through which they were passing. Tiny drops of water hung glistening in the rough hair of the ponies' mane and clung to the outside of their bundles. Gradually animals and humans became soaked in a layer of cold moisture.

This was the kind of weather Kiri least wanted for her patient. In an attempt to keep the moisture from his face she had Pasang rig up a canopy from odd pieces of stick and canvas which they appropriated from one of the ponies' baskets, but their materials were too flimsy to make a strong enough hood, and it kept collapsing on to the general's face. He supported it patiently for some time with his own hands, but then he became irritated with the contraption and tore it off.

From first light to last no landmark appeared to guide the travellers. Only the compass told them they were moving mainly west. But then, after their midday break, they came to a place which Stirling was perfectly certain he had never seen before.

For the first time on the whole trek he became physically frightened of the mountains. As they were ascending the side of a valley, the mist parted to reveal a precipitous chasm gaping beneath them. Gradually the track narrowed until it was a barely negotiable niche scored across the face of a precipice. Stirling, in the lead, felt his balance becoming uncertain. Every time he looked down, his legs turned to jelly. He tried to lean inwards, feeling the cliff with both hands, but there was no room to achieve a better equilibrium. He thought his pack would drag him over the edge.

Then he came to a place where half the path had fallen into the abyss. Here it was not possible to walk at all; at least, not for him. Shaking all over, he went down on hands and knees and crawled across in a quick, blind paroxysm of terror, of which he immediately felt ashamed.

Beyond the gap the path widened again. He sat down to recover and wait for the others. Then he got out the climbing rope. He would make sure Kiri was all right, anyway.

To his amazement, he saw the Nepalese advancing up that perilous ledge as confidently as though they had been on a main road. The bearer-team had reduced itself to two, and the men moved with extraordinary ease and assurance, stepping lightly and serenely, as though they were half-levitated by some inner certainty that gave them superhuman poise. Even when they reached the damaged section of the path they did not hesitate, but went blithely forward, as if in a trance. Afraid that he might waken them, Stirling said nothing as they passed him, and they continued smoothly up the valley.

The ponies also passed the damaged stretch with no difficulty, but when Kiri reached it, she had the same problems as Stirling, and he threw back one end of the rope for her to tie round her waist. The incident taught Stirling a profound lesson: that although he reckoned he was fit and walking well, he still had not learnt many of the mountain men's secrets.

Yet he was beset by a more immediate preoccupation. It was quite obvious that Mission Yak had strayed off its outward route.

'We never came down here, did we?' he said to Kiri.

'Jeeze no. I couldn't have forgotten a place like that.'

'That means we're off course.'

'What does the compass say?'

'A few points north of west. The trouble is, I think we should be a few points south.' He shouted to stop the column and brought Tashi back.

'I think we're on the wrong track,' Stirling began. Was it his imagination, or did the Khampa guide look shifty and ill-at-ease as Pasang translated? A long and laborious argument followed, the Khampas insisting that they were on the same route as they had used a few days earlier, and Stirling, supported by Pasang, denying it.

Inevitably the dispute proved inconclusive. Neither side had the evidence to win its case. Stirling could not even be sure where they had gone wrong – if they had. Had he been certain that at a particular point they should have taken an alternative path, he would have turned back as far as the junction. But in fact he could not recall seeing any junctions: all he could remember of the morning were endless, almost identical stretches of scrubby turf and rock hemmed in by drifting walls of fog.

He felt paralysed by irresolution. Normally he found it easy to take decisions, whether in the end they proved right or wrong; but now he found it impossible to make up his mind. The safest course would be to turn back, but to do so would be bad for morale and make them even later than they already were. Yet if they went on, they might end up comprehensively lost, and trapped in the wrong system of valleys.

'General,' he said. 'I don't know what the hell to do. What would you do?'

'You're sure you ain't been here before?'

'Absolutely.'

'But we're still heading in the right direction?'

'More or less.'

'Then I say go on. It'll work out in the end.'

'I just have this bad feeling that we could end up the wrong side of some bloody great ridge that we can't cross. Still, we'll have a go.'

They went on. The mist sat tight on the mountainside. After half an hour the angle of the path steepened and they began a ferocious climb. Now, every minute, Stirling's doubts were confirmed. Not only did the whole layout of path, cliff and chasm seem alien: the severity of the climb was something altogether new. Not since they came off Dhaulagiri had they been on such a precipitous track.

The higher they went, the colder the mist became. A thin wind came hissing down the path to meet them and flung crystals of ice fine as needles into their faces. Already the altimeter showed 14,500 feet, and this fact alone told Stirling that they must be wrong, since on the way out they had not crossed any pass as high.

'Now we've *got* to cover you up,' Kiri told her patient. 'Otherwise you're going to get frostbite in the face. Keep those arm exercises going as much as you can.'

The general allowed her to wrap his head in a sheepskin rug, leaving only a small slit for him to breath through. Kiri's great fear was that his body temperature would fall to a dangerous level. Physical exercise kept the marchers warm, but he, lying inert, inevitably cooled down in spite of his thick cocoon of wrappings.

By five o'clock Stirling was frightened. They were still climbing, and already, at 15,000 feet, the horses were finding the ascent an ordeal. Their thin flanks heaved in and out like bellows, and every few yards they stopped, with their hind-quarters shaking, in spite of the constant harsh shouts of the guides. A few moments later one animal refused altogether to go on. The Khampas took off most of its load and distributed it among the fitter horses. As they struggled with the ropes Stirling grimly calculated the position. They had only an hour of daylight left. They could not turn back, since there was nowhere remotely fit for a camp-site within an hour along the trail they had ascended. If they had to climb for another hour, they would be caught on the pass by nightfall.

They went on, with the Khampas urging the ponies forward by abrupt, automatic cries. The mist seemed to seize the small human voices and stifle them: no sound could live long in that ferocious wilderness.

Suddenly, on a large, flat-faced rock to his left, Stirling saw a maze of Tibetan characters. He recognised the universal prayer *Om Mani Padme Hum*, painted there by countless passing hands. Seconds later a high cairn of stones loomed from the mist, and beside it a stand of poles with coloured pennons fluttering from the tops. They had reached the pass.

Fifteen thousand seven hundred, the altimeter said. Around the cairn lay heaps of whitened bones – the relics of animals which had not survived the journey. As the Khampas came up each of them picked up a stone and added it to the pile. Then they reached down into the pouches formed by the tops of their shubas, to bring out pinches of tsampa and scatter them into the wind. Having thus placated the gods which inhabited that high place, they lost no time in starting down the other side.

Stirling waited for Pasang to bring up the rear, as usual. The Sherpa's face, normally so impassive, looked tense and drawn.

'We're lost,' said Stirling bluntly.

Pasang nodded. 'No good,' he said. 'No liking.'

Nineteen

Everything sparkled in the brave and brilliant morning. As the Cessna sat waiting on the access track for permission to turn on to the main runway and take off, the horizon ahead of Haller and his passenger was lined with snow peaks etched diamond-sharp against the blue.

'Here he comes,' said Haller, pointing right.

The morning DC8 from Delhi was on its final approach, tail down, appearing to sit and hover right above the runway as it hurtled towards them. Even in the bright sunshine landing lights blazed from beneath its wings. With a burst of smoke and a screech which they could hear through their headphones in the Cessna's cockpit, the tyres smacked into the concrete right opposite them, and the big plane went scorching down the runway to their left.

Presently the tower called, 'Cessna STOL Tango November, you're clear for take-off. Wind ten knots on two-eight-five.'

'Tango November, thank you.' Haller let off the brake, rolled forward, turned left, accelerated and took off with as little fuss as a motorist emerging on to a main road. In a few seconds they were airborne, climbing steeply, and already turning right-handed towards the distant snows.

'Fantastic!' cried Adair. 'Amazing lift.'

'Oh yes – she handles like a bird.' Haller dipped one wing, rolled and side-slipped so that the little aircraft tumbled like a falling leaf.

'O.K., O.K.!' shouted Adair hastily, clutching his seat. 'I believe you.' The plane was altogether too much like a flying box – and a box with very thin sides, at that. The door beside him was flimsy to a degree, and he could see down through a crack between it and the body on to the green-and-brown hills passing slowly beneath. He glanced stiffly back at his baggage heaped on the spare seats – his own rucksack and the three other substantial bundles, which so far he had managed to preserve from scrutiny. The heaviest bundle, declared to various customs posts as a magnetometer but in fact containing the automatic weapons and some ammunition, weighed more than 30 kilos. Adair was worried that the Sherpa, finding it too heavy for one porter, would try to split up the load before they got into the mountains.

Soon they were flying steadily at 10,000 feet, almost parallel with the great chain of snow peaks on their right, but edging gradually closer to them. Adair had the illusion of hanging suspended in mid air, while the phenomenal mountain panorama slowly unrolled past them. He had his own map spread out over his knees, and presently he called, 'You don't go direct, then?'

'My God!' shouted Haller. 'Go direct? Look where we would be. Crossing the main ridge of Annapurna! I would climb to more than 8,000 metres in this case. You must know, we have no pressure system in the cabin. Our ceiling is 6,000 metres only. Look, here is Annapurna already, with the snow.'

Far to their right front one peak was trailing a long, horizontal white plume. Only by looking carefully could Adair see that it was the highest summit of the chain – a giant flanked by other giants, piling back now in uncountable numbers towards the northern horizon.

'Must be a big wind up there,' he shouted. 'The way the snow's blowing.'

'Yes. That is the problem exactly. The wind. People think that to fly in the Himalaya is a picnic. No way. Here, the wind is not much.' He glanced at his instruments. 'Maybe fifteen, twenty knots. But in Kali Gandaki gorge – something absolutely different. I show you.'

They droned on, with Annapurna's snow-plume growing

steadily larger and the details of the vast mountain barrier gradually beginning to stand out.

'Macchapuchare!' called Haller. 'Here, on the right side. With the fish-tail top. The thin one.'

'Beautiful!'

Suddenly Haller gave a shout. The aircraft swerved violently and dived to its left as an immense bird, fighting to gain height, flashed past a couple of feet over the canopy.

'Jesus!' yelled Adair. 'What's happening?'

'Birds. Didn't you see them? Lammergeyers in a thermal. They weigh ten kilos. One of them through the windshield, and you have big trouble. When they get scared, they always try to climb – so I dive.'

'I never thought they came as high as this.' Adair was recovering from his shock.

'Oh, higher. Six, seven thousand metres – many times.'

On they went. Adair offered his pilot the map, but Haller declined it, saying that he knew his way around the Himalayas. Soon he turned right and headed straight in towards the big mountains.

'Now you see Pokhara – the big lake, down there. And now Dhaulagiri – all that to the west side.'

To their left front another mighty dragon's-back of peaks commanded the skyline. Haller had the plane climbing steadily, and as they met the first air-currents coming from the snow the Cessna began to bounce around exuberantly. Adair, already pale, began swallowing hard. Seeing his condition Haller called, 'If you feel faint, use the oxygen mask. It is automatic when you pull down.'

Adair just had time to say, 'Not faint – ill,' before he was comprehensively sick into the paper bag that Haller had thrust at him. Beads of sweat stood out on his forehead, but at least the act of vomiting eased his discomfort. He looked round gingerly for somewhere to put the bag, but Haller motioned him to throw it out of the window. He pushed the catch, slid the panel back a few inches, letting in a roaring rush of ice-cold air, and shoved the bag quickly through before slamming the window shut again. Although the expedient did not appeal to him, he realised that the chances of the bag landing on anybody, or even near anybody, were millions to one against, for by then they were over uninhabited hills of scrub-covered rock.

Haller shot his passenger a contemptuous look. He did not despise him for being air-sick. The poor fellow could hardly help that. But he did despise him for parting with so much money so easily. It was odd, Haller found, but that was the way it happened. An easy conquest left him contemptuous of the person he had defeated. More fight brought more respect. Yet in this case his contempt was increased by the fact that the man seemed so incompetent. But no matter, he wouldn't have much more of Adair's company.

Down ahead of them the gorge of the Kali Gandaki had come into view – a tremendous rift slicing northwards between mountains. In the open, before the gorge began, the turquoise thread of the river showed up clearly, snaking between its banks of ash-grey stone; but the gorge itself was so narrow that the water was hidden in its depths.

To show what he meant about the wind, Haller turned through 180 degrees, throttled back and descended towards the top of the gorge. Though the air-speed indicator needle remained steady on 90 knots, their speed over the ground – or rather past the mountains – began to fall sensationally. Soon the rock faces and patches of snow on either hand were scarcely crawling past.

'Look out!' cried Adair, scanning nervously from side to side. 'We're slowing down! We'll stall!'

'Don't worry,' said Haller calmly. 'It's the wind. Our air speed is the same. This valley is like a wind-tunnel every day of the year. Look at that.' He pointed at the indicator. 'The wind is 70 knots. Quite sure.'

'I believe you.' Adair glanced wretchedly below. 'Let's get the hell out of here.'

'O.K., O.K.' Haller opened the throttle to 100 per cent and eased the Cessna up out of the clawing blast, back on to

223

their northerly heading. They began to make better progress. 'Not just here, either,' he said. 'Everywhere in the Himalaya you get wind like this. Therefore you must know what to do.'

Adair did not argue. Gradually his spirits recovered. 'Incredible country!' he exclaimed. 'What mountains! Jesus Christ – I never saw anything like it.'

Excitement kept his fear at bay as they flew up the line of the gorge, just above the lip, with immense faces of brown pasture, rocks, ice and snow sweeping up towards the dark-blue sky on either side of them. Even so, he was glad when they began their descent towards the grey dirt-strip laid like a ruler across the green valley of Jomsom.

'Quite a trip,' he said appreciatively. Then he added an apparently casual question: 'You heard of a place called Rimring?'

'Rimring? There's a village called Pimring away in the west. Over there.' Haller pointed out to their left.

'No. This is Rimring, a monastery. Somewhere in Tibet.'

'Never heard of it. What about it, anyway?'

'Nothing. I guess I read about it someplace.'

'Well – Tibet is very close now. Over there. Earlier, we could see it.' He indicated their right front, but by then they were already down in the valley and sinking fast. The cinder strip swam up to meet them. Haller put the plane down so steeply that some men working on the runway had to sprint sideways for their lives. 'Ha!' he cried jovially. 'A new Nepalese record for the one hundred metres, I think.'

The aircraft hit with a bump. Reversing the pitch of the propeller, Haller brought it shuddering to a halt in front of the little control tower. A line of porters waited beside it, and two men came out of the building to help unload the baggage. Haller recognised one as Norbu, the Sherpa in charge.

He kept the engine turning over as they dragged the bundles out. '*Tik chai?*' he yelled above the noise.

The Sherpa smiled and nodded. Haller waited till everyone else was clear before bellowing his well-premeditated exit line:

'So long then, Comrade. *Dosvedanya!*'

The Russian's sunburnt face fell apart with astonishment and dismay. Haller pulled the door shut in front of his nose, gave him a smile and a wave, opened the throttle and took off, turning to waggle his wings derisively as he came back along the valley and headed for the south.

Twenty

Mission Yak had spent a wretched night. Darkness had caught the party at more than 14,000 feet, and the mist shrouding the unfamiliar track made it dangerous to go on. Pasang, ranging ahead during the last minutes of daylight, had come on a trickle of water, and this had dictated the site of the camp in an awkward, rock-strewn ravine. The one compensation was that the horses were still festooned with bunches of burtse kept from the day before against such an emergency, so that at least the humans were able to have fires, hot food and tea. For the animals there was no grazing, and nothing to eat but small rations of barley meal.

The general had been installed in his own bivouac, improvised by Pasang from the Nepalese army tent which they had captured on the Myangdi Pass. But though they had done all they could to protect him from the cold, in the morning he had a sinister cough and a rattle in his throat.

Not until the middle of the morning did the treacherous mist at last begin to clear. Even when it did break up, it went slowly, with fitful gleams of sun breaking through. By then the party was in another stony valley. There was, however, one major difference in their surroundings, which slowly became apparent as the fog went up: the western skyline – on their left – was closed by an immensely high, snow-covered ridge. Summits rose from it at intervals, but nowhere could they see any rift that looked like a pass.

By then there was no dissembling. Even the Khampas admitted they had never been in this valley before. Stirling's apprehension was increased by the fact that they were travelling a point or two north of north-west: they were no longer heading for Nepal, but further into Tibet. He suspected that the ridge on their left was the border. If he was right, they were marching parallel with it and about two miles inside Tibet – the most dangerous area of all, since it was most likely to be patrolled by Chinese border troops.

Maybe they should stop and lie up for the day. They might have done so, had there been any suitable place that would give them cover. But the horses would be impossible to hide in such a barren and featureless landscape.

There was no point in stopping, then. They might as well keep on. Or turn back. But even to reach the last stiff pass again would be the best part of a day's march. By the time they had retraced their steps and worked their way round to their original route, they would be days behind schedule. Better to go on. Might not the V now appearing in the horizon to their left front be another pass leading in the direction of home? For the hundredth time Stirling cursed the lack of a map. It seemed incredible that the people who had launched him on this marathon could not provide any map at all.

Presently they fell in with a small stream, flowing north-west in the same direction as their advance. At least Stirling knew they were starting to go downhill. The cheerful presence of the little river made him still more inclined to press ahead. But later the sun blazed out in full strength, and since it was nearly midday, he called a short halt.

Everyone subsided gratefully by the water, peeling off layers of clothes and luxuriating in the sudden heat.

'D'you think I'd be crazy to wash my hair?' Kiri asked. 'I've got one sachet of shampoo left.'

'Feel free,' said Stirling absently. He had greater problems on his mind than that of whether her golden mane would dry or not. He went over to the general.

'If that's the frontier,' he said, pointing, 'we're too damn close to it.'

'Sure are.'

'Supposing that V's a pass through – what would the Chinese have on it?'

'If it's a main route, there could be a six-man post, supplied by air from a forward base somewhere in back. They'd have a chopper up a couple of times a day.'

'So, if we had to force our way through, the time to do it would be in the evening, at last light – too late for any reinforcements to be flown up that day.'

'I guess that's right.'

'In that case we'd better keep going, and try for it tonight.'

Again Stirling swept the immense open spaces ahead with his glasses. Except for a large bird passing overhead, nothing moved. There was no house, no smoke, no sign of human habitation. Almost automatically he ate the food that Pasang brought him, endlessly turning over all possible alternatives in his mind. He could not shake off an oppressive feeling that something was about to happen.

They marched steadily through the pleasant afternoon. Slowly – inch by inch, it seemed – the dip in the horizon grew larger. But by three o'clock it was still several miles ahead, and Stirling saw they were not going to come level with it that day, let alone have time to climb to the pass itself. That meant another night in the valley.

It was four-thirty when they heard the engine. Kiri was the first to pick up the sound. 'What's that?' she said sharply.

As soon as the column stood still, Stirling heard it too: a mechanical hum, instantly out of place in the mountain silence. 'Aircraft!' he shouted. 'Aircraft! *Janu!*'

The best cover he could see was a small pit about thirty yards off the track to the right. The bearers had already set the general's stretcher down on the path. Stirling seized both front poles, Pasang the back two. Stepping carefully off the track, they picked their way through the stones to the hollow and set the stretcher down on the bank, with the patient's head steeply uphill. In that attitude he was well hidden, and could not be seen except by someone close overhead. Stirling pushed Kiri under an overhanging slab and made sure his rifle was loaded.

The rest of Mission Yak had carried out their drill impeccably. Already they were a hundred yards away and proceeding steadily along the track, like any other band of travellers.

The hum grew louder. In a minute Stirling picked up its source with his glasses – the dot of a helicopter flying up the middle of the valley.

'Chopper,' he told the general, who could not see over the bank. 'Coming up the river at about five hundred feet. Looks like he's on a routine patrol.'

'What colour?'

'Gun-metal – drab grey.'

'Chinese army.'

'He's seen them. He's losing height.'

The attitude of the aircraft changed as the pilot descended to scrutinise the column more closely. The ground was too rocky for him to land, but there was nothing to stop him hovering. Down he went, down, down, until he was within thirty feet of the ground, just to one side of the path. Dust boiled and swirled beneath the rotor, and the pilot lifted back a few feet to get a clearer view.

At first the men on the ground waved cheerfully at the aircraft. But then, as the horses began to plunge and rear with fright, they shook their fists and motioned the machine away.

'Climbing again,' said Stirling tensely. 'I think it's worked.'

It would have worked, too, if the pilot had continued on his original course, up the line of the stream. But something made him veer off a few degrees to his left and head straight for the hole in which the Europeans were hidden.

'Look out!' Stirling snapped. 'Nobody move a muscle.'

He himself lay like a stone with the rifle hidden beneath his body. Pasang was similarly stretched on the bank. Kiri huddled in her lair of rock. The engine noise swelled to a thudding clatter. The pulsing downbeat of the rotor buffeted them as the aircraft swept straight over. For a few seconds Stirling thought they had escaped unseen, since the plane kept straight on; but then it banked abruptly and came back in a narrow turn.

They hugged the stony ground. But the helicopter came remorselessly back, nosing lower at them until it was so close that they knew the crew had spotted them.

'They got us!' yelled the general into the engine-scream.

The shout galvanised Stirling. He leapt up, turned, brought up his rifle, all in one movement. Less than twenty yards away the green perspex bubble on the front of the cockpit glowered at them like the eye of a monstrous blowfly. Through the canopy he could see every detail of the two pilots sitting side by side at the controls. The mouth of the left-hand man was moving.

Instinctively Stirling aimed and fired, straight into the pilot's chest. He saw the perspex shatter into starred patterns as he fired again. Other shots cracked out beside him: Pasang was firing too.

With a sudden violent heave the helicopter lifted away and began to climb. Both men emptied their magazines into its belly. Stirling watched incredulously. It seemed impossible that he could have missed.

For perhaps five seconds the aircraft climbed normally. Then it went berserk. The engine note rose to a frantic scream. The machine tilted vertically on to its starboard side and began carving a wild horizontal sweep out of the sky. Stirling stood up shouting oaths. First he thought the plane must hit the ground. Then he saw it was heading straight for a line of low cliffs that flanked the valley. Without changing speed or attitude, the stricken helicopter smashed headlong into the vertical face of rock. There was a brilliant flash. A moment later the boom of a heavy explosion thundered at them out of the stones. The machine was transformed instantly into a skeleton of blazing twisted metal, which dropped like a crippled dragonfly to the valley floor.

'Christ!' shouted Stirling stupidly. His legs shook with

fright and excitement. 'That's that.'

Kiri was white with shock. 'Sorry, love,' he said unsteadily. 'It was going to be them or us.'

'Too right.' The general backed him up. 'They'd have got us. You see the rockets on that thing? Cannon, too. Boy – that was a knockout!'

Stirling shook himself. The rest of the party, still working to the letter of the law, were on their way back to the place where the column had parted company. 'Come on,' he said. 'Join up again.' He saw how short-lived the victory might be. Everything depended on whether the pilot had communicated with base and told them what was happening. He had been speaking, certainly, but maybe only to his co-pilot over the intercom. If he'd passed *any* message, reinforcements would not be long in arriving.

'It's no good staying here,' said Stirling, thinking out loud. 'We've got to find somewhere safer – a ravine, or at least some big rocks to hide in.'

'Right,' said the general. 'Get tucked into some place where the damned choppers can't see us.'

The rest of the party came back chattering with excitement. To calm everyone down, Stirling told them that although they had got away with it temporarily, they could be in worse trouble any moment, because another helicopter might come, full of men with guns, who might shoot at them out of the sky.

Sobered, the caravan went on. The time was five o'clock. The chances of another aircraft finding them that night seemed very small: an hour after first light next morning would be the time to watch out. Even so, Stirling walked with his ears strained for the sound of another engine, constantly imagining he could hear that deadly incipient hum.

'You see the markings on that aircraft?' the general asked.

'He shook his head. 'Can't say I noticed anything much about it.'

'Sinkiang People's Liberation Army, it was. That figures. They're responsible for policing the Autonomous Region of

Tibet.' He articulated the name with derisive exaggeration. 'Just stop anyone escaping from the Communist paradise. Stop anyone coming in.'

'Like East Germany.'

'Exactly. Only that's small enough for them to put barbed wire and mines all round it.'

The light had begun to thicken, and as the dusk drew in the nature of the valley at last changed. The level floor gave way to more broken ground, with sudden hillocks and huge slabs of rock lying at all angles. Instead of running straight, the track began to wind, following the stream as it twisted between the stony mounds. The descent became steeper, the stream noisy and cheerful. As the last of the light drained from the sky Stirling called a halt, in a place that seemed reasonably flat.

Only when the cooking fires were alight and the tents pitched did they realise that they were not alone in the valley. Pasang, who had circled the site in search for unforeseen hazards, came back with the news that other fires were visible in the distance. Stirling's scalp crawled: it was so long since they had seen anybody else that the proximity of other men seemed immensely strange.

He took his glasses and climbed one of the hillocks. Sure enough, a minute spark was winking from far down the track ahead. The binoculars magnified it, but could not reveal the nature of the encampment. A quick check confirmed that their own fires would not be visible to the neighbours, so that there was no immediate fear of detection. All the same, he felt intensely curious about the strangers.

'What do you think, Pasang? Chinese?'

'No, sair. I think Teebettan people.'

'How can you tell?'

'Chinese soldier no camping in this place.'

'Why not?'

'No special place, sair.'

What he meant was that there was no reason why Chinese troops should choose that spot. It was not a pass, or, as far as they could see, a site of any tactical significance. The people were more likely to be traders, on their way down from the north.

Stirling's anxiety to go and find out was numbed by physical exhaustion. His legs didn't feel as if they would go another hundred yards, let alone a mile.

'How far away are they?' he asked.

'Maybe one hour. Maybe more. You want me go looking?'

'Don't worry. It's too far. We'll leave them till morning.'

Again, in spite of his exhaustion, Stirling slept lightly, haunted by visions of fire-breathing Chinese hawks and gun-battles in frozen passes. The thought of that lonely spark shining from far off in the night also pressed in on him. Echoes not of King Lear but of Edward Lear rang fleetingly through his dreams: 'On the coast of Coromandel, where the early pumpkins blow . . . ' and someone crying, 'A spark! A spark!' Suddenly he woke fully with a start and knew that the people of his nightmare were the Yonghy-Bonghy-Bò and the Dong with the Luminous Nose. Relieved at last of anxiety, he settled into a deep sleep. The next thing he knew, Pasang was shaking his shoulder.

They moved out as dawn was igniting a fiery sky. Stirling led at a fast pace, deliberately putting himself and Pasang well ahead of the others. Before they had been on the move an hour they sighted the night's strangers coming up to meet them, and they did not need the binoculars to tell them that Pasang's hunch had been correct. The column of yaks, sheep and ponies immediately revealed the people as traders.

Stirling relaxed and sat down on a high rock to wait for his own party to come up. The strangers, climbing the valley from below, appeared and disappeared as they wound in and out of its flanks. The spark of their fire had been much farther off than he had supposed: thank God he hadn't tried to reach it in the dark.

The two parties finally met at eight o'clock. The strangers' leading yak carried on his pack-saddle a short stick from which flew two white flags printed with red Tibetan characters. Like most of his fellows, the animal was loaded high with a huge stack of tea – hard black bricks of it bound into long, square-sided sausages and piled hoop-like over his back. Some of the yaks carried boldly striped brown-and-white woollen bags full of tsampa, maize, barley and butter. All looked cruelly overloaded – although the length of their hair, which hung nearly to the ground along their flanks, was the main reason for their appearing so droopy. There were over thirty yaks, a dozen horses and twenty sheep, also tripping along under substantial loads, besides a cavalcade of ragged, filthy, grinning men and women, whose faces shone like polished copper with the patina of dirt and exposure.

They had come from Nepal, they said in answer to Pasang's questions. The pass was two hours off. It was guarded by eight or ten Chinese soldiers. The day before, they had seen a huge iron bird, *with men in it.* It had flown right over their heads with a noise like thunder. The men chattered with excitement at the memory.

Stirling grew nervous. The iron bird's brothers might appear at any minute. The terrain, although more broken than the place they had been caught in before, was by no means good for concealment.

Incipient barter broke out. 'They liking Nepali rupee,' Pasang announced eagerly, and he proceeded to haggle for fresh supplies of tea, butter and maize. Stirling almost cut him short. Since they had more money than they needed, it seemed perverse to wrangle over a few pence. Yet just as he was going to intervene he stopped himself, for he realised that the very size of the Tibetan caravan would give them a measure of cover if a Chinese patrol did fly over. If Mission Yak were spotted on its own, its identity would be apparent; but if they stayed put, they might be taken for part of the Tibetan gathering.

Hardly had the thought entered his mind when again they heard the deadly hum of an engine. Fifty yards away an immense slab of rock projected at an acute angle from the valley floor, leaning steeply over to form a natural roof. In a flash he ordered Likpa to start a fire, Pasang to carry on haggling, and Kiri to help him secrete the general beneath the rock.

He knew she could manage one end of the stretcher for a short distance. Together they picked up the American and moved towards the shelter.

'I feel a real horse's ass, giving you so much trouble,' he grunted.

'It's no trouble,' Stirling gasped. 'As long as the Chinese don't shoot everyone up.'

They lowered the stretcher under the overhang, and humped it further in, one end at a time. They themselves wriggled tightly into the back of the little lair. The place felt like a fox's den. It smelt like one, too. With the comforting, solid rock above them, they peered out across the valley.

'My God!' said Stirling a moment later. 'There are two.'

'Same kind as yesterday?'

'I think so, yes. Today they're playing crafty though – keeping off at a safe distance. No they're not. Look out!'

After a preliminary sweep, the two aircraft came snarling in low, to hover right over the group of men and animals. Seconds later came the heavy, bumping hammer of cannon fire, followed by the howl of ricochets. Two bursts, three.

Rage seized Stirling. Surely the bastards weren't letting rip into the caravan? He crawled to the edge of the rock so that he could see round. Someone had raised a white flag on a stick. Apart from that one man, no one was to be seen. The animals had scattered. The helicopters sat malevolently in the air only fifty feet above the ground.

Stirling prayed for a sudden down-draught to suck them to destruction; but before his prayer could be answered the pilots lifted away, evidently satisfied. Scarcely waiting for them to reach a safe distance, Stirling ran frantically back towards the path.

People began rising up on all sides from the rocks behind which they had taken cover. The animals, though disorganised, seemed to be on their feet. In a moment he established that nobody had been shot. The guns had been fired over the people's heads, perhaps in an attempt to flush out the white element of the party. He sweated as he realised how close the ploy had come to succeeding: one more burst, and he would probably have been out there, firing suicidally at the Chinese, even though he could not possibly have accounted for both helicopters.

With a mixture of relief and indignation they helped the Tibetans round up their animals, completed their purchases, and went on their way towards the pass.

Twenty-One

'Take 'em at dusk, like we said,' the general croaked. He burst into a spasm of coughing. 'Excuse me,' he said weakly. 'Something in my throat.'

'At dusk, yes. But how?'

'It ain't no use going for a straight shoot-out. They have too many advantages. Number one, they're above you, in a fortified position. Number two, they'll have some sort of blockhouse they can shoot from. All the frontier posts have a concrete box of some kind. The poor bastards live in it while they're on duty. Number three, they have superior fire-power – automatic rifles, for sure. Maybe a machine-gun too.

'Therefore, I figure you got to take them by surprise. One thing in your favour is that you're inside the goddam place they're supposed to be guarding. They'll be looking out mainly into Nepal. You'll be coming from behind them.

'What you gotta do is get one guy up there on his own, unobserved, and slip a grenade into the blockhouse. That way, you should knock out most of them with one punch. Simultaneously, have a couple of guys posted with rifles in places they can pick off any survivors – anyone who happens to be outside. Your two best marksmen, they'd better be.'

He coughed again painfully, and gasped, 'That's what I'd do if I could.'

It was what they did do, too. In only an hour they came to a place where the path divided. They took the left fork and began climbing towards the dip in the skyline, now excitingly close. The path ran up the side of a narrow valley, at right angles to the one they had left. The group threaded its way through huge rocks and chutes of scree that had fallen from the ridges on either hand. Not knowing how far off the pass was, or how well the Chinese could see down his side of it, Stirling could only advance with the greatest possible caution, constantly using the binoculars to check the prospect ahead.

Once again, his deer-stalking techniques were invaluable. He moved from crest to crest, stopping short of each to scan any new ground that had come into sight. He felt as if he was approaching a group of stags which had occupied the pass: as always, the stationary party had the advantage over the one that was moving. Movement attracts the eye instantly, whereas animals or men standing still can often escape notice, even though in full view.

So it was. A movement finally betrayed the position of the encampment in the pass – though only a movement of smoke. Scanning with the glasses for the hundredth time, Stirling picked out a thin, white plume slanting in the breeze from the west. So long as the base of the plume remained invisible, he could be sure that the guards were unable to see them approaching.

They reached a point beyond which it was unsafe for the whole party to advance. Looking over the next small ridge, they could see the square outline of the blockhouse and occasional movements round it. Men and horses moved off the path and settled in hollows among the rocks, waiting for the day to die.

Stirling lay on a flat rock and examined the ground ahead. Half an hour would bring him to the pass, even moving slowly. Therefore he and his two marksmen, Pasang and Chimba, the second Khampa guide, must set out forty-five minutes before dark, at least, to give themselves the last fifteen minutes of daylight in which to work. The snow-line was just on the level of the pass, but it would not affect them, for there were plenty of bare rocks and gullies to give the snipers cover.

The wind increased and the clouds darkened. A squall

came blasting over the frontier ridge with flurries of snow: all good for the attack.

At five-ten Stirling checked that there was no one in sight round the blockhouse and gave the word to start. They moved up the track in single file. Now they could not afford to stop every few yards for further observations. Instead they kept going and trusted that the dusk, already collecting in the hollows, would swallow their movements.

In twenty minutes they could see the details of the blockhouse and its low retaining wall with the naked eye. The building was roughly finished, its concrete blocks left bare. One shuttered window faced Tibet, and there was a door in the wall beside the track.

Stirling chose vantage points for his snipers, high in the screes at either hand, and sent them off. 'Careful through the rocks,' he whispered. 'No noise. But hurry: the light's going already. *Tik chai?*'

Stirling looked hard at the two leathery faces. Both men smiled and nodded. 'Good luck, then,' he said.

Left alone, he loaded and cocked his rifle. Then he moved steadily on until a movement ahead froze him. A man in drab uniform, wearing a thickly padded jacket and carrying a rifle slung on his shoulder, had come round the corner of the building. His thin, sing-song whistle carried clearly down the evening wind. He sauntered idly along the parapet, then turned back.

Stirling stood rooted, willing the sentry to return to the Nepalese side of the hut. Darkness was coming down fast. They had only a few minutes left. Turning his head cautiously to the left, he searched the rocks for Pasang, but could not see him. Good: the Sherpa had also stopped. Two minutes passed. Three. Stirling swore to himself. Details of the landscape were blurring. A light shone through the cracks in the shuttered window.

At last the sentry idled back to the far side of the blockhouse. Stirling went forward again, much faster. Above him, on both sides, he could see black shadows creeping through the rocks. The pincer movement looked good.

The final fifty yards of the path seemed dangerously smooth and open. From the last safe cover he measured his task. The boards shuttering the window looked solid. He doubted he would be able to punch a hole through them, to get a grenade into the building. That meant he would have to use the door.

He took a deep breath, stepped from the safety of the rock, and sprinted. His legs seemed to work on their own. He felt no strain or effort as he sped uphill. He just seemed to fly forward. But when he flung himself down behind the retaining wall he was gasping desperately for breath.

He could hear voices in the building. An argument. Smells of tobacco and food came through the wall: delicious traces of frying.

Twisting up on one shoulder, he drew two grenades from his pouch. The strolling sentry was out of sight. He withdrew the pin from one grenade, holding the lever down. But at the very second he was about to jump the wall, the door opened from inside and a man came out. Through the loose rocks in the wall Stirling saw him disappear round the back of the building.

Something else nudged at the door from inside and shoved it wider open. A dog. Jesus: an Alsatian, or something like one. Big, thick and black. The animal came out and cocked its leg on the corner of the blockhouse, five yards from Stirling's nose.

He held his breath. He was downwind of the brute, but dreadfully close. Would it pick up bad vibrations? It did. It had. Suddenly its hackles rose and it gave a growl, lowering its nose so that it pointed straight at Stirling. It took a step forward, growling louder. Any moment it would bark.

Stirling was suddenly in trouble. He had a grenade in either hand. One was primed, so that he could not let go of it. The rifle lay on the ground against the wall.

He just had time to drop the intact grenade and transfer the primed one to his left hand. Then the dog charged with a volley of barks. It stood with its paws on the wall gnashing viciously at him. Almost without thinking he drew the .38 from his anorak, shot the dog in the chest, transferred the grenade back to his right hand and threw it through the open doorway. Before the seven-second fuse had burnt through he had primed the second grenade and flung that as well. Then he threw himself flat and hugged the ground.

The earth shook with the muffled crashes of the two explosions, about three seconds apart. Surfacing again, Stirling knelt with his rifle at the ready, peering over the top of his wall.

The door and window-shutters had been splintered. Smoke poured out of the shattered building. One of the sentries raced round the corner and stood dumbfounded, staring at the doorway. Before Stirling could even take aim, a single shot cracked out from the rocks high to his left, and the man pitched forward. Another shot spat from his right, then another. A second Chinese soldier staggered round the corner, trying to reach the sanctuary of the building. A yard from the door he collapsed and subsided on his face.

Nothing emerged from the blockhouse except the smoke, which was caught and whisked away by the wind. The smell now was not of cooking, but of charred cloth and flesh.

Stirling stood up and beamed a signal into the rocks on either side. He heard the stones move as Pasang began to descend. He turned and flashed the agreed message back down the pass: long and two shorts, repeated three times.

Pasang materialised like a ghost at his elbow. A minute later Chimba was there as well. Setting them to cover him, Stirling went forward to investigate the bombed building. Wisps of smoke still eddied out, clouding the torch-beam. Presently he made out the bodies of five men, two in the shattered remains of wooden bunks, three on the concrete floor. One had almost reached the door, only to be smashed back by the second explosion. Blood glistened blackly on the concrete. The charred wood in the bunks clicked and creaked as it contracted, cooling down. The weapons inside the blockhouse had all been damaged by the blast; but a box of ammunition had survived, and from the dead men outside Stirling recovered two new-looking 7mm. automatic rifles.

Night had fallen. The main party, on its way up, was invisible to the men in the pass. Stirling waited with an inexplicable but definite feeling of apprehension.

At last there was a movement below him. The torch beam picked out Tashi, leading the rear party. Stirling stood up and called softly, welcoming his men. There was a brief pause as they slung the heavy case of ammunition on one of the ponies. Then they started down the far side.

They had hardly gone fifty yards when an abrupt, vicious rattle erupted from above them to the right: a burst of firing, and the scream and whistle of bullets.

'Down!' yelled Stirling in automatic reaction. 'Get down!'

First he thought they were being attacked by someone who had come up out of Nepal. Then he realised that more of the Chinese troops must have been there all the time, hidden on some higher ledge.

Flashes spurted from the black mountainside above him. Ricochets screamed above his head. He aligned his new rifle on the flashes and began to fire bursts back. Beside him he heard the horrible, soft, full thud of a horse being hit. With a crash the animal fell to the ground. Now some of his own men were firing back as well.

Again he fired at the flashes, but he could not see his sights or tell where his own shots were going. The torch, he thought. He pulled it from his pouch, held it at arm's length, waited till he saw more flashes, and put the beam on the spot.

There: he had them. Two shadowy, dark forms huddled against a lighter background.

'Go on!' he yelled. 'Get them!'

He himself could not fire because he was holding the torch. But surely Pasang or someone would pick off the snipers? Seconds crawled past. At last shots cracked out from his own side. One of the forms crumpled and fell out into space, disappearing abruptly through the beam. The other kept

242

firing. Suddenly Stirling felt a stunning blow in his right shoulder. The torch beam veered up uselessly into the sky. He seemed to have lost control of his right hand.

Cursing, he moved across and picked up the torch with his left hand. He refocussed it on the ambush position. This time one of his riflemen fired instantly, and the second sniper toppled sideways, to lie full-length on the ledge. He held the beam steady on the prone figure. More bullets smacked into it, lifting it into the air. Then the firing petered out. Silence flooded back.

Stirling picked himself up. His shoulder hurt, but not too badly. His right hand was weak but working. He could move his fingers pretty well. He worked back along the line, calling to people to stand up.

One pony lay dead, blocking the path with its load. A bullet had hit it in the neck, killing it instantly. Further up he found something worse – a man dead: Chimba, shot through the chest. He went on in a state of shock, expecting worse horrors at every step.

'Kiri?' he called. 'Kiri – where are you?'

At last she answered in a small voice: 'Here.'

'Are you all right?'

'Yes.'

'Thank God. What about the general?'

'He hasn't been hit. But he's not good.'

'What's wrong?'

As if in answer, a harsh, tearing cough rasped out of the darkness.

'That's it,' she said. 'What I've been afraid of all along.'

'Pneumonia?'

'Looks like it. He's coughing up blood. Temperature's up, too.'

'It's very sudden.'

'I know. It got worse quickly this afternoon.'

'Can you do anything?'

'I've given him antibiotics. That's about all we've got. We could do with some oxygen.'

Stirling tried to answer, but suddenly he felt faint. The torch slipped from his hand and he slid to the ground.

'What's the *matter*?' said Kiri sharply.

'Stupid . . . It's my arm. Damn shoulder.'

She seized the torch and shone it on the neat round hole in his anorak and the blood running down his sleeve.

'You've been shot!' she cried, making a dive for the medical pack.

Sitting on the ground, Stirling felt less woozy. 'Where's Pasang?' he said loudly into the darkness.

'Here, sair.' The Sherpa loomed up beside him.

'You O.K.? Likpa O.K.?'

'Yessair.'

'Good. Pasang, we're in a mess. Got to get down out of here . . . ' Nausea engulfed him. He waited for it to clear, then began again. 'There's a dead horse. Split up its load. Put it on the others. A dead man, too. Better leave him here. Anyone else hurt?'

Stirling did not hear Pasang answer. He seemed to have drifted off again. Then he was aware of being carried and propped against a wall. He was next brought round by a sharp pain in the shoulder. He found himself lying inside the Chinese blockhouse with a fire blazing in one corner and Kiri working on him. She had taken off his anorak and cut away the bloodsoaked sleeve of his shirt.

'What's happening?'

'Keep still. You're lucky. The bullet missed the bone. Went right through the muscle. Only a small hole. You've lost a bit of blood, but otherwise it's not too bad. I'm just waiting till the water boils. Then I'll clean it out properly.'

As his brain cleared, the sense of urgency returned. 'We can't wait here,' he muttered. 'Must get away from the frontier.'

'I know,' she replied soothingly. 'Relax. Most of them have gone down already to find somewhere to camp.'

'Where's Pasang?'

'Right here. He's stayed to give you a hand.'

Stirling saw his indomitable retainer balancing a pan of water on the fire.

'Where's my pack?'

'You're leaning against it.'

'Was anyone else hurt?'

'No. Chimba was killed, but no one else.'

'And the horse.'

'And the horse. But we were lucky.'

'Fancy those two bastards being up on that ledge, keeping quiet all that time. But now I come to think of it, I had a feeling that something was wrong.'

'Come on now. This is going to hurt.'

Half an hour later, with the wound cleaned and dressed, with his right arm in a sling and with two pain-killing tablets washed down by a mug of tea, Stirling felt fit for the road. By hacking the remains of the bunk-frames to pieces with his kukri and feeding the wood to the fire, Pasang had made the blockhouse like a furnace, so that it was a shock to step out into the freezing darkness.

Stirling gasped and shuddered. But after a couple of breaths he felt all right. Pasang lashed his haversack on to the one pony which he had kept behind and led it carefully round the heap of Chinese bodies, which they had flung outside. Then, with Stirling behind him and Kiri bringing up the rear, they started down into Nepal under a thin moon.

Twenty-Two

'We've *got* to go on. If we sit around here all day, we'll probably kill him.' Kiri's voice was hard. Beneath her wind-tan her face was white from anger and exhaustion.

'Now that we've got this far, it would be crazy to walk into a Nepalese army patrol in full daylight,' Stirling replied doggedly.

'It'd be even crazier to kill the general by hanging about.'

'You really think one day's going to make all that difference? Specially a day as fine as this?'

'One *hour's* going to make a difference. He hasn't got that long to live, unless we get him to hospital.'

'Oh Christ.' Stirling leant back against the rock and sipped his tea. He hardly had the energy to argue. Immense bruises had come out across his shoulder and back, and his arm ached horribly.

Somehow, sustained by Pasang and by frequent halts, he had kept going for five hours during the night: five hours of torture, but mainly downhill. Now they were perhaps four normal hours' march inside Nepal – a safe distance from the border. The day was fine and hot. They had found a comfortable hollow with water and grazing. Men and animals were recovering from the night's ordeal.

Yet it was not the place's physical attractions that tempted Stirling. He genuinely felt convinced it would be safer to move at night. But the American . . . He struggled to his feet. 'Let's go and look at him.'

They walked across to where the stretcher lay propped to face the sun. Beneath their grey stubble the general's cheeks looked unnaturally flushed. Flecks of blood showed in the saliva at the corners of his mouth. His breathing was short and shallow.

'Hi, doc,' he gasped. 'How are we doing?'

'Thinking about moving on. How's the chest?'

'Hurts pretty much when I breathe in.'

She put her hand on his forehead.

'Stupid cough,' the patient croaked at Stirling. 'What about the arm?'

'Coming on.' Stirling suddenly felt moved by the sick man's appearance. The handsome face had become so old and ill and full of pain. He turned away and said quietly to Kiri, 'We'd better get going.'

It was an effort for him even to pack his things. But at last he was ready. As they moved off they passed beneath a swarm of vultures circling over a spur that protruded from the hill above them.

'What's attracting them?' he asked.

'It's the funeral of the man who was killed last night – Chimba.'

'I thought we left his body behind.'

'I told the Khampas to leave it, but they insisted on bringing it with them. Now they've cut it up.'

'*Cut it up?*'

'That's what they do – dismember the body so the birds can eat it.'

'Charming!'

'It's hygienic, anyway.'

'I'm sure.' Stirling felt his stomach tighten. 'It makes one even less keen to die in a place like this.'

They advanced south-westwards without incident until well into the afternoon. Stirling had forced himself to wear his pack, even though the pressure on the right-hand strap produced a savage pain in his shoulder. His mind and body both felt dull and heavy. It was hard to walk, hard to think. They must, he reckoned, be within a couple of days of the airstrip at Jomsom. Kiri had insisted that either the whole party, or at any rate she herself, should make straight for it and evacuate the general by air.

Stirling hadn't been able to argue on medical grounds. But he had still fought against the idea of walking straight into the arms of the authorities.

'O.K. – they arrest us,' Kiri had said, rehearsing the possible consequences. 'The general's half dead with pneumonia or maybe pulmonary oedema. They must see how ill he is. So they put him in hospital. He's physically incapable of talking much, so they won't find out anything from him.'

'But they'll throw you into gaol.'

'So what? What crime have I committed? Nothing – except that I've been in a closed area. They'll deport me – that's all.'

'They'll interrogate you about the general. Maybe they know about the Bible. They'll want to know where I am.'

'I've never heard of the Bible. I'll just say I went with you to rescue the general, and that you were shot in a battle – which you were. I won't have any idea where we were at the time – a typical woman.'

So they had gone on. Kiri had worked herself into the worst temper Stirling had seen, and now, as they walked, he could feel it still simmering.

At about three-thirty they began to descend a steep-sided valley which bent gradually round to their right. Stirling was in the lead, and as he came round a corner he at once picked up movement far below. The binoculars revealed a column of men, ten or a dozen strong, climbing to meet them. He steadied his glasses on a rock and saw to his amazement that the leader was a European.

He wiped the sweat off his forehead. Who the hell could this be, stepping out in the middle of a no-go area, so close to the Tibetan border? Taking care not to show himself, he slipped back up the path to warn his own people. He would have liked to get the general away, off the track and out of sight while the strangers passed, but here there was no chance of that: above and below the track the side of the valley slanted smoothly. A confrontation was inevitable.

'People coming up,' he told Pasang. 'Get everyone to wait in this corner while we have another look.'

They went forward together to the bend. The party below had disappeared temporarily, but soon it came into view again, crawling up one of the many zigzag pitches by which the path climbed the mountainside. Pasang took a look through the glasses. 'Sherpa and porter,' he announced.

'Yes – but what are they doing here? No trekking here, surely?'

'No, sair.'

'Do they have guns?'

'No gun, sair.'

They went back to their main body. 'All weapons out of sight,' Stirling ordered. 'General – please don't speak to the man at all, whatever he says. We'll say you had a fall climbing. Hit on the head – can't talk. O.K.?'

They waited in the hollow of the hill, where the track bent inwards in a kind of elbow. From the vantage point on the corner Stirling had plenty of time to study the leader of the other private army, in his loud blue-and-white check shirt and clean-looking biscuit-colour trousers. His head and arms gleamed pink with the sunburn as he sweated up the hill.

When he was thirty yards off Stirling stepped suddenly into view, affected astonishment, and stopped with his hands on his hips. The other man really was astonished: scared, too. He started to duck back behind the shelter of the Sherpa following him, then straightened up and stood his ground. Stirling grinned and stuck out a hand.

'Dr Livingstone, I presume?'

The newcomer looked baffled. 'My name's Adair – James Adair, Junior.'

'My name's Bill Carson. I never thought we'd meet anyone out here. How *are* you?'

'Hello, Bill, pleased to meet you.' Adair shook hands, but he was looking over Stirling's shoulder. 'What's that you got there? Somebody sick?'

'Just that. Had a fall. We're bringing him down. How

about you, though? You've got a lot of men along.' Stirling gestured at the line of porters, who were still closing up with quiet hooting and wheezing sounds that put him instantly in mind of the Human Bellows.

'Sure, sure.' Adair looked back at them. 'I need 'em, too. Geology's my line. Making a study of the Mustang glaciers. There's stuff in the moraines up here you don't get anywhere else in the world.'

'Is that right? What sort of stuff?'

'Oh . . . you know: rocks. Quartzes, schists. That kind of thing. Say, who's the guy you're rescuing?'

'A British Government official. He was on a walkabout – you know, one of his tours. But he fell down a cliff between one village and the next.'

'Is that so? Do you need a doctor?'

'We have one, thanks.'

'Oh, great. Who's the girl?'

'That's the doctor. Dr Nelson. I brought her out with me to look after the patient.' He waved Kiri forward. She came down and shook hands, looking cold as a glacier.

'How do, ma'am,' said Adair oafishly. 'Mind if I have a look at your patient?'

'Yes I *do* mind. Leave him alone.' She spoke with such venom that Stirling was startled into a keener awareness. The stranger began making casual conversation, mainly about New York, and for a few minutes Kiri swapped reminiscences civilly enough, but Stirling could tell she had sensed something wrong. Now the man was talking to him.

'Which way are you heading?' he countered. 'You ought to be careful. You must be pretty close to the Tibetan frontier.'

'Is that right? You know where the frontier is?'

'Not exactly. But it can't be far. Watch out you don't end up in Tibet. I don't think the Chinese are all that friendly.'

By then Kiri's face was contorted. She was giving him furious and desperate looks.

'Well,' he said easily. 'We'd better press on. Best of luck with your rocks, Mr Adair.'

'Thanks, Bill. Best of luck to you, too. Goodbye, doctor.'

Kiri gave him a wintry smile and moved back to the general's stretcher. To Stirling's amazement he saw her shuffle the porters like a pack of cards so that she had a solid human wall blocking the stretcher from the path, and Adair could hardly see the sick man as he passed, let alone speak to him.

'What's all the manoeuvring in aid of?' Stirling asked a minute later.

'Didn't you see?' she snapped. 'That man's phoney as hell. I don't know what he's doing, but he's no more American than you or me.'

'How d'you know?'

'Couldn't you *smell* him? All that cheap scent – that's not American. That's Russian. He looked like a Russian, too. Didn't you notice he'd never heard of Dr Livingstone? Hadn't a clue who he was. But what really gave him away was the way he talked about New York.

'That restaurant I mentioned – the Sea Horse. He said he'd been there just the other day. But the place doesn't exist any more. It was burned out this time last year. Everyone in New York knows about it. There was a bomb – the Mafia, everyone said. That idiot hasn't been in New York for years. And yet he said he was there in September. It's rubbish.'

Stirling stared at her. 'In that case, the further we put ourselves from him, the better.'

'Exactly.'

'Let's go, then.'

Pasang came back looking agitated. 'Sherpa my friend. I speaking with him. He say, these porter having guns. They going Tibet also.'

'Bloody good luck to them,' Stirling retorted. 'They'll have a good fight for their money in the frontier pass, anyway. Come on.'

They went off at a sharp pace. Shock had cleared Stirling's head remarkably. 'If you're right, and he is a Russian, he can only be our friend from the Kremlin who was harassing me before.'

'The K.G.B.?'

'The one and only. It's taken him some time, but he's on our trail at last. What's more, he must see that he's been scooped. He saw the general. At least, he saw we were carrying an injured man. He must realise we've got the Bible. Therefore there's only one thing he can do.'

'Turn round and come after us.'

'Just that. We could be in for an uncomfortable night.'

He turned round and walked backwards for a few steps watching the valley above. The other party had disappeared for the moment. But presently, as he searched again, he saw them, still climbing. The glasses confirmed that Adair was still in the lead.

'He's gone on for the moment, anyway,' said Stirling. ' guess he'll come in the evening.'

His mind was revolving round extra sentries, diversions and other possible forms of bluff when suddenly, below them a wooden bridge appeared, carrying the track across a deep ravine. The sight of that fragile viaduct, laid precariously on a ledge of rock at either end, at once gave Stirling an idea.

Several times on the way down they lost sight of the bridge but in the end the path brought them to it. A quick glance round confirmed that the place was ideal, as it was out of sight of the higher ground. Stirling stopped the column and unloaded one of the horses, burrowing deep into one of its bundles for the bag of special equipment which until now he had not needed: a 100-yard roll of fine wire, small pulley wheels, angled levers, nails and other aids to remotely controlled detonation.

He needed someone to help him, and guard him while he wired the bridge up. Pasang was the obvious choice. By then Kiri was quite experienced enough to choose a site for the night's camp, so he asked her to go on down for another hour and then bivouac in the best place she could find. She seemed glad enough to do that: anything to get the general to a lower altitude.

The bridge was even better suited to Stirling's purpose than he had hoped when he first saw it, for it was made of two tree trunks laid about two feet apart and joined by boards nailed on cross-wise. The hollow beneath the boards and between the trunks made a perfect place for the concealment of grenades.

He watched and counted carefully as the first of his porters went across. Moving warily to keep his balance, the man took nine seconds to cross the rickety planks. The general's team, reduced to two men for the crossing, took ten. The quickest movers were the ponies, who showed a total disregard of the thirty-foot drop to the water raging through the rocky channel below, and tripped over as boldly as if they were on solid ground.

As soon as his team had gone on, Stirling set to work. He felt jumpy, for the noise of the water filled the air: even someone descending the track carelessly would come on him unheard. He set Pasang, with his rifle, to guard the corner, and summoned his aid only when he could not get on without it.

Every movement of his arm hurt, but he forced himself to use it normally. Lying flat on his stomach along the bridge, he lashed two pairs of grenades into position beneath the planks. The whole contraption might have been made for the purpose: the boards were wide enough apart for him to bind wire round the main poles, between them, but not so wide as to leave the wire visible. With his weak arm it was no easy job to hammer nails and pulley-wheels into the underside of the poles: he hung over the side of the bridge, half mesmerised by the hurtling torrent beneath, and hammered feebly upwards, against gravity and towards his own chest. It took him twenty minutes to get the trigger apparatus adequately anchored. Unable to hear anything but the stream, he glanced up every few seconds to make certain that Pasang was still on station. One wheel and several nails fell into the river, but in the end he had everything to his satisfaction. Then he threaded the wire and linked up several different strands so that a single sharp pull from the far end would draw the pins from all four grenades simultaneously.

Having got so far, he waved Pasang across the bridge and moved up into the rocks on the far side, unreeling the wire as he went. Because there was no tree or piece of wood on which to make fast another pulley, he had to leave the wire lying on the surface, in the open. When he pulled, it would rise into the air, and there was a slight risk that Adair would spot it. But Stirling felt confident that he would not return till dusk, and that when he did come, his attention would be fully occupied with the business of not falling into the water.

As a double check, he sent Pasang back across the plank one last time and got him to walk down the path towards it at a normal pace. Given the seven-second fuses in the grenades, he could tell the exact point at which he would have to pull the wire to catch Adair half-way across. He could, he realised, just blow the bridge with no one on it. But he wanted to eliminate the pursuit rather than merely delay it. He was taking no chances now.

In a stony redoubt commanding the lower end of the bridge, they settled to wait. Already the sun was low, and soon it went off them, leaving them suddenly chilled. High in the sky an eagle wheeled on gilded wings. Once it gave an abrupt, explosive scream which rebounded from the rocky faces all round. Stirling thought the bird might have been disturbed by men moving, but no one appeared.

They lay still, hardly speaking. Occasionally Stirling shifted to ease his aching shoulder. Blood had seeped out of the bandages and was showing through his anorak again. He needed Kiri to re-dress the wound. Kiri: he felt worried about her. For the past two days she had been uncomfortably hard and distant. He told himself it was only the worry that the general was causing her. But suddenly they had started arguing – something they'd never done before. Probably it was exhaustion, too: they were all more tired than they admitted.

254

His mind flew home to Deepwood Cottage. But was that home any more? He and Kiri had talked about going to New Zealand together . . . when they got out of the Himalayas. *If* they got out. Merely to escape would be easy enough: just walk down to Jomsom and hand yourself over to the authorities. A good spell in gaol maybe, deportation . . . Easy. But no good. To do that would be to throw away everything they had come to achieve. The Nepalese would get the Bible and probably sit on it indefinitely. The Khampas would be left without their promised help. The Emerald Goddess would be cut off in her thundering cave.

He felt fierce loyalty to the Khampas. They had kept their part of the bargain handsomely. One of them had been killed on his behalf. He was not going to let them down if he could possibly avoid it.

Still nothing moved in the narrow valley. Out above the end of it the snow peaks took fire one by one as the dying sun caught them. Huge pillars of cloud, drifting slowly on the evening wind, were lit by a flaring pink and yellow glow as they piled into the high corries. Every second the colours changed, first deepening, then suddenly fading, until only the two highest summits were left gently glowing against the gun-metal sky. Then that last glow also faded, and suddenly both mountains were black and white, dead masses of rock and snow.

Movement. Movement on the path. Suddenly in the dusk shadowy figures were advancing on the bridge. One moment the track had been empty: the next, the men were there. The binoculars revealed Adair leading. Yet neither he nor his companions looked anything like they had in the afternoon: they had shed their packs and carried short machine-pistols at the ready. They came down the path warily, as though expecting to make contact.

Stirling took up the slack in the wire. Beside him Pasang cocked his Chinese automatic rifle and aligned it on the track.

Just short of the bridge Adair stopped and spoke to the

man behind him. Their voices were drowned in the roar of the river, but the glasses showed their mouths moving. For a second Stirling was afraid that Adair was telling his second-in-command to cross the bridge ahead of him. But no: he seemed to settle whatever point was worrying him, and turned forward again to cross the river.

Stirling pulled the wire firmly. He felt it give a satisfactory amount and imagined the well-greased pins sliding from their sockets, the levers springing open, the fuses hissing faintly (but drowned by the river noise). He kept his head up for a count of three and had the pleasure of seeing Adair stepping cautiously out into the middle of the rickety planks. At four he lowered his head, blocked his ears, closed his eyes and held his breath.

The thump of the explosion seemed to hit him in the chest. The shock-wave came through the ground, buffeting him from underneath. He kept down a few seconds longer, expecting debris to rain on his back, but when nothing landed he peered over the shield of rock.

It was as if he had performed a brilliant feat of magic and caused the man to vanish. The bridge hung there shattered, with most of the cross-planks blown off, but of Adair there was no sign. His body must have fallen straight into the torrent below. On the far bank the second-in-command had been knocked off his feet by the blast, but a few moments later he got up again, apparently none the worse. He and his three companions crouched against the hill, looking desperately in all directions. Then suddenly they sprang to their feet and ran, back the way they had come.

Stirling wound in the remains of the wire so that it could be used a second time. He waited ten minutes to make sure there was no follow-up. Then he and Pasang went down to find their own people, secure in the knowledge that the man who had called himself Adair would never trouble them again.

The path was good. The dark seemed friendly, rather than a hazard. Stirling trod lightly, feeling that a weight had been lifted from him. Even his shoulder felt easier. Now, he thought, the rest of the trip should be plain sailing: tricky when they got the Emerald Goddess to an airstrip, but until that moment simple.

Yet his euphoria was short-lived. He had told Kiri to camp after one more hour on the trail, at most. But after he and Pasang had gone fast for an hour, they had come on no trace of the others. At every corner they looked ahead in vain for the cheerful glow of fires.

At the end of another half hour Stirling became seriously anxious. It was impossible that he and Pasang had overshot the site: if the party had been forced to move far from the path, they would have left a scout on the track itself. Equally, it seemed impossible that they could have continued so far.

'Something's gone wrong, Pasang.'

'No passing others.'

'No. We can't have gone past them. But why the hell have they gone so far?'

There was nothing for it but to carry on in the icy darkness. But they had only been going a few more minutes when they stumbled over something lying across the track. Stirling felt at once that it was a body, still warm; but only when he shone his torch on the man did he see that it was Kali, one of their faithful porters, and that he had been shot through the chest.

Twenty-Three

'Gentlemen,' Patrick Smith began formally. 'First of all I should like to thank you for coming to Katmandu so promptly. It was the Ambassador who requested this meeting. H.E. is worried about an important mission that's overdue. So are we all.'

He paused, and the two men looked at him expectantly. Flight Lieutenant Terry Bond wore his blue R.A.F. uniform. Captain Eugene Black, U.S.A.F., was in civilian clothes.

'I hope I needn't reiterate that every detail of what we're going to discuss is highly confidential,' Smith went on. He glanced from one man to the other. Both nodded. He then gave them a quick outline of the task of Mission Yak, and explained that Carson had failed to return.

'Talk about needles in haystacks,' said Bond with a hint of desperation. 'This is like looking for one particular bolt in a scrapyard covering hundreds of acres.'

'I know.' Smith's voice was soothing. 'But we've got to try everything we can to find him.'

'I don't get it,' said the American. 'You mean the Nepalese don't know what your man's doing?'

'Not at all.'

'Why in hell don't you get *them* to help, though? It's gotta be in their interest to know what the Chinese are planning.'

'True,' said Smith patiently. 'But you don't know the Nepalese. You can't imagine how touchy they are on the subject of the Tibetan border. The thing's like gunpowder with them. They'd never have sanctioned this operation in a million years. Sending an enemy agent through the frontier, at the Chinese – out of the question. So it had to be done without their knowing.'

The recent arrival of the R.A.F. contingent in Nepal had been entirely coincidental, and had nothing to do with Mission Yak. The small reconnaissance team had flown out from England in a C-130 Hercules transport to begin planning a major famine-relief operation – an air-lift of food into the Western Himalayas, which was due to start as soon as the snows melted in March. Their job was to establish a base-camp on the airfield at Bhairawa, and to prospect routes into the high valleys where maize, rice and wheat would be dropped as soon as the weather improved. The plane they had brought was one of those that would be used in the air-lift itself: a large, heavy workhorse, and by no means a nimble flyer. Yet in Smith's eyes it had one overriding advantage as a means of tracking down Carson: the Nepalese authorities had given the R.A.F. *carte blanche* to make reconnaissance flights wherever they wanted.

'Trouble is,' the American was saying in his southern drawl, 'a C-130 ain't the baby for this kinda search.'

'What's wrong with it?'

'Too big, too heavy. Stall-speed too high. Can't cruise low enough or slow enough. Otherwise it's great.'

Smith sidestepped the sarcasm. 'Well, as you know, it's the only plane we can possibly use, the Nepalese attitude being what it is. We'll just have to make the best of it. No American aircraft would get permission.'

'Point taken.' Black smiled. 'The question is, what are we gonna do?'

'Well – start from here.' Smith pulled the map closer to him and put the point of his gold pencil on the line that marked the Tibetan border. 'The Chinese have just complained about an incident here, at Frontier Point 121. Somebody shot up a border post. That was three days ago. I guess it was our man on his way out. If it was, he must be somewhere in this area.' He indicated the maze of hills north of Jomsom.

'He'll be trying to reach Jomsom, I expect. Or he may possibly cut across north of that and come down to Dhorpa-

259

tan, here. If he does that, it'll take him longer. Either way, it would ease a lot of people's minds to know where he is.'

'So we fly the tracks, huh? These red lines?' The American traced a couple of the main paths.

'That's about it.' Bond also followed some tracks with a ball-point. 'Shouldn't be difficult, provided the weather's reasonable. If we see him, we can drop an emergency pack, at least.'

'What's that got in it?' Smith did not mind displaying his ignorance.

'Rations, blankets, medical kit, flares.'

'What I don't see is how that's gonna speed him up any,' said Black. 'Just to drop him food and stuff ain't gonna get him out any faster. He can't get his dossier into the aircraft.'

'True.' Smith smiled disarmingly. 'But if we knew where he was, we might be able to organise something on the ground. You could drop him a message, too, I suppose?'

'Certainly.'

'Boy!' Black scratched his head with both hands, one above each ear. 'I'm glad it's him rather than me. Sure looks some terrain out there.'

'Wait till you see it for real,' Smith told him.

A knock on the door cut him short. A secretary came in and announced that Brigadier Bahadur had arrived. Smith glanced at his watch. 'He's early. But tell him I'll be with him in a minute.' He turned back to the others. 'The Minister of the Interior,' he explained. 'It'll be to do with your operation, Flight Lieutenant. Maybe you'd stand by in case he wants to ask you anything. Meanwhile, you two can start working out what you're going to do.'

Smith received his distinguished visitor in his office. The brigadier seemed on edge, and wasted less time than usual on courtesies. Refusing tea or coffee, he perched on the edge of a chair opposite Smith's desk and at once apologised for his intrusion.

'I will be quite frank with you,' he began in his squeaky voice. 'The fact is, we have a problem. And what is more, I find myself largely to blame.' He shifted around. 'The thing is this. Two weeks ago I authorised the issue of a visa for geological exploration in Mustang. I was under the impression that the applicant was an American professor of some repute. Now it has come to my knowledge that he is in fact an agent of the Soviet secret service.'

'The K.G.B.?' Smith had no need to conceal his surprise.

'Yes, the K.G.B.'

Smith felt his heart accelerate. Had wires got crossed? Could the brigadier be talking about Carson?

'What's his name?' he asked casually.

'The name he gave was Adair. But in reality he is called Ortsov.'

'How do you know, if I may ask?'

'Our Internal Security Department has established his identity.'

'And what do you suppose he's after in Mustang?'

'Nothing. If you ask me, I think he has gone into Tibet. You know the border incident at Point 121?'

'Of course.'

'That was him, for sure.'

Smith took a deep breath. 'What does he want, though?'

'Ah.' The brigadier spread his small brown hands. 'He is on a sabotage mission, I have no doubt. The Chinese have satellite monitoring equipment up there. Something on those lines. What I want is to make sure we catch him when he comes back.'

'Quite.' Smith looked steadily at his visitor. 'How can we help?'

The brigadier hesitated, then said suddenly, 'With an air-lift. I want to move two companies of infantry up to Tomsom immediately, so that we can close all the tracks coming down from the north-east. As you know, we have only small aircraft. What I wondered was whether the Royal Air Force can help us with their Hercules.'

'The aircraft's supposed to be on a reconnaissance mission.'

'Yes, yes. But this is of overriding importance.'

'Well – the man to answer the question's right here in the building: Flight Lieutenant Bond, leader of the R.A.F. party. I've just been talking to him. Shall I get him in?'

'Please do.'

Smith pressed a buzzer and asked the secretary to fetch Bond. In a minute he was sitting at one end of the desk.

'Delighted to be of service,' he said. 'But it depends on two factors. One, the shape of the Jomsom valley, and two, the state of the airstrip. We need a lot of air-space – not so much to get down as to take off again. Also, the surface of the strip needs to be pretty hard. When sixty tons of aircraft hits it, that's quite a thump.'

'I can get you the data,' the brigadier began.

'We'd have to look at it,' said Bond. 'On the ground.'

It was agreed that two of the R.A.F. team would be flown up to Jomsom in a light plane that afternoon. With this action set in train, the brigadier promptly took his leave, and as soon as he had gone Smith reconvened his earlier meeting.

'He's played right into our hands,' he told the others. 'Whether the Herc can get into Jomsom or not, he's given us a perfect excuse for flying around that area.'

'Yeah – but who are we looking for now?' the American asked. 'Your guy or the Russian.'

'Our guy, emphatically.'

'And how do we know which is which? From the air one party on the trail's gonna look just like another.'

'Except that our party will have a stretcher with a man on it,' said Bond. 'Isn't that right?'

'That's right,' said Smith. 'Unless . . . It depends what the Russian's doing. He may have gone on a sabotage mission, but I don't think so. It's too much of a coincidence that he should turn up just there. I've a bad feeling he's after the same thing as we are. If anything's gone wrong, it could be *his* party that has the man on the stretcher.'

He paused, thinking. Then he added, 'The least we can do is to get messages ready for dropping, to warn Carson that the approaches to Jomsom are blocked.'

'Seems to me your guy's got just about everything against him,' said Black. 'The mountains, the weather, the Chinese, the K.G.B., and now the Nepalese army as well.'

'Exactly,' Smith replied. 'That's why we've got to find him.'

Twenty-Four

Stirling felt exhausted and physically sick, as though he had been hit in the solar plexus. He could still hardly take in the disaster that had shattered Mission Yak.

He and Pasang had not waited long to find out what had happened. A few minutes after they had stumbled on the body on the track, they had seen two dark figures creeping back along the path towards them. A whistle had been answered from a distance, and seconds later they had been reunited with Tashi and Likpa.

The column had been ambushed – captured whole – by a Nepalese army patrol. They had come round a corner and the soldiers had jumped out on them – fifteen men, at least, all armed. It was useless trying to escape, Tashi said. The one man who had attempted it had been shot. The two who had succeeded in getting away had waited until after dark and then, with the column still marching, they had jumped over a bank and fled downhill. Likpa had gashed his arm, but was otherwise intact.

Now, the following afternoon, the survivors of Mission Yak were in a poor way. They had lost nearly all their equipment and creature comforts. Stirling's kit-bag had gone, and with it most of his spare clothes. Still worse, their tents, food and cooking equipment had been lost, on the backs of the captured horses. All that Stirling had left was what his haversack contained: the Bible, the .38, his binoculars, the torch, the money, a couple of jerseys, his washing kit, and a small tin of medical supplies. Pasang's pack also contained a few essentials. Tashi had a bedding-roll strapped over his shoulders. Likpa had nothing.

Besides, as they crouched on the side of a mountain high

above Jomsom, they could see that they had stirred up a hornets' nest of activity. Through the glasses Stirling watched a procession of stumpy, squat aircraft come gliding in to land. Other aircraft – or perhaps the same ones, unloaded – were constantly taking off. Evidently an air-lift was in progress: men were being ferried in, no doubt to seal off the area.

There was no immediate danger. They were five or six miles from the airstrip in a direct line, and many more than that by hill track. But as Stirling watched he thought desperately of Kiri and the general. By now they must be in custody. Perhaps they were already back in Katmandu. Had the general been put in hospital? Was he still alive? And Kiri – was she being interrogated? What would she tell them? He would back her to reveal the minimum, whatever they did. He tried to remind her telepathically to say that he had been shot and killed, so that there was no point in looking for him. But would they swallow that? One accidental word from one of the porters would blow the story.

Thinking about Kiri made him feel even sicker. They had parted on edgy terms, in the middle of an unresolved argument. God, he could do with someone to talk to – someone with whom he could discuss things properly. Yet he knew what they had to do. They could not go down towards Jomsom: to do that would be to walk into the arms of the military. No – they had to go west, across the Kali Gandaki, to rejoin the Khampas as planned. At least the Khampas would give them food.

Food was the most urgent necessity. They had not eaten for more than twenty-four hours. Had they been able to keep still, it would not have mattered so much. But to keep still was just what they could not afford to do. At all costs they must put distance between themselves and Jomsom. To do that, their bodies needed fuel. Hunger was contributing to Stirling's sick feeling, he knew: he felt hollow from lack of food, and from drinking too much water. One blessing was that his shoulder seemed to be healing cleanly. Kiri must have done a good job washing and disinfecting the wound.

He had one fresh dressing and some antibiotic tablets, but he decided not to use them until he had to. For the moment he could carry on.

None of the party had any exact knowledge of the country they were in. They could not predict where the next village would be. There was nothing for it but to start walking again. They were still high up, and slowly traversing an enormous slope that faced south and west. The track was only faintly marked, and evidently not much used, which gave Stirling hope that the army would not be covering it.

Their luck changed just before dark. Suddenly they smelled smoke rising to them on the breeze, and as they came over a shoulder they found houses right below them – a hamlet out on a spur. While the others sheltered in the lee of a rock, Pasang went down with some money to try to buy food.

He was gone a long time. But when he came back in the dark he was carefully carrying a large iron pot in both hands. Steam rose from it, and a thin smell of curry or spice. He set it on the ground, and without ceremony all four of them began to eat, dipping their fingers into the hot, stiff maize porridge. Stirling could have eaten the whole potful himself, and when he had finished his share he was still ravenous. He craved meat, or something solid. But at least the slushy pulp was warm and put something inside him.

Pasang explained in whispers that in the first house he had gone to the people had had no food to spare. The second had been the same. But in the third he had persuaded the woman both to sell him some maize and to cook half of it. He had promised to take the pot back. But what should he do now? They needed the pot badly, as they had nothing else to cook in. But Pasang clearly did not want to take it from a family so poor. Stirling didn't like the idea either. Nor was it any use leaving money, for there was nowhere to buy a new pot. Perhaps the woman had another? With heavy consciences they took the pot and disappeared into the night.

By noon next day they were in a better position altogether. Again blessed with fine weather, they spent the morning asleep in a sunny hollow and restored some of their energy. On a fire conjured out of practically nothing, Pasang boiled the rest of the maize. Without salt or spices of any kind, it tasted like slightly sweet blotting paper, mashed and sodden. But again it filled them up.

Yet the best feature of the day was that Pasang suddenly recognised where they were. The big river, he said, was over the next hill. They would reach it that evening. The bridge would be almost underneath them. On the other bank, the Khampas would meet them.

They went on in the afternoon. Stirling's spirits were higher, not least because it was so easy to move with a small, tightly knit party. The removal of the stretcher-borne patient made everything a great deal easier. He felt hunted, but at the same time pleasantly unencumbered.

In the early evening the track brought them to a point from which they could see down on to the Kali Gandaki and the bridge. There they got a shock, for the glasses clearly revealed not one army tent on either bank but several – a whole military encampment. The guard was obviously too strong for them to force a way across.

'What now, Pasang?'

The Sherpa did not seem put out. 'We finding boat,' he said.

'Where?'

'This side.' He pointed upstream and said that on the east bank, below them, lived a family who owned a small boat and used it as a ferry. 'They taking us,' he said confidently.

The crossing took place at dead of night, in Stygian darkness. Having waited for dusk, the party slipped down to the river and set off northwards, up the east bank; but the house was farther than Pasang had remembered, and they did not reach it until nine o'clock. By then the night was soot-black, the sky overcast.

More by feel than by sight Stirling found that the boat was a tiny coracle made of leather braced over hoops of cane. Deafened by the roar of the river, he groped his way into it and felt the skins bulging taut from the pressure of the water below. With himself, Pasang and the helmsman aboard, the minute craft scarcely rode the hurrying water; yet as soon as they had settled, the owner pushed out into the stream and sent them spinning on their way.

Stirling felt the boat twiddling round and round like a leaf. Icy spray burst over the side and switched him across the face. Unable to judge their progress, or the width of the river, he could only sit there and clutch his precious rucksack to his chest. Throughout their gyrations the helmsman stood upright in the stern, occasionally making a sweep with his single oar.

Suddenly a terrific jolt nearly hurled them all into the flood. Clutching at a rock that loomed up even blacker than the night, Pasang heaved himself ashore. Then he reached back to give Stirling a hand. Finally the ferryman himself climbed out, and immediately afterwards hoisted the boat out behind him, lifting it easily and settling it upside-down on his back like a prefabricated carapace. Thus burdened, he set off on foot along the bank to make enough ground to repeat the manoeuvre with the second half of the party.

Of the days that followed, Stirling afterwards remembered few details beyond the first chilling discovery that the Khampas were no longer where he had left them. Either by a fluke, or by an amazingly efficient piece of bush telegraphy, a guide met them on their second day across the river and told them that the main Khampa body had been forced to move on by pressure of army patrols. Nor could the man say exactly where they had gone; all he knew was that they were moving in the direction of so-and-so – and he named places unknown to Stirling's map.

The result was that for day after day they travelled westwards, with the colossal bulk of Dhaulagiri passing steadily on their left. Then, as they slanted away to the north, the great mountain seemed to recede and diminish until its snow summits had ceased to loom as individual giants and became part of one huge dragon's back.

At one stage they walked back on to the area covered by the map, and Stirling sought eagerly for a short cut through to Mukut, where the Khampas were alleged to be. But the guide told him that all the passes had been closed by the winter snows. Gazing up at the immense white ramparts, Stirling could not challenge the Tibetan's verdict. Though the days were still hot, the nights had become colder and the snow-storms more frequent. The mountains as a whole were whiter than on the outward journey. The snow-line had descended. They could do nothing but keep going west.

At night they sought shelter in whatever village they came to, and slept huddled together in smoky hovels infested by rats. Stirling felt grimly amused as he thought back to his normal preoccupation with bodily hygiene. Usually a great washer and scrubber, he was now in a state of indescribable filth – and none the worse for it.

At last their track turned and they started south again. Still Dhaulagiri seemed to dominate their lives, for now they were once more heading straight for its barrier ridge, and its peaks formed the whole of the southern horizon.

They found the Khampas comfortably settled in a high valley. Though not far beneath the snow-line, the humpy black tents stood on a dry, grassy slope facing south, and the yaks grazed contentedly in the sun.

Dawa Wangdi was delighted with Stirling's beard. 'Ha, my friend!' he cried in greeting. 'You have gotten very hairy. Like a yeti!' But he was far less relaxed than before. This time there was no ceremonial tea in his tent – only an urgent conference.

'You have been many days,' the Khampa leader began. 'Where is your American general? And your beautiful doctor?'

Stirling explained. He found it hard to apologise adequately for the death of Chimba, killed on the frontier. Wangdi heard him in silence. Then he in turn explained how he had been driven out of the previous camp by troop movements just to the south. Worse, a message had come up from

Andrew de Lazlo to say that the tracks south to Dhorpatan were guarded by strong army patrols, so that the Khampas were cut off from the airfield. The only option was to carry on to another strip at a place called Jumla.

'Jumla?' said Stirling sharply. 'Where's that?'

'It is to the west.'

'How far?'

'Eight days, perhaps. Nine maybe.'

'Nine days!' Another nine days. Stirling felt cold with exhaustion. Jumla. He had never heard of it or seen it on the map. But Wangdi was saying something else.

'My friend, I have bad news. Sahib Lazair is dead.'

'Oh my God! *Dead?* But you said you had a message from him?'

'That was two weeks back. But now, two days, we hear he is killed.'

'How?'

Wangdi shrugged his huge shoulders. 'We do not hear. We do not know where, how, anything. Just that he is dead.' He sighed and clicked the bones of his necklace. 'Sahib Lazair was good man, I think.'

Stirling felt shocked. All through the trip he had been relying on Andrew to organise the final flight to freedom. Andrew alone had had the contacts to arrange an aircraft from Bhairawa. Now that burden would fall on him too. How the hell was he to make contact with anyone outside? His mind spun with the difficulties. 'Yes,' he said in a daze. 'He was a good man.'

Wangdi was still talking. Most of the Khampas, he said, would spend the winter where they were. Only a few men would be needed to carry the Emerald Goddess to Jumla. The rest would stay at Mukut, since their ultimate objective was still to reach the refugee camp at Dhorpatan, and there was no point in their marching a hundred miles to the north-west, only to have to return on their tracks. Their best tactics would be lie low until all the passes were open and the hunt had died down in the spring.

'In that case, why don't you keep the Goddess here?' Stirling asked.

'The sign of the Goddess is bad,' said Wangdi ominously. Further divinations, he said, had confirmed that the image must leave Nepal as soon as possible.

It had been agreed that they should set out in the morning. But their departure was delayed by an odd and unpleasant occurrence. Soon after first light Stirling discovered the yak-herds in a state of great excitement. Their animals had been folded for the night in a natural enclosure with rock walls, and during the hours of darkness something had stampeded them so wildly that one had been killed and another severely injured. The dead yak lay stretched out like a small mountain of blankets, already stiff and cold; the other was crawling painfully about with its back broken and its hind legs paralysed. Stirling's immediate instinct was to shoot the poor beast, to end its pain, but the Tibetans paid no attention to it, so indignant were they at the turn events had taken.

'They saying it is yeti,' Pasang told Stirling. 'Yeti coming in night.'

'How d'you know it was a yeti?'

'He very strong – throw yak like this.' The Sherpa made a heaving movement off his chest, like an athlete putting the shot.

'Not a bear?'

'No bear so high, sair.'

'Why does a yeti come this high, then?'

'He liking moss, sair. Salt moss on rocks.'

Stirling walked across to the small cliff at the foot of which the dead yak lay and scrambled up. At the top he found something that made his scalp prickle. Leading away in a diagonal slant across a new snow field was a deep trail, freshly made.

He could see at a glance that the creature which made it had been walking upright, for every few yards on either side of the central track were dents where it had put down its hands – or front feet – for balance.

'Here!' he shouted down to Pasang. 'Look at this!'

The Sherpa was alongside him in a moment. At once he began yelling at the men below. Several of the Khampas swarmed up the rocks. They too began yelling and gesticulating in a frenzy of excitement, like hounds getting on a line. Also like hounds, they could hardly be restrained, but Stirling kept them in check for a few moments while he went forward to look closely at the trail. The snow was so powdery and fine that almost everywhere it had fallen back into the groove, choking the bottom; yet every few yards he found the print of a large foot, nearly twelve inches long and showing five distinct toes.

What did a bear's foot look like? Surely a bear had non-retractable claws? The creature that made these prints had no claws at all. He looked closely at one of the hand or front-foot prints, but they were no more than deep dents in the snow.

Armed with a couple of their ancient rifles, which had been brought up from below, the Khampas took off in a yelping, chattering rush. Whatever the animal was, Stirling reflected, it would be away like smoke with such a noise behind it. Even he, however, was excited that when he saw a movement in the rocks ahead he stopped with his heart thudding and feverishly whipped out his binoculars.

A small lump of snow, warmed by the morning sun, had fallen from a ledge, leaving a fine spray of crystals in the air: nothing more.

On went the pack, obliterating the original tracks as it followed them. But the chase proved short. Soon it brought the hunters to an immense slope of loose, bare scree, off which the snow had been blown, so that it carried no trace of the mysterious passer-by. For a quarter of an hour the Khampas swarmed over the rocks, looking for further traces, and blasting off long whistles into the scree, as the Sherpas had at the eagle. Then their enthusiasm wilted, and they trooped back disappointed.

'Why the whistling?' Stirling asked.

'Yeti noise,' Pasang explained. 'Yeti whistling also.'

Had any of the Khampas seen a yeti? No – but the father of one man had. What was it like? Very tall. The speaker indicated a creature at least seven feet high, walking upright and covered with dark brown hair, with a high, pointed skull and a face like a monkey. He spoke of it not as an animal, but as a low type of human being, with the contempt one would normally reserve for someone ill-mannered and coarse. The yeti killed yaks, he said, by seizing their horns and twisting their heads back to front.

Stirling felt uneasy. The Khampas' yak had not been killed by having its neck twisted, but by a rock landing on the back of its skull. The crippled animal had been hurt in the same way, by a rock falling from above. The stones *might* have fallen on their own – but the tracks proved that a creature of some sort had been up there.

In any event, they shot the injured animal humanely, skinned it and butchered it. The process took most of the morning, and although the delay was irksome, it did yield a huge pile of meat, on which everyone fell with glad cries, none more so than Stirling and his half-starved team.

At last the party formed up for the final stage of the journey. Wangdi himself looked magnificent in his huge bearskin coat which hung almost to his ankles, even when belted in at the waist. The other men who came all wore more modest versions of the shuba, and long, home-made leather boots. Eight yaks carried the party's rations, and a ninth was reserved for the leader to ride.

As the moment of departure approached, the Khampas advanced formally to the place where the Emerald Goddess had been housed. This cave was scarcely more than an overhang of cliff, from which a brown yak-hair rug had been hung like a front wall.

Four men disappeared behind the curtain, and a single figure in a yellow robe stationed himself before it. Stirling recognised the lama who had conducted the ceremony of exorcism. This time, instead of a drum and bell, he held a long, slender copper trumpet. Presently he began a chant, dipping his right hand into a leather bag that hung round his waist and throwing out small pinches of tsampa, first to the north and then to the west. While he chanted the curtain behind him bulged and shifted as the men inside touched it. Like stage-hands in a theatre, they were getting the show ready for the road.

Yet although the elements might have been those of some amateur production, there was nothing ridiculous about them. Far from it. Stirling found something intensely compelling about the slight, calm figure standing quietly at the foot of the cliff, with the tremendous buttresses of rock and snow piled to the sky behind him.

The lama stopped chanting and raised the trumpet. Its raw, ancient voice brayed in the crisp Himalayan air: a voice with the power to scatter evil spirits and stir the hearts of the living, a voice to raise the dead.

In Stirling's mind the call evoked confused echoes of past and present: an English master laying on his hounds; the Last Post; trains crossing the prairie; a single, red-brown animal loping upright through the snow. It evoked distance, loneliness, isolation. When it ended, profound silence gripped the scene.

Suddenly the curtain fell to the ground and the cortège came forth. At first Stirling was disappointed, for he had hoped to see the Goddess face to face in the sunlight. What he saw instead was the litter, apparently, of an important personage: an elaborate basketwork chair slung on bamboo poles, with the occupant riding in a dark, closed cabin. In a moment he realised that the part which resembled a cabin was in fact the box of black wood which housed the Goddess, cunningly built into the framework of the sedan chair. She must, he realised, be travelling sideways. Which way was she facing? As the bearer-party came past him, he found himself recoiling instinctively, as though the box contained something radioactive.

The entire tribe had turned out to witness the departure.

Men and women lined the path, and Wangdi addressed them briefly, but with dignity. Then he turned and mounted his yak, to lead the procession. The spectators prostrated themselves among the stones and lay motionless as their patron deity moved out on her great journey.

Stirling and his men joined the tail of the column. When he glanced back, he saw that the people still hugged the earth. The red-and-white prayer-flags, waving in the breeze, were all that moved in that infinity of rock and snow.

Twenty-Five

They travelled openly, moving by day and camping at night. Stirling doubted the wisdom of such overt progress: he was haunted by the possibility that news of their movements might filter down to the authorities in the south. Although no telephone or radio link existed, there was just a chance that someone travelling south on foot would reach a police or army post in time for word to be sent ahead to the airstrip at Jumla.

In the villages they passed through they were the objects of intense curiosity. Stirling himself, with his great height and red beard, inevitably attracted attention, and so did the mysterious dark palanquin whose occupant was never seen, even in the sunshine of midday. Whenever they stopped to buy food, they faced a barrage of questions, and Stirling feared that the answers, however guarded or deliberately misleading, must leave behind a trail of fact and rumour.

For him, it was a strange experience to travel backwards through the seasons of the year. On the Tibetan plateau he had already felt the bite of winter; but down here at 8,000 or 10,000 feet he had returned to autumn. Golden-brown leaves still clung to the walnut trees, and in the middle of the day the sun was hot enough to flood the pine forests with clean, resinous scent. Even so, the days were appreciably shorter, and the time for pleasant travelling less.

Wangdi proved a jovial companion. Although he sometimes rode his yak, he generally walked with Stirling at the head of the column, greeting passers-by with magisterial salutes and inquiring keenly about life in London. Yet when Stirling tried to question him about the origins of the

Emerald Goddess, he always became evasive. Either he pretended not to understand or he answered at a tangent, deliberately missing the point.

When Stirling asked how old the image was, he replied that they had guarded it in the mountains for twenty years. When asked what it was made of, he answered that no man could describe it.

'But it's not *all* made of emeralds,' Stirling persisted. 'Isn't there gold as well?'

'My friend,' the Khampa answered enigmatically. 'You cannot count such things.'

Stirling had tried a hundred times to analyse what had happened in the cave. Kiri had agreed that besides the three emerald eyes the Goddess had a fiery green headband, around the orange spikes of hair. But she had not remembered the change of expression which had scared Stirling so badly. Had he imagined it? Or did the image have some primitive mechanism whereby an unseen acolyte, standing behind it, could manipulate the contours of the face?

Whenever he passed close to the Goddess's litter he seemed to feel some burning emanation. As he drew near the swaying black box, with the Bible riding safely on his own back, he reflected with satisfaction that the twin objects of Mission Yak were moving in close harmony towards their destinations, and that if the conjunction did produce the arcane power he seemed to sense, it was only right.

The bearers never left the litter alone. Whenever one of the team wanted a rest, another took over, so that the carrier-poles were never left unattended. Even at night, when the bier was installed in a hide tent, several of the Khampas slept with it. Thus Stirling, in spite of his intense curiosity, never got a chance to feel the weight of the burden they were carrying. If he could just heft one end of the litter, he kept thinking, he might get a better idea of what the box contained. All he could do, in fact, was to observe the degree to which the bamboo poles sagged under their load; and from this he concluded that the box weighed a great deal more than the general on his stretcher: at least 300 lb. Part of it was the box itself, of course; even so, it left a good deal for the image.

Every evening, if he could keep awake, he put in a few minutes' study of the Bible, propping it open in the sickly yellow beam of his failing torch. Often as he fell asleep he reflected that even if he now lost the precious books, at least a good deal of their contents would survive in his head. Also in his head were multiple snapshots of Kiri, laughing, frowning, eating, crying. Even if everything else disappeared, he would have these left. The fact that they had parted on edgy terms meant nothing now. He saw that the tension had been caused by uncertainty. The thing he wanted most in life was to see her again.

Yet the main spur that drove him on was the knowledge that time was running out. The Chinese attack on Russia was projected for January 18. Already it was the second half of December. He just had to keep going fast.

Dimly he became aware that he was suffering from physical debility and deep-seated exhaustion. Though his wound had dried up, he seemed to lack his normal energy, and he found the struggle to keep walking increasingly hard. He should have given in and ridden one of the yaks, but pride prevented it.

He began to suffer mild hallucinations. Several times while walking alone he got the impression that there was someone behind him. Turning, he would find the track empty. Yet when he faced forward once more the sense of being shadowed stayed with him. On other occasions he felt he was walking beside himself: his body was there, proceeding mechanically, but he himself seemed to be a short distance away, alongside, observing the ragged traveller with detachment. At ever more frequent intervals he seemed to be losing contact with reality. Or was he *gaining* contact with it? He had always regarded the mountains as the most permanent feature of the environment, and himself as some transient being, a fly crawling across reality's face. But now that he was beginning to step outside himself, was he not identifying more closely with the life-force of the mountains? Was he not becoming part of some far more enduring creation?

Usually he was brought back from such mystical speculations by some small-scale, homely sight: a black-and-white dipper skimming up a river, or a wagtail bobbing about the stones. But his mind remained full of confused and disturbing images.

Day by day – inch by inch, it seemed – they left Dhaulagiri behind them and drew away to the north-west. Once more they had walked off Stirling's map, so that only his compass gave them an idea of where they were heading. By then they were all on strange ground. None of the men could name the new peaks which rose, ever-changing, to guard the white horizon. But always in the villages they found men who could point them on their way, so that they were never in doubt about which track to take.

One day, soon after the noon break, they saw a storm coming at them from the north. At two o'clock snow began to fall, and a blizzard came on so heavily that the yaks were soon piled high with snow, and moved silently over the soft new blanket like huge, self-propelled duvets. The storm passed on before dark, but Stirling felt particularly exhausted, and when they pitched camp he sat stupidly on a rock watching Pasang light a fire, instead of helping him. Now he, Pasang and Likpa all slept in a medium-sized felt tent which Wangdi had lent him: also he had a shuba of his own – a huge, fleecy garment of sheepskins in which he enveloped himself at night, instead of a sleeping bag.

Next morning the sky had cleared and the sun blazed out, so hot that even Stirling, inexperienced as he was, had premonitions of danger. Every time the party traversed a big slope he looked up apprehensively at the tons of new snow poised above them, wondering if the heat would start to dislodge it. For a couple of hours they continued unharmed; but when trouble came, it was so sudden that the travellers were powerless to take evasive action.

The only warning they had was a heavy boom from somewhere above them and a tremor in the ground. Stirling thought there had been an earthquake. His mind flashed back to the exorcism in the cave, when the earth had seemed to move.

Now the earth *had* moved: no doubt about it. Gigantic thuds shook the ground beneath their feet, accelerating into a continuous, cataclysmic roar. A blast of freezing air rushed down on them from above, and the whole world seemed to dissolve into violent motion. Stirling just had time to yell 'Avalanche!' before the first of the snow shot over him.

Pure chance ordained that for once he was walking behind the bearer party, in the Goddess's wake, instead of at the head of the column, where he would have been normally. He threw himself flat, but even so he was lifted bodily from the track and flung out into space. He felt himself turning in the air, falling. Thunder exploded all round him, both in the ground and in the sky. Day changed instantly to night. The firmament quivered and jerked as though the bowels of the mountain were being torn out.

Something came past him, giving a prodigious wrench at his pack. Or perhaps he had gone past something. He felt the straps of the haversack burst and clutched at them frantically. He was too late: the pack had been torn off. With a shattering crash he slammed down on his back. The breath was knocked out of him. The back of his head had cracked on something hard and brilliant points of light swam in his darkened eyes. Then the lights went out.

He came to slowly, not knowing where he was. As he opened his eyes something tickled them: snow. He was buried in snow. But there was light above him. He stuck up an arm and saw the light grow brighter. He swivelled the arm round and made a hole. There was the blue sky, straight above. Gingerly he moved his other arm and legs: everything worked. He fought his way upright and stuck his head up into the open air.

Snow-smoke hung all round him in iridescent clouds shot

through with rainbow colours. He tried to stand up, but fell over as the snow gave beneath him. He got up again, struggling to regain his bearings. He heard a shout from behind, turned round and saw the remnants of the column high up the face above him, gesticulating like stick-men against a white background.

As he watched them he heard a single, tremendous thud and saw a boulder the size of a house come vaulting out into space, driven like a cannon-ball by gravity and its own momentum. There was a vicious whistling of air as the rock hurtled past him, and more earth-shaking thuds as it slammed back into the mountain below. Looking down, he saw the whole valley smoking with clouds of snow and vapour.

Amid such elemental violence he felt weak and shaky. His eyes stung and ran, half blinded by the glare off the snow. He was afraid to move in any direction, lest he should precipitate another landslide. But the men above had seen him: one was starting to make his way down. He stood rooted to the spot, feeling his sodden trousers cling to his legs.

Suddenly he thought: the haversack. God almighty! The haversack. His hands went to his shoulders. The pack had gone. The Bible was in it.

He felt sick with despair. After so much effort. After all this distance, these thousands of steps up and down. And yet . . . He forced himself to think. He remembered the sudden wrench that had ripped it off. He felt sure the impact had been caused by him going past something, rather than by something going past him. He himself had been moving. He must have scraped past a rock on his way down. Perhaps the pack had not been swept away, but had come off somewhere above him.

He looked at his immediate surroundings more closely. He was in a natural crater, a pock-mark in the face of the mountain. This was what had saved him from being swept right down: he had fallen into this shallow bowl, and the main force of the avalanche had gone over his head.

Cautiously he began trying to climb out of his personal

crater, but as he floundered in the snow he saw a bank of it shift and slide. It went only a couple of yards, but the movement frightened him. His whole environment seemed dreadfully unstable. He waited a moment, then heard a shout from close by. He recognised Pasang's voice and shouted back, telling him to move carefully. A few seconds later he saw the Sherpa's head appear over the rim of the crater above him.

Pasang called to him to wait, disappeared briefly, then looked over again. Down came the snaking, twitching end of a rope – a climbing rope, white flecked with blue. *His* rope – Stirling's own. He stared at it with wild hope. It had been in his pack. Pasang must have his pack.

He put pressure on the rope and felt that it was securely anchored at the top. Using it gingerly, he floundered, crawled and scrambled his way out of the life-saving crater and dragged himself up over the rim. He found Pasang with the end wound round his waist, jammed between two rocks.

'Thank God!' he gasped. 'The pack! Where was it?'

'Here, sair.' The Sherpa pointed at his feet, between two big stones, where he was standing. 'I finding him here.'

Stirling shuddered all over. It must have been one of those rocks that had ripped the pack from his back – he had gone past it that close. If he had hit it, he would have been crushed like a fly.

Except for the straps, which had burst, the haversack was intact. They cobbled the severed ends together with pieces of rope and soon were climbing carefully back towards the track. Pasang did not seem to know what had happened to the rest of the column; he thought the middle was all right, but he was afraid for the front.

His fear soon proved justified. The central section of the party, including the bearers and the palanquin, had escaped intact, protected by a vertical wall of rock beneath which they had happened to be passing. The avalanche had gone straight over their heads, leaving them almost untouched. But out ahead of them the line of men and animals had been severed with surgical precision. One party of men and yaks had survived; the next ahead of it had vanished. Dawa Wangdi and the leaders of the column had been swept away. Nor was it only the living creatures that had gone: the entire surface of the mountain had been ripped off by the roaring torrent of rock and snow.

Stirling felt profoundly shocked. The other survivors seemed the same: struck dumb, incapable of showing emotion, they moved like ghosts to the edge of the abyss.

Stirling got out his binoculars and searched the valley. Judging by the smoke that still hung there, the main avalanche had gone down several thousand feet. Again and again he swept the snow for signs of movement, but there was none. It seemed impossible that any living being could have survived that appalling violence.

Even so, he felt bound to make a search. 'We'd better go down,' he said to Pasang.

'Too much dangerous, sair.'

'You think so?'

'Is very dangerous.'

'We must try, all the same.'

They roped themselves together and started down, but twice in the first hundred yards they set off minor landslides. The second built into an avalanche of its own. Stirling clung to a rock shaking as he watched the new chute of snow go rocketing down and heard the echoes thunder back out of the mountains opposite.

'You're right, Pasang. We'll kill ourselves.'

They regained the path and marshalled the survivors. They had lost Dawa Wangdi, two other Khampas, and three of the yaks. With the animals had gone a lot of the food. Only the dull realisation that there was nothing else to do forced Stirling to re-form the column and set it in motion again. Pasang translated his instructions, and the Tibetans obeyed them like robots.

With Pasang leading like a mountaineer on the end of the rope, they picked their way across the avalanche's track, glancing fearfully upwards in case further boulders should be dislodged by their puny movements. But the fury of the gods seemed to be placated, and they regained the path without further incident.

That evening, when he began to shudder, Stirling put the ague down to reaction, and to having got soaked through. He thought the responsibility of being in sole command had kept him going through the afternoon, and that now, with the burden suspended for the night, he was succumbing to delayed shock. Yet as the hours wore on and the shaking grew worse, he realised he had somehow caught a fever.

He began to pour with sweat and started getting sharp pains in his chest whenever he took a deep breath. If he coughed, he brought up phlegm, and he thought he must have pneumonia. Was pneumonia catching, he wondered wildly. Could he have caught it from the general? Impossible, surely: and yet he had it. Or did he have pulmonary oedema – water on the lungs? Kiri had told him it was caused by high altitude. Yet he had been at extreme altitudes for weeks, and now was lower than for many days past. Neither disease quite seemed to fit. Whatever it was he had, at least there were the antibiotic tablets Kiri had given him in case his shoulder flared up. They might help.

His torch batteries had finally died, and he did not want to wake Pasang, so in the dark he rummaged in his haversack for the small bottle of pills. He poured them out into his palm and counted them back into the bottle with shaking fingers. There were eight. He had a feeling they ought to be taken two at a time, but in the circumstances it seemed better to economise, and he swallowed one, stowing the rest again carefully.

Needles, instead of blood, seemed to course through his arms and legs as he lay racked by shudders. His teeth began to chatter uncontrollably. This is ridiculous, he thought: I'm going to die. The prospect did not seem unduly disturbing. Indeed, in many ways it would be a relief. At least it would mean no more walking, no more struggling up hills beneath a cruel load, no more raging hunger, no more fear of frostbite.

Yet still determination burned in him, alongside the fever: somehow he had got to get the Bible to the British Embassy in Katmandu. Maybe he should give it to Pasang and get him to post it first class in the next village they came to. Register it, too. 'Your name, sir?' the post office clerk was saying. 'Address? I am sorry, I cannot hear you. I need your address to register this parcel.'

For some reason the clerk was Chinese. Of course the bastard did not understand. 'Deepwood Cottage!' Stirling yelled, and suddenly he saw the place, with the autumn trees bending before a strong west wind. Something distracted him. He glanced aside and when he looked back the flame-red beech-leaves had turned into actual flames, leaping from the roof and upper windows of the little house. His home was on fire! Dial 999! Good men – they were on their way at once, the engine arriving with a terrific roar. But could any fire engine make such a noise as this, thunder enough to shake the earth? The earth *was* shaking, and small wonder, for the whole mountain was on the move: down a precipitous slope came a cliff-high wall of snow, charging at the speed of an express train, and bearing on top of it a monstrous red-haired figure with gleaming green eyes and features twisted into a grimace of furious triumph. *Whumph*, it went, right over his head, so that he could not breathe.

He awoke sodden with sweat. The terrors of the dream gave way to anxiety about what would happen in the morning. If he was too weak to walk, would they leave him behind? Even if they did reach Jumla, would he have the will-power and presence of mind to lay on an aircraft for the Goddess's evacuation? The night seemed to last a year.

When morning came, he could hardly move. Though not paralysed, he seemed to have scarcely any power in his limbs. Now he thought he had meningitis, even though he did not really know what meningitis was. In any case, he had an excruciating thirst. He lay helpless, waiting for Pasang to wake up – the infinitely adaptable, apparently indestructible Pasang.

His appearance, and the croak which was all he could manage in the way of greeting, gave the Sherpa a fright. Dimly Stirling wondered what they would do: whether they would wait where they were for a day, or somehow drag him along with them. He felt too ill to enter into any discussion, and merely lay inert.

Pasang brought him sweet tea, which eased his thirst, and offered him food, which he declined. Then he saw them starting to pack up the camp. They were going to move! He forced himself to get up. Dragging himself out of the tent, he slowly sat up. His head spun so violently that he had to lie down again. He tried a second time, but the result was no better. Giving in, he turned on his front and wormed his way back into the tent so that he could stuff his things into his rucksack, which he did in the prone position. Then at last he managed to totter to his feet, though only by pulling on the tent-ropes.

By rearranging the loads yet again, Pasang cleared one of the surviving yaks for him to ride, and when the column was ready to start he was more or less lifted on to the furry back. His pack had been strapped to the animal's shoulders, in front of him, so that he could lean forward and clutch it for support.

Looking back on the journey afterwards, he supposed that he must have been barely conscious a good deal of the time, for he remembered nothing except short stretches of uncomfortable jolting. The next thing he recalled clearly was waking up in some sort of building. There seemed to be no roof, but there was a fire blazing in one corner of the stone walls, and when he came round Pasang made him choke down some thickly buttered tea. He was aware of more people in the building, and of a noise like bees, but beyond that he took nothing in before sleep swamped his brain.

Later he learnt that that was the moment at which he turned the corner. Unknown to him, Pasang had more or less done him up in a bundle and transported him inert for three days, loaded on a yak like a sack of maize. Then they had come to an abandoned summer grazing and pitched up in it for the night. Likpa had climbed down five hundred feet into a gorge, and up again with a load of wood, so that they could make him a fire; and because they despaired of his life, they allowed one of the Khampas to perform a ceremony of exorcism, for driving out the devils which the Tibetans could see infesting him.

Coincidentally – or (who could say?) maybe because of the Tibetan's gyrations – he had come round at the very moment when the incantations ceased, and the Khampas were gratified, though not surprised, to see their methods succeed. For the patient, who had not heard the torrent of abuse that put the demons to flight, it was a blissful relief to sink into a deep, untroubled sleep, the first for nearly a week.

Next morning Stirling woke feeling weak but wonderfully clear-headed. In a flash he saw how he would get a plane: he would send *Haller himself* a message saying that the cargo had arrived. Instead of trying to work round him, he would use him. Haller would come like a rocket, Stirling felt certain. They would load the Goddess into the Cessna. He, Stirling, would get into the passenger seat and as soon as they were safely airborne he would hijack the aircraft. His .38 – so far not fired in anger at a human being during the whole trek – would persuade the Swiss to fly to Bhairawa instead of Katmandu. If Haller argued, he would shoot him dead and fly the plane out himself.

Stirling lay comfortably in the half light, enjoying the simplicity of his plan. Then he heard someone moving at the other side of the room, and presently he saw Pasang's face illuminated as he blew up the embers of the fire.

'*Namaste!*' he said brightly.

The Sherpa turned to him beaming. 'You better, sair?'

'Much better. Fit again.'

'You nearly dying, sair.'

'I know. Thanks for all you did.'

'It is nothing.'

'It is everything. How far are we from Jumla?'

'One day, sair. We coming Jumla tomorrow.'

'One day!' Stirling was amazed. Not knowing how long he had been ill, he had thought they might still have a week to go. One day! He'd better get up.

Twenty-Six

Jumla, they found, sprawled over low hills beside a long, narrow valley running roughly north and south. When Stirling first saw the place his stomach churned, for the floor of the valley was covered by a smooth blanket of snow. Thinking of the airstrip and seeing in his mind the Cessna landing on it, he had not expected snow to be lying at that level. What he had failed to realise was that even the floor of the valley was at more than 7,000 feet, and winter had already closed in.

They watched for an hour before dropping off the last hill. The airstrip was deserted, abandoned for the winter. The small, square block of a control tower stood at one side, flanked by a couple of sheds, but the snow round the building was unmarked. No one had been there for days. The town itself was visible further down the valley – a jumble of dark houses from which smoke was rising.

Another fear gripped Stirling's overstretched imagination: that the police radio link, like the airfield, would also have been closed until the spring. If that proved to be true, there would be no means of getting a message out except another fearsome trek.

By the time they reached the valley, frost was sharp in the air. Finding a convenient recess, with water and wood, they settled into it and made camp. Then Stirling went on alone with Pasang to try and make contact with Katmandu.

As they passed the landing-strip they walked out on to it to test the depth of the snow. The ground was level and the blanket even, varying from four to six inches. Stirling did not know whether that would be enough to cause the Cessna difficulties.

They soon reached the first of the houses. From the doorways of smoke-blackened hovels smoke-blackened children stared at them with enormous dark eyes, frozen by fear and curiosity. The place looked terribly poor. For trousers the children wore strips of hessian sacking wound round and round their legs, puttee-fashion, and some had arm bandages of the same makeshift material. A few scrawny chickens pecked about in the main street, where the chocolate-brown snow-slush was beginning to freeze again.

The police station was a house no different from its neighbours. They banged on the wooden door, and presently it was opened by a man wearing a khaki shirt and pullover. Stirling's hopes lifted at the sight of the uniform: however scruffy, it gave promise of an organisation, a network, that might be able to help them.

The man, however, was not going to help them if he could avoid it. He took them into a small, bare room which, even in that remote mountain fastness, had not escaped the dead hand of some distant central bureaucracy. There was a badly made desk of bare wood, three hard wooden chairs and a rickety table, all clearly government issue; a few yellowing sheets of instructions were pinned to the walls; a single naked light-bulb hung from the ceiling (unlit), and the air was thick with smoke, some from cheap cigarettes and some from the stove in the corner. Yet none of these dreary details depressed Stirling in the least, for his eye had fallen on the radio transmitter built on to the wall at the back of the desk, and the pair of headphones that hung beside it.

A long discussion began. Where had they come from, the man wanted to know. Stirling had primed Pasang carefully with the sort of answers that might be needed, and he understood enough of the conversation to know that he followed the brief well. They had been trekking, Pasang said. Had the foreigner a permit? No – he had had a permit, but they had been attacked by bandits, and all the Sahib's papers had been stolen. Hearing the word *badmash*, bandits, repeated a few times, Stirling judged it the moment to display how he

290

had been wounded, and he peeled off his clothes to show the puckered, livid scars on his shoulder.

Now the policeman showed a slight interest. Where had the attack taken place? When? How many bandits? What sort of people? Pasang made suitably evasive answers, and pointed at Stirling, repeating *birami*, sick, several times. It was no trouble for Stirling to produce sepulchral coughs to emphasise the truth of the assertion.

Pasang worked skilfully round to the need for the sick man to be evacuated. It was essential that they get a plane from Katmandu, he said. They must send a radio message as soon as possible.

By then the policeman had his feet comfortably on the desk. He smiled complacently. It was impossible for any aircraft to come to Jumla now, he said. The airfield was closed for the winter. The air-controller had gone away until next year. Unless the tower was manned, nobody could be given permission to land. Besides, had they not seen? The airstrip was covered with snow. That alone made the suggestion of an aircraft impossible.

Stirling's temper rose. The man was a professional wrecker. The stuff about the air-controller and the need for permission was nonsense; having seen the dash with which Haller landed at Pokhara, he felt certain he would fly into Jumla whether the airfield was manned or not. To talk about air-control here was like saying you couldn't swim in your own pool unless the lifeguards were posted. The snow was another matter.

'Tell him we must radio Katmandu even if the plane can't land,' said Stirling. Pasang translated, and got another dose of bureaucratic negatives. First the man said that he was not allowed to start the generator without permission from the chief, who was away. Next he claimed they ran the generator only on Wednesdays (it was then Thursday). Finally he said that the generator was broken anyway.

'I don't believe anything he says. Tell him I may die if I'm not rescued.' Stirling got off the hard chair and with an ostentatious groan lay full-length on the floor.

The man grew agitated. He took his feet off the desk and spoke sharply to Pasang. 'He say no staying here,' the Sherpa translated.

'Tell him we stay here until he gets the radio going.'

'He say generator broken.'

'Ask him how much it would cost to mend it immediately.'

This question produced some confusion, but after a bit of bluster the man repeated his request that they should leave.

'Get nastier,' Stirling ordered. 'Tell him it was the police's fault that the bloody bandits attacked us. Tell him Nepal isn't a safe country for foreigners. The police haven't got control of it. They ought to be ashamed. Ask him his name, too. Say that I shall mention him when I get back to Katmandu.'

All this had a distinctly good effect. The man was rattled and showed it. But he stuck to the claim that the generator was out of order.

'Where is it?' Stirling demanded. 'Say I'm a mechanic. I'll mend it for him.'

This produced further lies. The shed was locked. The chief had taken the key with him. He always did. Besides, the chief was the only man who knew how to operate the radio set: it was not like a telephone. One could not just pick up the receiver and ask for the number.

The way the man shifted his ground convinced Stirling that the generator was in working order. After more futile exchanges he reverted to the subject of money, but more openly than before.

He sat up and took his wallet from the breast pocket of his anorak. 'Keep at him,' he told Pasang as he began to extract 100-rupee notes, handling them slowly, one by one. When he had collected five he put the wallet away and held the notes in a fan like a hand of cards.

Much as he disliked such crude tactics, they took effect. After a few more diversionary remarks, during which his eyes remained glued to the money, the policeman at last agreed to see if he could make the generator work. Stirling pocketed the notes again for the moment and stood up. Through the single, grimy window-pane he could see that the light was already fading. Clearly there was no hope of Haller flying in that day.

The policeman left the room and went outside. In a flash Stirling was at the radio set. Around the edge of the tuning dial three or four pre-set positions had been marked with black ink. These, he guessed, were the frequencies of the only stations with which Jumla ever made contact. One of them must be Katmandu. Even if the policeman refused to help, he should be able to work the set himself. The microphone and transmitter-button were straightforward.

They felt the generator start in a room immediately below them. Considering its various ailments, it was in action remarkably soon, and the overhead bulb wound itself up into a flickering, feeble light. Stirling realised that far from being the dingy, modern means of illumination which it appeared, the bulb was probably a status symbol of a high order: the only electric light in Jumla.

The man returned and switched on the transmitter, which glowed and hummed in a promising manner. 'Now – your message please,' he said, suddenly breaking into perfectly presentable English. Now it was Stirling's turn to feel disconcerted, and he cast his mind back feverishly, wondering what insults he might have let fall when he thought the man could not understand him.

'Please say there is a sick man here who wants to contact Klaus Haller, the Swiss pilot.' Stirling laid Haller's visiting card, carefully preserved ever since Pokhara, on the desk. 'Ask the tower in Katmandu to telephone Haller and get him to come to the radio. There's his telephone number. But they know it anyway.'

The man stared at the card, laboriously spelling out its unfamiliar lettering. 'Haller,' repeated Stirling several times. 'Everybody in Katmandu airport knows him. Haller.'

The policeman put on the earphones, adjusted the dial and pressed the transmitter button. A green light went on at the top of the panel, and the note of the generator rose as the engine stepped up its power to meet the extra load.

'Katmandu, Katmandu,' he began, and added something which clearly meant 'Can you hear me?' or 'How do you hear me?' The question produced no reply. He tried again, then again, adjusting the dial slightly after each two or three attempts.

'Katmandu, Katmandu . . . ' The chant became hypnotic, stupefying, in the close little room. Outside it was nearly dark. Beneath the floor the generator drummed steadily. The electric bulb flickered. 'Katmandu, Katmandu . . . '

At last the man sat forward. He called again, adjusting the dial minutely. Then he began to speak the message.

Stirling crouched at his elbow, straining to divine what was being said; but the earphones gave out no sound. The man repeated what he had said, louder, speaking slowly. Obviously the contact was bad. Stirling waited in a fever of impatience until the policeman eventually gave a nod and took the earphones off.

'They telephone Sahib Haller now,' he announced.

'Fantastic! Will they call back?'

'The circuit is open now.' He handed the earphones over and Stirling tried them, listening for a moment to the earsplitting roar of interference. It sounded as though every demon in the Himalayas was competing for air-space. He returned the headphones.

'Bad interference,' he remarked casually.

'It is. But that is normal.'

A minute later the radio gave a long bleep, and a new red light came up on the panel. The policeman listened again, then answered. Sensing what he was about to ask, Stirling had a minor inspiration. He was going to write his name on a piece of paper, but at the last instant he changed his mind and instead of putting CARSON wrote CARGO.

The policeman took the headphones off. 'They speaking

with Sahib Haller now,' he said. 'He wants to know who is sick man.'

Stirling shoved the piece of paper across and listened with approval as the word CARGO was several times spelled out. Haller might take it as a corruption of Carson, and if he did it would not matter; but more likely he would recognise the codeword he had given Kiri before she left Pokhara.

Again Stirling waited breathlessly as more shouted exchanges took place. The policeman signed off with the word '*Dhanyabad!*' – 'Thanks!' – and switched the set off.

'Sahib Haller come to Katmandu radio,' he said with a smirk of self-satisfaction. 'They call in one hour.'

'Thank *you*! said Stirling enthusiastically. '*Dhanyabad!*'

The policeman smirked still more widely and looked in a pointed way at the breast pocket of the anorak. Stirling ignored the glance and prepared to leave. 'Let's get out of here,' he said to Pasang; and then to their oily ally, 'We come back at six o'clock.'

Outside in the freezing dusk they had themselves directed to a *chaikhana*, or tea-shop, Jumla's one and only approach to an inn. In a small room full of smoke, lit by guttering oil lamps, they drank thick, milky tea from filthy, chipped old glasses and ate handfuls of roasted maize, while messengers sent out by Pasang scoured the town for the things he wanted to buy: a chicken, eggs, potatoes and rakshi. No chicken could be found, and the only three eggs for sale had certainly seen better days. Nevertheless they bought them, and they did better with their other requests: a man arrived with a bagful of sound-looking potatoes, and also – luxury of luxuries – some onions. Then a boy of eight or nine staggered in bearing an earthenware jug of rakshi.

At five to six, back in the police station, they found the radio already switched on.

'If Sahib Haller comes on the air, let me talk to him, please,' Stirling suggested. To his surprise, the policeman agreed.

They waited. Six o'clock came and went. Five minutes

passed. Ten. 'Why not call *them*?' Stirling asked – but realised immediately that it was not a sensible suggestion. The delay could mean two things only: either that Katmandu was already on the air to someone else, or that Haller was late at the rendezvous.

Even as he worked this out, the set gave its long bleep, and the red light came on. The policeman listened, and as soon as he began to speak English, Stirling knew that Haller must be at the other end. When the policeman got up, he slid into position before the desk and slipped the headphones on.

At once he heard Haller's voice, wowing and twanging amid fiendish interference, as though he were reporting from the moon. 'Yes, I can hear you!' he shouted. 'Can you hear me? It's Bill Carson, in Jumla.'

'*Ja*! I hear you O.K. You have my cargo, yes?'

'I have. I . . .' Stirling began to say something else, but too soon. Haller also was speaking. Everything was garbled. Must wait longer between sentences. He held his breath until Haller began again, 'Hello, Jumla. Hello. Do you hear me? Over.'

'Yes, I hear you. Over.'

'How big is the cargo? Over.'

'Three feet by three feet by two feet. I say again: three feet by three feet by two feet. Over.'

'Yes. O.K. And how many kilos is it? The weight, please.'

'About one-fifty. One hundred and fifty. Over.'

'So. Is good. I come tomorrow, yes? Over.'

'Good. What time? Over.'

'Eleven o'clock. Over.'

'Roger, roger. Hello? Hello? Can you hear me? Over.' It sounded as though Haller had fallen down a well. Besides twanging, the voice had started to bubble unintelligibly. Stirling waited till the air cleared, then tried again.

'One more thing!' he yelled. 'There's *snow* on the airfield. Over.'

'I'm sorry. We lost that. Say again.'

'*Snow* on the airstrip! About six inches deep. Over.'

'I hear you. You must trample a runway, please. Ten metres wide, two hundred metres long. Did you get that? over.'

'Roger. I hear you. Two hundred by ten. Over and out.'

He slipped off the headphones and found sweat running down his neck behind his ears, partly from the heat, but mainly from the effort of concentrating intently on the scarcely audible voice.

'Phew!' He blew out with relief. 'That's all right.'

'He will come?' the policeman asked.

'Yes. On Sunday. Three days.' Stirling stood up, got out the five hundred rupees and handed them over. Then, with the policeman distracted by a knock on the street door, he quickly reversed two of the connections at one side of the transmitter. It might be safer if the police in Jumla received and made no more calls that night.

'He's coming tomorrow,' he told Pasang as they walked back through the dark. 'I told the policeman Sunday, but that was to keep him out of the way in the morning.' By sheer luck Haller himself had asked all the questions that might have given away what they were discussing. All he himself had had to give were a few numbers.

By the time they reached the camp Stirling felt totally exhausted. But Likpa had built up a good fire, and he sank down by it while Pasang set to work to cook the potatoes. Suddenly he remembered the rakshi. For the first night in weeks he could have a drink.

He poured a generous measure into their one plastic mug, which he offered to Pasang. But the Sherpa declined it politely, so he raised it himself and said 'Cheers!' Pasang grinned at him so widely that the skin over his high cheekbones wrinkled like shiny old leather in the firelight.

As rakshi went, the brew was not a bad one. The first taste was almost that of vodka, and although the second was a cross between fuel oil and drains, Stirling found he could kill the blow-back by taking another swig.

The alcohol coursed merrily round his unaccustomed bloodstream, and in a very short time he began to glow with its effect. As it took a gentle hold, he felt more and more strongly the lack of a language in which he could adequately express his gratitude to the Sherpas, man and boy, who had given him such unbelievable service. To have praised them effusively in English would have sounded ridiculous – and he could not do it in Gurkhali. Pasang deserved a medal, at least.

And now, after dragging them all this way, Stirling was proposing to abandon them. Even if he managed to hijack the Cessna, he did not see himself flying it back into the Himalayas from Bhairawa. Nor did he suppose he would be able to get another aircraft to come in and pick up the two men. Only Haller's special knowledge and greed were causing him to come; other pilots wouldn't want to know. That meant Pasang and Likpa would be stranded for the winter more than a hundred miles from their home in Namche Bazaar. They had accepted the news with astonishing equanimity. Perhaps they had expected it all along. Even so, the thought of it made Stirling wretched.

He was roused from his maudlin ruminations by the smell of frying onions. Never in his life had he felt so hungry or smelt anything so delicious! Drawn irresistibly to the kitchen fire, he observed the preparations with naked expectation. Pasang had boiled and sliced a mountain of potatoes, and in due course he tipped them on to the onions in the frying pan. At the last moment he added two of the eggs – the third having turned out addled – and a minute later a magnificent rumble-tumble was ready.

They ate together, Stirling sitting on a box, the Sherpas crouching on their heels. All too soon the food was finished, and they were on to the inevitable tea. As he sipped from his mug, Likpa whispered something to Pasang, looking bashful. A short, playful argument ensued, with the man trying to make the boy himself say whatever it was he wanted brought up. But Likpa would not give in, and in the end Pasang had to speak for him: 'He say, he coming work for Sair Yeti in English land.'

Stirling smiled at the boy through a film of tears and slowly shook his head. 'Thanks. It's a great idea. But I'm not going back to England.'

'Other place, then.'

Again he shook his head. It was impossible to explain that, wherever he went, he would never again be in a position to keep a servant. Here, in the high mountains, where he depended so utterly on the Sherpas, the master-servant relationship seemed entirely natural. Impossible to explain why it would not work elsewhere. Impossible, also, to imagine what a lad as bright as Likpa would do with his life. Obviously – by Western standards – he ought to go to school and be properly educated. But almost certainly he would spend the whole of his life walking the mountains, like his uncle. Or maybe he would gravitate to some squalid urban existence in Katmandu or one of the towns of northern India.

As Stirling stared into the fire, an idea came to him. 'Here,' he said. 'I want you to have this.' From his anorak he brought out his best pocket-knife – a strong, finely finished knife with brass ends and a single, self-locking blade. Likpa had often borrowed it and praised it. Stirling knew that he coveted it above everything else. Not for years, if ever, would he have the chance to buy a knife like it. 'Take it,' Stirling said, holding out his hand. 'It'll remind you of me.'

The boy stared at the knife without moving, apparently hypnotised. Pasang quietly murmured something to him. Still he did nothing. Stirling tossed the present a couple of feet so that it fell on to the ground in front of him, and at last he picked it up, handling it gingerly as though it was dreadfully fragile.

'Look after it,' Stirling said gently. 'Sharpen it every day, like I showed you. Not too much. And put some butter on the lock, now and then, so that it doesn't get rusty . . . '

His voice suddenly caught in his throat. Tears had begun to course down Likpa's sallow cheeks. Pasang, normally as imperturbable as stone, stood up abruptly and turned away into the darkness. Stirling could not say anything else. He too stood up and tousled the boy's hair before stumbling blindly away to sleep.

Twenty-Seven

'My God!' cried Haller as he came back into the flat. 'He's got it.'

'What?' Kailasha looked up from the flame-coloured material that she was making into a dress.

'The Goddess. He is in Jumla. Jumla! No wonder he is so long.'

'Heavens! How do you know?'

'I just spoke to him on the radio.'

'What will you do?'

'I fly to get it tomorrow.' He poured himself a large neat vodka and sank down into a chair, running one hand through his long fair hair. 'After so long. It's incredible. I thought Carson was dead.'

Kailasha stared at him coolly. 'Why did he call you?' she asked.

'How you mean?'

'Why you? Why not somebody else?'

'I give him my card in Pokhara that day.'

'Yes, but by now he must realise that you put the New Zealand girl to spy on him.'

'So?'

'As far as he's concerned, you're the enemy. Why does he come to you for help? He must realise what you're trying to do.'

'He is desperate, I think. No one else will fly for him. I am his only contact.'

'You'd better be careful. He might try to hijack the plane.'

'No problem. I don't even let him get in the aircraft. I leave him on the ground at Jumla for the winter. He likes that.'

'Maybe you ought to take someone with you – a body-guard.'

'Really, Maus. In your old age you are getting – how you say? – windy. No, no: I take the Beretta. That is bodyguard enough.'

But when, a few minutes later, Haller rang Brigadier Bahadur to tell him the news, the Nepalese at once suggested the same thing.

'Certainly you must take two men at least,' he insisted. 'I'll have two soldiers ready for you on the airfield.'

'It's a question of weight,' said Haller wearily. "In the snow, you must know, the take-off is very much harder. I cannot carry so many kilos. And another thing: Jumla is very high, yes? The valley floor is at 2,400 metres. That makes even greater problems.'

'Well, if you have to, you can always leave the men there. But if they're with you, at least they can supervise the loading and make sure that Carson doesn't get up to any monkey business.'

In the end Haller stopped arguing and agreed to take the two soldiers with him. He arranged that he would fly straight back to Katmandu, where the brigadier would have an army truck waiting at the western end of the airfield, so that the Goddess could be transferred from the plane immediately it landed.

Haller rang off feeling vaguely irritated and unsettled. If only he could have had a proper talk with the New Zealand girl. As it was, he had been unaware of her return to Katmandu until he heard quite by chance that she was in the sick bay of the British Embassy. By claiming to be a friend, he had managed to get in and see her, but she had been under sedation, and had not even seemed to recognise him.

The nurse told him she was suffering from exhaustion, and that it would be several days before she was well enough to talk. He didn't doubt it. And yet there was something surreptitious about the way the girl had reappeared and the way she was being looked after – guarded, almost – which made him uneasy. He had the uncomfortable feeling that something important had happened without his knowing it. He sensed he had missed out.

Twenty-Eight

The day dawned fine and clear. Out of sheer habit the camp was astir by first light, although for once there was no hurry. Stirling did not want to appear on the airfield too early, for fear of attracting unnecessary attention. Ten minutes would be enough to reach the airstrip – fifteen to be safe. Half an hour would be plenty for trampling the runway. If they left camp at nine-thirty, they would have time to spare.

His own preparations took only a few minutes. The main one was to transfer the Bible from his haversack into the pouch formed by his shirt and anorak. Even if the pack should somehow be snatched from him, the priceless document would still be safe. Inside his clothes, against his chest, it was as secure as it could be.

As he did up the straps of the pack, another idea struck him. Haller might well suspect his motives and refuse to take him in the plane. Therefore he would bluff the Swiss by appearing as ill and decrepit as possible. Wishing he had Kiri to make a professional job of it, he bandaged up his left arm and made a sling for it from the remains of an old shirt.

At the last moment he paid Pasang and the Khampas. handing out all the rupees he had left. Also he gave Pasang and Likpa a hundred dollars each. The Sherpa tried to hand the money back, but Stirling refused to take it.

Then he had to face saying goodbye. When the plane arrived, he knew, there would be no time for farewells, so it was now or never.

'Pasang,' he began awkwardly. 'I've got to try to thank you.' He stuck out his hand, and the Sherpa took it shyly. 'I can't say it. Words – no good. But you've done everything. Without you, no trip. Without you I'd be dead. Thank you a thousand times.'

He hesitated. Pasang looked steadily at him, his leathery face solemn.

'One day I'll come back,' Stirling blundered on. 'Another trek. I'll find you in Namche Bazaar. See Everest.'

The Sherpa nodded and gave a sudden broad smile, and said very clearly, 'Sair, fare well.'

The expression, so unexpected and so formally delivered, knocked Stirling off balance. He turned to Likpa and seized his small hand, clapping him roughly on the shoulder at the same time.

'Goodbye, Likpa. Next time I see you, you'll be this tall.' He indicated a man of about six foot six. 'Big as a yeti.' The boy was in tears again. 'Where's the knife?' Stirling asked. 'Got it safe?' The boy silently patted his pocket.

'Good!' Stirling suddenly felt choked by emotion. Between himself and these brown, wiry mountain men there flowed a current of loyalty stronger than any he had ever felt in his life. Words could not ease the pain of switching the current off, of severing the connection. If anything, they only increased the agony. Action was the only hope.

'Come on,' he ordered gruffly. 'Let's go.'

He, Pasang, Tashi and one of the Khampas shouldered the poles of the bier. Likpa came with them, but they left the rest of the party behind.

Now at last Stirling felt the weight of the ancient image. The bamboo pole bit sharply into his shoulder and tugged at his neck when the black box swung inwards. He wondered again at the endurance of the men who had already carried it so far. But now they only had a short way to go.

The sun, though bright overhead, had not come into the steep-sided valley, and their breath smoked in the air. The landing-strip was deserted. They set the Goddess down beside the tower and cut the leather thongs that bound the carrying-poles to the black case and its wickerwork disguise.

305

Then Stirling ripped away the wickerwork as well, leaving the box naked in the snow.

With the cargo prepared, they set out into the middle of the field. The icy crust of the snow snapped and scrunched under their feet as they began to trample the prescribed runway. In twenty minutes they had done enough: by walking up and down in line abreast, they had packed the powdery snow down as tight as it would go without a machine to roll it.

Back at the control tower Stirling got Pasang to prepare a fire with sticks they had brought with them, so that they would be able to show Haller the state of the wind. Then, as they waited, he noticed a stack of empty oil-drums in one of the open sheds, and they humped four of the five-gallon cans to the corners of the trodden patch.

Now there was nothing to do but wait. Stirling kept glancing anxiously at the village, in case anyone should approach from the houses in the distance. Nobody came – but no plane came either. It was five to eleven. Surely, after so much preparation, Haller was not going to be late?

No – he was not. At last Stirling heard a hum, sickeningly reminiscent of the Chinese helicopters. 'Light the fire!' he ordered. Pasang struck his flint on to the carefully warmed tinder, and a plume of smoke began to build, slanting gently away towards the south. Soon Stirling picked up the black dot of an aircraft slipping in over the ridges to the south-east.

He put the glasses on it and instantly sensed trouble. Even at long range he could see it was not the Cessna: the body was too big and black, the tail the wrong shape. Besides, it had four engines.

The plane came up the valley about a thousand feet above the snow. With a terrific jolt Stirling suddenly recognised it as a Hercules, in dull green and ochre camouflage. A moment later, to his utter amazement, he saw the R.A.F. roundels on wings and fuselage.

He yelled with surprise, making the Nepalese jump. 'Look!' he cried. 'The R.A.F.! English plane!'

Involuntarily he ran forward a few steps, waving. For one glorious moment he imagined the plane had come specially to rescue him. Then he realised it could not possibly land on the snow.

But by God, the crew had seen him. The plane turned in a wide, slow circle, lost height, and came droning back along the valley, much lower. Again he ran forward, waving his gloves frantically. The huge plane waggled its wings as it went over.

Once more it turned, to make another run. Now it was really low – a couple of hundred feet, if that. The metallic, whining scream of its engines filled the whole valley. This time a door stood open in its flank. As it passed the tower something large and black tumbled from it and fell, to bounce on the snow.

The bundle came to rest not fifty yards away. Stirling ran to it and found a standard emergency pack encased in black sorbo rubber. Someone had taped a message under a flap of perspex: 'DO YOU NEED HELP QUERY'.

What a question! Yes and no. Stirling calculated furiously. He'd have given anything for the plane to scoop him up and take him effortlessly back. *And* his men. But he knew it couldn't land. Any other kind of help seemed equally impossible in the time available. Haller was late already. What could the Hercules do in a few minutes? Nothing.

The aircraft was making yet another run, higher again. As it went over, he raised his arms, crossed, in front of his chest and splayed them out and in, out and in, signalling 'Finished' or 'O.K.' Again the pilot waggled his wings as he lifted away.

On the spacious, sunlit flight-deck, the captain pressed the send-button on his radio.

'Three-five to base,' he called. 'Three-five to base.'

'Three-five, come in,' answered Bhairawa.

'Three-five. I have an immediate message for the British Embassy, Katmandu, attention Mr Patrick Smith. We've found our man. I repeat, we've found our man. He's on the airstrip at Jumla. We offered him help, but he seems O.K. There's a slight mystery about what he's doing. He seems to be expecting an aircraft to come and pick him up. He's got marker-drums out and a wind signal going. Request a check with Nepalese army to see if they have plans to lift him out. Over.'

'Roger. Wilco. How about you landing for him? Over.'

'Negative. There's snow on the strip. Can't tell the depth, but it could be a foot. Over.'

'Roger. What are your plans then, three-five?'

'We'll carry on with our recce to Serkhet. Then we'll look in at Jumla again on our way home to see if he's still there. Any change in the met. states? Over.'

'No change. All fields blue. Wind ten knots on three-three-zero.'

'Thank you, Bhairawa. It's a lovely day for flying. Here we go.'

From down by the tower Stirling watched the plane dwindle to a speck above the western horizon. Had he made a fatal mistake in sending it away? And what the hell was the R.A.F. doing here anyway?

There was no time to wonder. Suddenly he realised that the Cessna was in the valley and about to land. Distracted by the first aircraft, he had not noticed the second approaching. Now he saw that it had short, stubby skis fitted alongside the landing wheels. Hastily he crammed his left arm into the makeshift sling and glanced round his team. All of them, including Likpa, were armed with rifles.

Haller did not bother to make a preliminary circuit. He came straight up the valley, saw the smoke and marker-drums, and put the little plane down smack on the end of the trodden strip. There was a puff of snow as the skis touched. The Cessna bounced once and decelerated astonishingly: half-way down the prepared strip it was moving at an easy trundle, and the pilot turned to taxi straight at the tower.

As the plane came close Stirling got a bad shock, for

through the cabin windows he saw other heads beside that of the pilot. 'Oh my God!' he said out loud. 'He's brought people with him.' But there was nothing he could do about it: already the aircraft was alongside.

Haller jumped out with the engine still ticking over. He was wearing a beautiful new three-quarter-length sheepskin coat and pale-blue suede boots that reached to the knee. His hair was brushed upwards and backwards, kept in place by a pair of dark glasses pushed up above the forehead. His appearance struck the sharpest possible contrast with that of the filthy and battered group awaiting him. Behind him two neat little men in dark olive combat uniform decanted themselves into the snow and stood holding machine pistols.

'There it is!' shouted Stirling above the grumble of the engine. 'Where d'you want it?'

The Swiss stared at him, trying to reconcile the wild-looking, red-bearded scarecrow with the well-equipped trekker he had seen once before at Pokhara.

'You Carson?'

'No. I'm Charlie Chaplin.'

Haller blinked and pointed at his arm. 'What's the matter?'

'Broken.'

Haller nodded and slid back the cargo door, laying open the whole flank of the aircraft. He had taken out all the seats except the front two, and the floor was clear.

'Get your men to help,' Stirling shouted. Desperately he considered whether or not to precipitate a shoot-out there and then. He could probably kill both the soldiers with one burst from his Chinese automatic rifle. But supposing Haller had a gun and fired back? Somebody might shoot the pilot – and Stirling was not confident of his ability to take off in such unfamiliar conditions.

Under direction from Haller the soldiers squared up to one end of the ancient black box. With Pasang and Tashi at the other corners, they carried it crabwise across the snow and hoisted it up beneath the high wing. The soldiers rested their end of the load on the cabin floor and scrambled aboard to drag the box further in. There was room for it to lie flat on the floor, and Haller signalled that they should shove it further forward, so that it was jammed against a ridge of aluminium that ran across behind the front seats.

Now Stirling's timing was critical. As the men were struggling with the Goddess, he had picked up his haversack. While Haller was securing the cargo door, he walked quickly round to the passenger door at the front and climbed aboard. For a moment Haller did not see what he had done and looked round for him outside the plane. When he spotted him on board, his face flushed with anger.

'*Nein!*' he yelled. 'Out! No room for passengers.'

'Rubbish. Let's go.'

Haller snatched the door open and stood there like an infuriated policeman, gesturing violently to show Stirling he must disembark. 'The weight!' he yelled. 'We have too much weight!'

'Bollocks! The box is no heavier than two people, at the most. You had six passenger seats last time I saw you.'

'You do not understand. It is the snow, the drag. The altitude also. You must know, we are at 2,400 metres already.'

'I do know. Get in and try it. If we have to, leave the soldiers behind.'

He thought the Swiss was going to drag him out physically, or at least try to. Looking down from his perch, he saw the man's nostrils dilating with fury. But Stirling's own rifle lay on his lap pointing straight at the man's head, and behind him stood Pasang with another rifle at the ready. Seeing the weapons fore and aft, Haller cursed vigorously, opened the cargo door again and ordered his men into the back, where they crouched on the bare floor behind the box. Then he ducked beneath the fuselage and scrambled up into the pilot's seat.

'You are mad!' he cried 'Mad! We may crash. My God, why do you do this?'

If only he'd switch off the bloody engine, Stirling thought. The noise induced a frenzied atmosphere and made argument impossible.

'I'm sick,' he shouted. 'I told you. This arm. Also I have pneumonia. I must get to a doctor quickly.'

'I come back for you tomorrow.'

'No thank you. Let's go.'

'*Schweinerei!*' The Swiss looked round desperately.

'Hurry!' Stirling shouted. 'There was another aircraft here before you. He may come back.'

'I know. The R.A.F., too. My God, I use up half my fuel waiting for them to go away.'

'Look!' cried Stirling. 'There are people coming.'

He pointed down the field at a group of men who had appeared from the direction of the town, alerted by the low passes of the Hercules.

Haller cursed again. 'At least get rid of the gun,' he demanded, pointing at the Chinese rifle. 'It is too dangerous flying with that.'

Stirling had expected this. As the final, prearranged element in his bluff, he swore but opened the door and handed the rifle down to Pasang.

The men from Jumla were less than a hundred yards away. At last Haller went into action and opened up the throttle. As they lurched forward Stirling had one last close glimpse of his faithful team. He waved to them, and they waved back.

Pretending to slump exhausted in his seat, he studied the controls intently. As they taxied he identified the throttle and pitch control, in the centre of the cockpit. The stick was a two-handed one, in front of the pilot, on the left-hand side. The compass, altimeter, tachometer and fuel gauges all looked straightforward.

They turned at the southerly pair of oil drums and faced into the breeze. Haller ran the engine up and started forward. Stirling hardly knew what the take-off run should be like in an aircraft of this kind, but even so he sensed that what he felt wasn't right. Their acceleration was sluggish. The skis seemed glued to the snow. In a few seconds they were at the second pair of drums with no sign of lift-off.

'So!' cried Haller in a high tenor. 'I tell you! It is impossible. We have not the length of runway.'

'You said two hundred metres.'

'But not with such weight.'

'I don't believe you tried.'

'You don't believe it? My God, try it yourself.'

'Me? Don't be ridiculous. I can't fly.'

'Then get out, please.'

'I'm not getting out. Drop the men.'

Haller glowered across at him, tapping his forehead. But suddenly he stopped in the middle of the field and shouted something in Gurkhali to the men behind. An argument broke out between them. Haller shouted again, and the stockier of the two reluctantly climbed out through the cargo door.

'So!' Haller cried. 'We try again.'

He taxied and lined up once more, revved up and shot forward. This time everything felt three times as lively. The plane sprang forward buoyantly over the snow. Thirty yards short of the far markers they lifted off.

Stirling said nothing as they climbed away in a right-handed turn. They skimmed low over the ridge bounding the eastern side of the valley and at once swung further to the right on to a compass heading of 135 degrees: doubtless the bearing for Katmandu.

Stirling's nerves were desperately taut. First, he did not know where Bhairawa was, except that it lay south of the mountains, out on the Terai, the immense plain at the foot of the Himalayas. But whether it was east or west of their present position, he was not sure. For all he knew, every minute might be taking him further from it.

His second major worry was the man in the back. He glanced round. The soldier was about six feet behind him, with his head and shoulders showing over the top of the box. What would he do if Stirling attacked Haller? Would he panic and start firing his machine pistol? If he did, it would be curtains for them all. Could the man even speak English?

Stirling badly needed a map – yet he could see no sign of one in the cockpit.

'Have you got a map I can look at?' he called.

'Maps!' shouted Haller derisively. 'Who wants maps? I don't need maps to fly in the Himalaya. You can see which way to go.'

To Stirling the remarks seemed singularly inappropriate. Beneath them, a bewildering maze of snow-laden ridges and valleys was slowly crawling past. Each looked exactly like the next.

In spite of his predicament, he could not help noticing the amazing contrast between himself and the foppish pilot. Haller sat there giving off a fragrance of lemon verbena, with his elegantly manicured fingers resting lightly on the stick. Stirling's own hands were blunt and scarred, the nails black and broken. He looked and smelt like a tramp, and he could sense the Swiss's distaste at having to sit beside so noisome a passenger.

But he could not wait any longer. Whatever the outcome, he had to act right away.

He unzipped the top of his anorak with his right hand and reached in. The first time he brought out a filthy rag of a handkerchief, on which he blew his nose. As he put it back his fingers closed on the butt of the .38. The metal was comfortably warm to the touch. With one smooth movement he drew the gun out and levelled it at Haller's heart.

'Now!' he said sharply. 'We're not going to Katmandu. We're going to Bhairawa . . . '

Before he could finish the sentence he saw Haller's right hand darting snake-like into the folds of his sheepskin coat. Instinctively he drove his own gun forward into the side of the other man's chest and pulled the trigger.

The explosion lifted the pilot half out of his seat. Concentrating coldly, Stirling snatched the man's right hand with his left. But there was no need. The strength had

313

already gone out of him. He gave a hoarse croak as he arched upwards and backwards. Then he slumped down in the seat. His eyes rolled upwards and flickered.

Holding him back to keep his weight off the stick, Stirling looked round at the man in the back. The soldier had his automatic levelled at the back of Stirling's head.

'Don't shoot!' he yelled. 'We'll crash!' He waved frantically with his spare hand, trying to obliterate the idea of another shot. Did the man even understand English? Jesus Christ what a mess!

Haller was dead. But in the few seconds since his hands had fallen from the control stick, the plane had lost a lot of height. Stirling suddenly saw ridges dangerously close beneath them: dragon-backs of rock and ice that would rip the Cessna to bits in a second if they touched down.

He reached across and yanked the stick back. They began to climb, but in a left-hand turn. From where he was, hampered by the body in the pilot's seat, it was impossible to fly accurately.

The only remedy was to get the body into the back. He twisted round again and shouted at the man to give him a hand. There was easily room for him to wriggle forward over the top of the box, but either he did not understand what Stirling was saying, or he was too terrified to move. He merely crouched behind the box as though it were a protective parapet, with the gun levelled over the top.

Again Stirling made scrubbing-out motions at the gun, and frantic signs that he needed help. But still the man would not move.

The final possibility was to get the body out. Stirling left the stick again and reached across to open the door. He unlatched it all right; but since the door was hinged at the front, the slipstream blew it shut again. Once more he unlatched it, and this time he jammed part of Haller's coat in the opening.

They had lost height again. He seized the stick and eased it back, leaning on the warm body. They climbed slowly. Now

314

he had a breathing-space. With all his strength he shoved Haller outwards head-first. The limp body rolled to its left and pushed the door wide open. A furious roar of wind howled into the cabin. Stirling heaved again, gasping in the icy blast. The body was half out. He saw the dark glasses whipped off and the hair fluttering madly in the slipstream. But somehow the feet were jammed. He bent down and wrestled to get the blue suede boots free of the rudder pedals.

He could feel the plane diving again. But first he had to get rid of the corpse. He fought it. Abruptly the feet came free and the body fell away. But as it went the fringe of the sheepskin coat somehow caught on one arm of the control stick and gave it a tremendous wrench.

The Cessna lurched violently and twisted downwards in a corkscrew dive. Stirling found himself being spun at a giddy rate. There was no time to change places. Instead he lay across the empty seat and fought the twitching stick. In a few seconds the aircraft's movement became less alarming. He began to anticipate the tugs that the stick was giving. Gradually he regained control and brought the plane back to level flight.

Now he did move across into the pilot's seat. Out of the corner of his eye he saw it contained a pool of blood. But there was no way he could avoid sitting in it.

Ignore it, he told himself. Slam the door. Level off. Get the plane in trim. Sort yourself out.

Again he seemed horribly low. To his left a snow peak blazed brilliantly in the sun, its summit well above him. Beneath him was a deep canyon with snow along its upper flanks. He tried to increase power, but found that the throttle was already fully open. Easing the stick back a little, he felt the plane start to climb.

He glanced quickly at the compass. To his consternation he saw he was on a heading of 345 degrees – a few points west of north, and almost exactly the reverse of what he wanted. His plan was to fly south until he cleared the mountains, and

315

found himself over the Terai. Then he would turn east and follow the edge of the plain until he came to an airfield. If he got into difficulties, it should be possible to land on any straight stretch of road.

Carefully, gently, he brought the Cessna round on to a heading of 180 degrees. From out of the cobalt-blue sky the sun blasted fire into the cockpit. He needed those dark glasses that had gone out with Haller. Screwing his eyes up against the glare, he concentrated on the instruments.

The altimeter gave him 4,000 metres, or about 13,000 feet. For a moment or two he felt positively euphoric, as if he were floating effortlessly among that fantastic array of peaks and ridges. But the pleasant sensation vanished abruptly when he realised that the plane would not climb any more.

He was flying along an immense valley. Yet to escape from it in the right direction he would have to cross a ridge ahead of him, and the ridge was plainly higher than the aircraft. He tried the pitch-control, but even a slight increase produced an uncomfortable vibration as the propeller began to snatch and chop at the air. Quickly he settled things back to where they had been before. The Cessna flew on more steadily, but still it would not climb.

Fear began to take hold of him, and suddenly its onslaught was ferociously increased by a new factor. From the apparent lateral movement he saw that he was caught in a strong local airstream. Some powerful current set up by the mountains had caught the plane and was clawing it fast sideways.

The force of it shook him. He had not the reserves of power to combat an airstream of that kind. He abandoned the attempt to clear the ridge ahead and turned away down-wind, to the west.

Now he was in another valley, flying below snow-laden ridges on either hand. Going with the wind, he was progressing faster, but still not climbing. An awful possibility began to dawn on him: that there might not be *any* exit from this valley. Perhaps it was a cul-de-sac. Or perhaps it was an open valley, but he was flying up it rather than down it.

Certainly the ridges in the distance ahead looked formidably high.

He had got to gain height. Maybe the man in the tail was upsetting the trim of the plane. He looked quickly round. The wretched fellow looked sick with fright – pale and grey. But at least he had lowered the gun.

'Come forward! Quick!' Stirling shouted, jerking violently with his right arm. 'Get in front. Otherwise we've had it.'

Whether the soldier understood him or not, he never knew. For whatever reason – lack of comprehension or fear of being assassinated like the pilot if he did come forward – the man refused to move. Desperately Stirling considered whether he could shoot him and throw him out as well, to lighten the load. But no: he couldn't shoot the man for failing to obey an order – and in any case, it would be physically impossible to eject his body without finally losing control of the aircraft.

In his dire straits another possibility struck him: that he could ditch the Emerald Goddess. Three hundred pounds less in the back would certainly make a difference. Again, the task seemed physically impossible: he would never shift that weight alone. Then he realised that if he canted the plane right over with the cargo door open, the box might slide out of its own accord.

The high ramparts ahead were starting to tower above him. There was no question of clearing them with his present load. He had only a minute or two left.

He turned and gripped the handle of the cargo door, reaching awkwardly back with his left hand. The handle gave and the door came slightly open, letting in a blast of ice-bound wind. But now the soldier suddenly came to life. With a scream he scrambled across and shoved his arm into the mechanism of the door, so as to prevent it opening any further.

'No!' Stirling yelled. 'You bloody idiot! It's the box I want to get out, not you!'

His words were lost in the noise of the wind and the engine.

The man in the back clung desperately to the locking levers. The door would not move another inch.

Now, thought Stirling, I *will* have to shoot the poor bastard. But before he could steel himself to the task the Cessna itself took a hand in the argument. Suddenly the engine faltered. It gave one hiccup only, but the jerk snatched Stirling's attention fully back to the machine.

Jesus – we're icing up, he thought. He looked frantically for some anti-icing switch. Or was it the fuel mixture? Again he searched the panel of switches and buttons.

The engine missed once more, worse than the first time. Far from gaining height, they were descending. They were not going to clear the ridge, or anything like it. They were heading for impact among the gigantic boulders and ice-faces which were resolving themselves out of the distance ahead.

There was only one thing Stirling could do: turn while he still had room. He swung gently to the left, sick with the knowledge that the aircraft would never escape from the mountains. The harsh face of rock and ice flowed smoothly past outside the right-hand windows. He kept the turn going and headed back along the same valley, flying almost north once more.

Now it was a question of finding somewhere that might be possible for a pancake landing – a sheet of snow or ice, relatively flat. But God, where *was* there such a place? Everything beneath him was in a state of primeval chaos – ravines, jumbled rocks, cliffs, with the precipitous sides of the valley descending to form a sharp V. No stream in the bottom, no flat valley floor.

The engine became ever more sick and rough, spluttering and back-firing. Stirling knew that it was a question of seconds rather than minutes now. Wherever he put down, there was going to be a bad impact. So as the Cessna slowly subsided into that unknown Himalayan valley he yanked out the seat-straps from underneath himself and drew them tight across his chest and lap.

He thought he was going to be killed. But the prospect no longer worried him. Rather, he was totally absorbed in the mechanical business of trying to nurse the plane down. Ice-cool, he watched the rocks and chasms and ice-slabs grow amazingly as he came down closer to them, but he felt absolutely no fear. All that mattered was the stick fluttering slightly under his fingers and the way the aircraft answered his commands.

Thus he was able to take advantage of the only chance that came. He could perhaps have flown for another thirty seconds, but suddenly he saw a relatively smooth, humpy shoulder of snow and ice very close ahead of him, on his left. Instinctively he recognised it as his only hope and turned towards it, into the hill.

Praying that the skis would stand the shock, he eased off the throttle and went straight in, tilting the plane to the right at an angle that matched the slope. In the final seconds he realised that the snow was dangerously rough and the slope diabolically steep, but by then he was committed.

Holding tight to the stick, he smacked the little plane down. At the first impact the Cessna held straight as it bounced back into the air. But at the second the upper ski and wheel dug in and spun the whole machine violently. Stirling felt himself being flung savagely through the air. Sky, sun and snow whirled madly about him; something hit him violently on the back of the head, and the daylight was extinguished.

Silence. The engine had stopped. He came round to feel blood running down his face, but not much. Cut again, he thought stupidly. He tested his limbs. They seemed to work, but he could scarcely move. Of course: the seat-straps. He began trying to release the buckles and realised that he was hanging in the harness with most of his weight on it. The plane seemed to have finished up on its left-hand side. The windshield had starred into an intricate pattern of small pieces. His haversack had come over from behind and landed in the passenger seat. Maybe that was what had hit him on

319

the head. But what had happened to the soldier in the back? He called out, but got no answer.

Painfully he braced himself against the door to take the weight off the straps. With the harness slack, he got the buckles undone. But as he moved slightly there was a sudden noise behind him – a creak or groan, almost human.

He screwed his head round and almost fainted with fright, for there, hardly a yard away, the Emerald Goddess had risen from the shattered remains of her travelling box and now sat upright confronting him face to face. Not only that: as he gazed in terror at the scowling mask, with its blaze of emerald eyes, he saw it move.

Rigid with fright, he watched the whole figure tilt forward as though bowing at him. It leant further, until the halo of stiff orange hair was almost touching his shoulder. It seemed to be trying to embrace him. There was a strong, musty stink, as of bats.

By God, the thing was alive! He screamed as it moved again. What if it *spoke* to him? He threw up his hands in front of his face to ward off the apparition. Unable to retreat in any direction, he could only brace himself against the hideous possibility of the thing trying to take hold of him.

Another movement. With a small, dry rustle the heavy embroidered robe fell away from the Goddess's throat and at last revealed the mystery which Stirling had pondered for so long. The whole torso was a huge, heavy sheet of beaten gold, roughly stippled with hundreds of tiny hammer-dents but glowing with a deep and ancient lustre. There was the weight. He stared at the ponderous golden breasts with fascination and horror. What else would the figure reveal?

Then suddenly the nightmare dissolved into movement. The wrecked aircraft gave a lurch; with a scraping noise and a crash the Goddess slipped down flat on her face and slid backwards through the open cargo door on to the snow. Stirling just had time to see the image accelerate away down the glassy slope when he felt the aircraft itself start to move.

The entire wreck was sliding. A different kind of panic

seized him. He forced himself half out through the door, backwards, grabbed his pack and kicked himself off into space. By then the plane was almost standing on its tail, so that he dropped fifteen or twenty feet. He landed upright, and the impact drove his boots through the icy crust on the snow so that he was held securely, thigh-deep.

Turning, he saw the wreck fall on its back and skid away downhill, its crumpled wing-tips scoring huge slashes in the white surface. Suddenly it cartwheeled and disappeared in a whirl of snow, through which the sun shot rainbows.

Stirling stood stunned. Two drops of blood fell from his head and dotted brilliant red stains into the icy blanket round his legs. Deliberately he kept still for a minute or two until he had collected his wits.

Then he slipped the haversack on to his shoulders and set about extricating himself from the deep holes in which his feet were anchored. He knew the surface was treacherous, from the way it had shunted the Cessna downhill; yet until he climbed out on to the shining crust he did not realise quite how slippery it was.

At the first step he took his feet shot from under him and before he could stand up he too was hurtling downhill on one side. Shielding his face with his hands, he turned on his front and hammered his boot-toes downward. At the second attempt he got one boot through the crust and scrunched to a halt gasping for breath. In those few seconds he had covered fifty yards. Another hundred would have taken him over the lip of the ravine that had swallowed the aircraft. The place he had landed on was not so much a snow-field as an ice-field.

Stamping through the crust for every foothold, he made his way to the lip of the ravine. At the edge he hung back and peered over. Below was an immense vertical drop. He could not see its foot, so steeply did the precipice go down; but out on the floor of the ravine were huge pockets of snow, any of which might have swallowed the Cessna whole.

For a few moments he stood still, panting from exertion and fear. The scale of the Cessna's graveyard was so tremendous that it took his breath away. But then he became aware of something still more alarming. As he craned over the drop, he realised that a familiar object was in sight a few feet below him: a circle of bright orange spikes – the hair of the Goddess. By a thousand to one chance the image had caught on a ledge only a few feet down.

The hair on his neck crawled from the feeling that he was in the Goddess's power. Her magnetism had drawn him to the lip of the chasm, and now she was about to draw him to the very brink, for he felt an irresistible compulsion to see what expression the ancient face wore at the end of its journey. There was no *point* in going forward a few more steps, he knew: the image was beyond rescue now. Yet he had to go, even if it meant being lured to his own destruction. He could not hold back.

He looked round. The mountaineering rope was in the pack on his shoulders, but there was nothing to which he could make it fast. He would have to go unsecured.

He took one step forward, then another. A third pace would give him the view he craved. But he never took it, for as he stamped his right boot into the ice-crust, he felt the whole area of snow beneath him shift. The edge of the snow-field was breaking away.

The movement shattered the spell. With a frenzied dive he began to burrow and scrabble his way uphill like a madman, fighting to smash holes in the crust and drag himself forwards. Terror gave him superhuman energy. But even so his breath soon gave out and he lay gasping like a stranded fish.

Everything was still. Shaking the snow from his eyes, he looked behind him. He was five yards or more from the edge. More calmly, he crawled further up the slope. From his new vantage-point he could see that a whole stretch of the lip had freshly broken away and dropped into the abyss.

From below, clouds of vapour drifted up sparkling into the sunshine. The rock on which the image had lodged was bare and empty now. The Emerald Goddess had gone to her final home among the eternal snows.

Feeling pole-axed, he began to climb again, and soon his eye was caught by something glittering on the ice. He bent and picked it up – a rough lozenge of green glass. No, by God! An emerald! Incredulously he rolled the stone around the palm of his hand. On one side (the back, he supposed) there were flecks of paste, where it had been wrenched from its mounting. The sides were covered with paste and grime. But the front was, clean and polished, and shone with a wonderfully rich green lustre.

As he stamped his way back to the point at which the aircraft had come to rest he collected six more; and then, at the impact-point, among splinters of black wood, a whole trail of nineteen almost in a straight line. Twenty-six altogether. How incredible! Kiri's next birthday was her twenty-sixth. He wrapped the stones carefully in a piece of the old shirt that had done for his arm-sling, and stowed the bundle in his chest pocket.

Still in a daze, he searched the area. A smell of kerosene arose from the icy snow, but there was nothing else to be found. With a jolt he remembered the soldier who had been in the back of the plane. By now he must certainly be dead – either killed in the crash, or crushed when the wreck went over the precipice.

Stirling sat down on a bare rock to think. His watch said one o'clock – but surely it must have stopped? He scrutinised it carefully. The second-hand was moving all right. He looked up and squinted at the sun, which was still high in the sky. Clearly the watch was right, even though his body and mind told him he had been through a whole day already.

He tried to take stock. He did not know where he was. He had no map, no food, no tent, no sleeping bag. What he did have was a compass, a few thousand pounds' worth of emeralds, and a document worth a great deal more than that clamped against his chest. Also, he had a very great desire to see a particular person again.

All he had to do, he told himself, was to find a valley that led south and follow it down. Even if that took some time, he would make it.

He got up and started slowly towards the ridge that had been too much for the Cessna. It was lucky he had crash-landed so high up the shoulder, as it meant that he had not far to climb.

In an hour he was on the ridge, and as soon as he came over it he saw that his luck was in, for there, deep in the next valley, lay the coils of a grey-blue river. Watching the water with his glasses, he saw that it was flowing south. All he needed now was to go down to that river and follow it. In the end, it must bring him to the plain.

Twenty-Nine

'I'm sorry,' Stirling stammered. 'I can't seem to make sense.' Every time he tried to say something he felt on the verge of breaking down. He knew that the sudden release from strain was the root of the trouble, but he could do nothing to counteract it. Luckily Laura Smith was as sensible and motherly as anybody could be.

'Don't worry,' she said as she drew the curtains. 'Everything's fine. Have a sleep, and you'll feel quite different. I'll call you in time for lunch.'

She closed the door. Stirling lay quivering between the crisp, white sheets. His fingers and toes moved greedily about, luxuriating in the incredible sensation of clean linen, but his mind seemed equally unable to keep still. Here, in the comfort and safety of the Smiths' house, he knew he should be able to relax; yet all he could do was to keep reaching up to make sure that the Bible was still there under his pillow, and glancing obsessively at the .38 which lay loaded on the table beside the bed.

Dumped by the friendly Indian lorry driver outside the gates of the British Embassy at seven o'clock that morning, filthier than he had ever been in his life, he had had himself driven to the Smiths' house and burst in on them like a bomb exploding. Patrick Smith, resigned to the fact that he was dead, had dropped the early morning tea-tray.

It had taken only a couple of minutes to establish the basic facts of the situation: that Stirling was alive and reasonably well and in possession of the Bible; that the general had reached Katmandu but had died in hospital; that Kiri had been ill but had recovered and had left Katmandu for New Zealand.

'But we wrote you off,' Smith repeated incredulously. 'We gave you up for dead. The R.A.F. reported seeing you at Jumla. Then we heard that Haller had picked you up – but his aircraft never came back.'

'I know,' said Stirling flatly. 'It crashed.'

'Where?'

'I've no idea.'

'My God! The R.A.F. and the Nepalese Air Force searched for three days. They never saw a sign of the plane. They assumed it had gone into a ravine or something.'

'It did. But I don't think we were on any normal route. We'd had engine trouble and got off course.'

'Didn't you see the search planes?'

'I never realised there were any.'

'What happened to Haller?'

'He was killed . . . in the crash.'

'But you were all right?'

'I was lucky.'

'The Nepalese seemed to think there was a soldier on board as well.'

'He was killed too, I'm afraid.'

'But why did you send for Haller? Why didn't you contact me or someone else in the Embassy?'

'I . . . Oh hell!'

At that point Stirling broke down for the first time. The idea of having to explain everything brought the whole ordeal back far too early. Recognising that he was exhausted, Laura Smith manoeuvred him into a bath while she got breakfast.

The sight of his face in the mirror had been a shock. An emaciated stranger with burning eyes stared at him out of the steamy glass. When he hacked off his beard (with borrowed scissors and razor), his appearance became still more bizarre: though his forehead, nose and cheekbones were burnt a mahogany brown, his cheeks were pale and hollow. The bath was magnificent, and so was the breakfast: coffee, orange juice, bacon and eggs seemed delights from another planet. But throughout the meal he felt on the brink of collapse, and straight after it Laura Smith put him to bed while her husband, in a state of elation, rushed off to break the news to the Ambassador and the Americans.

Now Stirling lay in the darkened, chintzy bedroom and tried to let his mind run down. But no matter what he tried to focus on, all he could think about was Kiri. Thank God she was all right. The worst thing was that she must think him dead. That was terrible. Obviously he would have to go through some sort of debriefing . . . but as soon as that was over he would take the first plane to Auckland and catch up with her.

He was dragged up from a bottomless sleep by a knock on the door. He had been out cold for nearly four hours. He sluiced cold water over his head, scrubbed his face with a clean towel, dressed in some loose new clothes that had been bought for him during the morning, brushed his hair and prepared to face the ordeal of lunch.

In fact it was no ordeal. The sleep had steadied him and made him feel more solid. Answering the stream of questions now seemed no problem. Apart from the Smiths, the only person present was a friendly, suave American, Ed Burrow, introduced as being from the United States Embassy but instantly diagnosed by Stirling as belonging to the C.I.A.

'The Pentagon's gone crazy with the news that you made it,' he said by way of greeting. 'They're sending a special plane to fly you straight to Washington.'

'Oh Jesus!' Stirling could not conceal his dismay.

'Don't worry. I guess it's the most comfortable long-distance aircraft in the world – bunks, bathroom, everything. I know, because I've flown in it. You can sleep all you like during the flight.'

'It's not that. I was hoping to go straight to Auckland.'

'Auckland? No problem. They'll fly you any place in the world after you've told them all about it.'

'I see.' Stirling tried to digest the news. 'What plane is it?'

'Converted 707. Right now it's on its way up from Calcutta. Take-off for Washington is at twenty-two hundred tonight.'

Twenty-two hundred. Ten o'clock. At least Stirling had the rest of the day to try and make contact with Kiri.

The meal passed pleasantly enough except for the moments at which Burrow's praises became uncomfortably effusive. 'The Pentagon sure is going to be mighty grateful to you, Bill,' he kept saying, and Stirling sweated with embarrassment. His other difficulty was in getting enough to eat. Several helpings of each course were piled on to his plate, but no matter how much he ate, it seemed to make little difference to the ferocity of his hunger.

When they moved through to the sitting-room for coffee Burrow politely asked whether he might look at the Bible itself. Stirling fetched it from under the pillow and carefully peeled off the protective layers of polythene. The two exercise books still looked amazingly clean and sound.

'It's not that easy to read,' Stirling warned. 'There are so many abbreviations. But I've made a list of the main ones – here, at the front. Then look at page 224.'

'O.K., O.K.,' said Burrow impatiently. 'I get the picture.'

He sat down in one of the windows, but almost at once he began uttering sharp exclamations and jumping around the seat.

'Boy!' he cried. 'This is incredible! Jesus Christ – it's dynamite!'

Stirling felt like an author whose work is suddenly recognised as brilliant. 'I thought you'd be interested,' he murmured.

The American stood up. 'Excuse me, but I have to go right to the Embassy with this. I have to get right on to Washington. It can't wait till tomorrow. Have you any objection if I take the book with me?'

'For Christ's sake keep a good hold of it,' said Stirling more sharply than he meant to.

'O.K., O.K.'

'Sorry – it's just that I've spent the last few weeks killing myself to make sure it doesn't get lost.'

'I know. I'll guard it with my life.'

Burrow took his leave, having arranged to meet Stirling again at nine that evening. As soon as he had gone, Smith took Stirling down to the British Embassy, driving the Mercedes himself. Stirling felt ill at ease and nervous that he might be recognised. To minimise the risk he wore a pair of borrowed dark glasses. Even though he felt bereft without the Bible on his person, he was glad that it had changed hands: even if somebody got him now, the object of the mission would be safe.

'I think I did for the K.G.B. man,' he said casually as Smith drove.

'Oh yes? Who was it?'

'I don't know. But I think if you check out a man posing as an American geologist, who turned up in Katmandu soon after I'd left, you'll find out.'

'What happened to him.'

'He won't bother you again.'

Smith looked quizzically across at his passenger, but let the matter drop. A moment later he said, 'Tell me how you got out.'

The movement of the car, the warm air blowing in the windows, seemed to make narration easy. 'I just kept walking south-west, basically,' Stirling began.

'I didn't have a map. But I did have a compass, and I remembered that the main alignment of the Himalayas in that area is from north-west to south-east. Also, I knew that the mountain belt is relatively narrow, and that, as a bird flies, Jumla couldn't be all that far from the Terai. So I reckoned that if I headed south-west, at right-angles to the line of the mountain chain, I should come to the plain quite soon.

'That's all I did, really. The first night was a bit tough. I had no food and nowhere to sleep except a hole under a rock. But in the morning I found I'd been kipping right on top of a meal. There was a pool in the stream with about ten thin fish in it. I diverted the stream, drained the pool, caught the fish and ate them. At least, I ate half, and carried the rest split open on my pack, to dry them.

'I followed a river down all that day. In the afternoon I hit a well-used track, and in the evening I found a village. The people gave me a meal and a bed – and after that I was never short.'

'You make it sound easy.'

'It was, after what we'd been through further north. Of course, the lower I got, the warmer it was, too. That helped.'

'And where did you come out?'

'I'm not sure. But I found a man who ran an incredibly decrepit taxi. He took me to Rexaul and from there I got a lift in this truck.'

'How long since the crash?' Smith counted on his fingers on top of the steering wheel. 'Eight days?'

'About that.'

'If we got a good map, could you work out where it was you came down?'

'I doubt it. Why? Are you thinking of recovering the aircraft?'

'Well – yes.'

'You might as well forget it. After it had come down, it slid over a precipice into an incredible ravine. No machine on earth could get it out.' Stirling's pessimism was calculated. He did not give a damn about the plane, but he was determined that the Emerald Goddess should be left in peace.

At the Embassy he put in a call to Kiri's number in Auckland. Then he had a brief, formal interview with the Ambassador – a short, dark man with bushy black eyebrows and a pleasantly direct, old-fashioned manner. Again, Stirling found being praised a strain.

'The whole thing was such a mess,' he protested. 'So many good people killed. The Khampas, Sulzberger, de Lazlo . . . By the way, what happened to him?'

'De Lazlo?'

'Yes.'

'We're not sure. He was murdered, perhaps in mistake for you. The K.G.B. man sent out several people after you. It may have been one of them, still trying to pick up his reward.'

The Ambassador paused. 'Sulzberger thought the world of you.'

'Oh?'

'He could hardly talk any more. But everything he did say was about you.'

'God, what he must have suffered. That's what I mean – he should never have lost his life.' Stirling shook his head.

'Your money,' the Ambassador was saying. 'How would you like it to be paid?'

'Can you arrange for it to go to Auckland? The Bank of New Zealand?'

'As you like. Do you have an account there?'

'No – but I will in a day or two.'

'That's fine, then.'

'Thank you.'

The interview was over. For the rest of the afternoon Stirling hung around the Embassy, waiting for his call to come through. But the only person who rang, repeatedly, was Ed Burrow, with a stream of questions.

At six Smith drove Stirling home again, for drinks and supper before he caught the plane. They gave the exchange the different number, but still the call did not come. Then, when they were in the middle of supper, the telephone rang. Uninvited, Stirling leapt up and sprinted into the sitting room.

'Your call to New Zealand is on the line!' cried the operator in a voice of triumph. Some anonymous international being said 'Speak up, please,' and suddenly Kiri was there, loud and clear.

'Hi, honey!' shouted Stirling. 'It's me.'

'Bill! I can't believe it. Oh, *Bill!*'

From 5,000 miles away he heard the explosion of tears.

331

'Don't cry!' he said fiercely. 'It's too expensive. Listen, how are you?'

'Oh, jeeze,' she gasped. 'How are *you*?'

'Box of birds.'

'But I thought you were dead.'

'I bloody well wasn't. And I'm not dead now.'

'Where are you, for God's sake?'

'In Katmandu. But listen. I've got to fly to Washington tonight, on business. Get there too.'

'What? I've only just got here. Are you crazy?'

'Only to see you. Get on the first flight to Washington D.C.'

'But I don't know when the planes are.'

'Hire one. Hire Concorde. But get there tomorrow.'

'Bill, you *are* crazy.'

'I can't help that. Where shall we meet? What's the best hotel?'

'Well – there's the Hilton.'

'O.K. I'll book a suite at the Hilton.'

'I can't believe it.'

'You will – specially when you see what I've got for you.'

'What's that?'

'It's a secret. But I'll give you a clue. It's a present from the Emerald Goddess.'

There was a gasp at the other end of the line, and then a click. The connection had been severed. But Stirling did not mind: it was always better not to have to say goodbye.